A Lord and His Lady . . .

Wrapped with her arms about him in the sweetness of the night, Emma wondered what would be the end of it all.

"There is your wife, dearest Horatio."

"She is very cold. She would never sanction any warmth in our marriage."

"My love, my poor, poor love. Never shall you chide your Emma on that score."

"To think that you kept all this beauty for Horatio! Through all those lonely years till now."

Emma sighed. She was far more afraid of the road which lay behind her, and she suffered tortures memorizing the black marks that had been chalked up against her virtue. The men who had held her as closely and as passionately, and who had drunk so freely from the same fountain. Nelson still believed her to be good. What would happen if he ever discovered the truth?

For the moment none of this mattered to Horatio, for he did not suspect it, and would have refuted any accusation with his own honor.

"All I ask now is to possess and to be possessed," he said as he clasped her to him. . . .

Also by Ursula Bloom from Pinnacle Books:

Love Is But a Dream
Passion's Pilgrim
Love, Old and New
Prelude to Yesterday

THE MAGNIFICENT COURTESAN

URSULA BLOOM

PINNACLE BOOKS • LOS ANGELES

THE MAGNIFICENT COURTESAN

Copyright 1949 by Lozania Prole

First American edition.
First published in Great Britain 1949 by Robert Hale & Company.

A Pinnacle Books edition, published by special arrangement with Robert Hale Limited.
First printing, March 1979

ISBN: 0-523-40542-1

Cover illustration by Bruce Minney

Printed in the United States of America

PINNACLE BOOKS, INC.
2029 Century Park East
Los Angeles, California 90067

The Magnificent Courtesan

I

EMY LOOKED back.

She glanced over her shoulder towards the village man, a smock bunched over his body, and carrying a hay-fork in his big red hands. She knew that he was looking at her and it was a sheer delight to Emma Hart to realize that she could make him stare. Only recently had she become aware of this power; it had budded in her since she was fourteen, increasing as she developed. He grinned at her, grinned knowingly, and she tossed her head and passed by.

She turned in at Mr. Thomas's gate. Emy had been born in Great Neston but had left that place before she could remember, and Hawarden was the only background that she really knew. She had always lived in the cottage with Grandmother Kidd, her mother coming to see them when she could, which wasn't often. Grandmother Kidd worked hard. Her hands were toil-worn and her pendulous breasts looped down on to a sprawling stomach that rose high. She wiped the sweat from her face with grey strings of hair, pushing it back under an old mob cap, though it always straggled down again. Although Emy was repulsed by her grandmother's appearance, she loved her all the same. Now Emy was going sixteen, and recently her child's cotton frock had become too tight, for her breasts were swelling and she knew that the village men glanced appreciatively at the frock with the splitting seams. There was no money for more, she'd have to be content and hope she did not develop further. Hope also that her chestnut hair falling in curls to her shoulders would hide it.

"Put it up inside your cap, so that the boys don't stare so," admonished her grandmother.

But it gave Emy a sense of completion when the boys stared, for she knew that she was pretty. She had first known it when she arrived to be a nurse-maid for Mrs. Thomas, and had heard Mr. Thomas say, "Far too pretty for a nursemaid," and grin.

"Hush," said his wife, who was a large, masterful woman. "You'll only turn her head! There's trollops enough without your making more of them."

So Emy, seeing which way the wind blew, looked down her nose, a modest enough child but proud in her own way that the men looked back at her. Not just the boys of the place, though that would have been pleasant, but the men, their eyes brighter, their mouths a little dry. She turned in at the Thomas gate.

"I saw you," said old Mary, the cook. She was on her knees, raking out the oven, her bird-like hands clawing at the ash grit, an ugly old harridan sweaty with preparing for to-morrow's baking.

"What did you say?"

"You'll regret looking that way at men, my girl. You'll be sorry enough, for all you think yourself so clever."

Emy sat down on the wooden chair. One day she would have Chippendales and Louis-Quinze gold chairs, for she had always been a dreamer. "I shall go far, you'll see," she said.

"Aye, as far as Ann Symonds," said Mary, for only last summer Ann Symonds had been delivered of a bastard boy in the new hay-rick, where she had strangled it, leaving the body going blue and wandering off. But the King's men had caught her; they had tried her at the Assizes, and hanged her with a rope marking her throat so that she dangled eerily in the wind, and she only seventeen! Emy shuddered! She was a compassionate child, and she hated to think of such things. She got up and stood watching Mary clawing out the ashes. She had the trick of falling naturally into exquisite poses, so that even Mary warmed to her.

"I must say that you stand pretty and look pretty," she admitted. Encouraged, Emy took a step forward and struck an attitude.

"One day I'll be an actress, and a lady, you'll see."

"Be off with you, you silly wench!" for now old Mary was hot and tired, and the grit stuck to her moist skin, pigmenting her so that she looked like a negress.

Emy went upstairs to the nursery, but Mrs. Thomas was coming across the landing, and she looked dour and disapproving. She had never liked this girl, possibly recognizing something in her that she herself lacked so hopelessly. "There's a parcel to be delivered," she said brusquely.

Emy followed respectfully, eyeing the fashionable dress with the kerchief tucked across the breast and wishing she could afford cashmere instead of cotton.

"Here's the parcel; deliver it and wait for a message, and don't loiter."

Mrs. Thomas was a big, plain woman; she had borne three children in four years with difficult, tormenting labours that had crucified her. Life held nothing ahead for her save childbed and weaning, then childbed again. Once she had believed that love was beautiful and men were attractive; she knew better now! She had been shocked by her husband on the first night of their marriage, and had never recovered from the souring disillusion of consummation. Emy curtseyed meekly and knew that the very meekness was an irritant to the disappointed woman.

Emy stepped out into the garden, glad to be in the drive again, with its wide border of June flowers, for soon Andrew Lack would be bringing the cows up the lane from pasture. He interested her. She saw him in church on Sundays, supposed to be singing, but staring silently at her over the top of the psalter as if he were hungry and the thought of starvation repelled him. She was aware of every expression on

3

his lustful young face, even though they had never spoken. But Emy knew what he would say—if he could—and to-day for the first time she saw the chance to be alone with him.

She danced along on buoyant steps, with the cows ambling towards her, the strong, sweet smell of milk and sunshine on their hides. She saw Andrew, a young man of twenty, standing on the very threshold of life, longing to drink from the cup it offered but as yet without the courage to lift it to his lips. He stopped.

"Emy?" he said, and as she looked at him, pushing back the curls and conscious of a power over him but not dreaming its capacity, "how beautiful you are!"

"Have you only just found that out?"

"I've looked at you so often."

"I know, and you're looking at me now."

He reached and took her wrist, and the pressure of his fingers almost hurt her. It seemed then that he transferred his own hunger to her, and for a moment she could feel it flooding her with the unconquerable desire to be possessed. "Lemme go," she said.

"Emy, why can't I see you sometimes?"

"Because you know that Mrs. Thomas'd forbid it. She'd whip me if she knew we were talking now."

"Oh, so she does whip her maids?"

"So they tell me."

"Night after night I've come to the shrubberies to look for you. Did you know?"

"Why do you do it? I'm never in the shrubberies."

"I know that. But one night you came down into the kitchen. It looked to me as how you was searching for something. You wore your shift and I've never forgotten that night. I go back and lie in the shrubberies looking for you. Hoping you'll come back again."

She was stirred by the way he said it. For a moment she felt childishly squeamish that he should

4

have seen her in her shift, then she squashed the feeling. "Perhaps one night you'll get your reward."

"Maybe to-night?"

"Maybe, who knows?"

"Emy, I'll be there. I'll wait for you. You know I'll wait." He would have drawn her closer and for a moment she felt the coarse linen of his smock against her shoulder. She could smell the strong human smell of his body, and disliking it, twisted herself away. The moment that she had broken from him she regretted that she had not let him kiss her, yet was proud that she had made herself unobtainable. She ran on to deliver the parcel and wouldn't look back though she knew that he gaped after her.

In the big mansion she was set to wait in the servants' quarters, perched mutely on the end of a form in the passage where the weeping stones smelt evilly of water. A footman walked past her, eyeing her with interest, and she smiled at him childishly. He looked back at her, knowing that the innocent smile had challenged him in an unchildlike way. He was dark with blackbird-bright eyes; all the way home she remembered the look in them like fires that do not smoulder, but flame and are avaricious. She kept on thinking about him, and the form in the beautiful uniform, and thinking how grand he looked, and how beautiful he was. But above her. Too far above her. That was how she dismissed him for the moment.

II

SHE WAS eager for the night to come, remembering that Andrew would be in the shrubberies and she could perhaps sneak down to the kitchen when all the others slept. The children went to bed with their nurse, whilst Emy slept on the floor of the boot cup-

5

board. She was young and thought nothing of it, sleeping easily. The palliasse was old and bulging, ripped in places, and it smelt of unwashed bodies and fouled feathers. She hardly noticed any of that, stripping to her shift, and unloosing her hair to let it lie proudly in a chestnut stream about her shoulders.

She lay there waiting until the place was quiet, with only the far sound of heavy snoring coming from below stairs, then she slipped out silently on her bare feet. She went into the kitchen. If anybody interrupted her she could always say that she had gone back for something that she had forgotten, or had thought that she heard thieves, or make some excuse, and she chuckled to herself thinking how easy it would be to cheat them.

The kitchen was dim; there were blackbeetles on the floor and the tiny chinks of starlight illuminated their iridescence. She lit a candle, sticking it in a heavy china sconce, and stood it by the sill, so that it flickered palely, a wan ghost in an eerie room.

As yet the June moon had not risen. Glancing out, she heard no sound from the shrubbery and wondered if Andrew was there. Could he see her, for she was so short? An idea came to her and she climbed on to the scrubbed kitchen table and stood there illuminated by the one candle. Hams in bags and bunches of dried herbs were clustered in the cross beams above her and an aromatic smell came to her. Here she was on a dais, a platform; she was the unobtainable, exalted above him, and following her desire she began to posture to imaginary music. She lifted tantalizingly the hem of her shift, she moved from one eager attitude to another, becoming so interested that she did not realize that a young colt of a man had drawn himself out of the shrubberies, and now approached the window, and knelt before it, staring in. His mouth was dry as a tavern floor with desire as he watched her marbled in the blue moonlight, her chestnut hair flung about her, concealing yet revealing her firm young breasts.

6

He was so intent and she so eager that neither of them realized that Mrs. Thomas herself had awakened, and hearing something unusual had come down. She had tried to rouse her husband, but he had been out with his kinsman Alderman Boydell of London, who was staying on a visit at the inn, and they had been to a cockfight at Megan's Barn, dining and wining over well, so that now he lay in a drunken stupor.

As she came down the stairs she took a hunting-switch from the wall, and her mouth set evilly. The moment that she neared the kitchen she knew that something was amiss; the door responded noiselessly to her touch, and the first thing that she saw was the young man's face pressed to the window intent and lecherous, whilst the girl postured on the table, the single candle irradiating her provocative body.

"You baggage!" she exclaimed. "Here in a respectable kitchen, inviting fancy men to watch you!"

Emy was so horrified by this unexpected turn that she could only stare helpless as a child, and all her courage ebbed. Until now she had been completely mistress of the situation, but now she was horrified, as she felt masterful and punitory hands pulling her from the table.

"I meant nothing . . ."

"I'll teach you to dance naked for village boys," said Mrs. Thomas. Her big body was muffled in a wrapper, and there was nothing lovely or kind about her, for she was a massive woman with a remorseless heart who felt that love was "dirty."

"I meant no harm . . ."

"That doesn't concern me." Mrs. Thomas was now intent on punishment; she laid firm hold of the girl's body, taking a grip of the chestnut hair which she twined round her left hand and swinging Emy towards her. Her intention became only too plain, and Emy screaming writhed to get away.

"Don't whip me, don't whip me!" she implored. If only Andrew had not been there she believed

7

that she could have taken her punishment, but Mrs. Thomas, resentful and vindictive, had forgotten that someone watched them. She pushed the girl's shift aside and began to beat her. It was the first time that anyone had raised a hand against Emy Hart, and the bodily pain was as nothing to the mental anguish. She was so proud of her body, and so ashamed that it should be exposed and striped red, for the hunting-switch drew blood. She screamed, clawing helplessly at her mistress's skirts, which availed her nothing.

Only when her arm was tired did Mrs. Thomas push the girl before her to the cupboard, and fling her down on the fetid mattress. All night Emy's body stung and ached; she could not move for the pain, and worse still was the knowledge that Andrew must have seen the bitter degradation that she had suffered.

She felt that she could not stay here like this, she hated the house, and the loveless, vituperative mistress; she must go away. She dressed next day, her pretty face swollen with crying, and her body still bleeding.

"Well, that'll teach you to behave better," said Mary who had been roused by the shrieks, "bringing your dirty ways into a respectable house! Girls of your kind want whipping."

Emy said nothing, only protesting that she was ill, and in the middle morning she crept out of the house and made her way back to Grandmother Kidd's cottage. By the grace of God her mother was home from London on a visit with her lady, who had parents in the neighbourhood. She saw the child coming in at the gate and walking soberly like a stiffened old woman.

"Why, what's the matter with my Emy?"

Kindness was too much; the girl flung herself into her mother's arms. "I can't go back, I just can't go back."

"And you shan't go back. You shall come right away to London where they know how to treat girls properly. Whatever were you doing to make the mistress so angry with you?"

"I went down to the kitchen in my shift looking for a cheese-cake because I was so hungry," she confessed; "a man was peering in through the window, and she thought I went to meet him."

"A downright shame." It was Grandmother Kidd who bridled up at that. "Why, Emy's going sixteen, and it's time she went to a good place where they don't think wicked things of her. She's pretty and she's good, and she'll go far."

"I'll make my respects and tell the mistress myself," said Emy's mother, and she went off up to the big house to explain what had happened.

Emy was considerably frightened. On her grandmother's advice she went to hide herself in the hayloft where the sweetness of other summers lingered in the strong, almost musty, scent of dead clovers and withered marguerites. It was comfortable in the hay, and she could lie there warmly drowsy, with the sunlight falling through the loft window, wreathed in the strong, coarse ivy that darkened it a little. Here her wounds did not smart so much, and with the buoyancy of youth she could feel her dignity returning.

As she lay half asleep, she heard a step on the wooden stair of the loft and knew that a man was climbing upwards to her. Andrew had come to the house—he had guessed that after last night's adventure she would run away—and her grandmother, thinking no harm, had directed him to the loft.

"Aye, but it was a rare beating," he said and grinned at the memory of it.

Emy squirmed in the hay, hating that he should recall it, and she began to weep. He crawled across to her, and drew her clumsily into his arms whilst she, turning, clung to him.

"Comfort me!" she begged.

"My pretty one, my pretty one!" He nuzzled his face into the crook of her throat. He liked the sweet body scent of her which was much like the hay itself.

He liked the way that she turned childishly and clung to him, and the softness of her forming breasts which he could cup with his hands. "My pretty one," he kept saying, bereft of other words with which to express his feelings.

He held her masterfully, and she knew by the way that he touched her, that she was disturbed. As though her body warned her! As though it throbbed and fluttered. Instinctively she drew back from the closer embraces of his arms.

"No, Andrew, you'd do me a wrong."

"I'd never wrong anyone so innocent, nor so pretty."

"My mother has told me that men mean a girl ill."

"All mothers say that. I'd never think ill of you, my pretty."

She thought of Ann Symonds and her bastard boy born and strangled in the hay. It was perhaps the hay that recalled it, and then she thought confusingly of love coming to her with the sweet dead scent of the flowers. "I don't know what to think . . ." she whispered.

"Leave yourself be in my arms, my pretty."

"I'm afraid, and yet so happy."

"I'll make you happy."

She could feel his quick breath on her cheeks, and the heat of his mouth as he sucked hers, feeling as though he had thirsted for this moment all his life, and now would never let it go. She had always known that love would be wonderful and exciting, but never so full as this. Unable to stay herself she lifted her arms and clasped them about him, and so they lay, locked together in the warm resilient sweetness of the hay.

It was her grandmother who disturbed them.

Old Mrs. Kidd came lurching laboriously up the loft stairs, a mild old woman suspecting nothing, and therefore undismayed. She could not manage the stairs easily, so that they heard her wheezing as she groped for a foothold, long before she ever appeared through the square shaft of the open trap-door. This provided them with time to spring apart.

"Your mother's back, Emy."

"My mother's back? Surely not so soon?"

"She's been two hours, and she has news for you, my dear. She has seen her mistress and made all manner of arrangements. You are to go to London."

"To London?" The girl sprang up, supporting her body with her two arms thrust back into the hay. London was news indeed, she could hardly believe it! Her mother had been to see Mrs. Thomas, who had told her a stern story of which Mrs. Duggan—as she liked to be called—did not believe a single word. She had faith in her beautiful little daughter, and was proud of the fact that she was by far the best-looking girl in Flintshire; she believed that the whole story was a tissue of lies provoked by jealousy, for everybody knew that Mrs. Thomas was older than her husband, heavy with childbearing, and that she did not love Mr. Thomas. Undoubtedly it was envy of Emma's beauty that had raddled her.

Leaving after a somewhat stormy interview, Mrs. Duggan had gone to see her own mistress at the big house where she was staying, had explained the facts and they had consulted together. The mistress knew of a suitable situation in London, in the home of a respectable tradesman who lived in St. James's Market, and who would hire Emy Hart. The girl, she said, could easily go there in the coach.

When this was explained to Emy, she knew that even the thought of London did not fill her with enthusiasm; she had come to the idea fresh from the hayloft and a lover's caresses, and had every reason for wanting to stay here. Now she longed to see more of Andrew and seemed already to be part of him, as he of her.

"Must I go so soon?" she faltered.

11

"The sooner the better. The village will only talk about you leaving Mrs. Thomas's so suddenly."

"If I could stay but for one short month with my grandmother?"

"No, Emy, it's time you were away. You're a big girl now, and London's a fine city. It will make a woman of you."

She stared falteringly at her mother. "I have loved Hawarden," she faltered.

"I know, and that's right and proper, but all the same you'll go to London in the next coach, and I shall be back soon, and you'll find that you are a lot happier there."

"Very well."

And that night when she lay down to sleep on the straw bed, she remembered stories she had heard of London, of the fine gentlemen, even of the King himself. Young Tom Jarvis, in the village, had already told her a good deal about London. He had been a servant at Brooks Club before he came back home to marry his Nellie and settle down. And what he had had to say about the gambling that went on there had made Emma's eyes gleam with envy.

She felt inside her that if she were given a chance she would take to gambling as a duck takes to water. Unfortunately for her, this was all too true, and in later life she was to curse that urge to back her luck with money.

But that, of course, she could not foresee, and for the moment, as she sometimes listened to young Jarvis, her vivid imagination transplanted her from the humble village surroundings into a world where cards flashed on baize tables, and the light from the great chandeliers lit up the brilliant clothes and jewels of the people around the tables.

He told her of the great gambling parties at Brooks, where £50 was often the minimum wager, and as much as £10,000 lay on the table at one time; where some of the more regular gamblers even adopted a kind of uniform covering their beautiful

12

lace ruffles with leather cuffs, and wearing high-crowned hats with wide brims to shield their eyes against the lights.

There was the brilliant Mr. Charles Fox, the young politician, sitting hour after hour at the faro table, watching the game with feverish eyes, unable to tear himself away from the pastime which was ruining him. Already, at the age of only twenty-five, they said, he had run through a fortune of £140,000, and most of it had been left behind on the green baize of the gaming tables.

Once young Mr. Fox and some friends had run a bank for days on end, continuously, day and night, each taking turns to keep the bank open; and food and wine had been brought in to them; and other players came and went, but Mr. Fox and his friends still kept the bank running.

And though he had won a fair amount to start with, he lost in the end, and in fact ended up "£30,000 worse than nothing." So that soon afterwards people in St. James's Street, who had nothing better to do, filled in an hour or two watching the moneylenders packing up Mr. Fox's clothes and books, and carting them off from his lodgings.

Emma listened to all these stories from the great city with eager, open eyes. One day perhaps all those dear dreams she had fostered would come true, and she *would* be a great lady. She forgot this afternoon when she had lain in the hay with a young labouring man whispering passionate ecstasies in her ear and turning her drab world to rose and silver. She looked ahead. There was adventure, silks and satins, sedans and compliments. It was in that spirit that she left Hawarden.

Her cotton clothes had been stitched and repaired by mother and grandmother, and then made into a bundle for her to carry. Her one pair of shoes was hurriedly cobbled. She was just sixteen and starting along the path to destiny; probably she herself was the only person who realized how much lay ahead.

13

When the coach entered the village the boys ran after it to the inn where Mine Host himself waited to receive it. He was rubicund as an apple, with little Emy Hart near him, her muslin cap pulled down over her curls, her cotton bundle in her hand and all her worldly goods neatly folded inside that bundle.

"Now be a good girl, Emy, do what your mistress tells you and work hard."

"I'll come back rich and then I'll make a lady of you," promised Emy and that was a promise that the girl never forgot.

They might think that the moment had endowed her with illusions, but that wasn't true. The dreams were within her.

She saw the beautiful ladies who travelled inside the coach, the postillions with the horses, flecks of foam dripping down their shining harness. She herself was too poor to afford a seat inside, but had to travel on top with the gentlemen and the less illustrious, whose pockets compelled the outside journey. It was a warm enough night. There would be stars, and as long as they were not beset by highwaymen it should be a pleasant trip. Emy was young enough to wish secretly for highwaymen, for she wanted all the adventure that life could give her.

She climbed the iron ladder up the side of the coach, her blue print frock swaying in the wind, her hair creeping from under her cap redly gold. She found that a man with brown eyes, seeing her coming, leaned down for her hand and helped her.

"That's better, my little wench," he said, then seeing her more closely, noted the fact that later on would become immortal. "Gad, but it's a woman!" for in her eyes was knowledge.

"I'm sixteen," she told him.

"A redoubtable sixteen," he challenged her, "and the prettiest that ever I did see, I'll warrant."

"I thank you, sir, but you watch me too closely."

"It is not often that my eyes have the good fortune to see so fair a face."

14

She laughed at that, for now she had recaptured the delicious feeling of power again. She felt as though she trod a mountain-top exhilarated by the air, with the world beneath her, hers for the asking.

This was indeed a gentleman; he wore a Dark Major wig, his coat was a good brocade and his overcoat fanciful, with frills of the kind that she most admired. The villagers never wore clothes like that, and she had been brought up in the atmosphere of coarse, harsh linen and of fustian coats. Even Mr. Thomas, who was rich, dressed soberly without fal-lals, and she eyed these with interest.

"And now you're watching me?" he said.

"You have been gracious to me, sir."

"And we're travelling companions." He edged a shade closer on the hard seat and she did not repulse him. She smiled warmly, and he took her hand in his fine gentlemanly one, with the soft skin and fingers so that she knew by the feel that they had never worked.

As they sat there hand in hand she was quite glad that she was going right away from the village. Suddenly by comparison it had become sordid. Everything that had ever taken shape in her life had gone, and she was seeing the dreams that lay ahead. They were bold dreams and she had faith in them and believed that they would carry her far.

Now the driver had vaulted into his place; there was the sound of the horn, and the little boys were running out into the village street to watch the excitement of the coach starting for London. Mine Host smiled and waved to them. There was the flinty echo of the horses' hoofs against the cobbles of the yard; then the coach lurched clumsily forward with a tremendous hallo from the horn, and it racketed off down the village street.

Emy Hart, the immortal Emma, had started for London.

III

AT FIRST the girl chattered, exuberant at the prospect of the journey, then when the shadows began falling, she drowsed to sleep innocently enough, with her head lying against the epauletted shoulder of her fellow traveller. She breathed lightly, her lips rosily parted, her lids blue-veined and heavily lashed against her transparent cheek. Glancing at her from time to time, he wondered how it was she had attracted him when he had first pulled her up to the coach top; for now she looked to be no more than a child. He would have placed her age at about fourteen.

At the first inn where they stopped to change horses, she woke with a jolt, and the older travellers scrambled stiffly enough from their perches. The girl, however, was lithe, and swung herself down, walking like an eager child. He took her into the inn and bought her a cheese-cake and a glass of red wine, so that she slept all the sounder on the journey towards London.

"And what will you do when you get to the great city?" he asked her when they climbed back into their seats and the coach started again with fresh and more vigorous horses.

"My mother has arranged for me to go as a maid-servant to a situation in St. James's Market."

"You're far too pretty to be a maid."

"What else would I be?" she enquired. For one moment those violet blue eyes asked a question which he knew set all his pulses quivering.

"You should be somebody's love," he replied cautiously.

16

"Faith, sir, but I'm too young!"

"You've thought of love, I warrant?" he ventured.

"I've thought of it," and she dimpled at that. For Emy had thought of love, and anxious to unburden herself she told him haltingly of the affair with Andrew Lack, who had hidden in the shrubberies to watch her as she posed on the kitchen table. It had been amusing, with her only in her shift, and the candle in its sconce at the far end. She had known that she looked her best, glamorously irradiated, and had appreciated the effect, for Emy Hart was an exhibitionist and loved nothing better than to exploit her charms.

Her words tempted the fellow passenger, and he felt his throat constricting. His hands wandered to the cotton bodice, tight across those young warm breasts that swelled with a girlish spring-time demanding more freedom. But he told himself that she was only a child, and, determined to make no mistake, held back.

The coach arrived in London with a new day only recently born. The city was an intricate maze of little streets and close alleys, with filthy, stinking gutters where pariah dogs and the kites scavenged. A few late sedan chairs were tottering home, the lackeys' eyes swollen for want of sleep as they staggered tiredly back. Emy was fully awake and her eyes danced as they went down the Strand and she saw London for the first time; she could smell the dull air with its strong tainted smell so different from the freshness of Hawarden, and she could see the roses blooming red and white on the bricks and rubbles. There were mercers in their tie wigs busying themselves, and beggars trying to excite compassion by squatting in the disgusting gutters asking for alms, or searching with claw-like hands in the garbage in the hope of food.

"But how will I ever find my way?" she asked, turning to her companion. Instinctively he knew the

17

way that she would find, but for the moment everything was an adventure.

Eventually she did make her way to the house in St. James's Market, fronted by stumpy posts of stone which darkened the already gloomy entrance down the area steps to the servants' quarters. She descended to the dingy basement. Blackbeetles crawled in the crevices, leaving that intimate and sickly stench which mingled with the humidity of stale bodies and moist paving-stones and the fungus that grew stealthily under the larder shelves. But she was used to poor quarters and she thought nothing of it, for London passed the door, and London was adventure.

In the first bewildering hour she met Jane Powell, a little maid a month or so Emy's senior, never as beautiful but with much the same plans for living.

"Oh, it's not bad as places go," said Jane casually; "the mistress is sharp and master foolish, but the young master's gay enough. He likes me and has promised that if I will do little kindnesses for him he'll get me to Drury Lane and make a great actress of me."

"Oh, surely?" for Emy was in rapt admiration. It stirred a flame within her, and she thought now of Drury Lane as a mecca. She wanted to have the plaudits of the crowd, to be admired and petted, and although once she had heard Mrs. Thomas say that only whores acted at the Lane, she thought it would be wonderful.

From the first Emy did not take to the house in St. James's Market, for the mistress was too sharp and the master too frowsty, with his wig for ever awry. The young master was already busy with Jane Powell, and at night Emy acted as watchman for them. She and Jane purported to share a corner of the stairs that led downwards in uncovered stone from the sumptuous ground floor to the servants' quarters. But every night Jane flitted up those stairs to the room where the young master slept, and Emy would go after her, a little watchful ghost for them.

18

Waiting in the chill she thought covetously of warm arms and hot kisses, and of the two locked together in the big comfortable bed whilst she stayed without, aching for the same pleasure. Because she was Emy, she passed the time by posing to amuse herself before the big rectangular mirror which reached from ceiling to floor, posing with arms upraised and body tilted. Once, illuminated by the light of the chandelier, she was disturbed, and turned only as she heard a step beside her.

"A man?" she gasped, and drew her shift closer to conceal the beauty that in her excitement she had exposed.

It was not a man, however, it was a lady of fortune, Mrs. Trowling, who was staying with the family at the time, and feeling faint, had gone downstairs to find a cup of wine. She paused.

"Oh, my pretty!" she said and smiled toothily, the knowledge of Eve in her appraising eyes. Emy knew she wasn't angry.

"You—you will not tell on me?" she faltered.

"You are far too pretty," said Mrs. Trowling, "you are wasted here, you should be on the stage. How many gentlemen would sell their souls to taste of so much beauty?"

Emy was enchanted at the turn of the conversation and she said with modesty, "I am very young."

Mrs. Trowling came closer. "You should come to my home," she said, "there you would have opportunities denied to many. You would be my personal maid and the life I lead would force you to meet people—the right people."

"But I dare not ask my mistress to leave!!"

Mrs. Trowling nodded, for she had already made up her mind. "I shall take you away, Emy, and what *is* your name really? Emy is no name at all."

"I was christened Amy, it was my Grandmother Kidd who called me Emy, and some people Emily."

"Emily is too ordinary for an extraordinary person. I shall call you Emma," and as she said it, Mrs.

Trowling had the feeling that the name Emma would be emblazoned in gold so that all the world would read it. Not only Emma, her lavish imagination went on ahead, it would be our dearest Emma. "I believe that Emma will go a long way," she whispered, as though with premonition, as she touched the exquisite shoulder, its faint tracery of blue vein lying translucent on the pearl of the flesh.

However, there was one person whom they had not reckoned on, for when Jane Powell heard that Emma was leaving to go to Mrs. Trowling's she was almost jealous. "Oh, but how fortunate you are!"

"I know, and I'm delighted."

From Jane's point of view the young master was too tardy in fulfilling his promises, and although he was ardent at night, the actress of Drury Lane did not come any nearer. The nights spent in the big bed with the sealed windows, the scent of pomanders and his rose hair pomade, were almost too much, for Jane wanted the work at the theatre to materialize. She began to be afraid that all he wanted was to make her his mistress and not to see her famous before an appraising crowd.

"One day we'll be at Drury Lane together," said Emma, lifting her arms and striking an attitude. She was like marble, a lovely cold statue, but her heart was vitally warm. As yet she was virgin, but the day would come—and soon—when she would lose virginity to some gentleman, and, thought she, once those gates are broken down how shall I ever resist the joy of pleasure in his arms? She trembled in ecstasy as she thought of it.

When she came to Mrs. Trowling's house it was far more beautiful than the one in St. James's Market which she had not liked. Now she was given a little room high in the eaves with a magnificent view of London spread out before her. She could see the clustering houses, and the verdantly green fields where Tottenham Court Road straggled across them with the wetly shining marshlands radiated in drifts of sunlight. She could look out on the woods that stood round Portland Place, and away to the right was the rural tree-grown district of Islington.

"Mrs. Trowling is fond of girls and will do anything for them," said Ann Buckle, the withered maid who had run the home for years and had seen life pass by in service. Old Ann's wrinkles horrified Emy; 'before this happens to me I will at least have tasted the true joy of living,' she promised herself.

Mrs. Trowling entertained lavishly; her husband, who was younger than she, was a vigorous man in the late thirties, and Elizabeth Trowling blinded herself to his infidelities, believing that she satisfied every want with her money. She trusted the husband so much that she never hesitated to introduce beautiful girls to the household.

"She knows that beauty amuses me; she knows too that she is the only woman for me," he lied from the head of his table as he leered at her between the spiral silver candlesticks.

He glanced at Emma as she filled the wine-glasses for the first time; his lips said nothing, his eyes everything.

"You come from the country?" he asked her in the end.

"From Hawarden, sir."

"They breed them fair at Hawarden."

"Yes, sir," and she dimpled.

She filled the glasses for a week, and once when she passed the master at table she felt his hand creep against her thigh under cover of the heavy linen cloth, creep and caress. No one could see and for a moment she felt a catch in her throat, as though half afraid, but she gave no sign of it. Once on the stairs when she went up to bed, he was coming down carrying a huge candle in his hand. He lifted the carved silver sconce, holding it so that the flame illuminated the girl's face.

"To bed so soon?" he said, then under his breath leering a little, "with whom?"

"Oh, sir, you do me an injustice," said Emma, but all the time her heart pounded and fluttered.

"You may be only sixteen, but you look to be a woman. If you do not know love, it is time some man taught you," he told her, his pendulous face coming nearer. He lifted hers with one finger set under the chin so that he could stare at her enquiringly with avaricious eyes. She admired the smartness of his wig, the smell of the pomade that he used, his shaven face smoothly clean, whilst his eyes teased her own.

"In good time," she said, and wished that her heart would quieten.

"One night you will find me willing and at your door."

"Oh, no, sir, no, sir. Mrs. Trowling would be very angry. She would dismiss me, and rightly. I would have nowhere to go. I am a poor lone girl, sir, I would not have that happen."

"It will happen," he said, and his hand closed masterfully over hers. "You were born too tempting, Emma Hart, I pray that you were also born generous. One night I shall be at your door and you must open to me. I shall expect that of you."

When she got to her room her breath was coming in little gasps, and she pushed a small chest against the door, barring it because the lock was broken. Suddenly she was afraid. This was indeed adventure, but if it went too far it would most certainly entail dismissal. He did not come. Nor was he there the next night. On the third she did not bar the way with the chest because she knew that she was disappointed. Why had he not come? He had promised. Was it that he did not find her fair enough? Or were there too many watchers? Not only Mrs. Trowling, but Ann Buckle. Ann Buckle had had experience of the master before, Ann Buckle was the woman to guard against.

'I have got to be careful,' thought Emma.

IV

ON THE fourth night when Emma was starting for her room, the study door opened and she saw the master framed in the lintels. She thought that he must have been drinking, for about him there was the strong smell of brandy. He stooped a little, his body too copious for his years, and somehow he did not look attractive.

"To-night?" he asked.

"Sir, I beg you . . . you will get me into serious trouble."

"You will get me into serious trouble if you keep me dallying too long," and he shut the door abruptly.

She went to bed with the curious sense of elation mingled with a pleasurable alarm. She did not push the chest across the door but she sat there to listen to the watchman below in the street: "Eleven o'clock and all's well," and for a while she dreamed. Then she began to undress, hanging up cotton frock and petticoats; she undid the coarse grey stays that were necessary for so firm a figure with no tendency to spread. It was a relief to be free of them, and it delighted her to see that tonight of all nights they had not marked her body as sometimes. She wished she had a better shift. She envied fine ladies; there was Lady Charters of the fashionable world, who had taken tea with Mrs. Trowling only today, and who wore enchantingly fine clothes. But, Ann Buckle said, Lady Charters had been a great actress and had become famous in the oldest—even if the more usual—profession. She attracted men. 'Lovely, lucky Lady Charters!' thought Emma.

She brushed out her hair, curling it round her fin-

23

gers in ringlets, and as they dropped she heard the stair creak, and was instantly alert. She opened her door a knife's breadth and peered through the yellow chink. George Trowling was coming cautiously, holding a candle high to light the way. He had removed his outer clothes and wore a bedgown and a velvet cloak which trailed. The softness of the rich material fascinated her, she was indeed lucky, yet now she felt afraid that the untasted pleasure might be too sweet. She remembered Ann Symonds of Hawarden who had swung on a gibbet, her head crumpled forward on her breast, her neck broken. Now there was no time to push the small chest before her door, for the master was on the top stair. What shall I do? she asked herself frantically.

He came in, and, seeing her, hesitated for a moment, his mouth filling with appreciation. He was no longer the man who sat at the head of the table and touched her thigh under cover of the cloth, he was a man in her own position of life; the man who wanted her.

"I knew you were beautiful, but not as beautiful as this," he stammered.

"Sir, you have no right here."

"I should have been here a couple of nights since, but thought a little anticipation would make you more anxious," he said and set the candle down on the small chest which was there.

Suddenly afraid that he would hurt her, she said, "No, no, you must go. I will call for help."

"You're not afraid? Not truly afraid? You're too lovely to be afraid, my pretty one."

"But, sir, you do not realize. Never yet have I known a man." She confessed it almost as a guilty secret.

"Blame the men for that. You have lived with a backward lot," and he laughed. Over-sensitive, she recognized a certain harshness about his tone that repelled her.

"You will get me dismissed."

"But first I will love you, my sweetest enchantress," and he kissed the hand that he held. His kisses ran up inside her arm to where the shift but half-concealed her body. She did not know if she were fascinated or awed, but suddenly wrenched herself free in an attempt at affronted modesty.

"For pity's sake!" she begged and moved away.

"Emma, in your life you will give much to many men. Give me a little now. My wife is old."

"She has been kind to me."

"She is not kind to me. I know she is rich, but you cannot buy love. She doesn't realize that."

At this moment Emma was almost sorry for him as he looked at her so tenderly. He was big and powerful whereas she was small and brittle; the strength of his body would almost break hers, and he alarmed her. "My mother would chide me," she faltered.

"That is foolish for she will not know. And, my pretty, do you suppose that your mother has never been in a man's arms, else how were you born?"

She glanced at him half slyly. "I was born in wedlock, sir," she said.

"Gad, but you've clever! You know the answer." He sat down on the bed under the window which she had with such difficulty opened when she first came here. For Emma coveted the air that so seldom seemed to filter through this fetid city which stunk of garbage in the gutters where the kites scavenged. Sometimes she wondered however the people lived and did not all die of fevers.

"Come, you wear too many clothes, and I do not permit that," he said as though more desirous.

He plucked at her and she knew suddenly that she could not go through with this. "I cannot," she besought him.

"You must not think to put me off that way." He had firm hold of her, and she realized how strong he was. He forced her to kneel on the floor between his knees, her body pressed back so that she could not turn her face from his kisses, even though they almost suffocated her. Her spine seemed to bend, and she struggled frantically to escape. Once she screamed but his mouth on hers silenced it.

"I take what I want," he told her imperiously. "I am a hard master and a compelling lover."

"Please, sir, let me go."

He probably would not have released her, save that whilst she protested, trying to thrust him away, the door behind her slowly began to open. He saw it first and paused dismayed, she could feel his hands relaxing. Then, seeing that the chink of light widened, he pushed her from him behind the bed-head, where she lay cowering, praying that it might not be her mistress.

It was not her mistress.

Ann Buckle stood there with a heavy cloth shawl worn over her stiff linen nightdress. She said nothing. Without a word, George Trowling got up from the bed, sobered of adventure and alarmed. He went across the room with the humpy floor, his wig awry, his velvet bedgown bunched about his hips. He said never a word but passed Ann Buckle not even looking at her. She said nothing either. When the last sound of his incautious footsteps had died away in the open newel of the curling stairs, there came the sound of a door shutting and a key rasping to, then she said to Emma, "Come out."

The girl crawled out. "Oh, Ann, what have you saved me from!" and began to cry bitterly.

"Why did I save you? Dear God, it will only happen again."

"But you came in time. He mauled me, but I am still a maid . . ." and, as if she were thankful, she clung protestingly to Ann. The gaunt woman lifted her in her arms as though she were a babe, and she laid her on the bed.

"You cannot stay here in this house, Emma Hart, he will be here in this room again, and more cunningly. Next time it may be that I cannot save you. You must go away. You must leave this house."

"Now? Now, whilst it is still night?" she asked aghast.

"No, not to-night, to-morrow. Before another night is born and brings opportunity again. You must be away by to-morrow night."

"But where can I go?" and she began to cry. She did not seem to keep her places well, and not through her own fault. She hid her face, alarmed at what would happen if she were left alone in this big city.

"Listen," said Ann, fondling her as though she were her own child. "Listen, I have thought about this, and there is Lady Charters. She said that she wanted you and I am sure that she would take you in. You must go to her." She stroked the girl's shoulder with her tired, work-frayed hands. "I never had a daughter, but had I had one, you would have been the child that I would have asked. All the same, Emma, you have no place here, and you must go to Lady Charters."

"But how can I tell her about this?"

"She will know. I am always saving girls from him and it will continue until the rheumatics get me, and I am too old and decrepit to get up the stairs in time. But this shall not happen to you, for greater than he shall taste of your sweetness, my pretty one. Remember what old Ann said to you to-night, your man will be a great hero and a great lover."

"Ann, how good you are!"

"I will despatch a message to Lady Charters in the morning, and I know that she will understand."

They slept that night together. Suddenly Emma knew that she was drawn to this woman with the malevolent eyes, and the sparse hair plastered down almost to her gaunt cheeks; the woman wanted an emotion that she had never tasted, the joy of passion and the agony of childbirth, as fruit of the insufferable sweetness, and a daughter of her own to hold in her arms.

In the morning it was Ann who told her that she

27

would leave for a more fashionable world. She had done with the middle classes and a star was rising in the sky; the star was our dearest Emma.

Long after Ann Buckle lay in the sleep of early morning, heavily tired, the girl lay there seeing before her a dream illuminated by flame. If one has courage and youth and faith a star may rise, so great that it will radiate the whole sky. She knew then for certain that her dreams were not misleading. She would be famous.

V

ANN BUCKLE was as good as her word: she saw Lady Charters the next morning and the whole thing was arranged on the spot. Mrs. Trowling raised no opposition. It might well have been that recently she had come to the conclusion that there was something suspicious about her husband's behaviour. When he was dressing one morning sitting on the edge of the communal bed, pulling on his silken hose, his gnarled legs exposed, he remarked that Emma had a pretty face, and more—that was prettier—under her frock. He said things like that to nettle his wife, and she refused to grab at the bait, but at the same time wondered if it had not been folly to tempt him with such beauty.

Perhaps the seed of the idea germinated. It would not be uprooted, so that she was not regretful when Lady Charters' sedan was set down outside her door and enquiries set afoot for her personal maid.

"By all means take her with you," said Mrs. Trowling, "she is a petulant little creature, for ever giving herself airs and graces," for she had not forgotten her husband's ribaldry as he thrust his legs into the silk stockings.

The chit should go at once! Emma, her few clothes wrapped in their linen covering and carried like a baby in her arms, demurely followed her new mistress's chair through the street. The fashionable home was in a better quarter. It was grandly luxurious, and its rectangular windows were heavily hung with brocade. Over the door an exquisite fanlight caught the sun and glistened like diamonds. Lady Charters alighted. Emma admired her powdered wig tied with turquoise bows, and her frock of bunched silk which fell so voluminously about her. Lady Charters loved pretty things and was grievously extravagant.

She took the new maid into the great hall that was colonnaded and paved in marble.

"We shall get on well, my pretty one," she said; "you must have grown tired of Mrs. Trowling, and George is always so ardent. Here you will be a great attraction. Do you sing?"

"I have never yet tried."

"Well, sing me a note or two now!"

The girl hesitated a moment, then gave a little impulsive trill. Though untrained, it was sweet and true.

"You will shape. Maybe you dance also, or mime?"

Looking at her Emma poised on a toe, her arms outstretched, and about her at that moment there was a piquancy and a delight that were enchanting. Her face had become the face of a little madonna, tipped up to the light; her hands shadowed on the marble of the floor were flower-like. Lady Charters was quick to note the sensitiveness of the interpretation. "Lud, but the gentlemen will be intrigued," she said, "and you shall exhibit at my evening parties. We always seek something new, and it shall be Emma and her attitudes."

"I shall be most happy, milady."

Emma was allotted a small bedroom adjacent to

her mistress's powder closet, so that it was for ever sweet with the scents of pomades and toilet waters, instead of the garbage of the city gutters. Pale green shutters framed the long windows and shaded the mulberry satin hangings. Never had the village girl slept so grandly, and she could not believe that this was really happening to her.

On the second afternoon her mother came round, for Ann Buckle had told her of the change in little Emy's fortunes.

"Oh, indeed you are the lucky one, Emy," said Mrs. Duggan; "now whatever happens, make up your mind to stay with this mistress for some time, for few have such chances."

"Of course I shall stay, and what is more, she wants me to sing and act at her evening parties."

"Do what she asks, that is wise."

There was no Lord Charters in the home and when Emma asked the cook about it, she laughed and said that "the gentlemen would have a job to discover the master, she'd warrant," and nudged the housemaid with her horny red elbows, ogling meanwhile the little negro page that Lady Charters kept. It was the fashion of the moment to have a negro boy and Lady Charters delighted in Sambo.

In the early evening the girl was sent out to buy custard tarts and cheese-cakes for to-night from the Chelsea Bun House, famous for its pies.

"Can you find your way, coming from the country?" asked the cook.

"I have a tongue in my head."

"And you'll need it. The men ask pretty girls all manner of sly questions," and the cook smacked her lips.

"I can take care of myself."

"You'd better take young Sambo with you. He's not a bad child. Here, Tar-Brush, you . . ." and she called him up.

Emma took the boy along to the Chelsea Bun House, and whilst the cakes and pies were being packed into her basket she waxed confidential and told the serving woman of her new place.

"Ah, with Lady Charters, and you so pretty too," said the woman rejoicingly, and she went to the doorway that led into the bakehouse, calling to the men who stood kneading the dough in the wide wooden troughs. "Here's another of Lady Charters' pretty innocents," she said and they all laughed significantly.

Somehow Emma felt hot and uncomfortable, and she turned without a word and went out to Sambo, who led her home prattling of the parties. She would see every kind; distinguished writers and singers, artists of all sorts. Here she might even meet old Dr. Johnson, for he had visited them once, and had made trouble because someone angered him. And once, said Sambo, the King in his chair with the Yeomen of the Guard, and peering out of them with a red, bloated face and wig awry. Also he had spoken with so broad an accent that they had had vast trouble to know what it was he meant.

Emma returned with her cakes, stepping daintily with the river on her right, the old landing steps flanked by statues of Tritons and Nereids, that fascinated her. For about Emma there was the salty flavour of the sea. She loved the sailing ships, and would have spent hours watching them, though perhaps it would have been more truthful to say that she loved those who sailed in them.

Her mistress had given her a lovely frock to wear for to-night. "It'll never do for you to look too simple in a cotton gown, and so disgrace me," she laughed and she tied the little grey frock with a pale blue ribbon sash and a muslin fichu that crossed the breasts.

"It is beautiful."

"It is wonderfully becoming."

"What will you want me to do?" asked Emma, who believed in Lady Charters and yet was apprehensive.

"At first I want you to watch the procedure; later

31

you will act as my maid and one of these days assist with the entertaining."

It was that first night that Emmy's country eyes were opened wide to the new fashionable world in which she found herself. Grand gentlemen came into the salon in silk and satin brocaded coats; their wigs were beautifully tended and tied, they paid exquisite compliments and dangled lace handkerchiefs. Emma stood behind her mistress's chair, and occasionally she saw a pair of roguish eyes looking towards her, but took no notice, behaving modestly as she believed became her, her eyes downcast on cheeks that were blushing.

Lady Charters sang and played the spinet. She recited poetry, and then in crueller vein, imitated her friends so that the audience cheered and applauded vigorously. As the evening progressed, the air of the luxurious room became hot and heavy, and although the company had already drunk enough, more wine was brought and served to them. It was then that Emma, a little tired of so much excitement, became aware of a younger man than the others who stood a little mournfully in a corner. He watched her intently, his dark eyes set under heavy brows, and she saw that his coat was of cherry silk, braided, but not so fashionably as the coats of the older men. Indeed he looked to be poorer than any of them. Recognizing the ardour of his look, she deliberately took a goblet of mulled wine to him and offered it herself.

He said, "What is your name? You are indeed quite the most beautiful creature that I have ever beheld."

"I'm called Emma Hart, and I am new here."

"You resemble a flower. I'm an artist and beauty so rare as yours should be painted. It is indeed the most perfect that I have ever seen, I could hardly believe that you were real."

Emma was flattered. There was nothing that she would like better than to sit for her picture to some

32

great artist, and thus be made immortal. "You are famous?" she asked innocently.

"Not yet. One day perhaps—one never knows. My teachers say that I hold great promise, but it is a hard road to tread and I am a poor man," and all the while his eyes were admiring her across the rim of his goblet. "If there were time could you sit for me?"

"I do not know if Lady Charters would permit it."

"She would not object. She is the most generous patron and would understand. I would love to paint you as you look to-day. My studio is in the street immediately behind this one, you could come to me and no one would know."

"I—I should love it," she faltered.

"My name is Charles Vere."

"Charles is a very beautiful name."

He touched her hand artlessly on the glass rim. "May I hope? Dare I desire?" he asked.

"I must have Lady Charters' permission; she is my mistress."

"And you are no man's mistress?"

"Lud, sir, what things you say!"

"Forgive me. You are so beautiful that I cannot imagine the men will long let you remain a maid."

She glanced at him again from under her downcast eyes, and blushed; he recognized that such modesty was tantalizing. A sudden hush came to the room, and looking up they saw that Lady Charters was standing in a tragic pose as an elusive muse. The onlookers clapped vociferously. ('I could do that as well, and better,' thought the girl, but naturally said nothing aloud.) Neither did she promise anything to Charles Vere, knowing that he had attracted her, but all the time she was aware of the somnolent fires in his eyes as he still watched her.

It was during another party that she herself started to give her "attitudes." Lady Charters suddenly tired of doing it all herself, and called the child to her. "This," said she, addressing the audience, "is my little country flower. You shall see what she can do.

33

She falls charmingly and naturally into exquisite poses. Play music for her."

For a moment Emma was shy, she glanced nervously about her, then summoning all her forces, fell into some of her simpler attitudes: The young girl at the well. The maiden surprised in the wood. The contrite Venus. She knew that she was a success, for she could sense the tenseness of the atmosphere before the applause broke. All the time Charles Vere was watching her. She had the freshly virginal charm so rare in the sophisticated salons of London at that date. She was intolerably beautiful.

"Where did you find so sweet a prize?" asked one or two, and old Sir Frederick Hayes—said to be Lady Charters' lover—nodded over his cup to the girl, eyeing her as though she were ripe fruit ready for the plucking. But it was Charles Vere who pressed closer and, inclining his head to Lady Charters, asked for permission to paint the pretty chit.

"By all means. Of course the little one shall sit for you, Charles. To-morrow if you will." He was instantly enchanted, and rendered speechless with wonder. "But," and milady laid a detaining hand on his arm, "there must be nothing more than painting. No teaching in other directions. I shall expect my little flower to return as she left me. That is understood, isn't it, Charles?"

The other men chuckled at the remark and he, reddening slightly, bowed, professing that no other thought had entered his head.

"But how shall I know the way to the studio?" asked Emma uneasily, and now it struck her by the other men's faces that Charles was accepted as a roué, although he had seemed so innocent.

"Sambo shall escort you," said Lady Charters, and as Charles would have interrupted, "No, that is accepted. Sambo goes with the child, or she does not sit for you at all."

It was during this party, too, that she was engaged in conversation with a serious-faced man with penetrating but compassionate eyes. Although for a while they spoke of little but trivialities, she deferentially and shyly, she soon became aware that he was not like so many of the other men she had seen in London. There was something intense yet wholly good which radiated from his personality.

He began to talk to her about men and women, old and young, who had transgressed the laws. To Emma's surprise, he almost seemed to be sorry for them.

"But surely, sir," she asked timidly, "surely they must be punished by being sent to prison for a spell, if they are lucky enough not to be hanged? Would you have them go free? I do declare, sir, it would be a dangerous land if all such people were unpunished."

"Prisons!" said her new acquaintance bitterly. "Yes, indeed, they should go to prison, in the hope that later they may reform their ways. But have you, my child, ever seen one of our prisons? But no, a silly question, you are far too young and innocent and I pray you never shall. For they are in truth like some horrid imitation of Hades! Picture, my child, men and women, old and young, rough and gentle, of all kinds and conditions, some healthy, some sick, some clean, some verminous, all together. Crowded together, in places where there is often no water supply, and very little air.

"Many of these places have no sewers. Others have sewers, but they are choked up. Such are our prisons, dens where felons and poor debtors who cannot pay their bills, prostitutes and poor apprentices who have stolen a crust of bread; all, all are cooped up together, unwashed, often starving—for in about half our country gaols there is no allowance of bread for debtors—sick, unloved, and, in many cases, forgotten. Small wonder that thousands die of gaol fever and smallpox!

"Nine years ago," he concluded bitterly, "it was agreed that no more convicts should be transported to America. Men would be kept in ships' hulks in the Thames and elsewhere. Now they tell me these hulks cannot hold any more, and that next year once again they will be sent overseas to toil under the blazing sun amid swamps and flies and disease. Working for heartless employers, dying like——" He stopped, made a gesture, and moved away.

All the rest of his life he was to devote to the betterment of prisons. Emma enquired his name, and was told it was John Howard. A sentimental dreamer, they said, who went about sticking his nose in where it was not wanted, and causing trouble and bother to the authorities and even to—worst of all—men's consciences.

VI

SAMBO KNEW the way. There had been a time when Charles Vere had painted milady in her new pink satin gown with the pearl embroideries, and they had been friends, said Sambo. He chuckled as he recounted the time when he had caught them unawares on the floor of the studio, the pink satin gown rumpled, the skirts torn. He had thought it to be most amusing.

The studio was a long, low house which stood in a meaner street. A red rose straggled lushly about the door, hanging down with heavy, sweet-smelling blossoms. The man who answered to them was slipshod, his wig frowsty, his uniform undarned and unbrushed. He gave a second glance at the beauty of the new model, and then enquiringly at Sambo.

"So, it's you again, young Tar-Brush?" he said, aiming a cuff at the boy's head which was thick with black, ropey curls.

Inside the studio Charles Vere waited with some impatience. Now he was wearing a heavy painter's smock over prune velvet trousers, and the smock reminded Emma startlingly of those moments with Andrew Lack in the hayloft, when he had drawn her to him and had drenched her in his hot, sweet kisses.

"So here we are," said Charles, and he ushered her to the dais. She sat down in her best grey cashmere frock, with the blue sash that reflected the colour of her eyes and the leghorn hat in her hand. He watched her appreciatively, trying to sum her up.

"I shall make a sketch of you first, Emma."

"Thank you, sir."

"You must not call me 'sir'. Charles is my name, and as all my friends call me Charles, you must too."

He made a rough sketch and brought it across the studio to show it to her.

"It is very good, but not too like," she ventured.

"How can it be very good if it is not too like?"

She tried to explain, pointing with her finger. "It is me, and everybody would know that it is me, yet in a way it is not me. Too haughty and grand and you know that I am not haughty or grand."

"I do not know you well enough."

"Yes, perhaps that is the fault."

"I always dare to venture that no artist can paint accurately the woman he does not really know. They ought to be one in body, if not in spirit." He said it tensely, surprising her, for at the party she had thought that he was a gentle if not a rather mournful personality, and now it seemed that he was overknowledgeable. She turned to him dismayed.

"What is it you would ask?"

"I think you know, oh sweet and lovely Emma."

"But I am only sixteen."

"You seem older. You have a generous heart that tells you to give widely, and to give of yourself. I shall never paint you with sufficient beauty until my body has merged with yours, and become part of you.

37

Then in painting you I shall be painting something of myself."

She was no longer dismayed; she felt surprisingly calm and laid her hand upon his brow compassionately. It was feverish. "How hot your head is!" she told him.

"It is desire. For years I have been ill and some say that it is a decline and that I may not be here very long. Now when I become deeply concerned, I burn as with fever. You will help me?"

She glanced first at the sketch of the picture as it stood on the easel; she recognized the tilt of the head, and the poise of the chin, and the directness of the eyes. "I should have said that you were doing well without help," she suggested.

"But it is not you. It does not live, and a picture must be alive. Yours is the beauty a man must taste to paint."

"Did you taste all your models?"

"Most of them," he confessed, and she thought of Lady Charters in her late thirties, so that the stay laces had to be pulled hard and her powder and paint carefully chosen and applied thickly. His kisses would have disturbed so much make-up, and Emma was thankful that, as yet, she needed no such aids to beauty. She dare kiss and be kissed without fear of disruption. Watching her, he followed her thoughts.

"I know how you feel, but the rich are my patrons. A young artist to be successful must have a patron, or he starves. Starving is a painful procedure. You would not have me starve, my loveliest Emma?"

She put out her hand, leaning down from the dais, for the flattery enchanted her. She touched his hair, darkly glossy—he did not wear a wig—and as her fingers rumpled the thick luxury of that hair, she saw the quick fire responding in his eyes.

. "Emma, my own sweet Emma!"

She could laugh at the tone. "I'm so happy. I love life. I am so glad to be alive, it is all such ecstasy."

He caught her hands, kissing them again and again

38

with a mouth that burnt. She thought of the other men: George Trowling, the strong smell of brandy clinging to him; Andrew Lack, of the fields, with the earth scent and the uncouth body; the fellow traveller in the Dark Major wig, a fop, powdered and scented. But Charles Vere had only the essence of himself. The fire in his eyes needed no brandy to ignite it, and he stirred her. He gave her the impression that she was a queen who was conferring a favour and kissed the hands she folded so demurely on her breast. Then his lips went to the base of her throat firmly white. Acting upon a sudden impulse and moved beyond measure by him, she clasped his head to her softness, so that his lips found her bosom.

"Dear one!" she whispered.

"Oh, lovely Emma!"

"This is perhaps only the beginning of so much!"

"Dare I hope for more?" He glanced at the easel. "Before I colour that perfect outline, and catch the rapture of those eyes, shall I have tasted the inner sweetness?"

"I cannot promise, but I will not be ungenerous."

Then she heard the sound of Sambo knocking at the door, and knew that the time had come for her to return to Lady Charters. To-night she was to stand before the gentlemen posing as some of those my- thological figures that she loved to represent. But to- morrow she would be here again, returning in the thrilling knowledge that an enchanting danger lurked in the studio. Charles Vere would not be able to re- strain his desire for her for long.

She went out into the street curiously elated. There was the supreme joy of having met the danger face to face, and for the moment having circum- vented it.

When she arrived back she found that her mother had been at the house. Mrs. Duggan had called in some agitation. A young kinsman, one of the Kidd family, had been taken by the press gang, and she had only just heard that he was a prisoner at Greenwich. She sobbed bitterly as she told this news, and distressed Emma, but what could she do? Mrs. Duggan said that something must be done. The man to approach was a Captain Willet-Payne; he had it in his power to order the release of the young man who had been commandeered. Emma, deeply upset, told Lady Charters what had happened.

"Oh, but I know Captain Willet-Payne," she said; "he is a very likeable fellow, and if you wish I will write you a message to take to him which will ensure his seeing you."

"But, milady . . . ?"

"You could ask him yourself. I am sure he would not deny you."

"Milady!"

Lady Charters was a sweetly impulsive creature always anxious to help. "It's a shame that your kinsman has been press-ganged, and the whole thing shall be squashed. Come, my pretty, you shall go to Greenwich to-morrow."

"Oh, milady!" for standing there Emma experienced that eager looking forward which always enchanted her. She knew at last that she would be brought into contact with the sea, and the sea stood for destiny in her life.

Mutely she watched whilst Lady Charters wrote the letter.

VII

EMMA WOKE the next morning, determined that if anything could be done to free her kinsman from the press gang, she would do it. She put on the grey cashmere gown that Lady Charters had given her, knotted with the blue ribbons, and composed herself for the coach journey with the precious letter in her hand. She was convinced that she would succeed.

"You'll get set upon," said the cook, busy with the food in the capacious kitchen. The scrubbed table was sprawled with freshly killed capons, a baron of beef and lambs' hearts, for they fed well.

"I can see after myself."

"No girl with so tempting a face could be expected to see after herself," grunted the cook, stripping the feathers from a capon lying limply in her hands, "and one of these days you'll meet your match."

Emma said nothing. She bade farewell of Lady Charters, who had an early morning doldrums as she sat up in bed sipping her hot chocolate. "Jack Willet-Payne is a great man," she said, "and good-looking enough though hot-headed. He'll do his best for you, but mind you he drives a hard bargain."

Emma went by coach from Westminster, quite unafraid of what might be. It was a beautiful summer's morning, and from time to time the fellow passengers glanced at the lovely child who had tucked a pale pink rose into her fichu, and whose lips were as desirable as the petals. Although it was unusual for a girl to ride without male escort, this child could carry off the situation, for she had poise. The road wound its way through wild country. The little village of Blackheath rose on a peak to the right, whilst the desolate woods of Shooter's Hill lay beyond.

She was elated when first she saw Greenwich coming into sight, lying at the far end of the flat marshland, and the little houses spread right down to the water's edge. Here the river straggled like a silver serpent, dotted by small ships. There was the smell of the bog mist, and a dead horse lay rotting at the roadside, its belly hideously puffed out whilst ragged children played round it regardless of the stench. Once she saw a gibbet crucified against the sky; it stood on a rising with a body dangled from it, the head sunk mutely forward on to the chest and the

41

corpse drifting lamentably this way and that in the wind. It was a highwayman, hung there to warn others of the futility of such a career, and the girl's eyes misted as the coach passed too closely to be pleasant, and she thanked God piously that she could not see the collapsed face, but only the bent head with thin hair drifting like faded flower seeds away in the wind.

"Poor fellow," she whispered.

A stout attorney, riding beside her, glanced at her smugly. "He deserved his fate."

"Surely, good sir, none deserve death! He might have done well had he been better directed."

The attorney was a hard man, and even though they passed the gibbet, the rope creaking as it tilted the pitiful body, it failed to stir his heart.

"Faith, sir, and have you no mercy?" she asked.

The small houses of Greenwich clustered pleasantly along the water's edge; it was a town of seafaring men and smelt saltily of the sea. The coach stopped and Emma alighted at the inn, picking her way across the cobbles, and she asked the ostler where Captain Willet-Payne lived.

"Aye, he's captain of the *Cormorant*. He lodges in East Street."

"The number if you will?"

"Number Seven," and he was glad to render a service to so pretty a face.

So Emma Hart came to East Street walking with head erect in the sunshine, her eyes shaded by the leghorn hat. The clean fanlights sparkled diamondwise in the morning light and careful housewives had drawn silk curtains to spare the carpets from fading in the brightness. Number Seven was much as the others, and at the oak door a maidservant of about her own age came to speak to her.

"I have a letter here for Captain Willet-Payne."

The little maid put out her hand. "I will take it to him."

"No, I was instructed to deliver it in person."

"An it please you, the Captain does not receive ladies."

"The Captain will see me. Tell him that Emma Hart is here," she directed, but her heart was fluttering with fear.

At that moment the landlady appeared from the dim recesses of the house. She was a protuberant woman, with big breasts and wide hips developed but not in the cause of love. Her sparse hair was drawn back from a reddish face and she stared resentfully at Emma. "The Captain will not see ladies," she said abruptly and the girl knew by the tone that she inferred more.

"I come from Lady Charters," for now Emma knew that it would be a terrible thing if she could not even gain admittance.

"I do not care from whom you come. Give me the letter," and the woman would have snatched it from her.

It was then that Emma made a bold bid; she stepped across the threshold into the hall with the rush chairs, and the brass shining bravely in the corner. The stairs rose beyond, and she had already seen the landlady's instinctive glance of apprehension in the direction of the first closed door. It was a formidable door, and Emma realized that the Captain must be behind it.

"What are you doing? Where are you going? Come back," the landlady demanded imperiously, but Emma had sped past her. Light and fleet of foot she had bounded up the shallow stairs which offered her no obstacle. She beat on the door with her hands. "Help, sir, I pray you help me," she called.

She heard a heavy step within, and the door opened almost on the instant. Willet-Payne himself was standing there. He was a large, well-made man, with an intelligent face, his dark eyes set deeply under the overhanging brows, his hair blown loosely against his ears, for he wore no wig, and his collar rising high formed the centre piece for heavy gold

43

epaulettes which lay on either side and a cross-laced lapel.

"Mother of God, now what's afoot?" he demanded peevishly, then halted, surprised to see the rare beauty of her face.

Emma curtseyed, then slipped past him into the room. It was smallish, used apparently as a sitting-room, and she caught a glimpse of an untidy bed-room which lay beyond. There was the four-post bed with tumbled clothes piled high disclosing the ticking of the feather mattress; the cluttered, recently used washstand, the chairs with uniform straggling over their backs, boots worn and thrown aside, for the Captain had had a late night and was only just primed to face the day.

He closed the door and stared at her. "Hell's bells, but you are a pretty one!" he said. "Do you make a practice of forcing your way into reputable officers' rooms?"

"The matter is most urgent, sir."

"Indeed it must be! What is it you want?"

She handed him the letter, and, breaking the heavy seal, he read it whilst she stood before him. Then he set it down. "So you are Emma Hart? It's a pretty name."

"An it please you, sir."

"It pleases me very much. How old are you?"

"Going seventeen."

"You have come here to-day from the city of London to see me on a matter of some importance?"

"Oh, yes, sir, of very great importance. My kins-man has been press-ganged into service."

He pulled a face at her as he stood there, his arms folded on his breast, staring with those deep but viva-cious eyes of his, that looked right through her. "Many men are press-ganged into service every day of the year. After all, the Royal Navy must be fed."

"I know, sir, but I came to ask your aid."

"You do not wish the Royal Navy for your kins-man?"

44

She lifted her face to his. "Sir, I have always loved the sea, and the Royal Navy and the brave officers that serve in her."

"Then why do you not wish your kinsman to serve?"

She looked at him timorously, her small hands folded like some little madonna who having left her celibate niche has erringly starved for help. "I pray you not to refuse me," she begged.

"I see. First we will eat. I had a late night. Several of us were out together, and they must all have aching heads, I'm thinking. My head does not ache but my belly is empty." He rang the bell rope impatiently, all the time looking at her as though trying to size her up. The landlady, annoyed at Emma staying so late but afraid to say anything, brought up the tray with hot rolls and meat pies, steak, and a jug of piping hot chocolate. Emma watched him eating and she encouraged him to talk of his life at sea.

"And pray, have you fought so many battles, sir?"

He had fought the Frenchies with Lord Howe, he said, and instantly her face rosied with childlike interest. "You have a ship of your own?" she asked, knowing the answer for the ostler had already told her.

"I have the honour to command the *Cormorant,* but it is not my ship, it belongs to His Majesty King George the Third, and for His Majesty I will fight for ever."

"God save the King," she said loyally, and held her head high, for patriotism was a flame in the soul of little Emma Hart.

He looked at her with his senses sharpened. Like most men John Willet-Payne could chatter about himself, and once the conversation was unleashed, they went on talking and laughing until the woman fetched the tray. Then he drew the chairs to the window with the view of the river lying silver beyond and the *Cormorant* riding at anchor.

45

"Let us to business, my pretty," he said and now his tone had changed.

VIII

"IT IS for my kinsman and not for myself that I have come, sir."

"Do you believe that the press gang lets its men go once they have taken the trouble to get them on board?"

"I do not know, but I realize that you are great and powerful and that you could command it. One word from you, sir, would release my kinsman."

He was flattered by her faith in him. Was she as simple as she looked to be, this amazingly beautiful girl? She had nun-like eyes, and a dimpled smile. "It is true that perhaps I could help," he said cautiously, "but, my dear Emma Hart, why should I?"

"Because I would do anything to set my mother's mind at ease."

"Even if, in other ways, it disturbed her more?"

"She is desperately anxious."

He nodded. "But all this is a one-sided bargain, my pretty child. What is the reward that you offer?"

"I have nothing to offer. I am a poor servant girl employed by Lady Charters. It is true that I can sing and dance a little, but very little else. I cannot pay you, sir, I have no money, but you would do this for charity?"

"Some things are beyond price. It is not money that I would ask."

"What else have I?" she urged.

"Something rare. You look so good, my child, almost like a little novice. You *are* good?"

"Oh, sir, how can you ask me?"

"Could it be true that you are cold?"

She glanced at him, her lids dropping. "I hope I am not cold, sir," she whispered demurely, now aware that she was trembling violently. She did not know when she had been so disturbed.

He came closer at that and, taking her wrist, pulled her towards him. She knew that she was immature, and now she felt strangely young. This was not another affair like clumsy Andrew Lack, George Trowling, with the stench of brandy about him, and the delicate, sensuous urging of Charles Vere. This was a man indeed! She was stirred by the dark cloth of his coat, the gold lace, shining buttons, and the display of white, watered silk upon his lapels. His big mouth had a dimple at either end, and there was another lying in the cleft of his chin. He could stir her imagination with his power, not over her kinsman alone, but over her body.

"But, sir, you would not wrong me?"

He silenced her mouth with a kiss and, feeling his lips, she did not deny him. When he released her she sank into a chair and could have wept for sheer joy. She had never lived until this moment. It was a man who wanted her, a man who commanded her.

"Emma, listen to me. You know the price of your kinsman's release. You have but to say the word and he will be free, but you, my pretty bird, will not."

"You would not make me a prisoner, sir?"

"A prisoner of love. I would take you from Lady Charters. I know a room near Drury Lane Theatre which I would take for you, and come to see you there. No other man shall look at you. You understand that? I am a naval officer and I allow no trickery."

For a moment she said nothing, too surprised to find the turn that events had taken; all the time her searching mind was trying to manœuvre a way of escape, yet her heart did not seek to escape. It would be magnificent to become the mistress of so fine a man, and suddenly she knew that she was growing older. "Sir, I am but a village girl. I have known no man, and you force a hard bargain," she stammered.

"You said that you would do anything!"

"I must have time to think."

"Time spent in thought is wasted. Your kinsman will be aboard and the ship will put out to sea." She realized the truth of this and sat there nervously plucking at her fichu. "I am a lonely man," he added in a changed tone.

"Indeed, sir, I am sorry."

"If you deny me this, I shall raise no hand to help your kinsman," and she knew that he meant it.

She glanced down at the water flashing silver in the sunshine. A red rose looped itself about the window, pressing fat crimson cheeks to the diamond panes. "How can I deny you?" she whispered at last.

"Then you agree to the bargain?"

She wept, half with pleasurable anticipation, and she clung to him. "Oh, sir, I am afraid. I—I have the greatest fear——"

"You must not feel like that," he bared her shoulder with a sweep of his hand, and laid his head affectionately on her bosom. "I am not a hard master. First I will attend to the matter of your kinsman. Come now, does that please you?"

"You are too good."

She moved nervously about the room as he dispatched the message; then, when the door had closed again, he turned to her, his face irradiated. "And now to taste the sweets of victory."

"But, sir, not now? Not here?" She felt that she could not bear another moment; her heart beat frantically, and her limbs seemed to have become uncontrolled. "I—I dare not."

He poured out a glass of wine and brought it to her, holding the cup to her lips. "My pretty, you must have no fear for I will only give you the greatest joy. You have not yet tasted the sweetness of ecstasy and I am the man to teach you this."

All the time his big hands were guiding her to the

room beyond, with the tumbled bed that she had noticed when she first entered. Now strangely enough she felt only the desire to hold back, for she thought of Ann Symonds—always the ghost in the background of her life—and the man she had seen only this morning, mournfully dangling from his gibbet.

"I am a captain in the Royal Navy, my pretty, I will not see you discomfited," he promised.

"But ships put out to sea?"

"And return to love again. Do not think that I should allow so fair a prize to slip through my fingers. But this is no time to waste words."

He spoke thickly, breathing heavily, and she clung to him completely bemused and not knowing how she felt. She could only abandon herself to his arms and, lifting her, he carried her across his heart to the four-poster, hung heavily with fading maroon and dusty cerise. He whispered ecstatically to her, but she heard never a word, for now her heart was making far too much noise.

For an hour—or was it more?—they lay until she slept in exhaustion against him. So when day was past its full and the afternoon was waning little Emma Hart returned to London again, but not to Lady Charters. She rode in a private coach beside her sea captain, to the apartment he had spoken of off Drury Lane, and here she would be mistress of her own room. For to-day had changed her whole life. She had saved her kinsman and had given herself to Jack Willet-Payne. 'I love him,' she thought, 'he has been good to me,' and in this mood she did not care what lay ahead. She had reached a peak in her life, and trod the heights.

"Never ask what comes to-morrow, for to-day is all that matters," Jack Willet-Payne told her, "or is it more accurate to say that to-night is all that matters?"

"To-night, and every night! I do love you," she whispered.

"I bless the moment you strayed into my rooms,

and one day I will take you to sea with me, who knows?"

"Who knows?" and then with perhaps the first doubt rising like a cold wave in her heart, "You will not tire of me?"

He kissed her the answer. "Does anyone tire of life? You have the power, my sweet, to hold a man to you for ever. You have the beauty of Helen, and you are my Ariadne."

She quenched the doubts that had risen, and refused to think ahead. Maybe he was right, this was the only moment.

IX

MEANWHILE, EXCEPT in India, where Warren Hastings was carrying on the great tradition of Clive, and laying firmly the foundations not only of the Indian Empire but of the Indian Civil Service, things were difficult for England.

Her enemies, France and Spain, were pressing her sorely. In fact, in all the world, the foes of Englishmen were watching intently the unfavourable developments in the ill-omened war with the American Colonies, taking advantage of her preoccupation with this struggle to try to filch her gains from her; and in half the courts of Europe kings and courtiers were rubbing their hands with glee.

Holland and the courts of the North were hostile; France was coolly proposing that England should give up all India save Bengal; Spain had been besieging General Elliott and his redcoats at Gibraltar, and refused to make peace unless the Rock was surrendered; already, for a year, the gallant force had been holding out desperately against bombardment and famine in the glare of the Spanish sunshine. And though they did not know it, the gallant garrison were destined to hold out triumphantly for still two years more.

But one event happened in this year which made Emma's heart, with its love of the sea and seamen, beat quicker with pride. The great Admiral Rodney met the Spanish Fleet off Cape St. Vincent, and in an action which showed that the blood of Drake's heroes was still undiluted, so smashed and harried the Spaniard that a mere four of his ships escaped to seek ignominious shelter in Cadiz.

Emma Hart was now living the life of a lady at ease at Nerot's Hotel, where her apartment was booked. Jack Willet-Payne did indeed go to sea, but he always returned to her. He was a reckless lover, asking everything, and ever ready to satisfy himself at the full fountain of her passion, but in her heart Emma was often disturbed by the intuition that the present circumstances could not continue for long. She was also alarmed that her mother would discover what was afoot, but, although Mrs. Duggan did find out, she was not even angry.

"He is a kind gentleman," she said.

"I did not dare tell you before, dear mam, because I was so afraid of how angry you would be."

For a moment her mother looked strangely at her. Then she said, "Once I was a pretty girl, Emy; you may not think so now, but I found the gentlemen ready and willing. I could not be ungenerous for, after all, it seemed so little to give. How could I reprove you for something that I have done myself?"

"But will Jack stay faithful to me?"

"That, Emy, depends much on you. You never know with seafaring men; they are naturally inconstant, but bold lovers when with you."

Captain Willet-Payne was generous, and when he came back from sea delighted in pleasing his Emma. They visited the Adam and Eve, which lay off Tottenham Court Road, a rural place, its pretty gardens

51

hung with roses, where loving pairs could listen to the singing and eat good food. He took her to Ranelagh, more fashionable and select, where ladies and gentlemen sat listening to music in the Rotunda, and where the gardens were more formal and the manners exquisite.

Sometimes he introduced his little friend to some of the men they met, and amongst them was Sir Harry Featherstonehaugh, who took marked notice of her from the first. Sir Harry was a young baronet, with a long, slender face, smooth, gingerish hair, and a mouth that was avid for kisses. Emma admired the fine lace at his wrists and throat, his sporting interest in a world that lay so entirely outside her own, and as they sat sipping tea in the Rotunda, he talked pleasantly of Uppark, his Sussex home.

"You found him a bore?" asked Jack.

"On the contrary, he was most entertaining."

"That's a change for him. But don't let's discuss him, there are pleasanter topics." He hugged her arm, bruising the flesh, for he was over-strong, and not appreciating his strength she bore many a bruise as the outward pledge of his deep affection.

All the time the intangible fear lurked in Emma's heart that it would be terrible if, after she had learnt the joy of luxury and the ardour of a man's love, she had to abandon both again. She gave freely of herself, and delighted in his possession of her, but would it last? She knew that he was extravagant, and when on leave he would spend everything in the first few days, and then had a life which had to be vigorously pruned in consequence. He and economy were not good bedfellows, and she feared lest one of these days he might find her too expensive.

"Dearest one, you will not leave me?" she implored him.

"Leave you? Hell's bells, what gives you that idea?"

"Sometimes I fear you'll forget me."

"Not really. I may seem quiet but I have other

things to think about," and she hoped that his mind went to the Frenchies, and the wars, and nothing more. So quite artlessly she went on with the life.

One night he returned quite drunk and lay sprawled on the bed in Nerot's Hotel, incapable of moving. Over-anxious for him, Emma went to the apothecary round the corner, hoping that he would make up a draught for her. That night London seemed to be tense. There had been rumours all day and even Emma heard them, though she knew nothing of politics, and had never heeded stories of the fanatic Lord George Gordon. But to-night something was wrong. The dimness of the distance was flashed red with the glowering fires. Here and there in the deserted streets were a few flitting lights of the link-boys, and all the time she could hear the dull roar of anger like distant stormy waves.

"What is amiss?" she asked the apothecary.

"It is the rioters again. Wise folks have gone to their homes and drawn the barriers."

It excited her. Emma was always eager for adventure, and she wished to see something of the trouble. She slipped the little phial into her capacious pocket, and went down the hill towards the Fleet. In the distance she could see the surging crowd, and knew that they must have passed this way before, for human bodies were lying in the filth of the gutters. An ale tavern had been broken into and looted, and she could see the casks rolled out and lying in the street like rocks that the tide has left bare. Some of the rapscallions were lying in the road, their mouths sucking at the drawn bung-holes, drinking noisily. A man who passed her told her that the King's Guard had been called out by order of His Majesty himself, and now she could hear the distant sharpness of shooting.

Even whilst she watched, it seemed that the rowdies changed their course and now were sweeping towards her, trampling over the prone bodies. Men and women shrieked, but the noise was choked in their throats as they died. In the gutter beside her Emma saw a young boy, and stooping in compassion to raise him, felt his head fall back against her arm and saw that already his face had been pulped by feet. In horror she dropped him with a dull thud, and began to run, dismayed to hysteria. Her skirts impeded her. She turned back towards Jermyn Street again, hoping that the crowd would go to the river, and as she ran distractedly she saw a man with something that she recognized in his walk. Throwing discretion to the winds, she rushed to him, beseeching protection.

"Kind sir, have pity on a woman!"

He turned to look down at her, the light falling on his gingerish hair. "What are you doing out on a night like this, Emma Hart?"

It was Sir Harry Featherstonehaugh!

Relief came to her that she had found a friend, and she wept for joy. He was in no wise displeased that she had discovered him. "Take me back to Nerot's Hotel?" she begged.

"They say many have died to-night. Half the street trollops have been trampled underfoot, they tell me, and now the rioters are said to be marching to the Duke of Norfolk's mansion to fire it. I hear also that they have freed Newgate."

"I hope the poor prisoners have escaped."

He patted her arm. "You have an over-compassionate heart, my pretty."

Now the noise was lessening, and only the far growling as of savage beasts came to them, with the occasional echo of shooting which rolled out to the marshes towards Tottenham Court Road, and was there dulled by the bog mist. But the fires still burnt darkly.

Sir Harry returned Emma to the hotel, where the doors were bolted fast because of the raiders, and it was some time before the watchman could be talked into admitting them.

"It has been a most terrible night," he told them,

"but praise God the disturbance did not come this way."

Emma walked in and shook her clothes that were splashed with mud. On the hem of her quilted petticoats there were the dark red stains of blood that had drenched the gutters against which she had brushed in flight.

"I will go up to the Captain," she said.

It was then that Sir Harry caught her hand, his mouth twitching and his pale eyes afire. "Surely I may ask some reward for bringing you home so safely? Why not stay and talk to me, for I have much to say to you?"

"First I must see how he is."

"No, I insist. First you must stay with me."

And she was amazed to hear herself saying quite quietly, "Very well, sir, I will."

X

SIR HARRY made enquiries of her early life, and she told him freely of her poverty in the days when she had lived with Grandmother Kidd at Hawarden, of her own mother, and her work as a servant.

"How did you come to give yourself to Willet-Payne?"

"He has been so good to me."

"And you to him. But surely you cannot love him?"

"I am deeply grateful to him," she said, "and whilst he has need of me, I vow I will stay true to him."

Sir Harry expressed his disappointment at her avowal, and remarked that he had hoped otherwise. He talked some time, until at last she went upstairs to see how John Willet-Payne was getting on. He was recovering a little, for the street noises had disturbed his drunken stupor, and he was throwing off the effects of the amazing quantity of spirit that he had swallowed. Disgusted to hear that she had been out on such a night, he accused her with some quarrelsomeness of making free with the King's Guard.

"But I had to flee before the mob," she said, wide-eyed. "It was indeed a most dreadful night. I would never have ventured out save to fetch your physic. They say that Newgate has been freed, and some tell me that the prisoners are still clanking about the city in their chains."

"They'll shoot the lot." He struggled into a sitting posture, wearing only his breeches; his shirt had been flung open, exposing his gaunt, sunburnt chest, scarred with a zigzag wound that he had received in battle. The sight of that scar always stimulated Emma with intense pity.

"See," she said gently, "I have brought you some physic."

"What good is physic to me?" he answered, his blood-shot eyes staring at her, his square face bloated.

She brought the phial to him, insisting that she should give it to him, and shook the dark, syrupy mixture. "It is to help you," she told him. He swore, but finally drank it, gulping it in one mouthful, staring at her as he tasted its vileness, gulping again and then beginning to vomit. She was appalled to see that it should have so grim an effect. "My sweet one, my own sweet one, I had no idea that it would do that. . . ."

For a while he could not speak, but lay there, his forehead beaded with a cold sweat, whilst she bathed it until he slept. Then she crept downstairs to tell Sir Harry, but he was sitting talking to an officer from the Guard, who had fought bloodily on Holborn bridge and was now a little drunk with victory.

"The Captain is asleep," said Emma.

Sir Harry glanced at her. "And if he sleeps alone, and sound . . . ?"

"Indeed, sir, you wrong me."

The Captain from the Guard looked at her. "It is a wicked waste that so beautiful a lady should dismiss the precious hours of night," he said, and belched vehemently. She liked his fair hair and smiled, but Sir Harry had noted her glance and was irritated.

"Anything for a new face?" he asked, and the officer would have drawn his sword, being impetuous with drink, but it was Emma who stayed him.

"When men are in their cups they speak foolishness," she said, and to the young man, "I pray, sir, you give me an arm to my room."

He escorted her up the stairs, lurching a little. Through one uncurtained window they could still see the distant fire glowering along the houses on the horizon. He said, "To-night, sweet lady, I have been close to death. It is a miracle that I was not shot, but I am still alive and young. Give me some of the joy that makes life worth living, for your partner is asleep and will not know."

She kissed him lightly, smoothing back the fair hair that she admired. "Alas, I am not light of love as men think, and I swear by my honour that I belong to Jack Willet-Payne."

"Not of the *Cormorant*?"

"The same—God bless him."

"He tires easily of his mistresses."

She shook her head. "But maybe not of the one who knows the meaning of true faithfulness," she replied, and went back to his room smelling so foully of vomit. Willet-Payne lay sleeping uneasily, sprawled across the bed with his scarred chest bare. She went to the window, and opening it leaned out to breathe the freshness of the early morning air. Now the noise had gone; it was away like a spent thunderstorm, and the birds were singing.

When she woke much later, Captain Willet-Payne

had gone to Ranelagh with Sir Harry, so the maid said when she brought in the hot chocolate. To-morrow the *Cormorant* would be sailing again. Jack would be off to Greenwich at midnight, and she hated herself for having slept so long; she always grudged their moments apart. She made the room ready. She brought in new pomanders to scent it afresh, she powdered and perfumed herself, admiring her reflection in the mirror, and knowing that he would find her desirable.

Yet when he came back she realized instantly that he was almost cold to her. He delayed, dragging out the hours with petty and unconvincing excuses. Impatient to get to bed, she rebuked him, perhaps not wisely. "Leaving at midnight, how little time there will be for love!"

But he was in a strange mood, and when he came did not seek to strip the clothes from her, and bask in her beauty, but sat as one wrapt in his own thoughts; she had the feeling that he was surrounding himself with a fortress and that she could not pierce it.

"What is it? What ails you?" she begged. "Is it that you hate leaving me so much?" and she hoped for the answer that did not come. He kissed her tiredly, and as he did so she remembered the chance remark of the officer from the Guard only last night—he tires soon—and panicked that already Jack was growing cold and would forsake her. "Do I displease you so much, dear, dear one?" she implored him. "If I have done wrong, tell me, and you shall punish me."

He accused himself, but not convincingly; he said that he had eaten something that had given him the colic, and that he feared he was unwell. They would not love to-night, but would store all that exquisite emotion for the day of his return, when it would be an added delight; now he must sleep a little. She laid him in her arms, smoothing his hair and singing little songs to him. When the watchman in the street below called, "Eleven of the clock, and all's well," she was forced to stir him, and now there was hardly any time for farewells. He kissed her almost brusquely on the brow.

"My heart, what ails you? You must indeed be ill to be so cold to me," she said, but he did not heed. She heard the sound of his sword stamping out tin music as he stumped down the stairs and out into the courtyard. Suddenly she was hideously afraid.

In the morning she could not drink her chocolate. She could not imagine what had changed Jack to such an extent, for he had given no sign of colic. She was but half dressed when the maidservant returned to tell her that Sir Harry was below, and as the girl said it, Emma heard his step on the landing, and saw the door open again. He stood there, admirably coated in brocade and wearing a spruce new wig on his gingerish hair. He smelt of orange flower toilet water, the perfume that she loved best, but somehow she felt foreboding.

"Good morrow, my sweet one," he said.

She stared, unsure of herself, and he, coming over to the dressing-stool, dismissed the maid with a mere fillip of his hand cuffed in lace. He sat down surveying Emma, his eyes riveted on her breasts, for she had but her frock, with no covering fichu, so that they rose, swelling lightly as twin translucent globes against the banding of her bodice.

"Good morrow, sir; surely this is a little unseemly to penetrate to a lady's bedchamber?"

"Not when the lady is so sweet, and when her protector has left her."

"Sire, you are mistaken; he has but put out to sea."

"My fair charmer—for you are my fair charmer—we all warned you. I have come to talk to you. I do not want to see so fair a lady deserted."

"Deserted?" It was the word that she dreaded most, and she turned to him, aware that she had paled. "Oh, no, sir, that cannot be."

She recalled the tragic coldness of Jack Willet-

Payne but last night. His mumbled excuses which had had no real meaning, the colic, and realized how despicable it had been. He had not dared admit to her the truth.

"Be wise, sweet Emma. I promised Jack Willet-Payne that I would see after you, and I have come here to fulfil my promise."

"But, sir, have I no say in this?"

"I would not be a hard master. I would take you away to Uppark. It is my own mansion, and there in faith you would have a marvellous time."

She stared at him helplessly, her beautiful eyes reading the truth, her heart afraid to believe it. "Sir, do you suggest that I have been sold?"

"That is a hard word, my dearest Emma."

"Have I been handed on to you, into your keeping, as one would pass on a commodity?" and knowing now that this was the truth, she began to cry. She was pitiful as she wept.

He took her into his arms. "Faith, Emma, but I shall never understand you. First you weep because you think that you are deserted, then you weep even more bitterly, because you learn that your future is ensured."

"But I have no choice in this . . . no choice . . . ?"

"Only to be wise," he bade her, and bringing out his lace-edged handkerchief, dried her eyes with it, "and somehow I think that my pretty sweeting will be very wise."

XI

THEY DROVE down to Uppark in the Portsmouth coach, changing at Petersfield into his own chaise, in which they then went forward. She saw the battlements and spires of Uppark rising out of the clustering trees, and became ecstatic. Never had she thought in such terms as these. Emma knew that she had little with which to bargain for life; her own body was her only possession of any commercial value, and Uppark was a good exchange for the services that she would be expected to render.

In the coach down she had been silent and a little resentful, but driving up the Harting valley in the chaise, she warmed to the beauty of the countryside, and the kindliness of the man who sat beside her. I am lucky, she thought, and decided that she had no further tears for the shocking infidelity of Jack Willet-Payne; she must put all that behind her and start anew.

That day tales of a terrible disaster to British arms became the talk of London, and indeed of the country.

At first it was a mere rumour, passed from mouth to mouth in coffee-houses, accepted by some, dismissed by others as mere idle gossip put about by enemies of the Government.

Then it spread like lightning to the Exchanges, was carried eagerly to great business houses, thence to the drawing-rooms of the wealthy, to the coaching-stations, and by coach throughout the length and breadth of the land. Finally official dispatches arrived. The rumours were confirmed.

Cornwallis had surrendered at Yorktown; surrendered with all his army. The American Colonies were finally and irretrievably lost. Marching on North Carolina, it seemed, the general had been foiled by the refusal of his fellow general, Sir Henry Clinton, to help him. In desperation he had fallen back to Virginia and hastily entrenched himself at Yorktown, on the coast.

"Where was the British Fleet?" people asked in bewilderment. "Why was he not supplied from the sea?" "How did it happen?" Alas! for Cornwallis, the French Fleet were for a period in command of the seas around that ill-fated spot. Starvation faced him and his troops.

The King, it was said, was in a frenzy of rage. Lord North, on hearing the news, had paced up and down his room, waving his arms and shouting: "It is all over, it is all over." And had then resigned. Emma heard of it all, but her thoughts were mostly, on this occasion, of herself.

In the mansion she was given her own room, with its striped blue and white silk curtains, a heavy carpet and silver fitments. From the gazebo window she could see the park with the deer browsing under the chestnuts that were already ambering for autumn, and the mist rising like tulle from the lake where the swans rode as Viking ships. She dined that night in an extravagant rose-coloured gown that she had found hanging in the wardrobe, ready fitted out for her. She sat at the far end of the long table, with Sir Harry opposite, and between them the silver twined candelabra and the épergnes of hothouse flowers.

"There are horses in my stable, and you shall ride," said he. "You shall become a great lady."

"Sir, I fear that you will spoil me."

"Have no fear for I demand reward, and only the best and fullest satisfies me. I have a ready appetite, you know."

She believed that he was the kind who, until now, had only known wanton love. John Willet-Payne had been attracted to her modesty and reluctance, but Sir Harry asked for something more mature. For a moment she became half afraid that she would not be able to satisfy him, and glanced in some trepidation through the silver sconces to where he sat. That night he came to her.

"And I shall come to this room every night," he informed her.

She had been secretly alarmed at his voluptuousness; he had a hoydenish charm that she was terrified might revolt her. First she insisted that she must

62

show him the attitudes she had originally exhibited at Lady Charters', and she stood in a niche illuminated by crystal chandeliers.

"Exquisite," he said, and watched her but half impatiently as one by one she dropped the scarves she wore, until at last he beheld her immobile as a marble statue, slender and straight like a tree unbent by the wind. "My Venus, my Psyche," he said, and deeply moved, knelt to kiss her.

It pleased her to satisfy him, and delighted her at the same time to feel that she was creeping upwards in the hard world of mischance, and soaring to the social heights that once had seemed to be quite out of her reach. It was not her fault that her only means of progress lay in selling herself, and there was no escape from the barter; she had to go on in the way she had started. Had it all begun with Andrew Lack's face pressed to that window at Mrs. Thomas's? Or had it begun when Jack Willet-Payne, hungry for her, had carried her to his bed to possess himself of her?

She started learning to ride, and Sir Harry admired her courage and her poise. "I shall make much of you, my sweet," he said. "You have the blood of a thoroughbred in your veins. Who fathered so magnificent a daughter?"

She told him of the blacksmith, but even as she mentioned it, she recalled her mother's admitted lapses, and wondered if, after all, some greater sire had called her into being? The idea inflamed her. They rode together, and before a fortnight had passed she was proficient. Sir Harry was delighted with this, for he had arranged a house-party for that time and was anxious to display her at her best, and she was shaping well.

"You shall show my company what you can do. None of their women can behave like my Emma. Your attitudes—you shall show them those, too."

"But, sir, I could not do those in public?"

He looked at her and laughed. The mouth curled, she realized that until this moment she had been blind to its cynicism. "I command that you display your attitudes, my sweet; I shall most certainly insist on it."

"But you could not want all and sundry to see me so?"

"I am very proud of my bargain," he stated. "I declare that no other man has so sweet a sweeting."

She thought that he was teasing her, and let it pass, hoping that he did not mean it. It was not mentioned again.

The gentlemen came down from London by chaise and coach. They disturbed Emma with the noise that they made, and she took her meals in her own room. Sir Harry wished her to come down for the first time and to make a startling entrance after their dinner was ended. She was to wear the new over-flounced frock he had purchased for her, and the heavily powdered wig. Somehow the girl was alarmed at the thought, and speculated about it in her room.

When the time came to dress she looked in dismay at the cream flounces, the brilliant blue bows and yellow brocade of the frock, and took a foolish dislike to it. Acting on intuition, she locked herself in her room and put on the simple grey cashmere frock she had kept by her, the spotted fichu, and letting down her hair, wore it in a cascade of auburn curls. This would be the unexpected! The quakerish look of the girl with the perfect beauty. When the moment came, however, she was overcome with nervous apprehension that her protector might be angered with her for changing his plans. She trembled violently as the door opened and the dazzling lights were turned on to her. There she stood. The gracious lady that Sir Harry had bragged about, dressed primly, her babyish curls to her shoulders, her hands folded meekly before her, and between her fingers a single spray of white roses.

"Gad," said one of the men, not sober enough to

realize that he spoke aloud, "here, indeed, is the charmer above all others."

Steps had been set to let her walk up and on to the table itself. She came demurely down the room, her eyes dropped on to her hands. She lifted her skirts daintily, and climbed step by step to the table, with the glittering chandeliers above her, and the men staring amazed. From the far end, with one discreet glance, she could see the look in Sir Harry's eyes, and knew that he was not angered but all the more intrigued by what she would do.

Lifting her hands in a little helpless gesture, she dropped the white roses, the petals drifting like an early snow, to her feet. She untied the fichu, striking an attitude of young despair. A sudden murmur ran through the men who were watching her. The fichu fell to the rose petals, and now the delicate globes of her breasts were clearer. Urged on by the knowledge that she was succeeding, she untied the bodice, and the simple frock, unclipped, fell to her feet; there she stood in an austere linen petticoat that was cut low, and slotted up the side so that it should reveal the first enchanting roundness of a limb. She stood quite still. She might not have been alive.

"It isn't true!"

"Lud, but she is too beautiful!"

She turned at the sound of that voice, moving her arms in an inspired gesture of supplication, as though she asked him for her life. It was then that for the first time she saw the man's face, and knew instantly that every fibre of her being was drawn to him. It was the long, thin face of a scholar, the light hair waved back from a delicately modulated brow: the eyes rapturous and wondering, with the lightness of water in them and a dark pupil which, dilating, told her how he appreciated her. The long nose and sensuous, half-complaining mouth were beautiful. She knew that he was an aristocrat, she knew, too, that he had something far more compelling than passion or wantonness or desire; she could give him her greatest treasure, the full, burning ardour of real love.

The man was Charles Greville.

XII

THEY DID not actually speak till the day of Charles' departure, when Emma lingered in the minstrels' gallery. He was talking to a man on the step, and she leant down to whisper a farewell, and threw him a spray of roses. He stooped to pick up the flowers, and lifting his face to her, smiled as he touched the petals with his lips.

"Sir, you will return?" she implored him, because she knew that she could hardly live until he came back again.

"Maybe," he told her, and then had gone. In her heart was an emptiness, a disquiet, a sudden fever of longing that she could not tear out. She would do anything to attract so noble a man, she told herself, and although she had not seen him for more minutes than she could count upon her fingers, she knew that he had immense power over her. She over him, perchance; he sent her a little ribbon from London, mentioning her in his letter to Sir Harry, and suggesting that "the charmer might make use of it." When she came to writing back, she was ashamed that she spelt so ill and found a pen so clumsy.

"I do not expect that he will read it," said Sir Harry.

But Charles Greville did read it and replied to her. She prayed that he would come again with the next consignment of visitors for the cock-fighting, and was disappointed when she found that he was not included amongst the guests.

"Maybe as well," said Sir Harry, "for I would not stand for truancy."

"I would always be faithful."

"I hope so. If needs be I would force it as I would force a mare to do my bidding," and he menacingly touched his whip.

"There would be no need for cruelty," for she flinched at the thought of another whipping, and already knew that she had been unfaithful to him in her desire.

For this house-party the country squires and their red-faced lackeys brought their cocks for the fighting, which was indeed a gentlemanly sport. Sir Harry had had an old coach-house made into a cockpit, and enjoyed every moment of it. Emma had never seen any of the sport before, and was intrigued that it would be a new experience.

"But I want no faintings and women's screams," he said.

"No, sir."

"Blood does not sicken you?"

"I saw the riots, and there was blood enough, for my petticoats were stained with it," she answered.

"Ah, well, that may be so," and he let it pass.

He was a great sportsman, training his own cocks, and he revelled in the amusement they provided for him. Never had Emma seen such a crowd as came, and she watched them as they laid their stakes, amazed that so much money could be treated with such casualness. She was wide-eyed with interest.

She had watched the practice fights, which the men held occasionally to train the cocks. Then she had been vastly entertained, for the spurs were guarded by long leather guards (she herself had helped to draw them on), and there was never any real damage done, nor any show of blood. But to-night was a different matter as she saw at once when she first came into the cockpit. The air was blue with smoke and strong; it made her eyes smart and her throat sting, so that she choked. There was the predominant scent of spirits from the men's breath. She sat herself down uncomfortably, already a little nauseated, and then she saw that the protective leathers had gone, and now the cocks had metal heads fastened to their spurs, so that the fight should be even more vile than nature had meant it to be.

"I had not thought——" she began, then remembering her cautioning, made no further demur, only hoping that she would not vomit. Her compassion welled in her, and she clasped her hands closely, the nails spiking into her palms.

Sir Harry started the proceedings with a pair of Staffordshire Piles; they were lovely, crimson-combed birds, who strutted proudly, full of bombast as they ambled for position, tipputing saucily towards one another. She watched them, suffused with intense interest, then suddenly the larger bird darted forward and viciously spiked his bill into the side of the other. White feathers drifted in a snowy tumult about the ring; the blood spurted, and before she could recover from her first horror, the little bird had drawn his opponent's blood. It sickened her. She groped helplessly, to feel a man's hand take hers. Clinging to it, she was drawn outside, and whilst the noise about the ring was at its most furious, she had escaped. Outside in the air she could breathe, her raw throat and smarting eyes recovered, and she stopped retching. She was standing in the yard beyond the gaunt coach-houses, with the scent of chrysanthemums which always reminded her of ashes, and the starshine of autumn. Here was peace, for she had been considerably disturbed by what she had seen. For the first time she became aware that it was not a gentleman who had led her out, but that beside her stood a young groom, little older than she herself.

"I saw that you hated it . . ." he volunteered.

"It was very good of you. I believe that I should have fainted."

"I also hate it. They accuse me of being womanish, but I cannot bear to see the poor things killing and being killed. Your ladyship must not be angered that I dared to touch you."

"I am not a ladyship, and I am not angered." On impulse she had to tell him about herself, for in the excitement of the cock-fight the others would not miss her. "Where can we talk?"

He drew her inside one of the stables. There was a pile of clean straw lying just by the door, and they sat on it side by side. The chains of the horses rasped against the iron mangers almost musically, and about the place there was restfulness. She looked at his young, eager face.

"Your name?" she asked.

"I am Edward Strong, groom to Sir John Drew." She knew Sir John, a ferret-faced, aged baronet who had brought a pair of cocks to the fight and had staked more heavily than it was said he could afford. "I am staying here."

She recognized in him a quality that did not lie on the others she had met, as though he were one of her own kinsmen, and she listened as he told his story. He was a bastard boy, knowing neither father nor mother, but some said that a king had sired him. His village had none of him, and he had always been given the most menial jobs until he had come to work for Sir John. In a rough-and-ready way Sir John was good to him, and he who had had so little from life, certainly none of its sweets, turned a starved face to her, asking for favours.

"But women? You have women friends?"

"No women friends. I care not for trollops. I meet only the village wenches, and I have in me the blood that demands the taste of something sweeter."

She looked at him, wondering what he meant. It was strange that at this moment, with only the star-shine coming in through the open top of the stable door, and the shadows hiding them, they seemed to be one another's.

"You saw me before you touched me?" she asked

haltingly, perhaps for something to say so that she might conceal her embarrassment.

"Everyone saw you. You are the most beautiful woman that I have ever seen."

"Was that what you wanted to say to me?"

"Not all that I wanted to say. But I—being what I am—have not the impertinence to ask what—what I would ask."

She looked at him, her own lips moist, her eyes tender with compassion. With a swift movement she untied the ribbon of her frock and, opening her arms, drew him to her breasts. There was the smell of the straw, and only the chafing of the animals against their stalls, and here, for one stolen, lovely hour, these two tasted and adored, with never a sound save his impassioned breathing, and her swift sigh of content.

Those at the cockpit did not miss them.

The air became thicker, the excitement more intense. Courageous little birds strutted into the pit to their death, their brave display of feathers torn from them, their pathetically mauled bodies red and streaming to be flung out on to the dung-heap, there to flutter till they died, or already dead. But the fight went on.

Much later, Sir Harry, a little drunk, staggered to her room with the blue and white striped silk curtains, to find his beloved happily asleep, a smile on her face. She looked so completely satisfied that he did not wake her. Had he not been drunk, he would have questioned the seraphic look as she lay there breathing contentedly, so wrapt in sleep. But he made no comment. She was young, he told himself, a pretty creature not yet completely grown, and she tired easily. To-morrow night he would see to it that she did not sleep so well.

During the evening Sir Harry had made arrangements to go abroad for some four months to visit friends, and he would satiate himself of her before he left. He planned that she would stay on at Uppark, quiet and unmolested, for in the country he could rely on that.

When the morning came a groom brought the horses to the door, and he saw with surprise that Sir John's groom held the bridle of the one that Emma would ride. He was a good-looking young man with the proud bearing of a king.

"Changed your man?" he asked Emma.

She glanced at him with modest eyes, and smiled, though there was something of the sphinx in that smile. "Perhaps," she said.

XIII

WHILST SIR HARRY was abroad Emma spent her time in amusing herself as best she could. She had many visitors, for the neighbourhood knew that she was alone, and men came to call. She was far too amiable to be discourteous, and enjoyed their society.

Charles Greville came into the vicinity, happening to be staying at Petersfield, and he drove over in his chaise to present his compliments. He expressed the deepest regret at finding Sir Harry absent, but Emma hoped profoundly that at heart he felt no real dismay but that this was mere lip service.

They walked together in the gardens with the first powdering of snow lying on them and the trees wearing black lace mantillas of leafless branches. She was enchanted to find herself with Greville, who warmed to her with his exquisite manners. He admired that sweet illusion of adolescence that she still retained.

She wished to attract him and detected an occasional irritation in his manner which alarmed her.

She asked a trifle reprovingly, "You are angry with me? Most gentlemen are overkind to Emma."

"Perhaps that is the cause of my concern."

"Or are you cold?"

"I do not touch the fruit that belongs to another."

"Meaning . . . ?" and she faltered, for in the noise of her heart she understood his meaning.

"You are under Sir Harry's protection. If he were not in charge of you, then things might be so different."

His very stand-offishness aroused an urgent passion in Emma. She felt reckless, wondering if it would not be possible to disrupt her present position, and fling herself upon his mercy. If only she could be sure of Charles's affection. But she doubted him. She knew as she walked in the garden that she loved him and it disturbed her. His face was impressed for ever on her heart and she knew that if she could not have him, she wanted no man.

"I am not happy as I am," she faltered.

It was true. She had always resented the method by which Sir Harry had acquired her. There was a certain distaste in rendering herself to him night after night feeling as she did, but she was terrified by the thought of the poverty that threatened her if she left him. Willet-Payne had sailed in the *Cormorant* and she had not given him a second thought, nor did she reproach him; all her distaste was for Sir Harry.

"But do you think that whilst there is a question of Sir Harry protecting you, I would so much as glance in your direction, pretty as it may be?"

"But if he were not here?"

"Then, as I say, it might be different."

Never had she known a man so aloof, and she burning with her desire for him. "I am so simple," she confessed, "I know little of the world and its ways, and I am indeed most unhappy to find myself in my present position."

"If ever you are in need you could write to me."

"Oh, sir, I would be so indebted."

She gained no more from him, and finally watched him drive away in his chaise, his profile which was so Grecian silhouetted against the window. Then, because he had the power to move her so deeply, she wept.

At Christmas there was a message from Sir Harry that he would return in February when they would meet in London and have a little gaiety together. Emma invited her mother down to stay, but dared not keep her too long in case people talked of it. She confessed her present position, unsure of what Mrs. Duggan's reactions would be, but Mrs. Duggan was a practical woman and she entreated her daughter to be wise and tire not too easily of Sir Harry's attentions, clumsy though they might be. At least they offered the girl security.

"He is so rich, Emy, he can give you safety."

"But I love Charles Greville."

"He has only five hundred a year. I have worked at Warwick Castle and know a great deal about him. You stay where you are, Emy, flitting after too many men will end by attracting none."

All the same Emma felt quite ill about it, and after her mother had gone had to admit to an indisposition for the first time in her life. She turned queasy in the early mornings, refusing the hot chocolate because it made her sick. Affrighted at the continuance of it, at her pallor and beringed eyes, she finally went with some reluctance to the village physician. He was an oldish man, grey-whiskered above the creased white cravat, and his seedy coat was grimed with the dirt of ages, and smelt of the dried blood and pus with which it was infected. He asked the formal questions, and in the end smiled broadly.

"But surely, ma'am, you had thought of this?"

"Of which, kind sir?"

"That you might be with child? For that is the answer."

She stared at him in horror, for temporarily she had forgotten poor Ann Symonds and her strangled bas-

73

tard, and now she was brought up with a jerk. She had been foolishly blind to all the tell-tale signs of her body, and she did not know whose child it might be. The physician gave her details and counsel, but the date was an unfortunate one, coinciding as it did with a conception that could only have occurred when Sir Harry was absent. She was distraught over this. She did not know what to do, and had wit enough to know that even if Sir Harry could be duped into thinking that the child was his, he would resent a period of time when she was spoilt for him, and might easily dismiss her from his company.

She wept as she retraced her steps to Uppark, and would have been at a sad loss had not the old cook spoken to her. The old cook looked like a witch, but was kind, and she knew a wise woman in the village who could prevent birth. "With little pain," confessed the cook.

"It is not that I fear pain."

"The wise woman asks much money, but she does her work well. One day she'll hang for it; they took old Mother Windham to the gibbet because she choked Sarah Walker's babe, but the wise woman is too clever yet."

The girl was inflamed with the idea. She felt that her whole future depended on this, and although her being welled up with dismay at what might happen, she determined to have courage and be rid of this child.

She went alone in the dimness of the January night, carrying the lantern to light her way. There was snow lying on the ground which already had a frosted top so that it was slippery, and she moved awkwardly, afraid of falling and harming herself. As she went along the lonely road she saw the bright light from a cottage window, and drawing closer heard the sound of heavy sobbing from within. Emma—over-compassionate as ever—paused. She knew the young woman who dwelt there, and who darned fine lace, and fearing that something might be amiss she pushed open the gate and went within.

As she stood on the threshold about to lift the latch, a piercing shriek rent the air, startling in its intensity. Horrified, Emma blundered inside believing that it must be a murder. The downstairs room was in confusion. On the straw palliasse in the corner she saw the young woman's body, half-naked, distorted and writhing on the bed, whilst the village midwife, an old hag with greasy hair prying out from under her filthy cap, tried to hold the girl down. Again and again she shrieked, and Emma felt her own body ravaged by the reflection of that pain, and her brow growing sweaty as she tried to shut out the sight. Suddenly the screaming stopped abruptly, and there was a gulching sound, mingled with the determined hoarse croaking of an infant. The midwife plunged down into the straw with her arms, and drew the babe up triumphantly, folding him in a filthy shawl.

His mother, so quickly quietened whilst he screamed on, turned to look at him squirming in the shawl. Emma saw the girl reach up to take him. There was love in her eyes, and rapture as she gathered him to her, and pressed him, still crying, to her body. Neither she nor the shrewish old midwife were aware of the proximity of Emma, as she stared at the most human of all scenes, then slipped out of the door again and into the frozen lane beyond.

Desire possessed her. Desire to clasp her own son. No longer did she turn to the wise woman, to have a living being deliberately destroyed within her. She was not afraid of the pain, even the intense anguish that she had seen had not terrified her. Beyond that agony lay the exultation, and she knew that willingly she would suffer the one to gain the other.

She retraced her steps to Uppark, now walking forcefully, with a smile on her face. Fate had decreed that she should bear a child; she would continue with it.

XIV

IN FEBRUARY Emma went by coach to London to greet Sir Harry. She did not wish to establish herself again at Nerot's Hotel; there they knew of her relationship with Captain Willet-Payne, and she decided that the moment Sir Harry appeared, she would ask him if they could not go somewhere else.

During the late afternoon he walked into her room, looking very prosperous, for he was fond of himself. "Faith, Emy, but you're looking peaky," he said, and his eyes expressed their noticeable disappointment in her.

"I have been unwell."

"Where's your pretty colour gone? And what are those rings under your eyes? Are you sure some man has not been keeping you awake too late?" and he grinned bawdily.

"It is just the malady of which I have been suffering."

He made a small grimace. "Nerot's looks dull enough after the gaiety of Parisian hotels. Why did we ever think this place so bright?"

That was the opening she had wanted. "Indeed, that is true. I hate being here. Could not we go somewhere where we are not known?"

"Or do you mean where *you* are not known?" and he slapped her hip roundly.

He did not pretend to understand her in this new mood, but later in the evening when a meal had been brought to their room and he was a little drunk, he learnt more. She could not hope for long to continue with the mystery.

76

"You see," she said, "nature insists on having her own way and you are to have a son."

"A son?" He was dismayed. "But surely not? I do not need a son."

"I am afraid . . ." she faltered.

He was instantly suspicious. Sobered by this news, he asked more questions, and when she gave the answers stared at her stolidly. "This is not my son, this is some other man's child and you have been unfaithful to me."

"No, no, on my honour . . ."

She was at a loss. She could not remember when she had been so utterly helpless with a man, and he, turning sulky, rasped back his chair and stared at her with dulled eyes. "Ah," he said at last, "now I begin to understand why you wanted to be in a quieter place. To-morrow you shall go into a little lodging that I know round the corner; that will be quiet. So much for the gay time I had planned. I am not likely to have much gaiety with a pregnant woman."

"But, sir, you should have thought of this before," she faltered, her eyes brimming at his words.

He said he would go out to make the necessary arrangements, and, although she waited up half the night, he did not return until it was almost dawn and she had fallen into an exhausted sleep, her cheeks still wet. The next morning they moved into the lodgings in Jermyn Street where a sour old spinster kept the place and eyed Emma with malice. The place was clean and tidy, but Emma hardly noticed this because she felt so heartbroken.

"A nice homecoming this is for me!" said Sir Harry, "and I had made an assignation at Ranelagh."

"Go without me!" she urged.

"Faith, your eyes are so red with crying that I shall have to."

She waved him good-bye and, turning indoors again, spent the afternoon in furbishing up her frills. Her mother had been right; it was folly to resign herself to grief and she must attempt to attract her lover, not let him go. Little did she know that he had already gone.

When he did not return she went next morning to Nerot's Hotel to enquire, but there she was told that he had departed yesterday and they did not know whither. The hawk-like eye of the malicious spinster at the lodgings was already upon her; Emma had the feeling that she knew that her lodger had been deserted, abandoned to her fate, and that she was completely desperate. She did not know where to turn. For hours she paced the room, frantic with anxiety. Then she sat down and wrote a pathetic letter to Greville. He was the only one she could think of, and he had told her to write to him. It was ill-spent, Emma Hart was no scholar, and, as she wrote, her tears blotted the page.

What shall I dow? Good God, what shall I dow . . . ? What else am I but a girl in distres—reall distres? For God's sake G, write the minet you get this and only tell me what I am to dow. Write to me, G. Adue, and believe (me) Yours for ever

EMILY HART

Don't tel my mother what distres I am in and dow afford me some comfort.

The pathos of this letter would have stirred any man, and Charles Greville immediately sent her money, advising her in the most guarded language to return home to Grandmother Kidd at Hawarden.

She read that cold letter in anguish. The thought of retracing her steps on the journey home was one she detested. She had already come so far, rising from the village girl in a cotton frock who had lain in the hayloft with Andrew Lack, to the lady of Uppark in silks and satins. Now that was over, passion spent, what could she "dow"?

The village would know she was unwed and would

-78

point a finger of scorn at her, yet what else could she do? She made that journey by coach half-way, and continued it in wagons. So, in the early spring when the first violets were in moss ditches and the primroses in the Flintshire valleys, she came to the cottage where she had been reared, and now she was heavy with child.

"My Emy, my lamb," said her grandmother, receiving her into her arms. The grey strings of hair still fell from under the spoiled cap; the figure was more bent, the breasts dropped lower on the pendulous stomach, but her heart was still kind.

They ate a meagre meal on either side of the cottage fire, and Emma told her tragic story. The woman listened; she knew life and knew so often love worked this way. As they sat there was the sound of the cows returning to pasture, and, looking through the diamond-paned window, the girl saw Andrew Lack, thickened, older and stouter, walking towards the field driving the cows before him.

Her grandmother saw the direction of her glance. "He married Fenella Stokes," she said, "and she gave birth to a beautiful boy in the autumn. They're happy."

She did not know why the girl burst into sudden tears, aware that had she stayed and followed the formula of all village wooing, she also might have been his wife and happy. She made it an excuse to step out to the gate as he returned. There, under a pussy willow furred yellow with blossom, she looked at him, and he gave one glance and saw only the usual sight of a woman who was pregnant, her time advanced, and standing staring wistfully at the evening. He did not give her a second look.

'What else am I but a girl in distress—real distress?' she thought to herself.

Her grandmother comforted her, smoothing the lustrous hair from the tired little face. "It will pass, Emy. These things do pass, and you are too fresh and lovely to let them mark you. I'll keep the child

79

and you'll go back to the world. I have faith in you and things will work out well."

But Emma knew that the only way they could work out well would be if Charles Greville stayed in her life, because she loved him. Like this, reduced to extreme poverty and in addition saddled with a child, she could not see how their union could ever come about. "I am the most unhappy girl in the whole world," she sobbed.

"Don't distress yourself," whispered the kind old woman. And what she did not know was that her sweaty body smell sickened the girl after the toilet waters and pomanders of better times. How she hated the coarse linen, longing for the silks and satins now for ever excluded from her life. She had returned to a daughter of the village, and even the man who had once loved her in the hay had failed to recognize her.

That night she wept herself to sleep.

XV

IT WAS in the time of harvesting that Emma's child was born. All Hawarden knew of the girl who had returned in shame, and at the cottage it was difficult to make ends meet; for although Emma had sought to take in sewing for the big houses around, she received hardly any work, ladies not thinking it proper to employ a girl who could not keep herself respectable.

She wrote to Charles Greville, and again he replied enclosing a little money, and that was all she had, for Sir Harry had ignored her entreaties to Uppark. In truth he had never given her a second thought and tore up the letters, for he had installed another sweeting at Uppark, a big woman with jetty hair and a coarse wit that he thought was sporting.

It was a hot afternoon when the pains first came to the unhappy girl. She lay down in the room with the smell of cut corn and barley coming in through the open door, and her grandmother strove to soothe her.

Late into the night the pain, increasing in intensity, racked her shuddering body so that she would not have believed that it was possible to suffer so much and still live. Then it seemed as though she were suddenly struck by a forked dart of lightning, and split in two like a tree with agony. Swift on the heels of that too terrible pain, she heard the husky crying of an infant and knew that in triumph she had reached the hilltop of destiny and had a babe to hold in her arms.

"A girl, another Emy," said Grandmother Kidd.

The child was like her mother in features, and although Emma eagerly scanned the small face she could find no trace of the fatherhood that lay behind her; as yet the baby gave no hint of the root from which she had sprung.

"She's pretty as a picture," said the grandmother, greatly relieved to have the business through.

Whilst she was lying in, Emma's mind went ahead. The moment that she was recovered her one desire would be to return to London. She wanted to go back and start again, to climb back into the realms of the lady of fashion. She would have to get back somehow, and made desperate plans, but of course the lack of money was a shackle to her. Little Emily was a month old when Emma left her. She promised to send her grandmother money for the child's upkeep when she could get it, but when that would be she did not know.

"It'll come," said her grandmother, who had faith in her.

Emma had to beg her way on that journey, getting

lifts from passing wagons. She climbed up into the capacious backs of great loads of hay, and would lie there amongst the sweetness as they jogged forward. Then, when they set her down, she would stand at the roadside begging for yet another lift.

Once she stood all the morning outside St. Albans city, where the abbey was stuck on the hill squat as a sitting hen, its roofs spread like wings. Eventually a red-headed man came along, driving a heavy, covered wagon of cheeses for market. Delighted by the sight of her pretty face, he gave her a lift and made her a bed from his overcoat. At Mimms he stopped the horses under a cluster of trees, and then turning climbed from the front of the wagon to where his pretty passenger lay, his eyes ogling and his mouth wet with desire.

"Too pretty to lie alone?" he ventured.

She feigned to have innocence of his intention, and tried to thrust him from her. "I am from the village and simple."

"Even in villages the wenches learn of life," and his clumsy hands would have ravaged the strings of her frock.

"I am indeed grateful for the lift towards London, but I prithee do not force me to walk the rest."

"Then give me a kiss?"

"Your payment is too high."

"Thou'rt been kissed before, I dare wager?"

He would not be denied but drawing her mouth up to his, sucked at it vigorously, and she, nauseated by the contact, tried to draw back. Again and again he kissed her, his searching hands asking more, but, summoning all her strength, she pushed him from her, and, caught off his balance, he fell back among the cheeses, his legs shooting up in the air displaying the patched fustian of his breeches. That angered him. He picked himself up from the humiliating position and, swearing at her, went back to the driver's seat. So they came without another word through the quiet fields of Elstree, with the blackberries thickening amongst the red leaves and the first yellow curls of leaves blowing in the elm tops.

Emma was thankful when at last she could see the outline of Whitefield's Tabernacle standing alone as a monument against the sky, and knew it meant that they had come to the pleasantly rural surroundings of Tottenham Court Road. The horses were tired, so that they walked slowly across the marshlands. The beggars were standing knee deep in the brackish water that smelt so strongly, their naked legs exposed to decoy leeches. It made Emma shudder to think that men and women should sink so low as to try to attract leeches to sell to physicians for a pittance, and she hid her eyes so that she should not see.

When at last they came to the Tabernacle, she crawled across the cheeses, tapping the man on the shoulder. "If you would put me down here?"

"Am I to have no pay?"

"I told you that I had no money."

"Then I'll put you down where I will," he said pettishly, and drove on into Fish Street, with London Bridge lying beyond.

Here was London just as she remembered it, with the stench of the full gutters, and the snarling of pariah dogs nuzzling in the filth. Thinking nostalgically of it in Hawarden, she had forgotten how airless it was, and now she knew that she longed for a breath of country air, and as she stepped to the ground turned to the man who had driven her. "I wish I had money wherewith to repay your goodness."

"I did not ask money; what I asked you would not give me."

"Kind sir, I am a good girl."

He looked at her lecherously, his eyes indifferent. "You won't be good long with that face in this city," he assured her, then whipped up the tired horses, so that the wagon went up Fish Street, his face grim and sour over the reins.

Emma stood there with her bundle in her arms, and now she did not know where to go, and already it was starting to rain in small, thin drops. That night she slept in the unyielding shelter of a doorway; it was the only accommodation that she could find, and with midnight the rain increased, and the melancholy dripping soaked her through. She could sleep but little, alarmed at the beggars who lurched out of the shadows in the cover of the darkness to molest passers-by, and if their appeal failed, to try robbery. Also there were the bawdy women, their faces painted, who, with no attempt to hide their trade, plied it in any doorway. She was trying to sleep in the region of St. Sepulchre's churchyard, and from it there came an overpowering stench which gave her the ghastly impression that there must be ghouls at work, disinterring recently buried bodies to sell to the hospitals.

When morning came she knew that she could not bear a repetition of such a night; she must get herself properly established as a maid before another night fell. The dawn was cold, flecked through with a bright salmon red, significant of further rain. When she rose she was cramped and chilled, and very hungry, but she had so little left that she dared not venture it on so much as a custard tart. She walked down Fleet Street towards St. Mary-in-the-Strand where the air freshened, for the wind was blown off the water, and so she turned to the Adelphi.

A few late chairs were being jogged home, the link boys looking palely worn in the brilliance of early day. Some drunks lay where they had fallen, but the main people were the milk boys, their full pitchers dangling from wooden yokes, and the countrymen in smocks bringing their live hens for sale, and alert for good marketing.

'I must get some work,' she thought, trying to stay her own panic.

She saw a middle-aged, quiet man approaching her, walking in a leisurely manner. He was comfortably dressed in good clothes that were not over-trimmed, and he wore a sedate wig tied neatly. Because he glanced at her with a fatherly air, and also because she was so desperate, she stopped him.

"Good sir, do you happen to know where I could obtain employment as a maidservant?"

Immediately attracted by her beauty, Dr. Graham hesitated. He had slept badly, perplexed by doubts; could it be that suddenly fate was showing him the solution to his difficulties? "You are from the country?" he asked.

"Yes, sir. From Hawarden, seeking work."

His eye ran appreciatively down the beautiful proportions of her body. "I believe that I might be able to give you work. What is your name?"

"Emma Hart, an it please you, sir."

"I live in the Temple of Hymen in the Adelphi. It is quite close."

Emma had no idea what the Temple of Hymen could be, but by this time she was so tired and cramped that she could only be thankful for the kindness of his tone, and she said, "I would render good service, sir, and you would find me faithful."

He bade her follow him and she went timidly at his heels and came to the important-looking house, with an elaborate porch over which was inscribed TEMPLUM AESCULAPIO SACRUM. She glanced at the words, wondering what they could mean, but for the moment did not care, and he realized that she was exhausted. This was no time to make a bargain, so he handed her over into the charge of a kindly looking woman who directed her to a slip of a room on the top floor. There, completely worn out, Emma fell asleep.

XVI

DR. GRAHAM was a quack, trained at Edinburgh, who had soon developed along ideas of his own, claiming to have discovered "the innermost secrets of nature," and had established his temple in the Adelphi, which was well known throughout London.

He expounded a theory that all health sprang from the satisfaction of the body, and declared that in the temple he had an apparatus which could rejuvenate, bring back youth and promote such complete happiness "from the merging of the body" that it was a sheer delight.

When he had started his temple in the handsome house, his famous apparatus enshrined in crystal glass pillars, he had had great success, but, unfortunately, recently his star had begun to wane. His lectures on the satisfying of the sex interest had had a tremendous mode, but had lost favour. He had, it is true, fanned the flame of favour for a time by introducing a novelty, known as the "Celestial Bed," where for a payment honest citizens could be accommodated to serve their wives, who would in turn produce male children "of such surpassing beauty as left nothing to be desired."

As much as fifty pounds would be charged (and paid) each time. For such as could not afford the price demanded for the use and blessing of the Celestial Bed, with the gilt dragons, soft music and dim lighting, there were less expensive mediums. There was a nervous balsam that he sold, which could not be surpassed for those growing older, or more tired. There was an electrical aether that had never failed. There were pills, potions and remedies, wherewith women could be warmed and men made potent, so that their life afterwards would be a series of delightful seductions and passionate moments, also leaving nothing to be desired, so the literature assured them.

Nightly Dr. James Graham lectured in his Temple of pure and delicious health, and he had had great encouragement in drawing to his temple the fashionably interested. The whole affair was conducted with the greatest show of respectability and under the seal of medicine, but recently, most unfortunately, attendances had begun to lessen, and undoubtedly there was not the same interest.

No longer did the crystal pillars and carved marbles intrigue the curious. Even the staircase shaft which looked down upon a marble statue of Venus ceased to enchant. Dr. Graham knew that he had to find some delicate novelty, and for that reason was moving his establishment to Schomberg House, where he hoped, with the assistance of a Gala opening night, to introduce newer and more elegant attractions for a still higher fee.

The Celestial Bed had produced some girl children, and indignant citizens had come demanding the return of the outlay because the promises made so glibly had not been ratified. They blamed his bed and not their own glands.

The doctor was toying with the idea of hanging a niche in the concert hall of Schomberg House, with black velvet curtains and effective lighting, and there exposing a nude girl as the goddess of perfect health. Cold marble was overdone. He wanted to find a girl who could hold the cornucopia of fecundity in her arms, and whose appearance would stir the senses, setting old men agog, and making impatient the tissues of sensuous youth.

Seeing Emma, he had realized that fate was playing into his hands, this indeed was the very girl for his work. She had even disturbed him—used as he was to beauty—and he was very delighted with his find. The moment that she awakened he sent for her, and she appeared, standing meekly before him awaiting orders.

"You are too good for the work of an ordinary maid," said he.

"I am fully prepared to work, sir."

"You know that I am a physician? I lecture here on how to obtain perfect health."

Emma knew that. The pleasant woman who had taken her to the slip of a room had confirmed it.

"I need someone to demonstrate at my lectures, someone who can portray perfect health." He found those quiet violet eyes very disturbing as they watched him. "When I saw you, I realized that you would make the perfect Hygeia."

Instantly Emma was intrigued. "I have posed before," she said, and gave a modest interpretation of her "attitudes," which did not impress the doctor.

"Yes, yes," he said, "but this would be different. To give the complete picture, the body must be exposed."

"But, sir, that would not be good?"

He had expected this. "Very well, but I am not asking you to decide all on the moment."

"Pray, sir, does it mean that I would have to stand naked before gentlemen?"

"It would be in the cause of perfect health for all."

"I know that, sir, but . . ."

"Think it over," he suggested, dismissing her.

She went back to the room deeply distressed that this should have happened, and she wept. Below her windows in the Strand she could see beggars holding out lean hands in the gutters. At this time of the day the taverns were full to overflowing, and behind them lay the brothels, and she was terrified that one day she might find herself in one of those houses of ill fame, and that she could not bear. She could not spend another night sleeping in a doorway with the stench of rotting corpses, the bawds plying their trade, and the hideous beggars picking filth from the gutters.

She heard a tap at her door, and opening it, saw a handsome young man standing there. He wore a white gown after the nature of a priest's, and seeing the look in her eyes, told her that his name was John Newman. Indeed he was an assistant here, for he served as a "junior priest" in the establishment.

"Junior priest?" she faltered.

"It must seem strange to you, but it is one of my duties to escort husbands to the Celestial Bed, to pray with them and then to set the music astir whilst they lie together."

She thought he was mad. "It sounds—foolish," was all she could say.

"That is because you and I are young, healthy people. We do not need the vitality that others come here to buy. We have no desire to stimulate our longings and passions, our greater need is to repress them," and he looked at her with ardour.

"It does seem very strange to me, sir."

"It is not really strange. You would be doing the men and women good service if you stood for the goddess Hygeia. Have you thought how many fathers you would help to conceive the children of their desire? How many women to bear fine, brave sons?"

She recalled her own longing for a child when she had stood in that lonely cottage at Uppark, and had seen a babe actually born there. "But," she stammered, "I have never stood naked like that."

"In the name of art and to help the nation it is not wrong. It is to benefit the whole world." He put out a hand and touched hers gently. It was so long since a man had touched her kindly that she felt she could not bear it, and began to cry.

"I do not know what to do," she sobbed.

"Believe me, this is not wrong."

As she stood leaning against him, she became aware of the warm throbbing of his body close to hers, and believed what he said. She saw across the street below her window a white glove tied to the knocker, betokening that a birth had taken place in the home. At that moment it seemed to be almost an omen.

Perhaps he was right and it was her duty to help others in this way? And once she was in the niche none could touch her. She would be a lovely display, a live statue, nothing more.

"Perhaps," she faltered.

"I assured the doctor that I was convinced that you would not withhold yourself. It means so much to so many," said the "junior priest."

"How kind you are!" and now suddenly she was no longer afraid. It was at that moment for Emma Hart that the die was cast.

XVII

ON THE opening night of the new Temple of Health, Emma Hart was to make her first public appearance. The handbills sent round to advertise this phenomenal production had excited comment, and the concert hall was booked to capacity at a price far above anything that the doctor had so far been able to charge at the Adelphi.

Schomberg House was admirably adapted to his plan. He had indulged in stained-glass windows which gave a mellow, religious effect, and Emma was to stand in a curtained niche which, when revealed, would be lit by red lights. She would be entirely nude, but motionless, and supporting a huge cornucopia, which would be stocked with the produce of Covent Garden, bought late in the day and therefore at a most reasonable price.

The Celestial Bed had been enshrined in another part of the building, in a room especially designed to hold it, and here John Newman escorted sterile couples. The husband would be given a draught of the "elixir of life" in the ante-chamber, whilst it was part of Emma's duty to discuss matters with the wife, superintending her partaking of a particular powder, and then escort her to the Celestial Bed itself. The bedroom was dimly lit, with a madonna reigning over it to give the religious influence. After the couple had been shut in together, John Newman set in motion the mechanical device which churned out a tinkling music, and started little wooden gargoyles jogging along the reredos at the far end.

Emma had written to Charles Greville announcing the opening night of the new temple, and she hoped that he would come to acquaint himself with what was happening, but he made no reply. She looked apprehensively for some message, but none came, and she was deeply depressed to think that he had failed her. When night fell, even the little doctor became anxious and disturbed. He was venturing so much on the success of this evening, and was alarmed that the venture might not prosper, but at the appointed hour everything seemed to be going very well. The chairs started to arrive.

"I feel most anxious," Emma told John Newman. "I have never done such a thing before, and although I know it is in the cause of good health, to me it still seems strange."

But he reassured her. "Your beauty is so perfect that you need have no fear, maybe the Prince of Wales himself will come to pay us tribute."

That thought stimulated Emma. Although not a prepossessing young man, the Prince was the hero of all manner of stories which ran up and down England. He was considered to be both a roué and a rake; he knew too many women and always indiscreetly. His sojourns at Brighthelmstone already aroused comment, and Emma thought of him with delightful anticipation. It would indeed teach handsome Charles Greville a lesson if she could fly for still higher game, and it was not outside the limits of possibility that the Prince might come to the Temple to-night, and could easily be enchanted by the nude posed in the niche balancing the cornucopia of fecundity in her arms.

She stripped to her shift, then wrapping herself in the velvet cloak that the doctor had bought her, she came down the stairs. He was waiting in some agitation in the ante-room. Already the concert hall was full, and she could hear the liveliness of their chatter. The organ was playing religiously inclined music, for this was the card Dr. Graham always played. He knew the people well.

"Let me sing to them whilst they wait?" she suggested. "I need not be seen."

She sang tunefully in a sweet, untrained voice, and the audience applauded, but growing impatient, demanded more. It was then that the doctor arose to give his lecture on the vitality of health through love.

"I am all of a tremble," Emma confessed as she waited with John Newman beside the curtained niche.

As junior priest it was his duty to help her into it, and take her clothes from her. She saw that his hands quivered as he lifted her shift, but he said nothing, only staring at the exposed beauty as though he could not believe it. The firm flesh was alabaster, and she looked quite perfect.

"To-night," he whispered, "the world will rave not of the doctor and his Temple of Health, but of the beautiful Emma Hart."

"You have helped me immeasurably, and I am grateful," she whispered back as she poised the cornucopia on her shoulder.

In the outer hall the lights dimmed, and there came the hush of expectancy. The curtains were withdrawn and the men in the audience turned, enraptured, to see the beauty of the girl who stood there so artlessly. The long line of smooth thigh, her young, out-pointed breasts, and the rounded shoulders as she turned her classic Grecian profile towards them. Never had they anticipated anything so perfect, and broke into cheers of appreciation. What had the old doctor done to lay hold of so adorable a charmer? Health through love indeed! What man was there who did not long to possess the beauty, and incidentally perfect health as an outcome of the union?

All the time Emma was only thinking if Charles Greville were there. She wished that she could see, but the lights were too dim for her to be aware of the men who gazed so greedily upon her. She thought— it is for *him* that I am standing here. Surely, when he sees me, he will not be able to resist me? Surely . . . surely . . . ?

After a moment or two the curtains fell again to allow the doctor to continue with his lecture. Emma rested on a couch wrapped in the velvet cloak. There was an immediate sale of elixirs of youth, stimulating pills and potions as the lackeys now passed to and fro amongst the audience with trays of them for disposal. It was John Newman who told Emma that never had there been so great a demand, and the doctor was very well pleased, as indeed he should be, for she had helped him so much. Many, he told her, were asking the name of the beautiful goddess who had enchanted them, and they pressed to know more of her. At least, they argued, it was only fair to present her to them in the flesh.

But Dr. Graham was obstinate, and he insisted that this was a medical temple and no place for profligacy. On this point he would not stir. Long into the night the lectures and the passing glimpses of the fascinating Goddess of Health continued. It was almost morning when the last sedan had been joggled away, and the final pony chaise had rattled from the door.

Flushed and excited, Emma stood alone in the concert hall where the lackeys were dowsing the candles. Now she was aware that one man had stayed behind after all the others had departed; he sat in a plush chair at the very back of the room. For a moment, strangely moved by the thought that it might be Greville, she felt her heart beat madly, and went to him. She moved down the long room impeded by the heavy folds of her dark velvet cloak, with her auburn hair lying untied in voluptuous curls to her shoulders. The tresses caught the last light, and gave the effect of a halo, a golden mist which suffused her head. The man was watching her. Now she realized that his aesthetic face had none of the compelling beauty of Charles Greville's, but that the dark hair curled a trifle and his eyes were kind. He had not the robust air of Jack Willet-Payne, but a tenderness that was almost womanish, and he watched her all the time.

"Kind sir, it is over for to-night."

He still stared at her as though he could not see enough. "Are you real?" he asked.

"Yes, sir, my name is Emma Hart, of Hawarden."

"And mine is George Romney."

"Surely not Mr. Romney, the artist?"

"The same, most exquisite lady."

Now she forgot the excitement of the night, her fever of anxiety that the Prince would attend, her desire that Charles Greville should see her. This man, now at the height of his fame, could make her immortal.

"You are the loveliest woman that ever lived," he said, and his quite voice was deeply moved.

"I am glad that I please you, Mr. Romney."

"Will you permit me to paint you?"

"Sir, I shall be honoured."

"Is that a promise? I will not leave here until I am sure that you mean it. If I can propagate your beauty, then indeed I shall not have lived in vain."

She put out a hand and took his in a friendly clasp. "It is indeed a promise, sir, and I keep my promises. You shall come to learn the truth of that."

"To-morrow night I shall come back here. I live in Cavendish Square. It would not be too far for you to come?"

"I am a country girl, and my legs carry me where I will. I shall indeed find the walk pleasant," and she glanced apprehensively at the lackeys waiting with their long extinguishers to complete the dowsing. "But you must go now."

He walked to the door as in a dream. Turning he looked at her, his eyes misted. "Emma is a superb name for a superb woman," he whispered. "Immortal Emma. That is what it should be."

XVIII

EMMA WENT up to her room hardly able to think, for after all there had been nothing distasteful about standing in the niche in the nude. On the top landing the first rare light of the dawn was chinking through the curtains, and she saw that John Newman was waiting there. He still wore his junior priest's habit, his arms folded on his big, square breast, whilst he looked at her from under his lowered lids.

"Emma, I thought that you would never come."

"But, John, why are you here? It is late enough in all conscience, surely we all need rest?"

"I could not rest."

She choked down some apprehension. "But why not? We have worked hard enough and long enough. Dr. Graham is already asleep. He was snoring when I passed the door. He sleeps and he is satisfied."

"But I cannot sleep, and I am certainly not satisfied. Emma, my sweet Emma, when I took that shift from you, what did I see? Surely you would not tantalize and deny me?"

She had never expected that he would make overtures to her, and turned half bemused. "But now, with the dawn breaking? You must be mad. I am tired out, and I must sleep." Going into her room she shut the door, and because it had no lock pulled a heavy table in front of it, but she need not have been anxious, for John Newman was not a trespasser. She was so exhausted that she slept until late in the day when the street cries disturbed her. She had forgotten about John Newman until she came down, a little dark about the eyes and pale of complexion.

"You must rest before to-night," the doctor told her. "We cannot have the Goddess of Health looking unwell."

Because she felt that fresh air would help her, she went out into the streets to market to buy fresh fruit for the cornucopia. There were plums with the bloom still on them, yellow pears and rosy apples from the old market women's baskets. As she returned, picking her way along the Strand, she thought eagerly of Mr. Romney, so eagerly that she did not see a magnificent sedan approaching. Outrunners were before it, women curtseyed, and Emma saw the chair stop and from it alighted the Prince of Wales. He was over-plump, tallish, with a round, amused face, a pink skin, and light brown hair. Recovering just as his eyes lighted on her, she curtseyed. The Prince never missed a pretty face and came towards her. Her eyelids fluttered and she wished that she was not burdened with so much fruit. She should have dispatched a lackey to carry it for her.

He said, "Surely I have seen this pretty face before?"

"Emma Hart, at your service, Your Royal Highness."

"It is a pretty name. Emma Hart."

"From Dr. Graham's Temple of Health."

People were collecting, and she felt the colour coming to her cheeks, knowing that this was an enchanting moment and one that she had long waited for. The Prince himself was speaking to her.

"I must visit the Temple of Health if it reveals so much beauty," he said, and smiled. The smile was curved like a scimitar. She curtseyed low, and when she looked up again he had passed on with his gentlemen, and she felt singularly disappointed.

However, she hurried back to Dr. Graham, who was delighted with what had happened, and made sure that undoubtedly to-night the Prince would attend. Emma in her own room was so exhilarated that she wrote yet another letter to Charles Greville, an ill-writ, blotchy letter, sprinkled too hurriedly with pounce, and sealed with a wafer before dry.

> "You should come to this entertainment," she begged him. "People say that my posing is remarkabul, and I dow want you to be here. To-day the Prince spok to me. My cupp of happiness is indead full."

She dispatched it, but she knew that Charles Greville was an aloof creature, and that it might be impossible to break down the impenetrable walls with which he surrounded himself, and because of this she was fated to love him even more.

John Newman came to her room. "Mr. Romney is coming back to-night, he is coming to see you, the message said."

"He is very charming."

"Be careful of him, Emma. He has a virtuous wife and children in Northumberland, and they say they are living in poverty, whilst he earns thousands of pounds here."

"But surely that is none of our business? Mr. Romney is charming and paints beautifully."

"In some ways, Emma, you are still the village girl. He does not bode you well."

"I do not see how you mean. If I am happy, what else matters?"

He came across the room, and laying his hands on either side of her slender waist, stood staring down at her. "You have a great power over men, my sweet. Only rare beauty like yours can do so much, but you

97

yourself are your own enemy. Because of that power I know that you may tread the heights, but you will also walk down into the darkest valley of despair. . . ."

"Oh, John, I hate it when you talk like that."

"Because it is the truth. In your heart you know that it is the truth, and nothing hurts more than that."

She tried to thrust him from her, but he was possessive and held her to him as though he would never let her go again. "I would take you away from all this, hide you in some village where there would be serenity. You should have a strong husband and children of your own."

At that moment she wondered if she dared to tell him of little Emily at Hawarden with her grandmother; only yesterday she had sent half her earnings for the child, but now prudence held her peace for her. The thought of serenity tempted her, but at the same time her ambition overrode her. "I must prepare for to-night," she said gently, and after he had gone she felt in a measure as though she had betrayed him. He, of all men, who most wished her well. When she thought of to-night, of the possibility of Charles being there—she put him first—and of the Prince attending, she forgot simple John Newman.

She washed her body, anointing it with perfume and orange toilet water, and powdering; then drawing on the velvet wrapper, she went down. A couple were being ushered towards the Celestial Bed, and Dr. Graham was talking to them, for the man was a stout city alderman, his hair receding, his chin slumping, and his rather timorous wife. Five years wed and as yet no pledge of their love. The pathetic eyes of the wife caught those of Emma, for she recognized in the girl that warmth and wealth of fecundity that could give a man his desire, and coveted it. Emma went to her and took her into the antechamber, realizing that she was afraid.

"It seems so wrong, so difficult," the woman whispered nervously.

"Drink this and it will change it all."

"But will it make me ill?"

"Surely not; it will make you happy and content, and send you a fine son."

The woman drank it doubtfully, and stared helplessly at Emma. "It still seems wrong," she said.

"There is nothing to be afraid of," and Emma quietly led her down into the dim room where the church music was already playing and the dancing figures stood as yet quiet in the almost majestic lighting. John Newman had helped the alderman to disrobe. The man was eager, for he wanted a son badly, and would endure any strange rite to fulfil his desire.

"You will have a lovely boy next spring," Emma told the wife, and patted her hand affectionately before she finally left her. She hoped that a lovely boy would be theirs, for she liked the rather frightened little woman. But when the door had shut on them she had other things to think about. Had the Prince come? Would Greville be here? She went downstairs where the concert hall was already crowded. John Newman whispered that Mr. Romney was already there, and "in a fever of impatience for the show to begin," but the Prince had not put in an appearance. He could not tell her about Greville, for he did not know him by sight.

'Ah, if only he were there!' she thought as she went to the niche where the cornucopia awaited her. Now she knew that nothing would satisfy her save to climb the heights. This was not enough, she had to go further. There was a time ahead. It was curious as she mounted the steps of the niche that she should hear a sound as of the waves of the sea. Or was it the beating of her heart? At that moment she could not tell.

XIX

GEORGE ROMNEY was watching the doctor's exhibition with the keenest interest. In truth he could not tolerate the actual performance, which he thought to be crude, recognizing behind it the idea of pandering to the prurient. No wonder half London flocked here! He thought, also that anything so lovely as Emma Hart should not be here at all, and framed her against the background of his spreading studio in Cavendish Square, with the Chippendale chairs, the jars of brushes, and the unfinished canvases propped against the wall. There was a background of the general *déshabille* of beauty, and far more wonderfully would she ornament it than here.

He looked eagerly round as the black velvet curtains parted and disclosed the statue, though he was instantly nauseated by the vociferous acclamations of the men around him. They thought of this girl as being theirs for the taking; they did not appreciate her delicate charm and the fragility of a beauty that was superb.

When the lecture was finished he made himself known to Dr. Graham, asking leave to present his compliments to Miss Hart. The doctor was a snob; naturally he realized only too well the importance of encouraging the "right people," for the success of his venture largely depended on attracting bloods to it. Mr. Romney was a society pet. If he could paint Emma it would increase the clientele and would be yet another way of making his temple better known. He would do anything he could to foster such a proposition.

"Of course, my dear sir."

"She is indeed beautiful. It surprises me that no one has painted her, perhaps I will do so myself, but anyway, kind sir, allow me to see her."

He was introduced to her as she reclined on a couch in the ante-room, and she was enchanted to meet him again. He sat beside her with those fever-bright eyes of his that she had recalled before. She told him of meeting the Prince to-day, and confided in him, not knowing why she should confess her weaknesses save that his gentleness impelled her, her deep and sincere love for Charles Greville—quite unrequited—and using such affectionate language as she spoke of him.

"Do you know him, kind sir?"

"I do indeed."

"Then could you not help a poor girl by taking him a message and telling him that his Emma stays faithful?"

"Sweet lady, he is not worthy of so great a love."

"The man a woman loves is always worthy of her," she said with truth. "I wrote to him begging him to attend to-night, but he is not here, and it saddens me that he should stay away."

"I have a proposition to make to you."

"A proposition?"

"I intended to ask you to come to Cavendish Square to sit for your portrait. I want to paint you in a hundred different ways."

"You are too kind, sir, but what would the doctor say to this?"

"He tells me that it delights him."

"Then I also am delighted. When shall we start?"

"The day after to-morrow?"

"Certainly." She gave him no inkling that she thought it very soon.

"This is my address, and we will begin when the light is good. Shall we say at noon?" and he eyed her keenly, for there was more that he wished to say. "I want you to know, my sweet child, that for an artist it is impossible to paint unless he knows something of the temperament of his model."

"So I have heard, kind sir," for she recalled Charles Vere, languidly beautiful, who had loved her in the early days and who, so far, had been her only link with the studio.

"Emma will not be unkind to her humble servant?"

"Emma is never willingly unkind," she faltered.

It was already time to return to the niche, and she went back and took up the pose, her lovely eyes trying to pierce the gloom of the concert hall, searching in vain for Greville's face. She was not thinking of the Prince any more, but ravishingly of Greville.

Without her dear Charles she knew that her life would be insupportable. She loved him. He had been so good to her when she had been forced to return to Hawarden to bear little Emily; his money had been all she had possessed, and she could only think of him with a deep affection that was greater than anything that she had ever felt before. She doted on him. Surely such love could not pass unrequited, even though he delayed in writing to her. And gave her no sign that he was alive?

But from the niche she could see practically nothing, for the faces of the avid audience were blurred discs, featureless and unrecognizable. Disappointedly she awaited her next call.

Two mornings later she picked her way daintily to Cavendish Square in the bright sunshine. She had not thought that the house would be so large and imposing, for Newman had mentioned Romney's family, supposedly impoverished, and she had thought that Romney himself was probably a spendthrift. But this was a beautiful house, and she was stimulated as she crossed the great hall to enter the studio which lay at the back. A minstrels' gallery of carved oak was across the far end; and the throne stood in a north light coming in from the oriel window. Before it was

Romney's easel. He wore a painter's smock over velvet trousers, and she saw that his hair was rumpled. She wished in some ways that he did not wear the smock, for it reminded her of Andrew Lack and the early adventure, now so childish that it hardly ranked as an adventure at all, though it still had the power to disturb her.

"I am here, kind sir!"

He took her hand and led her to the slender couch of striped yellow silk which stood beside the oriel. "First we must talk. We must learn of your thoughts, your ideals, your dreams. This is a confessional, you know."

He asked if she were wed, and she told him no, but in a second he discerned the shell-like colour creeping to her face, and the dropped silk of her lashes.

"There have been lovers? Well, well, and why not?"

"There have been too many."

She spoke of the day when she had travelled by coach to Greenwich to talk to Captain Willet-Payne, and the night spent in his arms. He had been a masterful lover who took what he wanted, and as he would. In loyalty she glossed over the way that he had passed her on to Sir Harry and the hours she had spent at Uppark, and there she had met Charles Greville. She said nothing of the flaxen-haired groom or the visitors who had smiled kindly upon her and had sneaked slipperless to her door begging favours. She recounted the tragic story of how Sir Harry had abandoned her and she had returned to Hawarden where her little Emily had been born with the smell of corn coming in at the cottage door. And then of the infinite courage of her return, determined to regain what she had lost.

"Oh, brave, wonderful Emma!" he said admiringly.

Now for the moment she was merely the statue at the Temple of Health, but in this she was accom-

103

plishing something, for she had already been able to send her grandmother money for the baby. Emma paid her debts. Her sterling quality was that she never forgot. Romney drew his knitted blue silk purse out of his pocket and said, "Please send her this from me," and she saw how feverish were his eyes.

"You are too kind, dear sir."

"I may ask you to be kind to me."

"I will most willingly sit for you."

"But that, dear Emma, is not all. I must be frank. No great artist ever paints unless he loves his models. Love guides his hand and changes the portrait to one of genius." As she listened she knew that she was immeasurably stirred. "Emma is not cold?"

"Oh, not cold, sir, too fond, perhaps," and she smiled encouragingly at him.

"Then we will start painting next week; will that be too soon?"

She shook her head, and he saw that there was deep emotion in her eyes. He put out his arms, and drawing her to him could feel the tantalizing beauty of her body beneath her gown. "Oh, Emma, my sweet, I hate to think of one so fair in the arms of young bloods like Sir Harry, and ravagers of women like Willet-Payne. Come to me, adorable Emma, and I will make you very happy."

It was then that she had the feeling that Romney could give her a quality of love that so far she had never tasted. He was gracious. Yet she knew even as she lay yielding in his arms that she could never feel the same absorbing passion for him as she did for Charles Greville, who apparently was unlikely to give her another thought.

XX

THE PRINCE OF WALES came to the Temple of Health.

Quite early one evening he walked in with a supercilious smile, and instantly there was a commotion. The doctor had known that some high personage would be visiting them, and five gilded chairs had been placed ostentatiously in the centre of the front row.

Although Emma had prayed that it would be the Prince, she could not be sure, so when John Newman slipped behind the curtains to tell her that His Royal Highness was already established there, she almost felt that she would swoon.

"Then he has come to see me?" she asked.

"Yes, he seems most interested, and the doctor is so excited and nervous that he is drinking quantities of port in the vestibule to summon sufficient courage to lecture!"

Emma felt that now everything depended on herself. Few young women got the chance to pose before His Royal Highness, who was known to be susceptible. This was the greatest opportunity of her whole life.

She waited on the couch hoping that her heart would not be too disturbing, because now she felt desperately frightened. As she went to her niche, however, she did not swoon as she had feared. Never had she stood so silent with never a ripple. In fact His Royal Highness vehemently expressed the doubt that so lovely a creature even breathed. When the curtains fell she returned to the ante-room, and five minutes afterwards Newman came to tell her that a gentleman asked leave to speak with her. She saw the door open, rose to her feet, drawn to her full height, her hands clasped before her. But the man who entered was not the Prince of Wales, it was Charles Greville!

She felt so utterly bewildered by the transports of joy that suddenly suffused her, that for a moment she stared amazed. "Oh, Charles, my dearest Charles, at last my prayers have been answered and you have come to me!"

"I came at your bidding, Emma."

"You have seen the exhibition?"

"I have." She thought that his lip curled slightly and hoped that it might not be in disapproval.

"His Royal Highness is here."

"His Royal Highness has a lecherous mind." Knowing as she did how much he cared for royal patronage, this seemed to be an extraordinary statement for him to make. "My sweet Emma, this is no place for you. You should not be employed in this wretched temple. It is hideously licentious, and you should escape from it."

For a moment Emma was at a loss for words. Any scruples she might originally have possessed had been dispelled by the presence of the Prince. "But, Charles, I have to live?"

"Must you live this way? It can only bring you ill repute."

"I do nothing that is wrong."

"You expose yourself so that all London may see you."

"But it is in the cause of good health."

"This is not true. This is not in the cause of good health and Dr. Graham knows that is so. This is lechery and I will maintain it to my dying day."

Emma felt her eyes dimming, and for a moment she said nothing, then she faltered, "If I left here, would you be kind to me, dearest Charles?"

"I have told you before that if you were living under no man's protection, then I would consider the thought."

"No man is protecting me now."

"No man, indeed, whilst you are working for the doctor, but any man can see you, any night."

"I do protest that there is no harm in it." She began to weep disappointedly; she had not thought that he would be like this. "Oh, Charles, I pray you to be kind to me. You are so stern, and I, alas, am but weak."

"If you get away from this extraordinary temple, then things could be different. I am selling my London mansion and it is just within the realms of possibility that I could make arrangements for us both."

Enchanted at such a prospect, she swung between the abyss of despair and a heaven of joy. She forgot that the Prince himself was in the next room, for she saw the greatest happiness of all within her grasp. "I should die from happiness," she whispered. "Perhaps I could leave here, and go into respectable lodgings in the vicinity of Cavendish Square. Mr. George Romney would help me to find somewhere suitable, unless you——" she hoped he would suggest a place himself.

"No, until you are absolutely free I can do nothing. But I desire that you shall arrange something yourself."

She clung to him innocently, so much in love that she could not see what manner of man he was. "Believe me, dearest Charles, whatever you wish is as a command to me. I have no other desire save to please you."

He rose casually; his very coolness was enchanting to her since other men were so over-warm. "When you are elsewhere then we will discuss the matter again," he said, and bowing low went to the door. But there he had to stand back for a moment for the Prince himself was entering unannounced. Portly and a little inclined to waddle, he smiled seraphically in recognition of Charles Greville, then came into the room, dismissing him with the merest flick of the lace-edged handkerchief with which he made so much play.

"I come to pay homage to an ectheedingly lovely lady," he announced, speaking with a slight lisp. She curtseyed deeply to him. Now she had forgotten that she was doing obeisance to the future King of England, for to her there was but one king, and he was Greville. She was deeply in love and because of it glowed like an opening rose. The Prince looked to be well pleased with her. "I pway that the lovely lady ith ath willing ath she ith fair," he said, and tittered a little as though a trifle nervous.

Emma looked at him with immovable eyes, for her heart was on Greville and she could think of no one else. "The lady is chaste, Your Royal Highness," she said.

"Doth it mean that the lady ith cold?"

"Not cold to the man she loves, Your Royal Highness."

The Prince had been drinking, and could never manage to retain both wine and faculties at one and the same time. He belched noisily, flapping his mouth with the foppish handkerchief afterwards to cover some confusion. Then he laughed a little, hoping that she would laugh too. "When a pwince ecthpotheth hith hand tho plainly, thùrely it ith for the lady of hith choice to be generwous?" he enquired in a last effort at persuasion.

She looked at him tantalizingly; at this moment she was probably at her most beautiful, and she curtseyed deeply. "When a prince exposes his hand so plainly it must be to a lady who is worthy of his affection," she explained quietly.

This was certainly not what Dr. Graham had promised to the Prince when he had sought the interview. The old doctor had assured His Highness of Wales that he would find the lady both amiable and willing and a very worthy bedfellow if he so wished. The Prince did not understand what had happened, and wished that he had not drunk quite so much because it confused him even if it did elate. Turning, he went to the door, and now he did not know whether to be angry or amused.

"Enough for to-night," said he and waved his hand imperially towards her.

It was then that quite suddenly she realized that she had denied him. She had refused the First Gentleman. For a second her eyes flickered towards him and, conscious of a social gaffe, she tried to recover the situation.

"There are other nights, Your Royal Highness," she suggested as she curtseyed low.

XXI

ALREADY EMMA was making arrangements to find accommodation away from the Temple of Health, for she had realized that she had no hope of pleasing Greville if she stayed where she was. For the time being she said nothing to Dr. Graham, but went to sit for George Romney, confident that she could solicit his aid and that he would help her.

"I am weary of the Temple," she explained, "I want to find some quiet room; somewhere where, for a while at least, I could live in peace. I could earn my living by darning fine lace and taking in sewing."

"But I will pay you to sit for me, and that should suffice?" he suggested. "I could easily find you a room. There are nice cottages near for it is countrified behind this square."

"I would not want to go near the Tottenham Court Road," for she had taken a dislike to the marshes where she had seen the wretched beggars exposing their skinny legs to attract the leeches, and standing up to their thighs in water that stunk.

"There is an old woman who lives in a pleasant enough cottage by the wood off Portland Place. I know her, and would speak to her."

"Oh, sir, I'd be indebted. I would not have much money, but I should not want luxury, for there is little Emily to be thought of."

"I understand." They were sitting on the wide steps of the throne, and he had his arm around her. "How cruel it is that some man should have left you with so great a responsibility! My poor and lovely Emma, you have suffered too much for one so young and so beautiful."

"But I am strong." She traced the outline of his face with her finger and brought her hand up to caress his sloping brow.

"And I am to paint you?"

"Your painting will make me famous for ever. Nothing could make me happier."

"But there is a penalty," he whispered and laid his face against her auburn hair.

"It can be no penalty, for surely such is an enchantment."

He thrust the ruffle from her shoulder and hid his face in the flesh. "How cruel it is that time should wear away such beauty! Youth's a stuff t'will not endure, that is the greatest tragedy of our life."

"But on your canvas my beauty shall endure, and for ever," she promised; "all the world will see it."

Shyly he slipped the shouldering back into place and she had the feeling that she had disappointed him. She was sensitive to atmospheres, and wondered what to do, for if they had a misunderstanding now it meant that he would not speak for her at the cottage off Portland Place, and the way would not be clear for her to go to Greville. She thought that she could not bear that.

With a delicate gesture she lifted her hand and untied the cross-ribbons of her bodice. George Romney watched her, his mouth working, his eyes fever-bright with anticipation. He found himself unusually moved, for to him the nude was as nothing, but this provocative girl had some rare quality about her. She could excite a desire that was unassuageable save at the one fountain. One by one she laid aside her garments until she stood there in nothing save the one abbreviated shift, and smiled at him with the confidence of a child.

"Will you help me?" she asked him.

His hands trembled so much that he could hardly reach her to take the garment from her. "I am clumsy," he said.

When he had taken it he gazed at her for a moment, fascinated almost intolerably by the close proximity of so much that was beautiful. Not easily stirred, he was amazed at the emotion she had roused in him. Then he said, "Oh, Emma!" and caught her compellingly to him, crushing her beneath his own body. Never had a model inspired him more.

For an hour they lay there on the step of the throne, whilst London passed across the square beyond the gate, and the street vendors called their wares, but the two were so enchanted that they never heard a sound. Nothing outside their two selves mattered. Whilst he held her in his arms and kissed and drank of her sweetness, time stood still.

Later he stirred from the sweet drowsiness that had suffused him, and immediately he started to paint. He worked carefully. Under his tapering fingers the beautiful face was transferred to the canvas; he caught the infection of her smile, her bright yet childlike eyes, and the delicate moulding of her cheek. He forgot that she would be growing cramped and tired, for she had such a capacity for holding a pose and yet staying fresh with it. Only when at last he looked closer, he recognized the exhaustion coming into her eyes and was angry with himself for having asked too much.

"Emma, my dear, you must rest now! I have been

111

selfish, I have thought only of myself and my picture," and flinging down pallette and brushes he went to take her into his arms.

She got up, stretching herself. She was like an eager kitten, every limb lithesome, and every movement with a gracious beauty of its own. "I'm all right. Please, George, do not distress yourself."

"Rest a while, then we will visit the cottage where I think they could find you accommodation. It is within a stone's throw."

"Let us go now," she said.

"Are you so anxious to leave the doctor? Surely he has been very good to you?"

"I am desirous of giving up the life and starting again," she confessed, but she could not tell him that it was for Greville's sake that she wished to make this break, thinking that it would irritate him.

They went into the street together, turning from the graceful Regency square, to the rural road with the smell of crushed hemlock and dogberry in the ditches. The lush fields sprawled beyond into the country. They walked arm in arm, and anyone seeing them might have thought they were some newly-wed couple from their manner.

The cottage was small and built of lath and plaster in the old-fashioned style, set skew-wise on to the corner of the road. A woman in a print frock came out to speak to them, and stood framed in the door, with the asters and zinias growing abundantly beside it. There was something about her freshness of complexion that reminded Emma of the women at Hawarden, and she knew immediately that she liked Mrs. Potts. The room she showed her was homely, very clean, and bearing no resemblance to Uppark, or Nerot's Hotel, or the sea Captain's room at Greenwich with its view of the harbour and the wooden ships riding at anchor there. The price that Mrs. Potts asked was moderate, and Emma made arrangements to occupy the room next week. As she walked away she knew that she should feel wildly happy that so much had been completed, but with the strange inconsequence of such emotions, had turned quiet.

"What is it, my Emma?" Romney asked her.

"It will indeed be difficult telling Dr. Graham."

"Why did you make such a quick decision? Could it be that some other man influenced you? Tell me, my sweet, for I shall not be angry. It is unthinkable that anyone so fair should not have many beaux."

"I saw Charles Greville."

"Indeed, but that makes me very sad."

"But he is so kind to me; he is the most wonderful man that I have ever met, and I think that I shall die of love for him."

"And he disapproved of the doctor?"

"Yes."

Romney shrugged his shoulders and made a little *moue* of displeasure. "I suppose that is understandable, but I always dislike and suspect Greville's prudery."

"But, indeed, he is no prude."

"I feel that Charles is a man who draws a velvet wrapping over a heart of iron. Remember that, Emma, his heart is hard."

"Indeed, I think you wrong him. He is forceful, he plays at many things, but, oh, his heart is gentle."

"I doubt that. I feel that he hides lechery under a distasteful veil of reserve. He has never earned the reward of the love of such as Emma Hart."

"Perhaps Emma Hart has never earned the goodness of the love of Charles Greville," she retorted with shining eyes, "but we will not quarrel about that."

He opened his mouth to say more, and then dismissed it. "We meet to-morrow?" he suggested.

"Yes, to-morrow, please, and indeed I will try not to tire."

"It was I who tired you. Yet if I were to say that there should be no more such tiredness, then I should be wrong. Or would I not?" and she knew that his feverish eyes were asking yet another favour.

"You would indeed be very wrong," she agreed, and curtseyed to him.

XXII

DR. GRAHAM was aghast when Emma told him that she intended to leave the Temple. Only a night or so ago the Prince of Wales had proved by his presence how the doctor's star was in the ascendancy. Dr. Graham foresaw a great future for himself, provided that he could vary the delights, and this certainly would not be for lack of imagination. Royal patronage had been all that he had required to make his establishment one of the sights of London, and he was in excellent good humour about it when Emma came into the room.

He had been busily combing out his most elaborate wig on its stand in readiness for to-night when she informed him that she would be leaving next week. He put down the comb, swallowing hard, and clutched helplessly at the lapels of his brown woollen jacket.

"If the money is not sufficient, I could pay you more," he gulped uneasily.

"It is not the money; it is that I have made other plans, sir."

An idea struck him. "The Prince?" he suggested archly, for after all princes are no more than other men.

"My plans have nothing to do with His Royal Highness."

He looked at her with some reproach, for it would have been a feather in his cap if the goddess Hygeia had become the mistress of the Prince of Wales, but this was not the moment in which to argue. He was already late—the wig had been tiresome—and there was a cheesemonger from Bow coming to the Celestial Bed, deeply desirous of a son and offering double fees if such a birth could be negotiated for him. His wife had already been brought to bed of three daughters in quick succession, and was not a compatible partner. She had taken against the thought of the Celestial Bed, and had been brought here entirely against her will, and the doctor had been told that she was making a scene in the ante-chamber.

"We cannot discuss it now, Emma, but you must change your mind. There is a client, a very difficult client, in the ante-chamber. Will you go to her for me?"

"Certainly I will, sir."

Emma knew that she had won her day and that it had been a great deal easier than she had expected. The woman waiting in the ante-chamber was smallish, very plain, her face mottled with recent tears and her lids heavily swollen. She stared resentfully at the beautiful creature who entered the little room, and although she disliked it, was relieved to see the tender compassion in the girl's eyes.

"I am sure that you wish to please your husband," said Emma sympathetically.

The cheesemonger's wife did not care if she did please him or not, and would have said so, save that the beautiful face was so unexpected and different from anything that she had anticipated. Emma held out a draught in a crystal goblet.

"It may be poison," said the little woman, as she eyed the drink.

"It is not poison, I can promise you. The doctor is clever. He knows which herbs make sons, and which make daughters."

The little woman drank the draught, which was bitter, and the taste, lingering, made her mouth sour. Emma, seeing what had happened, held out a custard

115

pie to her. She had produced it as though by magic from her pocket. "This will help; it is one of the best, I promise, so eat it quickly."

They went out of the room together, the little woman with weak knees, and clinging to Emma's arm. Already they could hear the deeply religious music—for John Newman had started the organ, and the stairway that led to the hall where the bed itself stood was dimly lit as though for a sacrament and smelt strongly of incense.

"I dread more children," whispered the woman. "I am afraid. You do not know what it is to bear them."

Emma laid her head against hers. "Hush," she whispered, "I do know, for I have a little daughter."

For a moment they stared at one another in the dimly religious light, then the woman, trying to read the truth behind those eyes, saw the massive doors swing open with the music in a crescendo, and her husband, bereft of his outer clothing, perched on the side of the Celestial Bed, with a white-robed priest bending over him.

Discreetly Emma withdrew.

Now she was glad that she would be leaving the Temple, because to-night she knew that it was all tawdry. The dcotor remonstrated with her for most of the next day, trying to tempt her with offers of better money, but she refused. She was adamant in her determination to escape this and go to the man whom she loved. It was George Romney who aided and abetted her.

In the handsome studio in Cavendish Square, she sat for him, and afterwards they talked together, she realizing what a tender and affectionate man he was. His wife had been cold, the daughter of a parson in Northumberland with no emotional warmth. At the time Romney had been nothing but a rawly developed boy, knowing little of love or passion, and it had been their kinsmen who had so desired the marriage. Later he had been to bed with a woman who loathed all passion and found it repulsive, and who

116

admitted that she had married him because she was frightened of the stigma of being left a spinster.

"Poor George," she said tenderly when he told her about it.

"We had two children, in faith, Emma, I have never discovered how! Now I have left all that behind me, she is back with her father blackening my name, and I am here."

"With me?" and she held wide her arms to enwrap him.

"Could I be with anyone sweeter?" and as he held her to him, kissing her, "Sweet, seductive Emma, do let me pray you not to waste so much loveliness on Charles Greville. Put him out of your life whilst there is still time, and forget him."

"You ask too much. Did Helen forget Paris? Or Cressida forget Troilus? Love is too strong."

She believed then that Charles was the one great love of her life, and was frantic to go to him. It was for this reason that on her last night at the Temple, she sat up late to write him one of her little ill-spelt letters, confident that she had done as he directed and that he could only be pleased with her behaviour.

MOST HONOURABLE SIR,

This is my last appearance at this abode, and tomorrow I gow to Mrs. Potts cottage in Portland Place, wear an it please you you will find me. Adue, dear Charles, and I pray that you will not kep your hapy Emma waiting long. The hours without you seem unending.

Your hopefull EMMA.

She dispatched this, her eyes misty with adoration as she peppered it with pounce, blew it away again, and sealed it closely with a wafer. Now she could only see ahead a golden path which led to the happiness she desired more than aught else.

For the last time the velvet curtains fell on the figure of Hygeia with her fecund cornucopia. For the last time the doctor, very distracted, pressed that she would not leave him but would stay and help to make his new temple the greatest success there had ever been. He was not to know that love had directed his Emma elsewhere.

Mrs. Potts believed Emma to be a discreet young woman, recently married, whose husband was at sea with the Fleet in foreign waters, and she accepted Emma as such. The fact that she was a friend of George Romney was sufficient. Every day the girl went to the studio and sat for the picture that was already a masterpiece, and both of them knew it as they watched it growing under his fingers.

On the third day Greville wrote to her. She read his letter in a transport of joy, and every word seemed to be imprinted in her heart:

DEAR CHARMER,

I have delayed until you had left the Temple, and the house of that odious doctor, and it pleases me much that you should be established as you are, away from other men, and completely free. I have sold my town house, and am taking a small one in Paddington Green. It is commodious though little, and there I think a man and his mistress could be very happy. May I call and explain what is happening? I should be glad to know the convenient hour at which I may pay my respects.

CHARLES GREVILLE.

There would be no delay in telling her dear Charles when he might call and pay his respects, and she wrote immediately, so uplifted by joy that she hardly knew what she did. A little house in Paddington Green where she might be established to render him the dearest services of all. Indeed she was a lucky girl! He could come to her at any hour, at any moment, and always he would be welcome.

The road ahead was golden. She could ask nothing sweeter of life, for her only sorrow was that George Romney did not feel as she did, but would still insist that Greville was not the right friend for her.

"Oh, I'm so happy, so tremendously happy," she laughed as she went to the studio to sit for him, and he realized that she could hardly contain herself for the sheer joy of living. He watched her, infected by her good spirits. She was a lark rising against the morning sky, its frittering wings gold-tipped; she was a rose opening to the sun. There was no doubt in his mind but that the beautiful girl was deeply in love.

"But what about us two?" he asked when, the sitting over, his arms would have detained her.

"Ah, no, George, that is over."

"Over? It cannot be over."

"All that I have now belongs to Charles. How could I give myself to any other, when I adore him as I do?" She lifted Romney's face, her hands lying like wings on either side of it, and set her lips to his brow. He recognized in the chastity of that kiss that she was right. She loved the one man; there could be no other for her. And out in Cavendish Square the women were selling lavender and crying it for customers. He thought of it as a lovely scent laid aside with summer garments, and redolent of spent sweetness. Was that a scent that now applied to their romance?

XXIII

ALMOST IMMEDIATELY Emma was established in the attractive little house on Paddington Green which Charles Greville had taken for her. Tall elms grew benignly beside it, and belted it with green or autumnal gold, as the seasons changed. There was a rookery at hand, and she could listen to the comfortable cawing of the rooks, busy with their nursery cares in springtime. She could see the rising larks above the fields, and the happy little finches who courted in the hawthorn hedges of Paddington. She insisted that Greville had been goodness itself to her, and that she had always known he would be a loyal lover.

"You shall be happy, my sweet child," he promised her.

He brought Emma to the house one spring evening, when the violets and primroses were blossoming in the ditches and the first leaf-buds thickening the trees. They drove in a phaeton, and with her hand in his he led her across the threshold, looking down at her with smiling eyes. If ever eyes could woo, they were the ones of Charles Greville, and she felt almost faint with desire for him.

"All past follies forgot," he said, "for me you were always more sinned against than sinning, my pretty innocent."

"Oh, Charles, don't let's think of such things."

"If for one moment I believed that you had allowed men to seduce you, and had acted the wanton, then indeed I could not bring myself to love you. But I have realized that you stayed pure, in spite of all appearances being against you. In fact, my sweet Emma, you were your own worst enemy."

She was distressed that he might discover the truth, and that she could not bear.

"Rumour declares that Sir Harry is impotent. At the Temple of Hymen you were only a lovely statue. 'Tis for me that you come to life."

"Think of me always with such kindness, dear Charles, for it makes me very happy."

"And now, my love, I shall have to train you. I am to be your master in more than love, for I am not satisfied that a country girl gives me her body. She must learn to be a lady."

"I was not born a lady, Charles dearest."

"I will make you one. I will teach you to write letters that a man can read; for the moment I admit that your spelling is execrable, but we will remedy all that."

"But, surely, Charles, if the meaning is so fond . . ."

"Alas, to a gentleman who is sensitive, it irks."

"But I love you sufficient, my sweet, indeed I do . . ."

"You are a child, and as a child you shall be taught. Sometimes I shall have to punish you, my pretty one, but I warrant you that the punishment will be very sweet."

So much in love, she felt that she could accept anything from him. He lay with her that night, and to Emma it was the most exquisite surrender that had yet come into her life. Charles Greville was less ardent than some; he could control his passion when she lay naked in his arms, and was never possessed by desire, but coolly masterful. The voluptuousness of his kisses, however, filled her with rapture, and he believed that he had seduced an innocent girl, and what he was taking from her was a maiden sweetness.

Afterwards she could not sleep for happiness, but lay with him clasped in her arms, his lids resting closed against his handsome cheek. Never had she beheld so much beauty in a man.

But, next morning, when coming downstairs to drink hot chocolate with him, she found to her amazement that is own pretty study had been transformed into something rigidly bare and uncommonly like a schoolroom. He had set a desk with a hard chair by the window, and awaited her, standing there with a strangely sensuous smile on his lips. In his hand he toyed with the supple little switch that he used when riding. He bent it almost caressingly, flicking it to and fro. Emma was surprised and not undismayed at this change of front.

"What is it now, dear Charles?"

He pointed to the desk. "That is where you will do your lessons, my dearest Emma."

She went to it suddenly unsure. Beyond the window lay the garden with the topiaried trees, and spread beyond the quiet pasture land with the comfortable farms dotted in the clumps of trees of Edgware. Here were clean paper and pens and fresh pounce awaiting her.

"What is it you would have me do?" and now his disdainful smile set her heart beating in apprehension. She had never felt like this before. Uneasy. Inwardly alarmed. He wished to dictate to her. His desire was to teach her to spell accurately, for alas poor Emma was no scholar. She made absurd mistakes, and had little desire to become educated save that it would please him. Her mistakes irritated him. He walked up and down the hearthrug, posing as some sort of schoolmaster, and she, believing at first that this was merely some new game, took down the dictation not troubling herself overmuch. But the moment that she passed the paper to him she saw that he read with a pucker of annoyance between his brows, and was instantly alertly anxious.

"Come, my sweet Emma, this is not good. You spell 'indeed' E-N-D-E-A-D, 'always' A-L-L-W-A-Y-S. Who taught you?"

"No one, my dear Charles. I had no learning."

"You must try again, my dear Emma, or put me to the pain of punishing you."

He handed back the paper with an elaborate touch of severity. She accepted it and now trembled, realizing that this was not a game; laboriously she began to figure out the letters that he gave her, but the sound of the words brought little understanding of their spelling, and she was all the more confused in that she realized how much she was displeasing him.

"Emma, my love, this is not good."

"I admit I am no scholar, Charles."

"I must teach you to be better. Some duties are odious, my sweet, but duties just the same and not to be shirked. Do you understand what a master does with a dog that will not come to his heel when he calls it? He beats it."

She stared at him in agony. "But, Charles . . ."

"It is pain to me to give pain to you, but what other choice have I? Put out your hand."

When she put out her hand the switch came down on it sharply, and she sprang back with her palm stinging, and amazed that he should hurt her with such cold deliberation.

"But, Charles, you are cruel! I have never had the opportunity to learn. No one has taught me, and now if you will be patient I will learn, indeed I will. But you must not punish me for something that is no fault of my own; it is when I fail to learn that you must punish me."

"You would dictate to your master, Emma? Surely you know that is not right? I think we shall have to teach you humility."

"Dear Charles, I have humility. I will do anything that you desire, you know that I love you enough for that."

"Then you must submit to me in all things."

"I will do whatsoever you wish."

"Then realize that I know what is right for you, and if I choose to punish you it is for your own good. Take off your clothes."

"But, dear Charles, I dressed but an hour since."

"Undress or you will compel me to do it for you."

She could not believe this of him, and felt her hands tremble as she untied her fichu, unaware of what might be passing through that strange mind of his. "Charles, is it that you do not love me?"

"So much that it is with difficulty I keep rein upon myself."

She undressed slowly, beginning to cry because she knew now that she did not understand him. Had

George Romney been right? But surely not. Was there about Charles Greville some strangeness that she in her ignorance had not yet gauged?

He grew impatient, becoming irritated by her tears which she, incapable of controlling her doubts, could not silence. She was unable to see the strings because of the mist before her eyes, and she fumbled so that he came to her deliberately, and losing control of himself, tore her skirts away from her, and beat her unmercifully.

She struggled not to scream because of the servants, cramming her handkerchief into her mouth, and afterwards when he had gone she lay where he had pushed her, so bitterly humiliated that she did not know what to do. Hours seemed to pass over her stinging, bruised body. Then the door reopened and Charles came to her. He knelt beside her, whispering such tender comfort, and kissing her in such exquisite consolation, that she thought she must die for love of him. Now she did not care if he whipped her, for nothing could take away from the glory of such ecstatic moments with him.

"My child, my sweetly wilful child," he said. "Other men profess to have known you, but they boast idly. I am the first to possess you."

"You are the dearest."

"Those others who protected you were not as I. I have made you all mine and have taken your chastity into my keeping."

"For ever and ever, dear Charles. And I will be eternally faithful."

Yet she thought apprehensively of the mornings when she knew that from now onwards she would be expected to sit at the desk and master her lessons, and that it delighted him to treat her as a rebellious child should he choose, and he would choose. She knew that. Now she was wise to the cruel streak in his nature, for Charles Greville was not flawless.

XXIV

CHARLES FORCED Emma to forsake all her old friends, save George Romney and Jane Powell, who was now an actress of some repute at Drury Lane. The others she had to pass by in the street, and she felt ashamed, for by nature she was a sweetly generous creature, so that the thought of being haughty with such people as Dr. Graham and John Newman hurt her; but Charles insisted on it. He knew by her previous history that she had not been entirely innocent, and one day she enquired of him about her little girl at Hawarden.

"She is such a sweet little thing," said Emma tenderly, "I wish that I could have her with me."

"That would be folly. I tell you I am having no children at Paddington Green."

"But supposing I bore you a son?" She glanced at him earnestly from under her lashes, for the idea had come to her frequently and put heart in her. Such a pledge of her affection could surely only make him love her more, but when she said it he looked at her coldly. He would never consent to having her little Emily here, though later he did send money for the child to be well educated at a good school.

"How generous you are to me!" she glowed, her eyes brimming, when first he told her what he had done.

It was entirely to suit his own purposes that he allowed her mother to come to them in the capacity of a housekeeper. Mrs. Duggan was an excellent cook, and it enraptured Emma to have her in the home with them. At the same time she realized that her mother did not like and never had liked Charles Greville, and that although she held her peace, she perceived the flaws in him to which the infatuated Emma was blind.

"Oh, matchless Charles," she told him.

"You love me?"

"My sweet, do you doubt it?"

But one trouble was for ever recurring in the home. Although they lived economically and Emma kept the closest accounts, brought up for Charles's weekly inspection, he was not affluent, and before long she realized that the closeness of his income might in the end oblige him to part with her. Now she did not believe that she could bear such separation.

"I will be thrifty, my dearest Charles," she said, and even regretted the halfpenny entered in her pathetic little accounts as "given to a poore man."

Once she asked him why he kept the disused powder closet so fast locked. Amusedly she had tried the door, only to find that it angered him unreasonably.

"Why, Charles, you look as if I were Fatima, and this a Bluebeard's closet!"

He did not laugh, and all day he was angered with her. He would not listen to her singing, and was pettish, but later he explained a little of it. His uncle, who was the Ambassador for His Britannic Majesty at the court of Naples, bought curios there and sent them home for his nephew to sell. Charles made a pleasing profit on these transactions, and supplemented his meagre income which, as Emma knew, was small enough. It is true that from time to time she had seen pottery statues, glassware and the Sicilian treasures that arrived in big packing-cases. The sight of them had made her avid to visit foreign lands—she had told him so—and harped on it.

"Some of the curios I keep for myself. That is why the door is locked."

"But surely your Emma may look?"

"They are not for my Emma."

Laughingly she came to think of this as being a

126

Bluebeard's room, and said so to Romney who bit his lip when told of it. She continued to sit for the great artist, whose pictures made her the most discussed lady of fashion, and this Greville encouraged. He always insisted that her mother should accompany her, "in case they do provoke silly chatter," but there was no breath of scandal about her friendship with Romney. He was a society pet and was immortalizing her on canvas.

Greville was possessed of the faculty of looking ahead. At one time he was thinking in all seriousness of marriage with "the fair tea-maker," but when he had discovered the bareness of the root from which she had sprung, and the fact that already she had a love child in Hawarden, he abandoned the idea. He could tolerate nothing that might produce "talk," and such a marriage, as far as he was concerned, was impracticable. To Emma he had never mentioned marriage, and she had not thought of it. She was so much in love with him that she was quite happy to be his mistress, and lived to-day for to-day only.

"What could he have in that room?" she asked Romney as she rested in his studio.

"Why not have a look? But maybe you do not know where he keeps the key?"

"Indeed I do, for I found it by accident. In the great stone vase on his study mantelshelf."

"Would he be very angry if you looked? But of course, anyway, he couldn't do anything to you."

Emma looked shyly at Romney. Then there was still something that he did not know and had not guessed. Charles was masterful; he stood over her private life with a rod in his hand, and already she had learnt the folly of tempting that rod, even though the pleasure of a sweet reconciliation might show her Greville at his best. A Greville grown infinitely tender. If Romney suspected anything, he did not breathe a word.

"You must do what you think best."

"Alas, I am distraught with curiosity."

"Then look when he is away. You have discovered the key, as you have discovered the key to most things in this world, my elusive Emma!"

"But Charles will be very angry. Some of the contents, he tells me, are souvenirs from Pompeii, from the ruined temples there."

Romney glanced at her uneasily. "I am not surprised, then, that he is concerned that anyone so sweetly innocent should want to see them," he said coldly, and she was surprised at the tone of his voice.

Her mother advised her to let well alone, warning her that gentlemen were gentlemen all the world over, which is as it should be. But curiosity still burnt Emma up, and refused to be dowsed by prudence.

One sultry afternoon in August, when Charles was at St. Stephen's, Westminster, she found herself taking the key out of the vase and fitting it into the door. There was a mischievous sense of achievement in her heart as she heard it turn over.

The lock groaned as she opened the door a trifle, seeing the smallness of the powder closet beyond, with the panelled walls. Her eyes becoming accustomed to the light, for the window was veiled as a woman's face in summer, saw that it was cluttered with fantastic ornaments. Immediately before her was a phallic symbol in stone, which took up a major amount of space and was so crude that she could not mistake its meaning.

Horrified, she held back a moment, her eyes wandering from one article to the next. Stone figures that were contorted and twisted stood there, undoubtedly the products of a warped mind. A woman's naked body corrupted by an amorous faun. A goat carved and exaggerated so that it sickened her, and she almost fainted at the thought that these things amused Greville so much that he kept them almost as some sort of a private museum and came here to entertain himself.

She would have cried out, save that at that moment she heard the door behind her opening, and a man's foot ringing on the threshold. She turned sharply, the Bluebeard's chamber as her backcloth, with its rows of evil ornaments leering down in gargoyle fashion at them both.

XXV

CHARLES GREVILLE was in a towering rage, and Emma had never seen the like before. He turned the shade of a tallow dip, his eyes seemed to recede into his head as though they hid at the far end of dim caverns, his hands clenched and unclenched. She had guessed, of course, that he would be bitterly angry, and that he would beat her, but his passion was too great even for that. The look on his face and his silence were worse than any fury.

She turned, but for the moment he did not see her apparently, but only stood staring to where the abortive phallic symbol stood.

"Speak to me, Charles! Charles, my dear one, speak to me!"

He made no sound. Dismayed by the fact that he could behave like this, she verily believed that now her Greville might desert her for her disobedience. And then "What shall I dow?" she wrote later to Romney, who was her father confessor.

She wept and rushed from him, hoping that he would follow, but an hour later Mrs. Duggan came to tell her daughter that Greville lay sick in his room. He was sprawled on the half-tester bed, his complexion pea green against his pillows, his eyes heavily closed, and not speaking a word.

"My dearest one, my own dearest," implored Emma as she smoothed back his hair and laid a cold compress on his brow.

She stayed there with him all night without failing or faltering, although at times he showed no recognition of her at all. Every little while he struggled violently, then half bemused would get into a sitting position, retch in agony and then sink back into yet another coma. Emma was distracted. She did not know where to turn for help, and only in the early morning did she think of Dr. Graham, and dispatched a messenger on horseback to him. Surely he would not fail her in spite of her having left him as she had done? The little doctor was flustered and surprised to hear from Emma again, but he came along at once in a chaise, and arrived at Paddington Green just as it was growing light.

"Oh, sir, this is indeed good of you. I feel that I have behaved very badly to you," she trembled. "I am weak and in love, and indeed that is a sorry combination for any poor woman."

The doctor understood her frailties, and he asked her to escort him to Charles's room. There he took the faint pulse, and laid a hand on the feverish head. Recognizing the malady, he resorted to only the simplest remedies; first an emetic, with strong salts to follow. He enquired what had happened to cause such an attack, and, although Emma tried to conceal the true facts, Dr. Graham grasped only too well the temperament of men like Greville, for they were the kind he catered for at his Temple of Health.

Late the following morning Charles awoke from a heavy sleep and asked for food. He was utterly exhausted and deeply touched by the tender ministrations of his Emma.

"My sweet and faithful child," he said, taking her hand, "I will never forget your goodness to me."

"And I can never forgive myself for what happened, dearest Charles."

He pretended to have forgotten the incident. "When I am fully recovered we will go to Ranelagh, for a little festivity will not come amiss for so fair a tea-maker," which was what he called her when he was pleased with her.

"Indeed, it would make me very happy," and she laid her cheek against his, but his skin smelt sourly of the fever, and the hair lay dankly on his brow.

They were lovers once more.

Emma was overjoyed that he should be better, and spared herself nothing to help him through his convalescence. She fed him from the soups that her mother had made for him, but never for a moment did she confess that, under cover of the night, she had persuaded Dr. Graham to come here and to treat him. A shrewd intuition warned her that Greville would not have been pleased at such ministrations, and she held her peace.

However, the illness had been sharp, and it took him several days to recover, during which time no mention was made of the Bluebeard's room, although an imposing new case arrived from Naples, and a bronzed merchant captain delivered it himself to the house. Emma had not wanted another consignment, and directed that it should be placed in the study to await Charles's pleasure, for she distrusted it.

She herself went down to pay the man, roughly bearded, a huge, towering creature with no finesse, but about him that brusque, salty tang of the sea itself. She was instantly attracted to him, perhaps because she remembered Jack Willet-Payne, and she noticed him as he watched her with his dark lustrous eyes. She would never know why she entered into conversation with him.

"Tell me," she asked, "is Naples as beautiful as people say?"

"It is a city of pearls, ma'am, slung round the neck of a fierce volcano. They say 'See Naples and die,' and faith, when I see Naples it is so beautiful that I only want to live."

He conjured up to her vivid imagination a city of gleaming piazze, of *casas* with the bougainvillea in

131

crimson and purple canopies flung about white façades; of wistaria in honey-scented veils of pale mauve against colonnade and pillar.

"One day, perhaps you will visit there, ma'am?"

"Oh, no, what would I do away from London?"

He surveyed her closely, and she was aware that as his eyes narrowed, he saw something written above her, something to which she herself was blind. "One day, ma'am, you *will* see Naples."

She turned amazed; he had conviction, here was something that he knew. "What do you mean?" she asked.

"Some say, ma'am, that sailors have second sight. They see an open book and can read it."

"You can do that?"

"For you, ma'am, indeed."

She put her hand into her little pocket and from it produced a new florin that shone. "They say," she said gaily, "that you cross the hand with silver. Here is a silver piece; now tell me what it is you see?"

He took the florin with care and then folded it back into the pink palm of her hand, closing her fingers securely over it, and holding them there with a firm, controlling grip. Beyond the tall rectangular windows lay the fields; they could hear the little English finches and wrens singing in the garden, yet he did not speak of Edgware. "There is written in your life so much," he said. "A queen in a crown. A great hero. A bold lover, and the sea. Marriage, but never to the man you love."

"The man I love is here in this house," she whispered breathlessly, with her colour coming and going. But the sailor was not listening.

"You have yet to meet the man you marry. You set sail for a foreign court, and soon. There you will rise as a star, and the whole world will know your name. Not London, but the world." Then he kissed the fingers that enclosed the florin and, bowing low, turned to leave her. She did not know what to think. It was a fantastic story, and it had rung with the very essence of truth, so much so that she was aware of how much it had stirred her.

She went back to Charles, but she did not tell him of the incident, neither did she mention the recently arrived case of curios that now stood in his study. It was later he went down to the room and locked the door. Afterwards she found the empty box pushed to one side, and recognized that the old, sardonic smile had returned to his lips; he must have gained yet another pleasurable thrill from the "treasures" that he had received.

Oh, how she wished that he was different!

However, a week later he remembered his promise to her and he drove with her to Ranelagh. For the occasion he had bought her a new gown, quilted in rose colour, with a bonnet arranged so that there were soft pink roses lying against her face. She looked radiant. She was so grateful that her dear Greville had recovered, and rejoiced to see the bright clarity in his eyes again, his step so firm and his love for her so ardent.

The day was warm.

She walked with him at Ranelagh amongst the flowers, and together they took a dish of tea as was their habit in the Rotunda. All the fashionable world seemed to be there, all the bloods and bucks, and a stringed orchestra was making pleasant music. Here was George Romney whose latest picture of her as a Bacchante had made London besiege his studio. Here was Jane Powell, richly dressed, for she was extravagant, and wearing an enormous powdered wig; her admirers were with her.

"It is the happiest afternoon of my whole life," declared Emma.

The talk stimulated her. And then the apex of the whole afternoon occurred when the maestro stepped down from the small rostrum, and making a low bow to her, requested that the loveliest of all ladies would sing to them. She glanced round her, flattered at the idea, and exhilarated that they should ask this favour of her.

"Indeed, and gladly," she said, and was led to the rostrum.

It was a delicious sense of power to be the centre-piece of the picture. Now Greville would see her captivating London. She stood there, struck one of her attitudes, and was vociferously applauded. It thrilled her to think that Greville would see her captivating London, and she sang tenderly, in that very sweet little voice of hers. When an encore was demanded, she changed to a gayer mood, and trilled a song of the country that her grandmother had taught her in the poverty-stricken days at Hawarden.

She hardly noticed Charles, so triumphant was she, so elated at her success; it was only when she returned to her place beside him, her head held high, her skirts lifted with dainty fingers, that she saw the heavy frown on his face. His eyes avoided hers, and she knew by his flushed cheek that he was furiously angry with her.

"Charles? My dear Charles, what is it?" she asked, startled out of her usual discretion.

He rose. "Now, having made this sorry exhibition of yourself, we will return home."

XXVI

THE DRIVE back was pathetic. She sat beside him hardly knowing how she felt. Just when she had been congratulating herself that this was her triumph, she had been consigned to the misery that only Charles could give her. She wept tearlessly, her grief too great to be borne.

"I thought that it would please you, my dearest

Charles. I thought you would rejoice to see how popular your Emma is."

"To a man who loves music, such singing is hardly likely to evoke pride."

"But it is the only music that I know. Pray do me the honour to be pleased by it!"

"It did not please me. Modesty becomes a woman. No man likes to see his beloved make such a sorry exhibition of herself."

But she knew that the gentlemen had been delighted, and had called for more, and was at a loss to understand Greville's attitude. "You wrong me, sir. How hard it is that I can please so many, but only anger the man I love!"

"Perhaps I demand a higher standard."

She knew now that if she argued with too much conviction she would only bring about her own undoing, so she held her peace, but it was with difficulty that she restrained her tears as she listened to the sound of the cantering horses, and saw the pleasant country views flashing past the windows.

"Oh, Greville, indeed, indeed you wrong me. My spirit is so willing, my meaning so kind."

He was completely silent.

Against the window of the chaise she could see his delicate profile turned from her. Why, she wondered, did she love so much this, probably the most difficult man of them all? She felt that the silence was like another of those thick walls between them, a bastion that she could not hope to penetrate.

Once she put out a hand in a childish attempt at reconciliation, but he ignored it. It lay upon his, his third finger jewelled with an agate ring given to him by his brother Fulke; then, without a word, he took her hand as though it had been a small parcel of no consequence, and laid it back in the pink satin folds of her lap; she wept silently.

"I love you so much," she whispered as they saw Kensington Palace coming into sight, peering out from the trees, and the orangery gleaming beside it.

When they arrived at the little house, she got out quickly and ran up to her room, unable to stay her tears a moment longer. She did not want him to see how deep was her distress. She tore off the new frock, and flung it aside. She blamed it for much. What should she wear with which to bring him back? Her love, her only love, she told herself vehemently. For a moment she played with the idea of going down to him, clad only in the velvet wrapper that she had brought with her from the Temple of Health, and flinging it suddenly aside so that he should see her, gleaming white against its darkness as she had stood in the niche. Then reason stayed her. Greville was not attracted by mere flesh and blood, and it might make him angrier still.

She looked into her cupboard and found amongst the frocks the cotton dress in which she had come to the great city as a village girl. Here were no pipings and laces, but plain hems with nothing to distract from the beauty of her face. She drew it on, slipping into it and tying the linen collar which was shaped like a quaker's. She lifted her curls and imprisoned them inside the folds of the simple muslin cap, so that now there was naught save her amazing beauty to proclaim her more than a little servant employed about the house. His servant—and for always, she promised herself.

As the ghost of her former grandeur, she went down to his study, tapping timidly at the door. He bade her enter, but did not look up. He was writing at the desk to his uncle, Sir William Hamilton, Ambassador at the Court of Naples. She guessed that he was thanking for, and enquiring after, further treasures!

She waited a moment, then curtseyed solemnly. "Your servant, sir!"

He turned to glance at her, and instantly his eyes were arrested by the sight of the simplicity of that frock. "Emma!"

"Oh, sir, indeed I am at fault." He went on staring, and unsure of his true emotions, she continued, "I—I have returned to my village ways. To that same modesty that once you were so noble as to admire. This is myself, dear Charles, the woman under it all. Oh, my dearest, see me as I truly am, once more before I go—for ever."

She stood there, her eyes downcast, for she did not dare to look at him. When at last he spoke his voice was moved. "Like that, Emma, how can I steel my heart against you even if I would?"

"I pray you, sir, do not try to steel it against one so faithful if so erring."

He rasped back his chair and came to her, standing with his hands on her shoulders, his eyes looking sorrowfully down upon her as he towered above her.

"Sweet one, I was too hasty. But then I could not bear to suppose that you would be so liberal with your charms. I could not bear to think that you could make so free."

"Free? Oh, no, sir, how could I be free with what belongs to another, and so dear a master?"

"I think of you as a violet, Emma, not as a flamboyant rose."

She looked so intriguingly simple that he knew she held him in the hollow of her hand. "What do I know of flamboyance, my dear Charles?" she asked.

"I could never tolerate faithlessness."

"There was no thought of such a thing. When a woman loves a man as Emma loves Charles, faithlessness cannot be."

"I believe you."

"Oh, Charles, trust me! I would never fail you. Far, far more likely that you—growing tired of a violet which after all must fade with spring—would fail me."

He bent over her and kissed her in a sudden uprising of passion. "I will punish you with kisses for so unworthy a saying," he told her.

"Such punishment is over sweet," she answered, and now she knew that she had won him back to her.

But there must be no more disagreements. No more arguments. Charles Greville had not the nature to tempt with scenes; the time would come when he would sicken and leave her, unless their lives could move along serenely. For one frantic moment as he kissed her, she thought in agony, what would I do if Greville deserted me? What would I do? Then she knew that she must not tempt him too far.

XXVII

EMMA KNEW that Charles had a will of iron and that, whatever else she did, she must not cross him again. Willet-Payne, Featherstonehaugh, and all the other men who had loved her had been as nothing to this one man, who demanded all and everything of her, yet was so prudish in his outlook. Never again would she exploit her charms in public as she had done so mistakenly at Ranelagh at the expense of Charles's bitter anger.

For a week or two she stayed in the seclusion of the Paddington garden with the quiet trees that sheltered it from the world, and she devoted herself entirely to Charles. It seemed that during this precious fortnight she grew even more beautiful, blossoming in the warmth of his ardour and he, taking the greatest pleasure in her, losing something of his austerity and being in his most caressing mood.

"My sweet one has learnt her lesson," he said one evening when they sat together in the bower that was wreathed with eglantine whilst the iris bloomed in the garden before them.

"I only want to please my dear Greville," she faltered, and that was true. Emma was deeply in love;

she cared nothing for what any of the others might think of her, doting on this one man, and, with the strange inconsequence of love, she did not care if he ill-treated her, for any treatment was rapture from him. To-night he was in a smiling mood.

"Does not my charmer find Paddington Green a little dull?" he asked, threading his tenacious fingers through her glossy auburn ringlets.

"Nothing could be dull with my dear Greville."

He replied, "I am well pleased with my sweeting, and I have planned a little treat for her! How would you like to visit the Vauxhall Gardens? They tell me that in these first warm evenings of early summer they are indeed most pleasant."

She turned to him, her eyes lit with excitement, for there was nothing that she liked better than gaiety. Then she remembered what had happened at Rane-lagh, and she dropped those eyes quickly, and began to falter as though to excuse herself. "But would you trust me?" she asked cautiously.

"I think you have learnt your lesson."

His compelling hands gripped her wrists, and for a moment she sensed that austere touch of Charles in that particular mood. She feared the punishment to which he often treated her, and quivered as though with anticipation; but he, feeling her tremble, changed his austerity to a far more congenial mood, bending over her in delight. He stooped to kiss her, and aware of his intention, she lifted her arms and clasped them impulsively about his neck. She drew his handsome face to her own, and kissed him again and again. He was so beautiful, she told herself, with that fastidious handsomeness that none of the others had had (unless it had been the groom in the clean, sweet straw at Uppark). Charles had none of Willet-Payne's dropping jowl and hard eyes; none of Sir Harry's weak, somewhat fatuous face with the pale hair that hung limply. Charles was a strong man, and Emma loved that strength, drawing from it her own joy.

"Very well, we will go to-morrow night," he promised her.

"Oh, Charles, that would be most exciting. I will be there and behave just as you would wish me to," and she paused, her eyes meeting his. For a moment she had almost said, "as you would wish your wife to behave," but had stopped herself in time. He knew what had been on the tip of her tongue and he warmed to her. On the impulse of the moment he replied.

"Perhaps one day you will indeed be that," he whispered smilingly, and she felt herself to be uplifted and drenched in such complete rapture that she could not stay herself from trembling.

"Oh, dearest Charles, that would make me the happiest woman in the world! I could not believe that so much happiness could be given to one poor humble creature," she faltered, the colour coming and going like damask roses in her cheeks.

"Very well; we will wait and see what fate has in store for us," he promised her, and stroked the small hand that lay so tenderly in his.

Emma could hardly bear the ecstasy of this moment, and the vista that it opened before her; marriage lines, a wedding ring, and the legal right to live here. She hid her face in his shoulder, and trembled so violently that he believed her to be weeping.

Next morning she spent the time in choosing a lavender frock to wear at Vauxhall to-night. It was a closely cut frock, with a deep cream fichu into which she fastened a pink rose. She added a blue ribbon, threading it through her hair, and she took great pains to look virtuous and modest. To-night there must be no repetition of what had happened at Ranelagh, for she could not afford two such mistakes, and must rein in her impulsiveness.

She was impatient to be started, but, as yet, Charles was in no hurry, and kept the chaise waiting whilst he arranged his hair, tying it with a black moiré band on the nape of the neck. Then they went

140

down the garden arm-in-arm, to the chaise, and she lifted her skirts with mittened hands and stepped daintily inside, Charles after her.

It was a wonderful evening, with the sun just setting and London in the blue distance before them. They drove through the country fields with Marylebone church rearing itself gauntly before them. She glanced at it, recalling what Charles had said about marriage, and thinking that she would swoon with joy to be married to him there. She did not know that it would be another man whom she would marry in Marylebone church, an older man, and she with the tears pouring down her face because she remembered the young beau whom she had loved with such misplaced faithfulness.

To-night, in the comfortable warmth, they galloped towards Vauxhall. Coming within earshot of the gardens they became aware of the tinkle of music, and the burr of chatter interspersed with laughter. Vauxhall Gardens were immensely popular, all society were there, and the music and refreshment were of the best. The sound of the music set Emma's pulses throbbing wildly and her little foot tapping on the floor of the chaise. Seeing it happen, Charles put out a remonstrative hand and said, a little reprovingly:

"My dear, you will be careful?"

"Oh, so careful, Charles. My dearest Charles, so very, very careful, indeed I do promise you."

They alighted and were ushered through the heavily embossed iron gates to the gardens within. They were a feature of the London of those days, lit by coloured budding roses wreathed about the stanchions and festooning little arbours set apart for the romantically minded. An orchestra on a flower-decked dais dispensed music and a young girl was standing singing. Emma glanced at her, realizing that she did not sing one whit so well as herself, then she glanced at her escort. Charles had seen the look and knew what she was thinking; she coloured and dropped her eyes, and they went arm-in-arm to the small table in the corner and sat down.

The place was thronged with aristocrats, with eager beaux and their sweetings, and many a glance was given to the lovely Emma as she sat composedly in her lavender frock with the pink rose at the bosom. Aware of the glances, she flushed a little. She knew that Charles was watching her closely, and not for the world would she have anything go wrong with this particular evening.

The leader of the orchestra came towards her with a flourish, and bowing low. He was a handsome young man with waving black hair and fine, sensitive eyes that lit up as with fire when they saw her.

"If the lovely lady would sing for us?" he suggested with a flourish of his violin and a deep bow.

Emma glanced at Charles who bit his lip; then she shook her head. "I do not sing in public," she said.

The young man was not looking at Charles, for indeed he had no eyes for any save Emma. "But I have heard . . ." he began, and again she shook her head. For one second their eyes met, his challengingly as though he could only think of her in one way, and before the demand of his ardour her own eyes fell.

"Go away!" said Charles brusquely.

The young man withdrew to his place on the dais, but now all the time Emma was painfully aware that he was watching her, and was a little distressed by it. Charles, on the other hand, seemed to have forgotten the incident and to be elated. Friends were here, and they came across and spoke to them both. They took wine together, compliments were exchanged and healths drunk, and it was extremely pleasant in this friendly atmosphere.

"We must come here often," said Charles delightedly, and Emma could have rejoiced at the thought. She was a gaily impulsive creature and would willingly have come here every night if he would permit it.

"We will, dear Charles, indeed we will."

"Let us dance?" he suggested.

She was amazed that he could propose anything of this kind, for it was quite unlike his prim disposition. They went to the far end of the garden where people were already dancing under the soft blue and red lights. The stars were in the sky, and they could see a young crescent moon like a scimitar rising above a cedar of Lèbanon from an adjacent garden. As they went forward together Emma felt herself almost at the zenith of happiness. Now nothing mattered save the fact that Charles's arm was about her, and that the orchestra was playing a gay gavotte.

The music ended abruptly.

She stood there clinging to Charles's arm, and flushed with triumph, and at that very moment became aware of a big, burly figure watching her closely as he stood at her elbow. A heavily built man had just finished dancing with a fly-by-night little girl, who struck Emma as being a light-of-love. There was something familiar about this man, and as she turned she felt herself quiver, for she recalled with a qualm the room at Greenwich, the forbidding-looking landlady who had sought to refuse her admittance, and the *Cormorant* riding at anchor down the river on the high tide. It was Willet-Payne!

She tried—too late—to turn away, but he had seen her. He must have been a little drunk, for he left his partner and came to her side, standing so that neither of them could hope to escape. Oh, not this, surely not this, she prayed, with horror rising in her heart!

"So we meet again, my sweet Emma?" said the Captain.

"Your pardon, sir." Charles had hold of Emma's arm, and his voice was glacial. It had the flavour of remorseless ice. Crudely aware of it, Emma would have turned away, but instead she stood her ground looking from one to the other. Willet-Payne was in no mood for play.

"I once knew your little friend," he said, "she was a servant girl then. What is she now?"

"Go away, sir"—Charles's nostrils were dilated—"or you force me to use the gentleman's prerogative."

Willet-Payne only laughed. Contemptuously he said, "No gentleman likes to think that the flower he wears has been worn—when fresher—by others," and he laughed more loudly.

That was when Greville lifted his silk handkerchief and struck Willet-Payne across the face with it. The crimson of that face turned to purple, and it looked as if the veins rising on the neck would burst. In an agony Emma did not know what to do; there was silence after the sharp scream of a woman standing by who had seen it.

"You will be hearing from my seconds, sir," said Willet-Payne thickly, and handed his card with a flourish.

Emma saw that the address was Nerot's Hotel!

"Mine will show no tardiness in meeting yours. I bid you good evening, sir," said Greville, and taking Emma's hand in his arm, he led her out of the gardens. For her the bright lights were dimmed by her tears. The rose scent was of rue and remorse! She knew that the waiting link boys, grouped round the gate and the sedan chairs, watched her as she stumbled into the chaise, and again she could hear the orchestra playing Cherry Ripe. Unwittingly she had become the talk of Vauxhall Gardens.

"Oh, how could he do it?" she sobbed on Charles's shoulder as they drove away.

Charles Greville was grimly silent.

XXVIII

WHEN CHARLES had time to cool down he recalled that he was not an adept swordsman, and a worse shot with pistols. Now he would have given much to retract the ugly scene in the Vauxhall Gardens, but it was too late. No gentleman backed out. His seconds were swift to accept the challenge on his behalf, the duel must be fought and the lady's good name defended.

Any thought he had ever had of marrying the girl was abandoned. Now the whole town knew that she had been a mere servant, and a light of love—he could well imagine the burble of amused conversation after they had left Vauxhall Gardens, the whispers, the incautious grins and the merriment at their expense.

They came home, he feeling very sick and Emma distracted.

"Charles, you must not fight him. He told me once when I asked where he got that cut upon his cheek that it was the dawn when he put his sword through young Bentinck in a clearing at Highgate. He has never lost a duel yet."

"At least I have the courage to die like a gentleman," said Charles, but it comforted him little.

"Charles, I love you so much. I would not have this happen for the world. And on my account! Oh, my dear, we must stop it."

He helped himself to snuff, closing the small gold box with a snap and elaborately flicking away atoms of dust from his embroidered coat with a handkerchief. "When I am dead, my dear Emma, you will know where the onus lies," he said.

She went to her room and wept copiously. She did not know what to do, working herself into an agony of apprehension. She knew that Charles could not retreat from the quarrel, and later the next day heard the names of his seconds, and that swords had been chosen. Charles would not tell her of the place, but she guessed that it was in the wooded hills beyond the marshes of Tottenham Court Road, and wept to think of it.

In the dead of the night an idea came to her. She knew where Willet-Payne was, and that it would be possible to gain access to him at Nerot's Hotel. Charles, of course, would probably dismiss her for ever if he heard of it, but to save his life she would do anything. And she honestly believed that his life was at stake.

She dressed herself demurely, putting on a hooded cloak so that she would not be recognized, and she waited until the following late afternoon when Charles was in the city seeing his attorney, for there were several matters to be put in order before he set forth to fight his duel in the morning.

Emma ordered the chaise, and set forth with a beating heart, as this was a mission that she had to accomplish satisfactorily. The streets were empty, for half the world was drinking Green and Bohea and talking little scandals. She had no doubt that her name would figure largely at tea-tables just now. Sedans were joggling along, and in the neighbourhood of Nerot's Hotel she saw the small clustering houses, and the grand ladies and bewigged old gentlemen with pendulous stomachs beneath their flowered waistcoats. She wished she dared have waited till dark, but then undoubtedly Willet-Payne would have been out, and that she could not have risked.

She came to Nerot's Hotel and crossed again the threshold of a door she had thought never to enter more. She had suffered agony here and she recalled it with horror. That awful night of the riots when Newgate had been broken into and the poor prisoners had gone clanking about the city, free, but yet unable to rid themselves of their chains. That time when she had been handed on to Featherstonehaugh, with never a word on the matter, unforgivable, but now she must swallow her pride and forgive it if she was to save Charles. And at all costs, however great the sacrifice, Charles must be saved.

The lackey recognized her; she had been good to him and he was quick to appreciate it. "I came to see Captain Willet-Payne," she said. "I have an appointment."

She saw the man demur, but, opening her little silken bag, she took from it a gold guinea piece and thrust it into his hand. His eyes brightened and he muttered thanks as he told her the room.

She climbed the shallow oak stairs, and soon the shadow of the landing, lit only by a rush light, received her. She came to the door and rapped on it, unable to hear the sound because her heart was making such a disturbance in her bosom. A gruff voice called to her "Come in!" and, opening the door, she went inside, shutting it behind her and standing there, both hands on the knob, her lovely head flung back and her eyes seeking him out.

Willet-Payne sat at the table in the window drinking tea. He wore breeches and his shirt was flung wide, so that she could see the crimson zigzag of a scar across the hairiness of his chest. He turned to look at her, then his eyes brightened.

"So it is Emma?" he said.

"Sir, I have come to ask you a favour."

"You have come to ask me not to hurt that pretty fop of yours?" He had gathered her mission with no difficulty, and she was dismayed to find that she had been so obvious.

"I love him," she said.

She stood there, the dark cloak flung aside revealing her in her virginal white frock with the blue sash and the deep fichu. Her hair, no longer held back by the restrictions of the hood, fell in clustering curls

147

about her shoulders. Willet-Payne had not remembered her as being so startlingly beautiful, for then she had not been in love; now he was surprised by her wide-eyed loveliness. How had he discarded one so young and radiant?

"Come here!" he said.

She did not move, only her eyes watched him, and they were exquisite.

"Your fop has taught you pretty tricks, and, by Gad, made you even more beautiful. Once I would not have believed that possible, but it is."

"Sir, I did not come to talk of myself. I came to talk of him. You are fighting a duel in the morning."

"At dawn." The Captain poured himself out yet another cup of tea and with studied calm. "And by this time to-morrow night one of us will not be here to regret it. That one will be Charles Greville."

She moved a little towards him, leaving the cloak a dark smudge on the floor, her arms clasped to her bosom. "Jack, I do pray of you not to do this thing. Go to sea, go away, go anywhere, but leave me Charles Greville. I love him so much that I could not bear to go on living without him."

Even Willet-Payne recognized the intensity of her fervour as she stood beside his table staring at him with despair in her eyes. He set down the teacup and looked at her.

"So you have come to ask his life?"

"I do beg his life of you."

There was a long drawn silence, with just the sound of the link boys in the street below, and Willet-Payne watching Emma, never believing that his appetite could have been so whetted. He leant towards her, his shrewd eyes narrowing, his lower lip bulging.

"And what price will you pay, my pretty?" he asked.

"I have nothing wherewith to pay as you do know, kind sir," she faltered, for she had given her last golden guinea to the lackey.

148

"To-morrow my ship could sail unexpectedly, I suppose. I could be away. The Fleet has need of her sailors." He began to laugh; it was a coarse, loud laughter which, after Charles's more cultured mannerisms, appalled her, but she gave no sign of it. "What would you give me if I do all this? What is the gift that you would give in return? This is a new Emma! It is a sweeter Emma. Perhaps now she knows the price?"

He sat back to survey her. For one instant she knew that she would give almost everything that she possessed to be able to turn and go out of the room and out of his life. He had betrayed her in the beginning and had abandoned her. All that had ever happened lay at his door, yet it was the will of fate that she must plead with him. She could not leave so easily. Charles meant more to her than that, for whatever happened in her own life, however she demeaned herself, Charles Greville had to live—for her.

XXIX

FOR A couple of hours Emma remained at Nerot's Hotel, then she drew her hooded cloak about her and made her way down the stairs. She knew that to-morrow Willet-Payne would have put out to sea again, and that when her beloved Charles went to the appointed place he would not be met by an opponent. In consequence he would live.

She slipped down the shadowy stairway, and she was glad that the day was dying and the covering dusk concealing her movements. She would have to pretend that she had been with the dressmaker, the usual woman's excuse, and undoubtedly Charles, with his mind so beset on the duel, would not be too particular about her movements.

As she came into the hotel hall a man spoke to her. She turned in some alarm, recognizing him as being Henry Forbes, the editor of a somewhat scurrilous broadsheet which diverted the bawdily minded by its revelations of society gossip. She had met Henry Forbes at the Temple of Health where he had called to enquire. John Newman had warned her of him, disliking him on sight, but she had found him amiable and kindly, and did not resent him. Save now, when she was anxious not to be seen.

"And what does the lovely Emma do in Nerot's Hotel?" he asked, lifting a glass to her with a significant gesture.

"I had business here, kind sir, please let me pass." She drew her lavender skirts aside, for the moment alarmed that he would detain her, but the hand that he put out was merely complimentary.

"Your roses are crushed," he said, and his eyes challenged hers. Did she imagine that his mouth had something of a leer about it?

"So they are." She had forgotten those roses when Willet-Payne crushed her to him in the final farewell. She glanced down, and coloured to see how they revealed what must have happened. "Please let me pass," she said again.

With her colour heightened she went out of the hall, sending a page to tell the chaise that she was ready. She stood there but an instant, though it was long enough to hear Henry Forbes' laugh and to know that he was bandying her name with the other men. For a second she trembled at the thought of his broadsheet, then she dismissed such a horrid idea, for Greville was too influential. Then she recalled that once Forbes had referred to the royal princesses—never beautiful and always gauche—and hated to remember that rank meant nothing to him.

She got into the chaise and drove away sitting in a corner. The seat was hard, the vehicle unsprung, and the country road bumpy and irregular. She saw the low hedges and the tall Marylebone trees, and eventually the lights of home shining through the haze. Whatever she had done, she had done well, for to-morrow Charles Greville would not die as once she had thought very possible.

Charles had returned before her and had gone to his room, leaving word that he required no food. A glass of wine and some macaroons had been taken to him, but that was all. She went to him. He was sitting in the deepest gloom on the side of his bed, staring before him, his face remarkably pale and quite haggard.

"Charles, you are ill?" she said with her ready sympathy.

"I must not be ill. For if that is so and I cannot go to-morrow then they will say that I was a coward and afraid."

"Charles, I have a premonition that everything is going to be all right."

He stared at her helplessly, and she knew that he was so depressed that he could not say a word. She went and knelt beside him, holding his body in her protective arms. She dared not tell him that fear was needless, lest he suspected the truth and so incriminated her. She could do nothing more for him.

So they sat late into the hours of the night, she struggling to comfort and console him and he past either. He knew with brutal certainty that if he crossed swords with Willet-Payne in the morning he could not hope to live. He held no illusions about his own prowess, and had not thought to die this way. He was sick at the thought.

In the end Emma fetched him hot chocolate, and into it she mixed a draught, bringing it to him and coaxing him to drink it. After that he fell asleep for a while, she keeping watch, but he woke with a start and a groan, to get up quickly and start fumbling into his clothes with hands that shook. His head was still thick from the draught, and his face desperately

151

pale. It seemed by the light of the rush lamp beside them, that already death had touched him with its tallow coldness. His face was shrunken and anguished, he looked to be a very old man. He did not speak to her, but held her at arm's length, then clutched her to him kissing her again and again with lips that were already like marble.

She wept after he had gone. Then when she had recovered a little, she dressed herself in one of her best frocks, and went downstairs to the garden. Dawn was illuminating the world with its own fine radiance, making it look almost unreally beautiful.

She gathered flowers of all kinds, and with the abundance of late May there were some of all kinds. Tall irises, and scarlet poppies, rhododendrons in great sprays, azaleas, the roses and lilies, the verbenas and sweet-peas. She brought them into the house to make a bower of it, then she went to the gate to await her beloved's return.

The countrymen were going by. Shepherd boys in smock frocks and old hats pulled down on long love-locks, with their flocks and their dogs, and one with a pipe that he played. The hay carts were cooing from the Middlesex farms, lumbering past her on their way to the Haymarket. Soon she saw the chaise coming back and stopped at the gate, and Charles—a rejuvenated Charles—stepping out. He alighted like a boy; his face was no longer lardy with dismay, but glowed, and his eyes were bright.

"Emma, he never came to the place appointed. He sent some message that his ship had been forced to put out to sea."

"Didn't I tell you, Charles, that all would be well?" and she clung to him, ecstatic that the horror was past.

"He must have been afraid," said Charles contemptuously, for that thought gave him infinite joy. He had acquitted himself bravely, he had gone prepared to die and he had been spared. Now he forgot that all night he himself had been sick with fear, and

152

could remember nothing but the self-congratulation of the moment.

"Charles, my dearest, come and eat, for you have had no food."

She took him into the flower-decked room, where the breakfast was already laid. Hot chocolate foaming in silver pots, a cold capon and a ham, patties and little pies, and a couple of trout, silvery fine on silver dish. He sat down.

"I have a monstrous appetite, my dear," he said.

It was good to find him in his gay mood, and after they went out into the fields like a couple of children. He spoke affectionately of little Emily, he was in his most amiable mood, and he said, "We must celebrate this great occasion. Next week I will take you to see the Derby race ridden, if you desire."

"Oh, Charles, that would indeed be wonderful."

She could not believe that he really intended this, but as the day wore on she found that he had every intention of going. The Derby had been run for the first time in 1780, and had instantly tickled the public imagination. It was said that great crowds assembled on the downs for the occasion, and that the gipsy women wandered from carriage to carriage and told the most amazing fortunes. There would be heavy betting, and there was nothing that Charles loved more than wagering his money on horses, or cards, or women, or cock-fighting. Charles had been born with an intensely gambling spirit which meant that very often he could not face his creditors. In fact, had it not been for his rich uncle, Sir William Hamilton, at Naples, he would before now have found himself frequently in most embarrassing positions.

He was entranced to have saved his life, and delighted that Emma should be so responsive to the suggestion of the Derby. He was in the mood that made him think sentimentally of marriage, of adopting little Emily, of behaving differently from his usual ways so as to become something of an angel.

153

That mood would pass, but Emma—always the most credulous of fair charmers—rejoiced, believing that he was reformed and that this would last for ever. As Greville's wife how content she would be! As the mother of his sons she could see the doorway to a joyful new world opening. And now she suffered no qualms, realizing that she had done the right thing in saving her darling even at the cost of herself.

"I love you so deeply," she told him.

XXX

THE DAY of the Derby dawned bright and very warm. Picnic hampers had been prepared overnight, and they were ready to put upon the coach. There was the best wine, and the fattest ham and capons, thick fruit pies with cream. Emma dressed herself in a pale blue frock of the simple type that George Romney had made famous in his pictures of her.

They started very early, for it was a long distance. Greville was gay, for nothing more had been heard of Willet-Payne; both he and his ship had gone from Greenwich, and enquiry at Nerot's Hotel had brought only the news that the Captain had been recalled to duty on the night before the duel. Now Charles felt that he could, as a gentleman, refuse to meet Willet-Payne should he ever return to demand satisfaction, though Emma insisted that the subject would never recur, it was done with and the thing to do was to forget it.

They drove in the blue haze towards Epsom. The country was quiet and they went through the rural little village of Chelsea, with its thatched houses and the pretty waterfront. They could see Battersea marshes lying flatly the other side of the river, and crossed in style into the wild Surrey country beyond.

They stopped for refreshment at a coaching inn on the outskirts of Totting Bec, with the road stretching into the distance of the Surrey hills. Travelling on the road grew busier, there were other coaches making the same journey, and here or there the gaily painted van of some gipsy, with lurcher dogs padding beneath it. It would be pulled aside to permit the gentry to pass, while the ragged gipsies stood, caps in hands, and women curtseying obsequiously.

The traffic intensified as they came eventually to the little market town of Epsom, astir with excitement. The day had become much hotter, and the sunlight fell on the lath and plaster houses round the market-place, above which a road, fringed with vividly green beech trees, climbed the hill to the downs.

The coach, drawn by the fresh horses, took the hill in style, for now Charles was in the very best of good moods, laughing and joking. He had come to enjoy himself, for the Derby Horse Race was the fashionable vogue and all society would be here. Suddenly the coachman drew the horses into the side of the road.

"Here. Go on. Go forward," Charles insisted, leaning out of the window to emphasize what he had to say with his ebony walking-stick, ringed in carved gold.

The coachman pointed half-way down the hill with his whip. A far more handsome coach with six white horses drawing it was coming cantering in their direction, and as it approached and passed by Charles drew off his hat, for he had seen the heavy features of the Prince Regent sitting within. The fine coach went on in a swirl of dust, and only when they had given it time to settle down a little could their own coach proceed. But no longer did they travel fast and in style, for as they were already on the steep of the hill the horses could not hope to recover the same energy as before.

Emma glanced at Charles as they climbed higher

and over the prow, with the glorious vista of the downs before them.

"It's a remarkable view," he said.

"It is indeed, dear Charles."

As they drove alongside the course, the crowds rolled back for them. Everybody was here, and the Prince the centre of the picture, with his gentlemen grouped about him. Emma craned herself round to see if Mrs. Fitzherbert was there, for as yet she had never laid eyes on this famous lady, and was disappointed to see that she was not present to-day.

When she had recovered from the first thrill of being here she could settle herself to view the proceedings. There was the race-course spreading before her, with the starting-point far away to the left behind Tattenham Corner, and almost out of sight. There were the touts and toughs, the men who made their living by picking wealthy pockets on these occasions, and the coarse-faced, vulgar brawling men who took bets.

"Oh, pray let me back a horse?" she besought Charles, yet was almost sure that he would refuse her. But for the moment she could do no wrong, for he was in his most amiable mood.

"Maybe you will have beginner's luck, my love."

"You must tell me their names."

He told her the names of the ten runners, saying that they were owned by half the peerage, and because she had the sudden urge that it would be fortunate to her, she laid her money on Lord Clermont's horse, which was ridden by a jockey named Hindley. Already she had seen the young man, and noted his bright, dark eyes, and the way that his hair waved back on his brow.

"I will put my money on Aimwell," she said, "it is an honest name and the jockey looks an honest man."

"He is not so young as you suppose," said Charles, who had seen her enquiring glance in the rider's direction. "He won this race in 1781, and that was the time when he rode Eclipse, and again in '83 when he was mounted on Saltram."

"What strange names they give to these horses!"

"Do you think so?"

"I do indeed. That is why I have chosen Aimwell. You have aimed so well at my heart, my dearest Charles, that it is because of that I chose a horse which I feel sure will be fortunate to me," and she turned to him, her limpid eyes full of the deep affection that she held for him.

They ate their lunch with society picnicking about them, the chaises and coaches drawn to the edge of the downs, and the lackeys, drivers and grooms picnicking discreetly well behind their masters and chaffing with the gipsies who came begging for titbits.

As the appointed hour approached the excitement intensified. Judging by the conversation some of the gentlemen stood to win or to lose fortunes, and wigs went awry with anxiety. Emma looked her loveliest beside Charles, her eyes strained towards Tattenham Corner where they would first see the horses flash towards them. Now she was feeling more herself, for at first she had been afraid that the Prince would remember her from that time at the Adelphi, when her heart had been with Greville. But he never so much as cast a watery eye towards her, for his time was occupied observing a somewhat plump lady of the party who had a rollicking, and Emma thought an unseemly, manner, and who led a little girl by the hand, a child so like the Prince in appearance that she marked it.

"Oh, so you have observed that also?" said Charles. "Many have remarked upon it, I can promise you, but the lady still maintains that the child is her niece. The little girl is allowed to address His Royal Highness as Prinny, which is in itself remarkable."

"You do not think . . . ?" she enquired, piqued with curiosity.

157

"Those who do not dare to think are perhaps the more discreet," he answered.

Emma was looking at him with a tender enquiry in her eyes, for if the Prince could permit his love child to be of the party, surely Greville could melt towards her little Emily left at home? Surely, she thought frantically, but this was not the moment, for all eyes were strained upon the distance. The Derby Stakes had started. There was a breathless moment, then round the far corner, brilliantly green with early June, there flashed the little knot of ten horses, coming like the wind, their jockeys carrying the gay colours of their owners in scarlet, and rose, and vivid blues and golds. Emma sprang up excitedly and clapped her hands.

As they watched they could see Lord Clermont's colours in the front group, crashing down the straight, and Hindley applying the whip, urging his horse forward. Two other horses, neck and neck, came closely behind him as they all arrived before them, with the assembly cheering and even the Prince himself waving a foppish handkerchief and crying "Huzza" in that Germanic hoarse voice of his.

Aimwell flashed past the winning-post, and Emma, who had been so thrilled that she could scarce breath, almost collapsed into Charles's lap.

"Oh, Charles, how much have I won? Tell me, what have I won?"

"You have done very well, my sweet, I promise you that."

"You shall have it all," she told him. "I only did it for you," for she was the most generous soul and there was nothing in the world that she wanted for herself. Everything was for him.

He turned to her with a smile. "Perhaps it would be as well if I took care of it for you. Too much money is not good for any woman to possess, and I will be your banker."

"How good you are! How kind to bring me here

and allow me to bet, and then take care of the profit for me!"

She could see no fault in her beloved, who was entirely perfect in her eyes, and she could not believe that there was a flaw in his character. She was content that he should accept the money on her behalf, and sat back well satisfied.

The great race was over. The belles and beaux had lost or won, some were elated, some furiously indignant. The Derby Stakes had been raced for for the sixth time in history; it was already becoming an historic race and gaining popularity yearly.

Emma sat back whilst Charles collected the winnings, and now she was watching the people about her with interest. Young men were selling broadsheets for which they seemed to have a very ready sale. The broadsheet was a popular form of literature, containing news of the day, some cryptic, some scurrilous. In particular it dwelt on petty gossip and gave rise to much comment.

She watched the boys, and the people reaching out for the sheets, reading them with exuberance and relish, and obviously interested in something that they held. She thought that one or two glanced in her direction with amused interest, but told herself that this could not be so. It must be her imagination, for she had done nothing to rouse comment, in fact, this was her first venture out into the social world since the unfortunate meeting at Vauxhall Gardens. It was true that she was living under the protection of Charles Greville, but then many young women were living under a like arragement with a beau, but she became a trifle alarmed, for Charles hated any publicity, and she was anxious lest something was afoot.

When she saw him coming back and making his way through the crowd to her side, she saw that he held a copy of the broadsheet in his hand. Apparently he had noticed what she herself had seen, and she knew by the expression on his face that something was deeply amiss. Oh, what have I done now, she thought in bewildered anguish.

He sat down beside her, the frown between his eyes a rugged line.

"You have the winnings, my dear Charles?"

He nodded and tapped significantly the blue, knitted silk purse.

"Emma, what is this I read?"

"I—I do not know what you read," she stammered, dismayed at the tone of his voice.

"This is no place in which to discuss it. The race is over and we will return to Paddington Green." He said it in his most final tone and his face was forbidding.

"But, Charles," she exclaimed in horror, "there are still other races to be run, there are diversions, and the Prince has not departed yet. We have come here for the day, and it is only middle afternoon as yet. Surely we cannot leave so soon?"

His voice brooked no argument. "You will do as I bid you," he directed her as he called up the grooms.

XXXI

IN THE coach, with the blinds all drawn, it seemed to be stuffy and dark after the bright sunshine of the downs, and the keen fresh air blown across from the Surrey hills. The grooms were obviously disappointed to be dragged away so soon, for theirs was the first coach to lumber off in the direction of London. Emma could not control her disappointment either.

"What has happened, my dear Charles?"

He brought the broadsheet out of his pocket.

160

"This wretched publication! It has bandied your name in the vilest manner."

"Please let me see, dear Charles?"

She took it from him and saw the paragraph to which he had taken such exception. As she read it she thought of Henry Forbes again, and saw him in a flash as he had been at Nerot's Hotel that night when she had sought out Willet-Payne to dissuade him from keeping his appointment with Greville. The paragraph queried that moment in the most ribald terms. Why did the lovely lady come down the stairs with the crushed roses at her bosom, and what had she been doing? The lady of Romney's beautiful pictures, some said the most beautiful woman in England, if not in the world, who was believed to delight so well a younger son of Lord Warwick.

All the time she knew that Charles's eyes were watching her and she was painfully aware of the rebuke in them. And, queried the paragraph which was determined to leave nothing to the imagination, was it true that an old love of the said virtuous lady had been upstairs, and was it notorious that he was not too old to love? She felt herself palpitating with horror at the inference. So Henry Forbes had known all the time!

"If that is true," said Greville coldly, "I will halt my coach and set you down here in the dust to which you belong," and she knew that he meant it.

She wanted to cry I-did-it-to-save-your-life-my-beloved-Charles, but she dared not say so. His mood was such that he *would* have set her down in the dust, and she would never have found favour in his eyes again.

"Charles, how could you suppose . . . ?" she faltered.

"Were you or were you not at Nerot's Hotel?"

"Charles!" She had to lie, she mustered all her efforts for it, and at that moment it seemed that the entire coach suddenly rocked as though it would break in two. There was the violent stampeding of horse's hoofs, the scream of a woman at the roadside and the sharp invectives of the coachman. "What has happened? Oh, indeed, what has happened?" she gasped as soon as she could speak.

Charles was already half-way out and into the roadway. It seemed that just as they were galloping away from the little town of Epsom a young boy had run out of one of the cottages, not looking to right or left of him, and the coach, coming rapidly round the corner, had had no chance to pull up, but had driven into him. He lay sprawled in the road, apparently dead.

Emma got out and rushed to him. All the tenderness and sympathy that were so abundant in her nature were suddenly aroused. She knelt beside the lad in the dust of the road and, thrusting away his ragged shirt, she laid her hand upon his heart. "It still beats," she cried, "oh, thank God that he is not dead."

She was painfully aware that Charles Greville was standing beside her, his face contemptuous and his eyes narrowing, for this was the kind of scene that he most disliked. He hated the crowds who trespassed under the wheels of his coach, and dared to excite public sympathy by getting themselves run over. He held no brief for the gutter-snipes as he called them, and stood there urging Emma to leave the lad and come away. But her compassion had been roused and she could not leave him until she had done what she could to help. She passed her hands gently all over him, his mother, who knelt on the other side of him, watching her closely.

"There are no bones broken," she said at last. "Come, we will carry him into your home. My coachmen . . ." and she called the men up.

"Emma, this is most undignified," Charles reproved her.

"Can pity ever be undignified?"

He shrugged his shoulders as though to wash his hands of the whole situation. She knew that he was very angry with her. She followed the men into the humble cottage, where they laid the boy. The place was much as Grandmother Kidd's had been at Hawarden, and it struck that friendly, homely note that had eased some of her most harrowing hours. The old grannie was crouching over a mite of firing, for with age her own fires had burnt low, and she watched the company from between strings of grey hair as though unsure of what was going on.

"Let us lay him here," said Emma to the mother, and she indicated the half-collapsed couch in the corner. "He is stunned, but I do not think that he is seriously hurt."

As she spoke the boy opened his eyes and turned to her, staring at her. "I am in Heaven," he whispered, "and this is an angel!"

Emma turned to Greville who had, most reluctantly, followed her into the cottage. "I want some of the guineas that I won," she said.

"Surely you have done enough?"

"It was my money, Charles."

She knew that had it not been for the watching crowd he would have refused her, but that he disliked scenes and therefore consented with a bad grace. He drew from his pocket the silk knitted purse, threaded through its carved steel rings, and he flung it on to the scrubbed table before her. "As you wish," he said.

She selected ten guinea pieces.

"The lady is indeed an angel," said the mother, and followed Emma to the door, for now Greville had retreated and she was going to join him. "May God send you fine sons yourself, dear lady, and an eternal blessing; but then you are born under a lucky star."

"You read the stars?" she asked quickly.

The woman nodded. Then she spoke in an earnest voice. "Do not condemn me as a witch, but oh, dear, kind, generous lady there is a star above you and a letter. The letter is an N."

Emma shook her head. "Alas, no, that is not right! The letter is G," she said, and then went out to join Greville.

The moment that she re-entered the coach she knew that he was deeply offended with her. He refused to speak a word to her, and the broadsheet lying discarded on the seat opposite to them reminded her that even deeper issues were at stake. There was nothing that she could say or do that would not incriminate her, and her eyes filled with tears as they drove in this forbidding silence together. She was reminded of her early home, for the simple cottage had been poignant with memories, and she recalled that never at Hawarden had there been disturbing scenes of this nature, and there she had been almost completely happy.

When they reached Paddington Green she went to her room, and that night Charles did not visit her. He was silent still at breakfast, and left her without a word. It was only from one of the servants that she gathered that he was seeing a certain Mr. Henry Forbes, and in consequence was terribly anxious.

In one of his most remorseless moods Charles had driven up the Strand. The red roses were flowering on the face of the little houses there, and the flower scent from Covent Garden Market came down the alleyways. The small carts and baskets of first strawberries were hurrying to and fro. The old Lyceum stood there, and he came to Fleet Street where the miserable writers lived in garrets and poured out their imaginings by the light of guttering candles. The Old Cheshire Cheese was in fine fettle, for Mr. Sheridan was expected at midday, and Charles could smell the scent of their famous pigeon pie and of their good wine issuing from the rustic door.

The tiny office of the broadsheet was atop a creaky stairway, so ill-lit that Greville stumbled, and with rat-holes in it large enough to permit of a man's fist. It smelt of frowst and strong spirit, for that same

164

strong spirit enabled many of the numbers to be produced and the inspiration to flow the more freely.

Greville blundered into the room with the humpy floor and closed windows, diamond-paned, with sandbags about the crevices even so late in the year. There was something nauseously thick about the air, and Charles choked as he crossed the threshold where Henry Forbes was working at a desk. He turned when he heard the sound, and for a moment did not recognize Greville.

"Your servant, sir?" he said.

Charles threw the broadsheet on to the dusty table. "My name is Charles Greville. This item refers to Miss Hart, and it mentions Nerot's Hotel."

Scenting trouble, Henry glanced at it then back at Charles. "I saw Miss Hart at Nerot's. It was one afternoon last week, one late afternoon."

"Miss Hart was not there."

Henry Forbes looked at him, and marked that Charles's remarkable face was paler than before; he knew that he had been impudent. "The lady was very like her," he stammered.

"No lady is like Miss Hart. No lady will ever be like her. Besides, what would you have inferred she was doing with her crushed roses at Nerot's Hotel?"

"Captain Willet-Payne was staying there, sir. I—I am very sorry if this has been disturbing. . . ." The barb had met its mark! Instantly Greville knew that the paragraph had been accurate, for Emma must have gone to Nerot's Hotel to see Willet-Payne. The first horror was eclipsed by the memory that the duel had been called off; undoubtedly his life had been saved and he moved a trifle uneasily. Henry Forbes was quick to see the change.

"I do crave your indulgence, sir," for he knew that one so influential could harm him.

"Miss Hart is never to be mentioned in your scurrilous broadsheet again."

"That I will willingly promise."

"I am absurd to acquit you with merely a reproval; you should be beaten. But I am a kind man."

"You are a very good man, sir. I do regret that I made a mistake of this nature."

"Doubtless you were drunk, sir."

Henry Forbes bowed politely. "Doubtless," he admitted.

Greville turned, believing that he had carried off the situation with dignity, not guessing that Forbes was laughing at him. He went down the crooked staircase with the rat-holes in it. So Emma had visited Willet-Payne, and had done it to save him! He smiled incredulously to himself as he got into his chair with the pomander dangling aromatically from the roof. So Emma had done this for him! She should have her reward, he told himself, and opening a golden snuff-box took a pinch from it.

At that same moment Henry Forbes was in the Cock Inn and laughing over a grog. He considered that he had got away with the greatest good fortune from an unpleasant situation.

XXXII

EMMA HAD been much disturbed, but did not dare to mention it to Greville in case—as she guessed he had done—he had discovered the truth. He never referred to his visit to Henry Forbes.

The reward came later. It was within the week that he asked if she would accompany him to the masked ball. He gave her money with which to select one of "those simple frocks that so become you."

Taking heart at this, Emma chose a white satin frock embroidered with true lover's knots in pale blue; she fixed the black velvet mask to her features, tying back her hair with a pale blue ribbon. She looked a mere child, and—she told herself—whatever happened tonight she must be discreet. She went to join him below, and he led her by the hand to the waiting chaise.

It was a night agog with anticipation. Link boys and flunkeys carrying torches were everywhere, and it seemed that all the poor had clustered outside the hall in the region of St. James's Palace to watch the aristocrats arrive. Emma saw the open doors and the men standing on every step wearing crimson velvet with powdered wigs. She took Greville's arm, and solemnly they mounted the marble stairs to the ballroom, where a minuet was already being danced. It was lit by the dazzling lights of thousand-candled chandeliers, and they sparkled like ice.

"Greville, I think?" said a lady, tapping him on the shoulder with her fan. "I would know the Warwick features anywhere," and, in a low voice, "I must introduce you to Lord Middleton's youngest daughter, in my charge for to-night. Beautiful and simple and a fortune of thirty thousand pounds to give to her husband. What a dowry!"

"Some man will be fortunate," said Greville.

"This is the child." The lady turned and put her arm round a youngish girl in white, her blonde hair curling, and instinctively Emma knew that behind the mask lay beauty. Just as she knew also that Charles was interested.

"At your service," said Greville with a sweeping bow, and Emma, watching closer, saw his lips move sensuously. They always moved that way when he was interested; when he was at his most forbidding, the moment his lips moved, she knew that he was melting to her. When he took her into his arms . . . She pulled herself up abruptly. Could it be that she had a rival?

She danced with Greville, and then stood back while he took Miss Middleton's hand. "It is just my duty," he said to Emma, and she agreed, but with pain in the eyes behind the mask, and settled herself on a Louis-Quinze chair, somewhat nervously. It was at that moment that a large, somewhat flamboyant lady stopped beside her.

"I believe it is Emma Hart, portrayed by Romney, wooed by Greville?" said the lady.

"It is indeed, ma'am."

"And Emma Hart is looking pensive! What is it?" asked the lady jokingly. Emma recognized her as being Lady Donruggett, well known as a coquette.

"I was thinking, ma'am, what I would do for thirty thousand pounds!"

"But that is a great sum of money. It is a fortune."

"I know that, ma'am. But I have need of a great sum of money." She did not look at Lady Donruggett, but at the couple dancing the minuet. *And still his lips move in that way,* her heart was telling her.

The lady leaned closer. "Maybe I could tell you how to make a little fortune. Maybe you and I could be friends?" she said enticingly. "Think of it. Come and see me to-morrow and we will drink a dish of tea! Be assured that I wish you well."

Emma turned to her. At that moment she had seen Greville deliberately take Miss Middleton's hand and kiss it. "Yes, indeed, I will come. I will and gladly," she said.

The lady slipped a card into her hand, but at that moment there was something of a hubbub, the music stopped abruptly and there was a pregnant silence. Then the music began again and Emma saw the Prince Regent coming into the ballroom—no mask would ever conceal those features—and with him a gentle and dignified lady. She knew instantly that this must be Mrs. Fitzherbert. Maria Fitzherbert walked in a leisurely manner, she was not over-perfumed or pomaded, and her frock was not extreme. Here was nothing of the adventuress or the bawd, and Emma, looking at her, was quick to perceive it. She curtseyed low.

Greville had returned from dancing and was now by Emma, and the Prince paused to exchange courtesies with him. It was at that moment that Emma found herself side by side with Maria Fitzherbert.

"You have a charming frock, my child," said Mrs. Fitzherbert gently.

"I'm happy that it delights you, ma'am."

"It becomes you. You should always wear pale blue with that red hair of yours. It is attractive. The gentlemen must admire you very much."

"Thank you, ma'am."

For one moment Maria Fitzherbert put out her hand; she said, "Be cautious, my child. Love can be the happiest, yet the most unhappy experience," and then she passed on.

Emma turned to Greville. "What a lovely person she is."

"You refer to Miss Middleton?"

"No, I meant Mrs. Fitzherbert."

"Oh, yes. Yes, naturally. Miss Middleton is charming too. I would that I could see her without her mask."

"She is an heiress, so they say."

Charles Greville was now too excited to be cautious. Emma did not know that recently he had had serious betting mischances and he owed money. "She has all the charms. What a wife for some fortunate man!" he exclaimed.

She could not answer, for she was too hurt. She thought of what Lady Donruggett had said. She knew where Emma could make a fortune, and a fortune was what she most needed. Was this the reason why Charles had never married her? And would he marry her if she could bring money to him? Never did she blame him for a moment; he meant too much to her for that. She saw him with eyes blinded by love, and he could do no wrong. She adored him.

At this moment Sir Godfrey Takely approached. He was an oldish man, his wig cockeyed, and a red mark across his face where the ribbon of his mask had been tied too tightly. He had taken it away now, and held it dangling in one hand. Charles had often held him up to Emma as an example of propriety. A city alderman, to be lord mayor one day, and immensely rich.

"I have an entertainment to offer you, Greville," he said, "if you and your sweet lady would care to accept my hospitality."

"Indeed, and what is the entertainment?"

Sir Godfrey stood fanning himself with the mask. There was to be a public execution at Newgate in the morning, and Sir Godfrey's office windows were opposite to it. There was a great demand for window seats, and he could offer them a comfortable time and refreshment. "It should be most amusing," he told them.

"What has the poor fellow done?" asked Emma, her heart turning over with compassion for the man who would die in the morning.

"Alas, my dear lady, he is a rascal, a ruffian. He stole a loaf of bread for his children, and it is only right that such dastards should die." Sir Godfrey twinkled at her amiably.

She thought with a sudden pang of the night when she had slept hungry in a doorway. These people well fed and housed did not know the misery of those who had neither food to put into their stomachs nor beds to sleep in. She quivered wretchedly, for she had known both, and for her part she could take no amusement in going out to see some unfortunate man die.

"It should be interesting," said Charles, "and we will be delighted to attend, and grateful for the courtesy of your hospitality."

"But, Charles . . . ?" For a moment she plucked furtively at his sleeve, then hesitated. Miss Middleton was on the other side of the room and Emma was only too well aware that there were a magnificent pair of violent eyes behind that little velvet mask. Suddenly she stopped, for Charles thought squeamishness was merely the hallmark of common breeding. "Very well, then. I will be delighted," she said in a subdued voice, but the tears were already pricking in her eyes.

The lights were being lowered, and the dancers were emerging to take part in the cotillion. Charles and Sir Godfrey bowed to one another, and they left him trying to refix the velvet mask with the too tight strings.

"Shall we dance?" asked Charles, extending his hand to Emma. But now she knew that all the time he was looking at Miss Middleton.

XXXIII

WHEN GREVILLE and Emma arrived at Sir Godfrey's offices the next morning, there was already a surging crowd pressing forward outside Newgate Prison. The day was hot, and there was the stench of the unwashed populace and of the putrefying refuse in the gutters which already made Emma retch.

"Charles, I am much alarmed that I may faint," she said.

"Nonsense. No lady faints. After all, the fellow deserved to die, and unscrupulous sympathy is very ill-bred."

"It was only that he stole bread."

"If all stole bread, how should we eat?"

There was never any answer to such questions, and she held her peace as they climbed the high stairway of the city house where Sir Godfrey dispensed tea from Ceylon. In the first-floor room chairs had been arranged before the window. They were high wing chairs, and a table at the back of the room was laden with good food, pigeon pies, gooseberry tartlets and larks in aspic.

Greville was now in the mood to be amused and full of stories. He had not seen so great a crowd since March, when Count Zambeccari and Admiral Sir Edward Vernon had made an ascent in a balloon from the Tottenham Court Road. Everyone had been there, and there had been much speculation that the balloon would never rise. And, said he, a certain Miss Grice of Holborn had wished to go up also, and got into the basket, but the balloon refused to rise, so she had to be put out again, whereupon she burst into tears seeing it go off without her at great speed. It had been snowing at the time, he said, and everyone requiring hot rum punch. And last year there had been Dr. Samuel Johnson's funeral at Westminster Abbey, with ten mourning coaches and all manner of private carriages and such a crowd as never was! But no wonder, for Dr. Johnson had been a famous man, and amongst the mourners were Sir Joshua Reynolds, Mr. Edmund Burke, and the Doctor's faithful black servant.

Emma could not bear to listen to the chatter. She had most unhappily been put well to the fore in the window and could look down at the crowd below. The well-to-do sat in windows, the less fortunate clustered on rooftops, but the street was full of the very poor, any one of whom might one day hang as the unfortunate man to-day.

Sir Godfrey pointed out the gallows on the raised platform with, for background, the dark, forbidding doors of Newgate, and the grilled windows. The prison had an austere face, and Emma remembered the night it had been broken open, and the wretched skeletons of men and women in chains who had wandered out of it.

"It all makes me very sad," she said.

The bell of St. Sepulchre's began to toll. It had a miserable insistence, and she could not think how on this bright sunny morning, when life was so exquisite, anyone could wish that someone would die.

"Now it is time," said Sir Godfrey with obvious

relish, and taking out a golden tooth-pick applied it to a tooth which had taken full toll of pigeon pie.

On the platform the executioner, a big, burly man, had taken up his stand, and with him two assistants. At last the prison doors opened, creaking like the doors of a vault, and the Governor and doctor came first, with the chaplain following, and the miserable little man supported between two immense warders, who dragged him to his appointment with death. The crowd, seeing his dismay, screamed their disapproval, for they asked that a man should die bravely, and this man did not wish to die.

The procession mounted the scaffold, and Emma's heart was making horrible noises, so that she thought she would vomit. The crowd, becoming frenzied, jeered the man, and he was given leave to speak and stood there mouthing out words they could not hear. Emma had the unbearable sense of suffocation, as though she could not bear a moment more of this.

Then the chaplain began to read from his book, and the executioner approached the man. She did not want to look, but could not divert her eyes, fascinated by horror as he was bound, and the hideous rope knotted with a relish about his throat.

Time would never finish it, for this would go on for ever, she thought in dismay; then the executioner moved away, and there in his acute agony the man was displayed for all to see, and a cheer went up. Suddenly he was there no more. He was just something on the end of a rope, something which jerked convulsively for a second, so hideously that the whole of her body shuddered at the thought, then sank into silence like a bundle of old clothes, past suffering. Past horror and swinging emptily into space.

At that instant a woman, dragging a child by the hand, flung herself forward and on to the platform. Emma thought that it must be the man's wife and child, but they acted strangely, going to the limp bundle with the executioner, who lifted the lifeless hand of the dead man, and stroked them with it.

"It is reputed to cure wens," said Sir Godfrey, "and they pay the executioner heavily for the cure." He laughed comfortably.

Now she realized that she had been so occupied with the horror that she had not noticed that Miss Middleton and her guardian were in the window seat with them. That Charles had been talking to Miss Middleton, looking composed and beautiful, with a large leghorn hat that shaded the violet eyes most becomingly. The girl had not even changed colour; it might be good breeding, but to Emma, distracted with compassion, it was hardly human. Charles Greville was being very polite to Miss Middleton, and when the hanging was over, and the street too full as yet for chairs or coaches to come for aristocratic guests (who would not be expected to walk), Sir Godfrey suggested that the time should be passed in gambling for the gentlemen, and chat for the ladies.

In one corner the men drew together, the ladies still sitting in the window, with the heat growing intense, and the crowd gradually dispersing in the streets below them, whilst scavenger dogs came and ate the refuse scattered in the filthy gutters. Miss Middleton was not talkative. She was a refined young lady, she was well educated, and Emma gathered that she sang and spoke several languages, and painted exquisitely. (I wonder if she can spell, thought Emma, remembering how her own faulty spelling had irritated Greville.)

She realized very soon that the gambling was not going well for Charles. Although he always hid his feelings, she knew by his pallor that he had already lost more than he could afford, and when finally the gentlemen pushed their chairs back, he said nothing, but came across to her and stood there with lips blue as lead, and face chalky. He was watching Miss Middleton closely, and she—aware of his gaze—returned it with interest in her eyes.

174

"I was saying, Mr. Greville," she said quietly, "money is the source of all evil, is that not so?"

"It is also the bedfellow of much that is good," he told her, and bowed politely.

Emma felt the pulse pricking in her throat; she could not believe that it was possible to suffer such torture; never before had she been jealous of another woman, believing—and with justification—that her own charms were sufficient in themselves. But now suddenly she was aware of the something this girl had, with which she could not compete. That something Greville wanted. Not only did he want it, but needed it. He needed that fortune with which she could endow anyone.

Emma clasped and reclasped her hands. If she had had any qualms about Lady Donruggett, they had gone now. Something must be done to keep Charles with her and for ever. She could not conceive a life without him, for indeed he was life itself to her. Much later he rose and offered her his arm.

"We must be away," he said. "The street is almost clear."

But even when they were in the chaise she could not speak of the subject nearest to her heart, but sat fanning herself, aware of the imminence of tears. Never had she felt so dreadful. At last she said in a trembling voice, "Miss Middleton is very beautiful."

"She has something more permanent than beauty," said Charles with a slight sneer, and she saw that his lips were moving again as with that sensuous apprehension which she found so disturbing. I cannot bear this, she thought desperately.

"Charles, you would not forsake me?"

He turned with obvious delight. "Can it be that my sweeting is jealous of a fortune?" he asked, and then, "Ah, well, there is much to say for money. It has an exceedingly comforting capacity."

XXXIV

IF EMMA had any doubts about attending Lady Donruggett's party that afternoon, they were now dismissed. She would not give up her hold on Greville's heart without a struggle, for she loved him too well and, indeed as she had said, she could not live without him. Charles went off on business, announcing that he would not return until late, and she dressed herself, hiding all traces of tears as best she could. Life had taught her how little they availed her, and she knew that she must have courage.

She went along to the pleasant house which overlooked the Greek Park, where the trees were enchantingly green and the loving couples sat hand in hand on grass banks.

She envied them their simplicity and romance. Now she was feeling the swift, high tide of the jealous emotion, and she knew that something must be done to stem it. If, indeed, Lady Donruggett knew of some aid, then she must avail herself of it.

The manservant who admitted her looked twice at her; she disliked his manner, it was officious and yet familiar; he had some air about him that was repugnant to her, almost as though he felt a personal interest.

"Your mistress, please," she said haughtily.

She heard the titter of childish conversation, young girls' laughter and a warning "Shush" as she crossed the somewhat over-decorated hall. Everywhere was sumptuous, if anything too sumptuous. She was taken up the stairs, past an oriel window through which the scent of syringa and red roses was blown. She was shown into a smallish room, no bigger than her little one at Paddington Green, simply decorated, its main feature being a bed canopied beside the window. Emma looked at it in startled distrust. She did not understand why she should be here. She seated herself on the little sofa with its hard bolster, and awaited the arrival of Lady Donruggett.

Presently the door opened and her ladyship herself bustled in at it, and was effusive in her welcome.

"How very good of you, Miss Hart. I am indeed delighted to see you, and here we can talk quietly. I thought it would be better."

Emma, still puzzled as to what was afoot, bowed her head, all the time surveying the lady with perplexity in her eyes.

"I understand," said Lady Donruggett, without the slightest nervousness, for she was obviously well used to this situation, "that you find yourself in need of a little financial assistance. It is, of course, well known that Mr. Greville is somewhat meagre in his arrangements of this nature. All the Warwicks have frugal minds."

"Oh, but that is not so, he has been most generous," for Emma would not hear one word against her beloved. "I have only to ask and Charles will give it to me."

Lady Donruggett bowed, but it was plain that she was not deceived by the statement. She said, "Indeed, but you still find yourself in need of financial assistance."

"Yes—yes, I do. I want to have some money of my own. Not money from Charles, but for myself."

Lady Donruggett narrowed her eyes, she was quick to read the truth behind this and not to be deterred from it. She knew readily enough that Emma had seen the first tendency of her star to fall when she had realized that Charles was interested in Lord Middleton's youngest daughter with the fortune that she could bring to the happy man who was to marry her. The girl had everything. She might not have Emma's superb beauty, but she had the greater attraction and—as Emma knew only too well—a man's fancy wanders. Charles had had everything for him, and she was prepared to give him her heart for eternity, but in the last few hours she had realized that he might not want her heart. He might want something more substantial, a bank balance.

She knew he was in debt. He lived too well. He spent money on himself and questioned every farthing disposed for the house. Her weekly accounts were as ever the source of trouble between them. She was only too anxious to save him money where she could, but if she were too meagre he challenged the lowness of her upbringing, and at times it was more than she could bear.

Lady Donruggett smoothed her taffeta skirt, pushing the creases aside with fat, over-ringed fingers. "Rich young gentlemen often seek me out," she said. "They know that I have several enchanting lady friends. They realize that only the most beautiful come to my house, and that all my rooms are pleasantly furnished."

She waved her hand in the direction of the bed.

Emma turned to look at it; for the first time its reason struck her and with force. She had heard stories of Lady Donruggett, of course, but had thought them unkind. With her over-generous heart she did not listen to common gossip. She considered it beneath her. The world was too harsh in its judgments.

"Do I understand?" she asked.

"The gentlemen who visit my house are kind. They pay large sums of money. A young lady of such exquisite beauty as yourself could command something that would probably surprise you, and"—she leaned closer—"Mr. Greville would be none the wiser. Is it so unusual for ladies to exchange a dish of tea together? The fact that gentlemen may be present, and that the dish of tea may be a cup of wine for two in a room of this nature"—she waved the hand again with an airiness that affrighted Emma— "is of little importance."

"But . . ."

"Ah, do not be too hasty," warned Lady Donruggett. "I imagine that at first this makes you feel bewildered. But you have need of money. A girl of your nature cannot earn a vast sum easily. This is the only way. Princes visit my abode. I have the pick of the gay young ladies of London. It is said that none but the most lovely come to my house, and"—in a kindly manner, as though she were sugar-coating the plum—"I have long had my eye upon you, my dear."

Emma was horrified. She did not know what to do. She wanted to refuse with emphasis, but knew at the same time that if she did so, she left as she had come. With no more armament against the perplexingly great armament of Miss Middleton with her thirty thousand pounds' worth of fortune.

She said, "I do not think that I can do it. It is not love, it is something so dreadful that it frightens me."

"You are a charming and sensitive girl," said the lady with that false air of gentleness which in itself was almost more revolting. "I would suggest that you come down and see the gentlemen at my party. You will not find that I entertain roués, but only the kindest and most charming. Here there is nothing rough and unmannerly. The gentlemen are here to be amiable, and they only ask a little generosity from my young ladies."

"I did not think that it would be like this," faltered Emma.

"And pray, what did you suppose? What had you else to offer of great worth?"

Perhaps she had been foolish! Perhaps in her immaturity she had not reasoned very well with herself. She got up feeling that she had a headache coming, that she felt strangely ill, and that she would have given much to order her chair and return to Paddington Green. But she could not do it. There were greater things at stake. Her love for Greville and everything that he meant to her. She must see this thing through. "Let me see the party," she said.

Lady Donruggett touched her arm with the professional wise touch of a woman who with experience knows the value of merchandise that she offers. The arm was smooth and dimpled. It was an exquisite piece of flesh, and as she knew, gentlemen had enquired why she had not so famous a girl as Emma Hart at her house. The place was notorious. And although Lady Donruggett conducted it with all the insincere ritual that her good name and dignity could lend it, it was nothing more than a brothel for aristocratic gentlemen who were choosey in their selection.

"I see that you are a wise young woman," she said, and went on ahead. "We will see you rich as well as beautiful, and that should make us both very happy."

They went down the stairs again, and the flunkey flung open the big double doors, on to the large room, where something of a party was being held. There were the most aristocratic gentlemen and young ladies of great beauty. Looking at them there was little to suggest that it was more than an ordinary party, and yet when one looked closer, there was— she knew—that expression on the men's faces, that certain flushed abandon about the girls, the ribbon of a modesty vest undone, a rose crushed to a bosom, the mark on a young white neck where a man had kissed too savagely.

She drew back alarmed. Then it was that she felt the compelling hand of Lady Donruggett urging her forward. "It is only the first step that is difficult," she said in a croaky voice in the girl's ear.

Half reluctantly, half desperately, Emma went forward into the room.

XXXV

A SILENCE had come on Lady Donruggett's party; men lifted eye-glasses, sparkling with cut marquisite, to approve the new beauty.

"Lud, but it is Emma Hart," they said, and nudged one another with approval. Many of them had suggested that they would pay a noble commission for the chance to speak with so fair a charmer. It was plain that old Lady Donruggett—the artful old bawd—had taken their words to heart.

Emma walked down the room with the charm of a duchess. She carried her body beautifully; she walked to the far end, where she had seen a small sofa awaiting her. She did not look at the avaricious eyes of the men about her, nor the jealous ones of the girls. She knew—without seeing it—of disarranged bodices, and crumpled skirts. She felt as though someone had struck her, for, what these people would not realize, was that what she had done had always been for love. How could she sell the gift she gave to men so readily? And if Charles ever knew of this, she would lose him for ever! She took her seat on the sofa, her eyes misty with anguish. Lady Donruggett close behind her, with much of the bustle of an old hen mothering a lone chick, came and sat beside her.

"A friend of yours will soon be here," she said.

"A friend?"

"Mr. George Romney."

The thought of seeing his kindly face suddenly delighted her. "Oh, that will be wonderful!" she said, and clasped her hands together in her lap.

Now the beaux closed round her, each vying for her favours. In a way she was in her element, in another she was disturbed. She must have money; she must have the means wherewith to keep Charles for herself. She dared not let him go to the Middleton girl, but what could she do? She was captious; one moment encouraging, the next prudish and trying to set traps for them. But her beauty was intensified as she sat there, aware that she was the target for their favours. Soon Romney will be here, she told herself. Yet when his friend John Widney arrived, he was alone.

Emma had met John several times; a tall, aesthetic man, he was a portrait painter of great merit, but not successfully, for he had an honest outlook. He refused to take age from the woman whose spring was far behind her, or give full summer high tide to the raddled beauty. He would not grant sophistication to springtime loveliness, but painted what he saw. This did not always give pleasure, and she had heard George Romney assure him that if he was to succeed, he must forgo his truthfulness of outlook and be wiser in his generation. The moment that she saw him coming into the room, and marked that he was alone, she got up urgently, and leaving the clustering beaux behind her, went across to him.

"John, is not George Romney with you? They promised me that he should be here. . . ."

He turned and looked at her with hazel eyes that were entirely sincere. "Emma Hart, what are you doing here? This is no place for one so fair and so brave."

"Lady Donruggett is my friend."

He turned, indicating the old woman, earnestly fixing a price with a foreign princeling, who spoke with a guttural accent and was uncertain of what the payment should be. Lady Donruggett was never uncertain! She was emphatic in her gestures, and one knew instinctively that he would pay to the uttermost farthing. "Lady Donruggett is the friend of no

182

woman," he said in a low, eager voice. "Go before you find it is too late. Greville cannot know."

"Greville has no idea. I came because I had to get money. It is very urgent to me."

"You mean that he is miserly with you?"

"It is not that. There—there is another fascinator. It has only happened within the last few hours, and, John, it has made me more intensely miserable than I dare say."

He looked at her dismayed, the colour starting to her cheek, her eyes downcast, the long lashes up-curling. "He could not jilt one so lovely," he said, half to himself.

"It is true. I would not deceive you."

He said, "You cannot do this thing. Have you thought what people would say if they knew that you were here? Come away with me. I have but come to apologize for my friend's absence, and that will take me but a moment."

"Why is George not here?"

"I will tell you—but later." He turned to Lady Donruggett who was just leaving the foreign prince-ling who looked discomforted. But she was elated, and was cramming money into the satin bag that she held in her hand. She had made a good bargain—for herself—as was her wont! John made his adieux, de-livering the message that George Romney had sent, and said, "Now I am taking Miss Hart with me."

"But surely not? Miss Hart has business here," said Lady Donruggett.

"Miss Hart has no business here."

Emma would not have believed that John could have been so strong. He put an arm round her waist and drew her through the heavy double doors into the street beyond. "But I have not made my adieux," she said.

"Never mind. That is unimportant at the moment. The thing to do is to get you away."

They stepped out into the street with the green park radiant in the evening sunshine. It looked coolly entrancing after the house, too censed with the perfume of wigs and of the powder the women wore. He took her hand and escorted her into the park, and there they stood amongst the poor lads and lasses who made this their place of assignation and dispensed the simple rituals of love under the hawthorns.

"About George?" she said quickly.

"George Romney is a very sick man."

"He was never a strong man."

"He gives too much to his art, you could not expect that he would be strong. Recently he has suffered a great blow. Can you not imagine what that blow might be?"

She shook her head. "How can I? I have not seen him for some little time," and—dropping her eyes, "my protector is very strict; if Greville were to discover that I had been here to-day, you cannot imagine what he would think."

"Indeed I can! And there he is quite right and proper in his judgment. But George Romney gave his heart to you, Emma. Do you remember when he first asked you to sit for him?"

She started a little, and the colour began to fill her cheeks, as the rose moves delicately in the cream of a shell taken from a beach. She did recall the moment, and when he had led her to that throne and had told her that, to understand the workings of his model's heart, an artist must know more of her. Those exquisite moments they had spent together, and—it was true—she had experienced for Romney something more than she had experienced for those others, unless it be Greville. Greville she always set alone. He was her star, and for him she would have suffered death itself.

But George Romney had been tender as a woman; he had touched her as though her frailty had been that of gossamer. His compelling had been of the most gentle.

"I could not come to see him," she said nervously, afraid that John accused her of being unkind.

"He knew that, but he said nothing. That was why! He has become much thinner, and much paler; he eats so little. Once, when he could stay himself at the full fountain of your love, he was fed, but now he starves."

She turned, dismayed. "He is in no danger?" she asked.

"I feel that he is in every danger. If this goes on much longer, he will be in his grave, and then how will you feel?"

She made an immense resolution. "I will go to him at once. Take me to him immediately."

But John shook his head. "Unless you can help him I will not be party to taking you to him. To set meat and drink in the sight of a starving man is cruelty. Unless it is for him I will not take it to him. He must die," he said.

For a moment she stood there, with the young thorn trees about her, so lately stripped of their sweet-scented blossom, and the country couples hand in hand. The birds trilled, and a sedan in which an ancient alderman joggled, was carried along the roadway towards Piccadilly.

"He shall not die," she said. "You must take me to him."

"To-morrow."

"Why not to-day?"

"To-morrow I will have prepared him. I have always told him that Emma did not wave good-bye to her old friends so easily; he never blamed you, but insisted that you had no other course open to you. Romney would never blame the woman he loved."

She laid her hand upon his arm. "Go to him and make an appointment for me to-morrow. I will come whatever happens. He was always my friend, he helped me when others were cruel to me, and never shall it be said that Emma Hart forgets her friends."

"If you break faith, I feel that he will die within the hour."

"It is as critical as that?"

"It is as critical as that!"

She lifted a face wreathed in tender smiles. "Tell him that I come to cure him. My remedy is perhaps the oldest in the world, but then also it is the most successful in the world. Take him my heart, and know that I shall not fail you."

Then she turned back to the roadway.

XXXVI

EMMA WAS distressed to think that George Romney could be so ill. Nothing should come between her and to-morrow's appointment, she told herself, for had it not been for his good offices, she would never have won the heart of Greville, and she must repay what he had done for her.

She arrived home and changed into one of the simple frocks that most pleased Greville, but he was delayed, and when he came in wore a worried look. He said he had been detained, for only to-day John Adams, of Massachusetts, had arrived in London as the First Minister of the United States, and it had been something of an occasion. He asked if anyone had been to see him, and seemed disturbed when she said no one. He was, it appeared, expecting a packet to be delivered by a messenger.

"What sort of a packet, Greville dearest?"

He took umbrage at this, and seeing that he looked to be so forbidding, she quietened and said no more. Nervously she fluttered beside him. Now she seemed to have lost her first tenacity of purpose. She tried the little wiles that once had coaxed a smile from him under all circumstances. Now he was moody, perverse, and when a sudden knocking came at the door, sprang up as if he were afraid.

"It is only the messenger that you expect," she told him.

He compressed his lips, listened intently to the loud voice emerging from the hall. Then the manservant came into the room, closing the doors discreetly behind him, and going across to Charles, acquainted him with a message that Emma could not hear. She saw Charles go very white, and knew instantly that something had happened.

"Can I help you?" she asked.

"It is Sir Leonard Cartwright," he said.

She knew the man by repute; forthright and vigorous, said to have a dreadful temper; rumour had it that he had strangled a manservant who had crossed him, and had flung the body into the moat about his country home.

"I owe him money for cards," said Charles.

He said it in such a tone that she knew he needed her help. She said, "I will go to him," and turning went out of the double doors, across the hall to the room where she knew Sir Leonard would be waiting. She saw him standing, his back to her, taking snuff from a china box he held in his large red hands. She had always disliked men so ponderous and so forthright, but she summoned all her courage and curtseyed kindly.

"You must forgive me, Sir Leonard. To-night, Mr. Greville is not well. He sent me to speak to you."

Sir Leonard knew Emma Hart by sight; by reputation also. If Greville thought he could fob him off with that stuff, he was mistaken. Sir Leonard was not a lady's man, his pursuit was wagering, and it was a wagering debt that he had come about. He looked at the girl who stood there. "This is man's business, and it is only with a man that I would speak," he said.

She motioned him to the sofa. He noted the delicacy of her gestures, the exquisite shape of her

187

hands. He had heard that she was the daughter of some village smithy in the country, but that he knew to be a lie. No smithy's daughter had wrists so elegant, and fingers so tapering! Against his wiser judgment, he sat himself down, and she seated herself before him.

"Greville has been unwise?" she said.

"He owes me five hundred guineas."

"So much?" she gave a gasp of dismay. "How will he ever pay?"

Sir Leonard knew how he thought Greville might pay, though maybe this was not the wisest company in which to express the opinion. "He might make a rich marriage," he said.

She did not flicker; even though she knew that such a suggestion meant that already the gossips had heard the rumour and were doing their worst by it. She said, "But if he is to make the rich marriage wherewith to pay his debts, surely you would not desire to hold him back? You have come to ask for the money, I presume, and to pay such a debt would mean the selling-up of all the assets whereby he might suppose to make such a marriage. Is that wise?"

He looked at her again. He had never thought that this little creature could be so diplomatic. Daughter of a smithy? Never. Some lady must have erred, and then resorted to the anvil with a wedding ring with which to guard her indiscretion. If this had been the daughter of a great ambassador she could not have made a more discreet observation.

"That is perhaps true," he said.

"I do suggest—in all humility, sir—that you hold back for a short period and see if Greville cannot provide himself with the means to settle this just—this most just—debt," she said very quietly, and it hurt her to suggest it.

"If Charles Greville marries, what will become of you?" he asked cautiously.

"I shall have great happiness in knowing that he is

happy. I love him so well that I would not desire to hold him back from a destiny that he felt was more befitting to him."

"Few are so generous."

"It is not generosity," she said in a small, quiet voice, "it is that I only desire his happiness, and that I ask above all things."

Even as she said it, she convinced herself that if it were for his happiness she would aid and abet it. But it was not! Lord Middleton's daughter could never make him happy as she could. She who knew all the lovely ecstasies of love, the gentle passions, and the tremendous sacrifices, she who knew better than anyone else in the world how best to lend her mood to his.

"I admit that Greville has chosen an advocate to plead for him with the sweetest tongue in the world," for now Sir Leonard was finding himself very well pleased with the young lady. "You urge me to defer my insistence."

"If you insist to-day, you cannot be paid. If you wait until to-morrow, you shall be repaid perchance and in full," she said. "Nothing is to be gained by pressing the cause to-day, whereas everything is to be gained by to-morrow."

In her own mind some desperate plan already was suggesting itself whereby, perhaps, she could find some of the money wherewith to imburse Greville. Something would surely reveal itself. And, if all else failed, there was already a rumour that Sir William Hamilton was returning soon on holiday from Naples, and he could perhaps be pressed into the gap and asked for help. She ordered wine, the very best that they had, for him, and talked sweetly. For now she knew that the cause was won!

An hour later he left her, believing that he had done the wise thing, and envying Greville so sweet a mistress.

Emma went to him. He still sat at the head of his

189

table, with the wine before him and the fruit on his plate. His eyes, grown haggard, looked at her.

"He is prepared to wait," said Emma.

"To wait? That is useless to me! I want the debt forgotten."

"Dearest Greville, we cannot climb too high too fast. The first step is to silence him for the moment. More than that we cannot hope for as yet."

She had been delighted with having won the old gentleman over, and went confidently to Greville's side, laying her hands upon his shoulders and her face beside his.

"But where will I get the money?"

She could not confess that there was the chance of the rich marriage. She said, "Maybe your uncle . . ."

"You mentioned that?"

"Indeed, yes, I mentioned it."

"I think you took too much upon your shoulders. Since when has the servant girl turned diplomat?" She fell back, stung by his mood. She could see that he had dwelt upon the matter, and that he had conjured up all manner of imaginary ills in the hour alone.

"I may one day make you regret that accusation, Greville."

"Sir Leonard told you of the sum?"

"He did mention it."

"Nothing more?"

She could not pretend about it. She turned swiftly and faced him. "He hoped that perhaps the gossip is true. And that you are really thinking of a rich marriage. How true is it, Greville?"

If only he would deny it!

He lifted a glass of wine and set it deliberately to his lips. He drank without hurry and looked at her again. "Why should I reveal my innermost thoughts to you?"

"Oh, Charles, my dearest, I have done my best for you. I have managed to rid you of this odious man, and I would always help you and gladly. Now you

190

can only chide me! I could not bear you to leave me. Promise me that such a thought has never entered your head and that you will never do this thing?"

She knelt beside him, clinging to his knee in the grey silk breeches, with the fine hose reaching them, and the small pearl buttons.

He said coldly, "Supposing then I say that I promise never to let this happen on the condition that you promise never to see George Romney again? What would you reply?"

Dismayed she sank back, pulling nervously at the strings of her bodice, her eyes misting with tears. George Romney was sick. He needed a friend more than he had ever done before, and she had promised she would go.

"I—I could not do such a thing, and you would not want me to be so cruel to a friend," and burst into tears.

XXXVII

THAT WAS a terrible night.

Emma and Charles had a bitter quarrel, and it was even more hurtful that she had been so helpful, rescuing him from the very difficult situation with Sir Leonard, then to find how angry he was. He reviled her when she refused to promise not to see Romney again; she argued that the great artist was a very sick man, and that his friend had said what a great difference it would make to him if Emma went to assure him of her goodwill. Greville's lip curled.

She clung to him pathetically, crying for the love that he denied her, but he had turned cold, and rising left her to her despair. She knew that he would not visit her again that night, and cried until she was utterly exhausted.

Next morning he left early, leaving a message that he had gone to the city, but secretly she guessed that he had driven to Lord Middleton's country house in Hertfordshire, and dreaded to think that it might be to ask the hand of his youngest daughter in marriage.

She dressed herself for the visit to George Romney's, her hands shaking, and her whole being much agitated. She did not know how she would bear it if she lost the affection of Charles Greville, for whom she had this deep and abiding regard. The emptiness of a life without him would be unbearable.

She came to the region of Cavendish Square, with the sweet countrified scent of the elder flowers blossoming in the hedges just beyond. She remembered how she and Grandmother Kidd had made elderberry wine, and maybe Grandmother Kidd and little Emily were doing much the same thing to-day. Only such a short while ago she had fostered such deep desires that Charles would permit little Emily to become an inmate of the establishment, and ultimately perhaps be the stepfather to the child. But now those dreams seemed to be further away than ever before.

The manservant ushered her inside the artist's home, and everything was as it had always been. She saw the double doors of the studio opening before her and stepped confidently across the threshold. The fine Chippendale chairs stood as before, the great colourful vases with the upstanding brushes in them, and the throne with the easel before it. But she noticed instantly that no half-finished picture was there, and she knew that was ominous. Had the flame of Romney's genius perished in his malady?

She heard a frail voice that she scarcely recognized coming from the far corner of the room.

"That surely cannot be my Emma?" it said.

She turned whence the voice came, and hardly knew that the man lying there was George Romney, for he had grown so thin and pale. His dark hair fell straightly over his brow, and the hand he held quiveringly out to her was transparent, the bones in ridges, and the fingers like yellowish ribbons holding the knuckles together.

Impetuously sympathetic she rushed to his couch. "George, what has happened to you?"

The shirt that had once been quite spare to his person now hung in bunches. His throat was full of holes and crannies, with a flesh that seemed to have withered on it; his eyes were caverns.

"My poor friend, indeed what has happened?"

"I am dying," he said.

She put her arms about him, drawing his body to her own which was so full of the urgent vitality of life. Her face laid against his smelt the nauseous scent of illness, felt the pappy, too relaxed skin, and the weakness of his whole body, but she strained him nearer, striving to fuse him with some of her own abundance.

"It is too late," he said.

"It is not too late. See, I will give you some of my strength. I will pour into you my own love of life, and bring the will to live back into you."

It seemed that for a moment he warmed a little, then his body grew limp again and he fell back as though fatigued against her. Now she was determined to save him at all costs, and she laid him against the pillows. She opened her bodice and drew him to her flesh, and it seemed that her warmth entered into him, for he turned his mouth to hers.

"My dearest," she whispered, and kissed him again and again.

It seemed that time ceased as they lay there, and gradually she watched the sick man recovering his strength, changing with every passionate moment, until something of the old Romney looked at her out of his melancholy eyes, and kissed her with that abiding fervour.

He slept after a while, and she beside him, yet all the time willing that he should live. She would never

193

forget how good he had been to her, how forgiving of those little sins that others considered unforgivable, how wise. So she lay with the day fading into its late afternoon, and the sound of the country carts returning to their little farm homestead, after leaving their provender for sales in London town.

In her anxiety to help an old friend she had almost forgotten Greville at Lord Middleton's. Romney had such need of her. Then, when the shadows lengthened more, she drew herself away, and, going over to the other side of the studio, began to tidy her frock.

Ten minutes later George Romney stirred and, opening his eyes, looked at her.

"Oh, incomparable Emma!" he said.

She went to him and laid her arms about him, burying her head against his chest. It seemed that he was warmer and more alive. "Oh, you are better!" she said joyfully.

He sat up on the couch and stretched himself, then buried his lips in the abundance of her auburn hair. "Do I not look better?"

"You look quite different," she said with truth.

He struggled to his feet, laughing at his weakness and overcoming it. "You have done this for me, most wonderful of all women. This is indeed a miracle."

"Love is always a miracle," she reminded him.

He walked a little unsteadily to the table, asking if she would ring for food. He had not eaten for a fortnight, he said, yet, when the man brought it, he ate ravenously.

"Not too much, too soon, dear Romney," she begged him, "lest you have a return of the malady, and do not live for Emma."

"I shall not be ill again. I know now that there is a magician who can always make me better," he smiled at her.

Was it her fancy that the skin was brighter, his eyes clearer and the faint sick smell leaving him?

"I must not stay too late," she warned him gently.

He did not want her to go, but knew the nature of

194

Charles Greville too well to brook any delay for her. He made her promise that she would continue her treatment when next the opportunity arose, and that she would do what she could to come to his side. Now, in the fullness of her own bountiful spirit, she agreed. She would make excuses to Greville, for George Romney had the primary call upon her and was indeed a good friend.

They kissed farewell, and as she crossed the hall she saw John Widney arriving into the house.

"So you kept your promise, Emma?"

"I kept my promise, and you will find that the patient is much improved; he is eating; he tells me it is the first time for many a long day."

"That is good news!" He slipped aside his cloak and would have passed her, then, seeing that she was about to leave, paused and said, "You will not leave him, surely? He will want to see you again?"

"I shall return," she said, "and there I will keep my word. Be assured about that. I shall come back and do what I can for him. I was deeply shocked to see him so distressed, but you must see him, he is wonderfully better now."

She went out to the street, with the first amethyst of evening cloaking it, and the flower scent quickened, and the echo of runners and horses' hoofs sharpened.

As she turned into the house at Paddington Green she realized, with something of a pang, that Charles Greville had not yet returned home.

XXXVIII

CHARLES GREVILLE had made up his mind that he must rescue himself from this embarrassing position. Although Emma delighted him, and he knew that others envied him his good fortune in having won so fair a charmer, he disliked the fact that she had managed his affairs, and had dismissed Sir Leonard with such ability. He disliked the wagering debts mounting up in the way they were doing, and putting him in such an ungentlemanly quandary.

Conscience stirred in his breast; a prudish conscience that resented the fact that he could not dispose of riches. A wife with a fortune would be the most pleasant way out of this dilemma, and he had been attracted to the beautiful Miss Middleton, and believed that she felt the same for him.

Charles Greville, sinister and forbidding as he might be, had a charm for women. Although he would not have admitted it, he had had several mistresses, and could treat them as he would. He was something of a social hero with women, though men disliked him.

All night he had laid awake, disturbed, and now he was determined to go down into Hertfordshire, where the Middletons lived, and there to ask Lord Middleton for the hand of his daughter.

He dressed with infinite care, powdering and perfuming himself, and wearing the handsome new silk suit, with the Dark Major wig, that was so becoming and jaunty. He took the long drive, and turning in at the country house appreciated the neat lodges beside the gates, the well-kept park lands, and the lakes spread like milk before the great house with its rectangular windows. Lord Middleton had no son. An idea formed itself in Greville's mind that perhaps he could so ingratiate himself in his lordship's good books that, as a son-in-law, he could gain management of the estates, and subsequently ownership of this excellent house.

He had, however, chosen an unfortunate moment in which to approach the old gentleman. Recently Lord Middleton had suffered a severe attack of gout, which was exceedingly painful. He knew perfectly well that his daughter was something of a *partie*; she had this redoubtable fortune from a maternal aunt, a spinster of a jaundiced complexion, who had been godmother to the child. The moment that Charles Greville was announced, the old man had a good idea why he had come. London gossiped. It knew that Charles Greville was reckless at wagering, and that, although his uncle, the ambassador from Naples, did occasionally come forward and pay up the debts, recently Sir William Hamilton had grown a little tired of a routine that was becoming over frequent. Also London discussed his relationship with Emma Hart. It was not that Lord Middleton was prudish; he knew that all gentlemen cultivated mistresses which were the proper mode of living, but Emma Hart had been discussed too openly. Her beauty was something more than usual, and Greville took her about with him almost as though she were his wife. She had in fact been introduced to the youngest daughter, which was hardly in the best of taste.

Greville entered entirely confident of himself. He was not one of the type to be modest or shy. He had come on a laudable mission and expected to be received graciously.

At first there was a mere exchange of compliments, and during the opening feints, Charles had time to absorb the surprising beauty of the room and the furniture, and to comment that probably, when the old man died, the daughter would inherit even more, which was a pleasant thought.

He approached the subject upon which he had called. He was complimentary and gracious. He had marked the young lady and wished permission to present his compliments to her.

"You want to press your suit?" asked Lord Middleton.

"If I have your lordship's permission?" said Charles, with a flourish.

"My daughter has a considerable fortune?" said the old man with some craftiness, and he eyed Greville from behind the over-laced handkerchief.

There was a moment's silence, then Greville said that he had heard of such a rumour, capping it with the assurance that it was the lady's beauty and modesty of demeanour that had attracted him.

It was one of those days when Lord Middleton felt that he could tolerate little more. He said that he had no wish to influence his daughter's choice, he was not a stern father, but he would be very disappointed in her choice if she looked to one of the Warwicks for a husband. He said it quite plainly.

There was a moment's agitation. Charles stiffened visibly. He descended into an argument; it was an argument in which he was bound to be worsted. Lord Middleton referred to his wagering debts, to his present mode of living, and to innumerable points that had come to his notice. His daughter was free to choose for herself, but he had faith enough in her discernment to believe that she would never become his wife.

Greville rose, pale and furious. He did not believe that the matter was at an end, for he intended to appeal to the young lady's generosity. He could manage women, and he did not see why he should fail with this particular one.

"I bid you good day," he said, bowing stiffly.

It meant, of course, that he would never inherit the house or the grounds he coveted. It meant that he would only estrange the daughter of the house from her father, but this he was determined to do. Antagonism acted as a barb to his desire. He went across the hall in a white hot fury of rage. He asked if the young lady were at home, and was told—most unreassuringly—that she had gone to the races with the second son of the Duke of Devonshire.

Paler and still more angry, he got into his chaise to return. He sat there fuming. But he refused to be daunted. As far as he was concerned it was not over; he would not be foiled so easily.

Half-way they stayed at a tavern. The landlord was a hoary old buffer who whispered of a cock-fight in progress behind the tavern. Charles, in one of his grimmest moods, went out to join in the amusement. It was a stable lads' fight. The place stunk of beer and straw and mulch, and of the sweatiness of human bodies as they grouped round the gallant little fighting-cocks. But the fun was fast and furious, and the betting strong. Several country squires had ridden over, for the tavern was famous, and Charles stayed here until sundown, winning on almost every bet. His purse and pockets were full.

He went into the tavern itself after, to drink with the others, and they were indeed merry. He drank heavily because to-night he had much to forget. He lurched to the chaise much later, when the night was descending in a dark pall, a starless, breathless night, fetid with summer heat, and even the trees grown still, significant of thunder.

He was very drunk.

As the chaise rollicked towards London, rolling from side to side on its springless frame, he belched uncomfortably. His hand went to his pockets; at least the day had been profitable. The pockets seemed strangely flat. Sobered a little he felt again, thrusting his hands down into the capaciousness, but meeting nothing at all. Again and again he felt, believing that in his drunken stupidity he had made a mistake, then he recalled dimly, as through a haze, the foxy-faced stable lad who had primed his glass for him, and had in the end supported him to the chaise. He remembered somebody laughing, and the foxy-faced one (the owner of two gallant cocks) almost lifting him into the chaise. He had been too drunk to be aware that the sharp, furtive hands of the stable boy had not been wholly well-intentioned. That, although they hoisted his body into the chaise, they cleared his pockets at one and the same time.

Anguished and indignant, he vomited violently.

When he arrived at Paddington Green his head ached horribly, as though a chasm yawned and closed, and yawned and closed yet again. He did not know how he got to the door, nor was admitted. How he went to the bottom of the staircase, and clung to the balustrade of wrought iron. Then it seemed that an angel came to him.

A woman's kindly arms helped him to his room and took his clothes away, and laid sweet-smelling bandages upon his aching head. He was aware of her proximity, aware that he murmured stupid and meaningless nothings.

"Never leave me, Emma."

And she—too thankful for this change of mood— clung to him and promised fidelity.

She sat beside him holding his hand until he fell asleep, and when he woke next morning she was still there, with clear, cold water for him to drink and more bandages for that head.

He was a little ashamed.

As he lay there he told her something of what had happened at the cock-fight, but not a word about Lord Middleton's. And she, putting the pieces together, was only too well aware of the fact that he had never gone to the city, for how could he have been in the city and yet find himself in Hertfordshire, cock-fighting at some low tavern? But she was too wise to air her doubts. She merely ministered to him, and eased his pain, so that by midday he was able to come out into the garden with her, and sit in the pleasant tree shade, paler and rather wan, but recovering from a dreadful day.

He said, "You must forgive me, my sweet Emma."

"Perhaps you and I have much to excuse in one another. But rest assured of one thing, that, whatever happens to you, I am always here to love you, and that you will always shine foremost in my heart."

"I do believe you," he admitted.

She decided that she would not mention Romney to him again. That would only serve to rekindle the dissention between them, and if the bickering were to continue she did not think that she could bear it. The whole thing must pass, and be forgotten.

"Is there no reward that I can give you?" he asked.

She thought of the child, and the elderberry wine at Grandmother Kidd's. Yesterday with the sweet creamy scent of the flowers in the rural hedgerows round Cavendish Square, she had been reminded poignantly of her own youth. She put her arms about him.

"There is my child," she whispered.

He did not stiffen visibly as she had anticipated. For a moment he said nothing, then very quietly, "We will have to think what we can do about her," was his answer.

"Charles, it would give me infinite pleasure . . ."

"Just for the moment, I doubt if it would be feasible. Sir William Hamilton is coming here."

"From Naples?"

"Yes. It would not do for him to find a child with us."

"But after he has gone?" she begged.

"After he has gone, there are many things that we will do," he promised her, "and then it may be Emily's right to be here."

She lifted her ecstatic face. "Oh, Greville, how good you are to me!" she sobbed with joy.

XXXIX

NEWS CAME from the Court of Naples that the Ambassador to His Britannic Majesty King George the Third would be returning to London on a short visit. Charles Greville, when he received the news, was elated.

"My uncle must stay here," he said. "I consider that it would be most unwise to permit him to go elsewhere, for it is urgent that he and I should remain as the best of friends."

"But will it not be a trifle difficult to explain my position?"

Charles looked at her coldly. Although he liked to think of her as a modest violet, he was at times angered at the thought that she knew so little of the behaviour of gentlemen in high position. "Naturally my uncle would not expect me to live as a monk. He is a man of the world, and he is accustomed to the ways of that world. But we have to put on a brave show for him as he is used to court life."

"But surely he cannot expect the same splendour in Paddington Green?" she asked, and laughed at the idea.

Greville was unamused. He had no sense of humour and saw nothing funny in a remark that derogated from rank, because he was peculiarly snobbish.

"At times, Emma, you annoy me. You have to remember how important it is that I should keep in my uncle's favour, because I am his heir. At his age he is unlikely to re-marry, and he has money to leave. I am unfortunately placed financially; it is a constant source of apprehension to me," and he glanced significantly at her ill-written accounts lying beside his desk. "I must help myself towards a more desirable end. It is not a matter for mirth and has never been considered as anything in the nature of a joke by my family."

"I am sorry. I did not mean to vex you. Oh, Charles, how is it that I—with only the desire to please—do so constantly irritate you?" and she looked at him in dismay.

"Your mother will make her best dishes for Sir William?"

"Naturally, dear Greville."

"And you will wear your prettiest frocks and be your most charming, you understand that? I insist that you shall be your most charming to my revered uncle."

"I will, indeed I will."

"I have a special reason for asking it."

"You have but to command me," and she busied herself to see that the home should be prepared and everything set in order for the important visitor now expected.

What she was not to know was that after these first few years together, Charles was beginning to tire. At first he had intended to wed her; to educate her and wed her, but, having seduced her, he had come to the conclusion that no gentleman marries a common woman, so he had abandoned that project. He had been happy with her for a time, but was a pervert who could never settle. Now, after the affair at Ranelagh which had affronted his dignity, he was searching for a means by which to rid himself of her.

Charles Greville did not intend to desert her, or to do anything that would lay the lady of his affections, and his personal conduct, open to criticism. Already George Romney had made the lovely Emma a famous character, and Greville realized that people discussed her. When she drove out, heads were turned to look after her, and she certainly had her following.

If he deserted her, he knew she would speak of it,

for she was very deeply in love with him, and this Charles Greville realized. He was searching about him for some plan whereby he could rid himself of an incubus, and yet do this "respectably."

Greville was a disappointed man; he hated being so limited for money, and, the great Pitt having entered on his long reign, Greville saw the red flag of danger ahead of him. He contemplated the project of marrying an heiress, if heiress he could find, though he knew that after his devoted Emma, it would be difficult to find a charmer so obliging. Also, in his heart, he was aware of the fact that an heiress might take exception to his "treasures" should she discover them, and might also be averse to the means of correction that he employed. Emma had come to accept Greville's strange ways as part and parcel of her life with him, and, because to her he had no fault, she did not dispute them.

"At times you hurt me severely," she once told him, but there were always those passionately sweet moments when he forgave her and, lifting her in his arms, blessed her. Whilst he "acted so warmly" towards her, she could not believe that in his heart he was contemplating ridding himself of her. However, George Romney warned her.

"Alas, dear Emma, do not trust your Charles too far. I have told you he is a strange personality, and I would not have you hurt by him."

"Why should you say such things? Charles has been goodness itself to me, and I would die without him."

"He was getting a reward."

She flashed on Romney, indignant that he should think basely of one she loved so well. "He has paid for little Emily's schooling."

"If he loved you, he would have the child at Paddington Green with you. Do you think that I would deny a mother her child?"

"But when the child was born out of wedlock? And is its mother's shame?"

"To me it would still be her child."

She looked down from the throne to where he stood painting her; the sunlight was falling on his head, flung back as he watched her; his finely intelligent eyes, his large mouth and rumpled hair, all had an attraction of their own. Sometimes she laughed at him, for she always vowed that he could never do good work unless his hair was rumpled.

"Charles is the most considerate of men to me."

"Sweet Emma, you know that isn't true. You cannot believe it, or has love blinded you to his failings?"

"Love is an enchanter."

"But the awakening may be cruel." He flung down his palette and brushes, and came to her reclining on the throne. "I care for you, my sweet, I want you to be happy, because anybody so beautiful and so vigorously alive deserves to be happy. I fear for you with Greville, and I tell you quite frankly that I do not trust him."

"If you want me to stay your friend, you will never say such a thing again."

"Then I will not speak another word, but I promise you that if ever you should want a friend you have but to command me."

"You have been goodness itself," and she melted in his generosity.

After all, if Romney had not helped her to find the cottage in Portland Place, she would never have been able to win her Charles, and she owed him a debt. She got up, drawing on her delicate gloves, and wrapping her cloak round her. All the while she knew that Romney watched her, his throat working, but he did not speak.

"Is—is this the final sitting?" she faltered at last.

"Would you like to see the picture?"

"Indeed I should."

He drew the cloth back from it, and she saw the portrait of a woman who was looking at a tragedy— her own tragedy—with such tremendous sorrow and amazement in her eyes as to be almost unbelievable. Silently she contemplated it, then turned to him.

"What have you done to me, George?"

"It is you as I saw you, for an artist can only paint what he sees."

"But there is such pain in those eyes . . ."

"If I could only prevent that pain for you? But I see ahead, sorrow, joy, rapture and despair in the strangest mingling of all adventures."

"You sound like the prophetic sea captain."

"Who was he?"

She told him laughingly about it. The queen in a golden crown and a city made of pearl, laced about with the sea. A great hero who would come to her, and emblazon her name across the world. She was surprised that he did not laugh at so fantastic a story, but he listened, his eyes devouring her.

"But—George, this does not seem to amuse you?"

"No, Emma, it does not amuse me, because it is the truth. That is the life written for you in the stars. You will go far, but I doubt if anyone will appreciate you for the goodness in your heart, the fidelity that your very actions deny, and the stupendous courage with which you face life."

"Alas, I am not brave, dear George, but thank you for thinking so pleasantly of me. I have appreciated the one staunch friendship."

He caught her to him in ecstasy. "I think you are the bravest woman that I have ever met," he told her.

XL

THERE WAS a stir about the house in Paddington Green on the day when Sir William Hamilton was expected. Charles was now very nervous. Emma appreciated how he felt and did her best to see that matters should run smoothly, but Sir William arrived sooner than had been anticipated.

Greville was still at St. Stephen's, where a debate was in progress, and he had fondly believed that his uncle would not be with them until the afternoon, so did not hurry. Emma heard the chaise draw up, and when the maid came to her was in the garden picking an elaborate posy which she had intended putting as a centrepiece on the table. Her hands were full of oxslips and anemones, the small grape hyacinths which grew so plentifully here, and some of the blossom with which every apple tree was so vigorously splashed in pink-tipped pearl. She wore her morning frock, her favourite grey cashmere tied with lavender ribbons, and a little apron to preserve the frock from the sticky flower stems.

"It cannot be Sir William?" she exclaimed, alarmed at having been caught unawares.

Sir William had followed the maid out into the garden itself, and turning, Emma saw him coming towards her. He was not very tall, of a stoutish build, though not preposterously so. He wore a short brocade coat in a deep shade of purple which was her favourite colour, and it was richly braided with amber silk. In that one look she noted that the buttons were made of the new gold, for which Mr. Pinchbeck had made himself famous and which only the fops and aristocrats yet wore.

"Oh, sir!" she said, and curtseyed deeply.

After the splendour of the Sicilian court, no scene could have been more entrancing than this, with the girl in her simple dress, her hands full of flowers, and Sir William was enchanted.

"You must be the lovely Emma of whom my nephew has written. What a sly dog not to have emphasized your beauty! I had no idea that it would be so rare."

"You flatter me, good sir, and we did not expect

207

that you would be with us until the afternoon, for Charles is still at St. Stephen's."

"Then we shall have a chance to get to know one another."

She felt that he had a kindly face and a most charming air, and she knew immediately that here was somebody whom she could trust. He offered her his arm and they walked towards the house so that she could offer him some refreshment. Within the next quarter of an hour they were sitting in the parlour, Emma reclining on the slender couch with its striped silk covering, whilst Sir William feasted his eyes upon her.

"You must have made my nephew very happy."

"I have done what I could"—she clasped her hands on the bosom that was swelling a little, for passion develops beauty—"I love him so much, Sir William. I cannot help it. I suppose women are weak when they are in love, and Charles is everything to me."

"He is a very lucky man. I hope that he appreciates his good fortune."

"Or is it that Emma is lucky to have attracted anyone so exquisite as Charles Greville?"

"You are a modest young woman."

"I come from the country, Sir William. I am not of London, and have none of the airs and graces of city ladies."

"If you will pardon my saying it, you have not only a rare beauty, but a natural charm of your own. If I am to stay with so fair a tea-maker, then do not be austere and do not call me Sir William."

"But, sir, what should I call you?"

"I am, in some ways, your uncle."

"Then I will call you Uncle."

"That being so, is it not permissible that the uncle may kiss a new niece?"

She extended her hand with a courtly gesture, but Sir William caught it, and going closer, stooped to kiss her cheek. He was prodigiously pleased with her.

When Charles Greville returned from St. Stephen's it was to find his uncle already installed and Emma completely at ease with the older man. He had won her confidence. But the thing that was worrying her under it all was that she could not understand how he had brought himself to send Greville those "treasures" which pandered so vilely to the worst side of him. That was a constant thorn in her heart. She left the two men closeted together in Charles's study and went out into the garden sweet with twilight. About it was the moist scent of springtime ditches full with April rain; of bursting leaves and dew-drenched blossom. She busied herself with the flowers, then, aware that she was being watched, lifted her eyes to behold John Newman standing on the other side of the hedge.

"John, what are you doing here?"

"I came, sweet Emma, because I had to. Oh, I pray you will let me speak to you?"

"What has happened?"

"The doctor is ill. He lectured, and had a seizure during the speech. Now he is lying sick unto death in Schomberg House, and when he could speak he asked for you."

The thought disturbed her, and touched her compassion. She threw discretion to the winds as she tore off her apron. "Of course I will come. Let me fetch a cloak and tell them that I shall be away for a while. You have a chaise here?"

"Yes, but you must hurry. Already his lamps are dimming," he urged her.

Never for a moment did the girl delay, but ran indoors, and brought down a hooded cloak. She rapped on the door of Greville's study, explaining that the doctor had been taken ill and that she must go to him. Greville came out to her, his brows knitted.

"But it is your guest's first night here! Surely you would do nothing of the kind?"

"When you were ill, Greville, the doctor came to

you. I shall always vow that he saved your life by what he did, and now he is dying and has asked for me. You would not have your Emma refuse a dying man?"

She saw Sir William standing behind his nephew, and knew by Charles's scowl that already he was very angry with her. "But an honoured guest is here. It would be unseemly to go."

"Death, dear Charles, takes no nay."

It was Sir William who interposed. "I admire the generosity of so warm a heart. You, Charles, are wrong, and she should go to this doctor. I am staying some time, and, although you will insist that I am a guest, I am no guest in that sense of the word, for am I not one of the family?"

Without more ado Emma fled down the garden, where John Newman, impatient at waiting, bundled her into the chaise, and they started post haste for Schomberg House. For a while she did not speak. The road was bumpy and full of pot-holes, and the chaise entirely springless, so that they were buffeted about, and had to hold on to their places. Then she listened to what John had to tell her. The doctor's overwork had produced this; he was eager to get added attractions to Schomberg House, and his audiences had been failing him recently. Even the Celestial Bed had ceased to attract as once it had done, for it had not fulfilled the gifts claimed for it. The old man had been embarking on a new series of quite original ideas, and had spent the small hours poring over plans, with the result that he had done too much.

They came to the house itself, and now the evening had fallen darkly over London. Upstairs in the gaunt room, the little doctor lay breathing stertorously. Beyond the shut window, which closed in the frowsty smell of body and stale clothes and bad air, lay London bathed in amethyst and warm with the lateness of an April night.

"I am here, dear, kind friend," whispered Emma,

and knelt down beside him, trying to take the stiffened form into her young arms. The old man turned, his eyes dim, and raising a hand attempted to stroke her.

"I knew my Emma would come."

He lay in her arms for half an hour, without ever saying a word, and died with his head against her shoulder; it was Emma who, murmuring a prayer, closed his eyes and gently laid him down. Now she was weeping.

"I have lost a true friend, and one whom I could trust," she said as she allowed John to lead her from the room.

"He worked too hard. In many ways he was a fanatic, but he believed in what he preached," and then, "Shall I take you back to Paddington Green?"

She shook her head. "Let me drive alone, for I am not afraid of footpads and such. I have nothing of which they might rob me, save that which a man took years ago."

Without an answer he pressed her hand in his own. He too longed to love her, but knew that now she was irrevocably sealed to Greville. He put her into the chaise for her return alone, her eyes still wet with tears. And, as the bumpy journey to Paddington Green began, she thought with chagrin of what lay ahead, for her Greville would be furiously angry that she should have left and would undoubtedly exact punishment. Now she began to weep for herself.

XLI

SIR WILLIAM had talked to Greville, and the strange thing was that when she returned he was not angered with his Emma. He received her so tenderly that she could not understand what might have happened. Was it that she had a kind friend in her new uncle? She believed that to be true, so set herself out to repay by pleasing him. She called him "Pliny the elder," and Greville watched her under lowered lids as they played together, for his plan was working. He himself now decided that he would have to marry an heiress whose fortune would stabilize his rickety financial position. His bills had been pressing down on him, though naturally he said nothing to his uncle of this. He did, however, mention his idea of marriage.

"But what would happen to the little tea-maker?" enquired Sir William. The conversation took place in Greville's study, with the first roses already budding about the windows and the rooks making their pleasant cawing in the high trees beyond. "If you marry, my dear Charles, it means that the lovely Emma would be forced to go somewhere else." The old man was anxious for the girl who had made such a great impression on him.

"There are other men."

"Would that I had the good fortune to win so fair a charmer! I have been lonely in Naples since your aunt died, and life has lost much of its joys. A girl with Emma's personality could make life very delightful for an ageing man."

This was the chance that Greville had been hoping for, and he could not believe that it had come about so easily. "Perhaps, dear Uncle, we could make some convenient arrangement."

"Surely you would not entertain an idea of that kind?"

"I would do much to please a favourite uncle. Emma has never travelled abroad, and the thought should charm her, I am sure."

"But how could we persuade her?"

Greville smiled that enigmatical smile of his. "I think it would be possible to get her to see you on the pretext of a visit. Under the circumstances, probably it would be wisdom to send her mother with her."

"But the adorable creature loves you. She loves you passionately, and would never consent to being parted from you."

"That I admit, but supposing we could tell her that for the moment it was not expedient for me to leave London, that she was going to Naples for a visit only, and that after a month or so I would sail to fetch her back. Then I think it would be quite a different story."

Sir William was not sure whether he admired the strategy or loathed his nephew for devising it. "But it would be deceiving a very pretty creature."

"If you will listen to me, dear Uncle, you will appreciate that pretty creatures are made for deception. You desire her, and I have no further use for her. It is in her own interest that she should come out to you on a visit, and I vow that she will give you the same ecstatic pleasure that she has given me."

But the older man was not so sure. "I am uncertain that the lady would be amenable."

"Ladies are amenable if the proposition is bright enough. Emma shall come to you for three months, it would be some kind of a test—forgive my frankness—and if you found her charming, as indeed she is, then she could stay awhile. I can assure you, my dear Uncle, I have no fault to find with her save that financially I am in need."

His uncle promised to reimburse him for parting with so artless a creature, and the matter was discussed as coldly as though Emma had been a parcel from the grocer's. It was a bargain, and neither of the men pretended otherwise. For, with Emma gone, Greville hoped to attract the youngest Middleton daughter, and saw for himself a more stable future in which he would not be haunted by the bogey of most ungentlemanly poverty.

"But remember, unless Emma feels the visit to be one of innocent pleasure, she will refuse," he warned his uncle.

"I agree. One would not attempt to force so sweet a lady."

"I would suggest that it is told her that she can have lessons in art and music in Naples. Emma delights in such things, and probably would attract some Italian painter to immortalize her. The whole idea must be that, in October, I would come to fetch her home again."

"And that she will think that absence makes the heart grow fonder," and the two gentlemen called for more wine, and drank to the very excellent bargain that they had made.

It occurred to neither of them, and certainly least of all to Greville, that they were behaving abominably. Emma was not virtuous, and therefore could be sold from man to man, whoever desired to possess her. Willet-Payne had dispatched her to Sir Harry with no qualms; Sir Harry, an irresponsible buck, had not even troubled to make any arrangements for her future, and would probably have excused himself from any responsibility by explaining that she was "with child by another at the time." Greville had been finicky about possessing her whilst she still lived under the protection of another, yet showed no such exemplary principles when it came to passing her on to his uncle.

Meanwhile the innocent Emma was completely unaware of any plans being made on her behalf. She entertained Pliny the elder, petting him childishly, and fondling him artlessly as she had been instructed, believing that she did all this to better dear Greville's financial position. When Sir William left he made some suggestion of a visit, but this she did not take seriously. It was much later that Greville mentioned it, and she realized for the first time that he actually meant it.

"But I could not live without you, Charles!"

"It would be but for a few months and you would benefit enormously. You could learn Italian, your

214

music would be improved, and you would sit for great painters there."

— "Naturally I should enjoy it, save that I can enjoy nothing without my dear Greville being at my side."

"I would fetch you back in a few months. Your mother would be with you. No breath of scandal should touch you," for Greville was a stickler for breaths of scandal not touching those with whom he was concerned, even though he himself was nothing more or less than an underhand seducer.

"Do you want me to go?"

"I take it to be the most generous offer on my uncle's part, and I much desire it."

"But, Charles, away from you . . ." She was frankly puzzled by the suggestion.

"How often have you said that my wishes were your commands?"

"But to send me from you? No, that could not be."

He was displeased, sulking all day, and now she realized that she had hurt him, and wept pitifully. Finally, on her mother's advice, she capitulated, and went to him, kneeling at his feet and begging forgiveness. Before he would kiss her he dictated the letter that the girl wrote to Sir William.

Emboldened by your kindness to me I would most joyfully accept. Greville, whom you know I love tenderly, is obliged to go for four or five months in the summer to places where I cannot with propriety attend him to. I would indead be glad to be a little more improv'd and dear Charles has out of kindness offered to dispense with me for a few months at the close of which time he will come to fetch me home. I would indead be flattered to be allotted an apartment in your house, and if you will also lett Greville occupy those apartments when he comes. I have full confidence in your kindness and attention to me.

She never thought that in writing this letter she was complying with her own dismissal, which was what it really meant. The holiday was postponed until the early spring of the next year, owing to illness, but the day came when she finished her last lesson in the house at Paddington Green, and passed the door that was locked on the "treasures"—it had always given her a queasy feeling of distaste—and when for a time London was to know her no more.

"Oh, Greville," she implored before she set sail with her mother in the *Veturine,* "the hours will crawl without you."

"For me also," he lied, "but duty must be done."

He was the richer by some thousands as he kissed her on the quayside and entrusted her to the boat that was to row her out. Her eyes were blinded with tears as they rowed away, and she did not see the last outline of her handsome Greville, whom she was to love for the rest of her life. She wept like a little child on her mother's shoulder.

XLII

EMMA HAD never boarded a ship before. She stepped on to the deck, a sharp wind blowing, whipping the water so that already it wore white ruffles, and she could hear the masts creaking as though with some memory of the trees they once had been. The ship rose and fell beneath her, but she was entirely unafraid. A man met her at the gangway, looking at her thoughtfully. He wore the blue jacket of a ship's officer; his face, bronzed and bearded, stirred her memory so that she stopped. "You—you once brought me a packet from Naples?" she said.

"I did. And now you are going to Naples as I said."

"Surely you do not remember?"

Her mother, her shawl blown about her by the wind, was agitated beside Emma, and the catpain, seeing it, called to a passing boy who held a lantern in his hand. "Show the lady to her cabin," he said, indicating Mrs. Duggan, and to Emma, "You shall come to mine. I have things to tell you."

He helped her down the vertical ladder into the darkness that lay below decks. He could not stand upright, she noticed, and about it there was the strong salt smell of wood that has been drenched in sea water, and the whining noise of live animals in the hold, where they would await slaughter as required. The thought horrified her. The queasy tang of oil lamps permeated everything. They went into his cabin, so small as to be hardly true. It was accommodated with but the barest necessities for living, and stirred her imagination as many a sumptuous chamber had failed to do. She could hear now the heavy splash of the waves recurring against the ship's sides.

"You don't feel sick?" he asked.

"No, should I?"

"It depends. I have the feeling you will not, for you are brave. Wine?"

"Thank you." She watched him as he poured it out and set it on the rough wooden table beside her, and she sat on the keg which served for a chair. Beyond lay his bunk, thin as a coffin, and furnished with a coarse, dark blanket and a hard little pillow that gave her the creeps.

"It's a small world," she said.

"Not so small, really. I felt that you would come here; even when I was talking to you in the house on Paddington Green I could see you here. You will go far."

"I am going to Naples."

"To the Queen of Naples?"

217

"Possibly. My husband's uncle is the Ambassador there, and I am going to stay with him."

"And your husband?"

"He will be visiting his uncle, and in a few months will fetch me back." She radiated as she spoke of her beloved Greville. The man watched her admiringly, but at the same time was convinced that none of this would happen as she anticipated. "I am so very happy," she told him.

"Stay happy. I hope you will have a satisfactory and comfortable journey, and love Naples. It is for a long time."

"No, only for a few months."

"I know that it is for a long time," he said.

Now she could feel the ship stirring resolutely beneath her, and knew that the west was darkening and they were putting out to sea with the full tide. The man beside her watched, giving no indication of his inner feelings, but he was not thinking of the putting out to sea, for he had been doing it all his life. This, to him, was the high tide of his life. He reached out a hand callused with work and laid it on hers. She did not sweep it aside, but looked at him questioningly, her eyes dark pools of enquiry, and little more.

"Ships come and go," he said. "They pass one another in and out of the harbours. They are storm-beset and tossed. When I saw you that day when we first met, I knew we should meet again in this cabin with a journey before you, and myself standing at the cross-roads of your life."

"But you have it wrong, my kind sir. This is no cross-roads in my life, for I go to pay my respects to a kind uncle; no more."

He held her hand in a compelling clasp and, fascinated by the lantern which hung from the deck above, stinking of oil, she watched it as it swung to and fro with every movement of the ship. The vessel lurched as she had seen the plough roll across the heavy fields at Hawarden; there the blade had plunged down into the earth, guided by the ploughman who steered apparently so clumsily. It was strange that she should never have thought before of a ship being like a plough, rising and falling, and for ever pressing forward. She was suddenly aware of the intentness of this man's eyes, of his proximity to her, and the smell of rum that lingered about him.

Afraid of his intentions, she said, "I have a husband," but her voice was low and vibrant, and not wholly convincing.

"You have no husband," he answered. "It is your lover who is behind you in England, and you are going to meet a fate far greater than you imagine. But for the moment you might call a halt with life, because you have me."

He drew her into his arms, his enormous height bending over her, and she knew that he was crushing her face against his harshly bearded one. It was extraordinary that she should be so afraid, yet not of him but of what lay ahead. She wondered if she could escape, and when he released her, slipped with her back to the wooden bulkhead and stood panting, her arms outstretched against it as one crucified.

"Indeed, sir, but you do me wrong. I love Charles. There is no one who would make me unfaithful to him."

"He is not faithful to you."

"That is untrue."

"I could prove it to you."

She shook her head. "Do not imagine that because you are a sailor you know everything, but you are imagining this."

"Yet I told you you would come to Naples."

"That may be true, guessing is a lucky game, but you may not be so fortunate in your next guess."

"You will see, sweet lady, for I know truth when I meet it."

A quick and demanding fire burnt in him, and she knew that she would have to think and act rapidly; there had been a time when she would not have troubled had he availed himself of her, but now with her immense love for Greville she could not lie lightly with any who asked it.

"I pray you, sir, you must not molest me."

"I thought a man could take when he desired?"

"Not if it is not freely given."

They stared at one another, the lantern swinging between them. This way, that way, as with the pulse of the ship. The sound of the water became all the more insistent, and the groaning of the ship was like that of some pain-filled body that has to express its agony, for now every timber complained as the prow lifted to the tide.

There was a knock at the door.

It opened to admit a youngish boy, with light flaxen hair that caught the light, a freshly alert face in which the eyes were blue as road flints. He had a message for the captain, and stood to offer it. He did not see Emma. Looking at him she knew that, had little Emily been a son, this was the son she would have yearned to suckle, and she slipped past him to the door. The narrow alleyway beyond echoed with the creaking, and there came up to her the strange, sweaty scents mingled in a sickly fashion so that they were nauseating. She clawed her way up the ladder to the deck again, and now she saw that the stars had come out, and the disturbed water was lit as with silver flutings on its ruffles.

A figurehead leaned forth across that water stretching out from the ship, and Emma knew that it was a madonna with a blue painted veil about her golden hair, her eyes for ever turned to the sky, her hands clasped pensively upon a full breast as though in prayer. With the wind stirring her dress Emma clung to a mast and watched. She clung because she was afraid, lest the plunging of the ship might cause her to slip, yet at the same time she was not afraid, only exhilarated by it. This was her place, she recognized it in every passion within her, this was her destiny, with the salty tang on her lips and in her throat and the ship rising beneath her.

She could see the grey outline of the coast of England with the chains of lighted houses like ghosts along the cliffs. She could see above her the panorama of the sky with the galaxy of stars. She was going out to meet adventure, and she knew that the sea captain had been right. She stood here with the spume and spray rising and splashing vigorously the wooden decks, and she wondered what else he had seen for her. Not happiness, his manner had conveyed that. She had known much pain already; hardhearted men who having drunk avidly of the full fountain of her body had sated themselves and turned away. But Greville would not be like that, she told herself. She was only going to Italy to perfect herself for him, to learn more art, to practise her music and to speak Italian. And perhaps when complete she would marry him.

The dream—a happy one—lingered but for a moment in the hopeful ecstasy that was born with it, then drowned itself in that same joy. In her heart she knew that was the one thing she must not expect from him, that was the great solace that she would deny him. But, because she loved him, the fact that she was important to his happiness sufficed her, and she smiled tenderly to herself as she stood there, with the spray against her cheek.

XLIII

IT WAS on the twenty-sixth of April in the year of our Lord, 1786, that Emma reached Naples, and it happened to be her birthday. She was eager as a child to see Italy, and as yet quite ignorant of the true facts that her coming here had paid Greville's debts, and that Sir William had drawn up a will in his nephew's favour as part payment of the debt he owed for the bestowal of his fair tea-maker.

Sir William's *palazzo* at Naples was situated on the Piazza Flacone, and looked out on to the bay of Capri. Beyond were the mountains, vividly blue against the sky, and to the east was the foreboding figure of Vesuvius with the smoke rising grimly from its summit.

The garden was entered through a carved iron gate, and there were scarlet scabious and lilies gleaming together; it was wreathed with wistaria in profuse bunches, and surely, Emma felt, there had never been a more beautiful spot! Paddington Green had been simple, but this was rare. Sir William also was kindness itself both to her and to her mother.

"Indead," she wrote to Greville. "I should be greatly happy were it not for your absence. Wright some comfort to me."

But Greville was not writing. Now he wanted her to forget him, and only waited for the moment when Sir William should inform him that the contract had been completed and Emma was entirely his property.

Sir William was affectionate in his manner and overanxious to please, also alarmed at making a false step. He engaged the best masters for Emma; the most exquisite salon was put at her disposal. Every morning a spray of flowers was laid on her tray beside the hot chocolate. He took her out on enchanting visits, to the Blue Grotto, to Vesuvius, and to ruined Pompeii. But although she was childishly pleased, she prattled all the time of the day when her dearest Greville would come out to fetch her, and could be included in their trips.

Her first introduction to actual court life came on the night of the Ambassador's ball. It was impossible to keep the fair tea-maker of Edgware hidden for too long, and this was something in the nature of a début. She had a fashionable frock for it—Sir William's gift—a pale blue silk with waterfalls of cream cascaded lace and sprays of yellow tea roses.

"I'm so alarmed that I shall not behave properly," she told her mother privately. But Mrs. Duggan was not worried for her daughter.

"Such beauty as yours, Emy, will shine however you behave."

The ballroom was brilliantly lit by the huge crystal chandeliers, as though the room were crowned with diamonds. The musicians were completely hidden in a bower of pink spiraeas, red roses, and clove carnations, so that the atmosphere was idyllic. The company assembled awaited the moment when Their Majesties should appear, and Emma could hardly contain herself.

Presently the golden doors were flung open, and alone Sir William advanced into the space, bowing low. For the first time Emma caught sight of the royal pair whom fate intended should influence her life so much. King Ferdinand was leading his Queen by the hand. He was not a tall man, and he had a long, fat face with bulbous lips and rather somnolent eyes. He gave the impression of being top-heavy, by reason of the over-ornate wig that he wore. But his Queen, the plainer sister of Marie Antoinette, sparkled with jewels as she advanced towards the assembly.

As Emma curtseyed low, she knew that she was remembering the sea captain's prophecies. A queen in a crown. A great hero. Was it that the little tea-maker of Edgware was already embarking upon a royal adventure?

The King had not overlooked her beauty, and asked to be introduced, though he hastened to assure Sir William that he was not sure that his Queen would approve. As Emma was presented, some of the court ladies looked amazed, for although there had been no breath of scandal against Mrs. Hart, as she was called—was not her mother staying with her to chaperone her?—everybody secretly felt that she

223

might be a light-of-love, and only staying here to oblige Sir William.

"I have always heard that the English rose is the most beautiful flower in the world; now I know that to be true," said the King of the Sicilies as she curtseyed.

Other men looked admiringly at her. She knew that her star was rising and the world lay at her feet.

"The little tea-maker of Edgware is turning everyone's head," announced Sir William proudly, for within the moment every man raved about her. They eulogized his Emma, who looked like a madonna. A prince pleaded for permission to carry her shawl. Painters asked to paint her portrait. Any suspicion that she might be the mistress of Sir William faded out, because now Naples was devoted to her beauty.

But in his heart Sir William grew impatient, for the bargain had yet to be fulfilled. The prize had been delivered to his *palazzo,* and in return he had made the will in Greville's favour, and had paid the debts (they had amounted to more than he had anticipated). He was growing older. Although young men in the lustful hey-day of their springtime could afford to await physical favours, he could not, for his fires were burning low. Even Dr. Graham's love elixirs would not prolong for ever his powers of enjoyment.

One morning he sent for Emma, and she came to his room in the white frock and sash for which she was already famous, and the wide leghorn hat on her auburn hair.

"You wanted me, my dear Pliny?"

"It is time that we talked, my pretty one. You have been here for some few weeks."

"Indeed, it has been some of the happiest time in my life. I have only needed Greville's presence to make it heaven."

This was not the tone in which Sir William wished to conduct the argument. He drew her down to his side on the couch, and so they sat together. "You miss Charles much?"

"So much. You little know how deeply I love him."

"My sweet child, when you arrived here, you— you hoped that he would come out to fetch you home to Edgware in six months' time?"

"I did, and he will." So great was her faith in the unscrupulous Greville that she did not for a moment doubt it.

"I have news for you, my dear Emma, and I consider perhaps it would be kinder for me to be plain spoken. Charles will not come out here for you."

She turned her wide eyes to him; for a moment she did not believe that she could have heard aright. "But that cannot be true. He promised me that he would."

"He promised me that he would send you out to me, and that you would be mine." Sir William was a trifle irritated and was perhaps forcing the issue, but he was impatient for her. Too well aware of the approach of the autumn of his passion, he had to press her before it was too late.

"I'll not believe it."

"I paid his debts and settled a will in his favour. Greville is intending to marry, and it is both right and proper that a man in his position should marry . . ." Then he stopped dead.

Emma had arisen. She was a calm woman, hardly ever stirred by even a small petulance, but now she was in a passion, for every atom of colour had been drained from her face, her violet blue eyes were dark, as though consumed by physical agony, and she stood with her hands clenched.

"You mean that he sold me, and that you actually bought me? That when I came here you intended to make me your mistress, and I was sold as a man sells a commodity for which he has no further use?"

Sir William was dismayed. He put out a hand and took hers. "My dear, sweet Emma, do not feel so

225

resentful about it. It is a gentleman's bargain, and one that is made every day of the week. It is a very usual transaction."

"Then more shame on the gentlemen who stoop to make it. Never will I believe such a shocking thing! Never, though Greville himself swears it to me and on his knees. Neither will I believe that you, who loved and respected me—or so I thought—would want me as a mistress, even if I were willing to render such a service to you, which God forbid!"

This was a turn that Sir William had not anticipated. He was an honourable man, and very much disliked people plunging with such words and challenging his honour.

"My sweet Emma . . ."

But she would not listen. Frantically she turned from him, her face overwhelmingly distressed. "I do not know what to think, for here are two men whom I loved and who have connived against me. I will never believe it. Nothing in this world would make me faithless to my dear Greville, even though he deceive me a thousand times, and I will not agree for a single moment that he has deceived me. . . ."

"My poor child, your innocent trust lies with a man who knows not the meaning of honour."

But nothing that he could say would change her. Even though George Romney had frequently warned her that Greville was treacherous, she retained her faith in him, and finally rushing from Sir William's room, locked herself in her own salon and penned a frantic little letter to her lover.

I have had a conversation this morning with Sir William that has made me mad. He speaks—no, I do not know what to make of it. . . . Greville, you will never meet with anybody who has a truer affection for you than I have, and I only wish it was in my power to show you what I could do for you. . . . My heart is entirely broke. I have lived with you 5 years, and

226

you have sent me to a strange place, and no one prospect but thinking you was coming to me. Instead of which I was told . . . No, I respect him, but no, never . . . What is to become of me? But, excuse me, my heart is ful.

She dispatched her letter and then flew to her mother's arms. For three days the door of her room was locked and she lay as in a coma, staring dully out across the Bay that was perhaps the bluest in the world, and wondering if she could ever hope to be happy again.

She was stunned that the man she loved so profoundly could have played this trick upon her, for gradually it was borne down on her that it had been a trick, and she had been merely the pawn in the game.

"There must be some explanation; he must tell me what was in his mind," she insisted. Mrs. Duggan could offer little comfort. She had suspected Greville from the first, for when she had been a maidservant at Warwick Castle she had heard his own brothers speaking of him. "That snake of a brother of mine," Lord Brooke had called him. It was as a snake that she personally thought of him.

Twelve days later when his reply came to poor Emma, Mrs. Duggan had hardly the heart to bring it to her daughter, for she held so little hope of it being good tidings.

"At last, oh my dearest Greville, now this will explain all," gasped Emma, and the colour returned as she broke the wafer. But she read the message, her eyes dilating and her cheek paling. It did not bandy words.

"Oblige Sir William," it commanded.

XLIV

GREVILLE WAS in a singularly bad mood. He had had his debts paid, and he knew that the will had been made in his favour, but his advances—he had penned an elegant offer of his hand to the youngest daughter of Lord Middleton—had only brought back a curt refusal from the lady, who did not even trouble to be polite, for she "could not abide him." This had coincided with the fact that his political career was being blighted by the reign of Pitt, and now it seemed according to Emma's appeal to him that there was trouble arising in Naples. If Emma were difficult, his uncle might demand his money back, though, as Greville soliloquized sourly, "It is the old fool's fault if he cannot lure the girl into some happier arrangement with himself."

Emma's pathetic letters arrived, and for the main part were ignored; in truth he did not know how to answer them, for she was continually adoring, still refusing to admit the feet of clay. But on one point she remained adamant. She would not give Sir William that which Greville had sold so lightly to him.

In the salon overlooking the Bay of Naples, the old man, who was now somewhat confused, tried to argue.

"I would not force you, dearest and most lovely creature, but by right you are mine. You would not have cause to doubt my sincerity, and you would not find me faithless."

"But I could not forget my Greville."

"Let us not discuss it. Let me make you happy here, for everybody loves you and admires you and talks of nothing but the exquisite Emma. For a while let us put aside any other thought and be just true friends."

Unhappily she wept like a child upon his shoulder, and he was deeply stirred with pity for her. "Oh, Sir William, I am so dreadfully unhappy. Surely you realize what it is to love, and then to find that love denied you?"

"My poor child!"

But now, out of the unhappy, tear-stained Emma, the new, triumphant Emma was to be born. Sir William beguiled her with gaieties, hoping with these to turn her head. She met royalty and statesmen, she heard profound discussions, and became one of a glittering throng. She saw ahead of her that greater rôle which she might be destined to play. Now she was rapidly making headway with the Italian language, and in fact now and again Sir William allowed her to play hostess for him. If there was talk, it did not travel far, for her charms covered that. Universally beloved, people forgot that she had come abroad with perhaps other intentions, even though she might have been ignorant of them herself.

"Have you not noticed, Emy," said her mother joyfully, "that these days even the servants call you 'Excellenza'?"

"I know, and I wonder why?"

"You are not still fretting for . . . ?"

"I shall love him until I die," said the girl vehemently, and turned her face away. She would have forgone all the glory that was coming to her if she could have kept her Greville's love. Now there were King Ferdinand and his Queen; the court; Sir William holding her hand and smiling ardently; her attentions to him as she brewed his punch, and petted him in a daughterly manner, rather than as a light-of-love. She, who had been Greville's devoted slave, was now living in luxury, and yet felt that she had so little left.

So when Sir William came to her one night, she was amazed. The scent of the oleanders blown cream and pink in the piazza and of the orange blossoms was filling the room. She got up from her bed, virginal in her white gown, her hair tumbled about her shoulders.

"Who is there?" she asked.

Sir William came in holding high a golden sconce, the pale flame from the candle illuminating his sparse hair and kind but faded eyes. "My sweet, I am tired with waiting for you."

"Sir William!"

"Not Sir William to you, only Pliny. Your own dear Pliny."

She shrank back to the edge of the little bed that he had ordered to be specially made for her. There were silver stars spangling the blue curtains, and through the uncurtained windows came the incense of the flowers. Down the street a Neapolitan plucked at a guitar as he sang a love song to some girl.

"You—you should not have come here," she said at last, and her mouth had gone quite dry. She was thinking of Greville; of how she had lain locked in his arms, his head cradled against her breast.

"I have long wanted to find the way to your room," he said, and set the sconce down on the bowed chest beside the door.

She rose then, looking strangely tall in the frothy white folds of her gown; she lifted a lace scarf and wrapped it round herself and over her hair, so that she gave the impression of being a nun, a novice not yet entirely avowed to eternal chastity, but trembling on the brink. Looking at her he realized that he had never seen her so disturbingly beautiful.

"The way to my room," she said, "lies not through that door, but through the church porch."

For the first time the thought cannoned into his mind, and he could feel his mouth dropping. Now he doubted his nephew. Had Greville really lived with this sweetly modest creature who stood pointing to the church across the street, silhouetted with its single breast of a dome against the starry sky? Had he

taken an unwarrantable liberty in daring to suggest
the warm and tender alliance that wears no ring?

"But, Emma . . . ?"

"Oh, no," she said, "you have misunderstood. I
have the warmest regard for you, the fondest affection, but there is nothing of this nature in what I feel,
and there never could be. I shall remain faithful to
the man I love, and for ever."

"But if we were married . . . ?"

He did not know why he suggested it, save that
now he was consumed with a passionate desire to
possess her. Try as he would he could not control the
senses that disturbed him so much.

"This is no place to talk of marriage," she said,
and her voice was icy. He recognized as she stood
looking at him that she was wholly virginal and bitterly reproachful.

"A thousand pardons, I entreat you, a thousand
pardons."

Blunderingly he retrieved the candlestick and went
out of the room. It had been a most regrettable mistake, and one that he would never repeat. In the
morning he promised himself that he would make her
a formal offer of marriage. He was now ashamed
that he should ever have dared to enter the room
with so foul a desire in his heart.

Left alone, Emma drew out pen and paper.

An idea, wild in the extreme, had begun to ferment in her mind. She had left behind her the childish ecstasies, the little girlish enthusiasms that had
walked so long with her and had made of her so beloved a personality. At last she was a woman.

She wrote to Greville.

Please write, for nothing will make me so angry and it is not in your intrest to disoblidge me,
for you down't know the power I have hear. If
you affront me I will make him marry me.

231

It was not a threat but a prophecy, and she folded the paper, putting it together and wetting the wafer with lips that were still moist with love of him.

She meant what she said, and her words conveyed the impression that already the plans were laid for her future. Unless Greville sent her some fond message, some driftwood to which she could cling in the seas that shipwrecked her, she intended to marry the man to whom she had been sold.

XLV

EMMA PRAYED that time might bring her a reply, but time only produced complete silence, for Greville had no answer to make. He had thought that her word about marriage was just an idle boast, though when he had first read her letter he had been stabbed by dismay, but had dismissed it. Many a young woman, piqued by the loss of a lover whom she worships, makes ridiculous threats, and men do not marry their mistresses. In his own mind he had little doubt that Emma had become his uncle's mistress, else why was she staying in Naples so long?

It would indeed be embarrassing if she did marry him, and would most certainly make Greville the laughingstock of people in England; she might even bear the old man a son—he wasn't as old as all that—and some quite uncomfortable doubts stirred Greville, though he dismissed them again.

But he gave no second thought to the agony of the girl whom once he had loved so fondly, to Emma as she had been to him in the little Edgware home, Emma so anxious to have her child with her, so willing to please, even if it was to submit to the whims of

Greville's perverted mind; anything to retain the warmth of his love, for she had doted on him.

He thought that the letter was an indignant threat, invoked by the fury of the moment; ambassadors to foreign countries have a high position to maintain, and would not readily marry wantons. To Greville's own knowledge Emma had been Willet-Payne's mistress, and Sir Harry's, too, and now he was not at all sure of the purity of the relationship with George Romney.

He made no reply.

For days the unhappy Emma watched messengers coming and going, praying that the dispatch-box might contain some smuggled acknowledgement from her beloved Greville. But, having recovered from the first hot fury, a cooler and calmer mood overcame her.

"Do nothing foolish," her mother besought her.

"I promise that I will do nothing foolish, because now I intend marrying Sir William. At least he will be kind to me, and so far in my life kindness is a companion I have met too seldom."

Mrs. Duggan privately thought that Sir William would not marry her, and therefore was all the more amazed when one morning he sent word to Emma that he wished to see her in his apartment.

Emma had just been going out in the early morning cool, for the day was coming up sultry, with a mist about the vineyards. Later it would be too hot.

In the streets below, the Neapolitan boys (their brass ear-rings jingling in their ears) were selling black and white grapes in small round baskets, the fruit lying against the heart-shaped leaves. As she crossed the courtyard, Emma saw a young boy just past adolescence, his lithe body poised as he leant against the railings, who sucked noisily at a pink-fleshed melon flecked with black seeds. He turned his eyes to her, aware that she was a woman, and beautiful, and he grinned with his wet mouth. She would never know why she stopped, certainly not wholly because he was poor. She took a golden piece from her bag—Sir William was abundantly generous—and she passed it through the railing to the boy.

"Here," she said.

As he took the money he caught her wrist and jerked her closer. Then he pressed his young moist mouth to hers in an unreined passion, and for the moment it almost made her drunk. When he released her he ran away like the wind. Now only the oleanders stirred with the little breeze of morning; only the scent came from the lemons, hanging on their pyramid-shaped trees, hot with the yellow sunshine, mingling with the odour of orange flower from the tangerines at the gate.

She wiped her mouth vigorously with her lace handkerchief, but nothing could wipe away the memory of the passionate demand of that kiss. If she married Sir William, there would be no more desire; only the quieter commands of age. She did not know if she could bear it, she who had lain in the arms of so many men, had drunk of them and had uplifted and been perfected by their strength.

She tapped on the huge door of Sir William's study.

"Come in," he said.

Guessing her mission she had purposely put on a muslin gown of blue, spotted white, and tied with the same colour. The gown reminded her of her early days when as a village girl she had worn simple clothes at Hawarden. She had tied her hair with blue to match, and she went into the room. The Ambassador was standing there wearing satin. It was the purple that she loved best, and braided with pale blue seemed to form some sort of a link between them. His wig was smooth, delicately powdered and tied, his ruffles beyond reproach, and he had just been taking snuff from the gold box given to him by the King himself, for it had the Royal cipher and Georgius Rex carved upon it.

"Oh, there you are, my pretty creature!" he said, and indicated a chair by the window, with the garden below and the street beyond that, where the Neapolitan boys were still busily selling their little baskets of black and white grapes. "I sent for you, my dearest Emma, because I have a proposition to make to you."

She smiled at him. "Yes, Pliny?"

"I was profoundly sorry for the episode the other night. I blame myself entirely. I should have known."

"I had forgotten that there was an episode, dearest Pliny."

"I have sent for you this morning to make you a formal offer of my hand and heart." He was feeling embarrassed, for he thought that she might refuse, and then he did not know what he would do next.

She looked at him. At that very moment Vesuvius sent up a scarlet streak of warning. It quivered in flame against the sky, and she saw it across the bay. The hot day was rising out of the sea, with the mist like smoke on the vineyards, and the crater belching and suddenly showing that one flash of warning for her future.

"You do me a great honour, Pliny."

"You would not do me the misfortune of refusing it, I pray?"

"You would make me Lady Hamilton?"

"Immortal, lovely Lady Hamilton."

She got up slowly and went across to him, lifting her hands and laying them on either side of his jowl, drawing his lips down to her. How different was this kiss from the one she had taken within the last few minutes from the amorous boy at the railings.

"Dear Pliny, I pray that you will never regret your immortal and lovely Lady Hamilton."

He was enchanted.

Where would they be married? When? How soon could it be? he asked. Emma insisted that they must return to London for the marriage, for she had her own reasons. Although she said nothing, she in-

235

tended to meet Greville again before she actually made the irrevocable move. She must give him the chance to prove to her how he really felt. Sir William, madly in love with the pretty creature, agreed that they should return and be married immediately.

Mrs. Duggan could not believe that this had happened, for now indeed her daughter's star was rising. Her marriage would put her beyond the pale of scandal; nobody could chatter now, and her early peccadilloes would soon be forgotten.

The engagement coincided with a dinner given in their honour by some Dutch officers who were in port in a frigate, and Emma was at her best. She was glad to have decided on her future—or almost. She sang when they dined on board, and the ship fired a salute of twenty guns and was dressed overall in her honour. Never had she been more enchanting than she was at the opera that night, where there was a gala in honour of the Spanish King's birthday.

"You shall be England's greatest ambassadress," whispered Sir William when they drove home, for he was very pleased with it all.

"I can at least do my best."

In the spring of 1791 they set out for London to be married.

XLVI

SO GREAT was Emma's love for Greville that she was not prepared to abandon him without one last bid. Arriving in London she felt that it looked a tired and rather dirty city after the loveliness of Naples. She had forgotten that here the balustrades did not glitter white in the yellow sunshine, nor were the flowers so luxurious, or the people so gay. Housed in an apartment with her mother, until the ceremony that would make her one with Sir William could be accomplished, on the very first night she went out alone.

"Oh, Emma, I implore you do nothing rash," said her mother, who still feared for her daughter's impulsiveness.

"I will do nothing but what my heart dictates."

She was wrapped in a voluminous cloak of blue, the collar studded with diamante and silver braid, and in this she looked strangely regal. She wore a scarf over her hair, a scarf of the same colour and spattered with stars, and she went out in her own sedan chair. It was gold, with a lining of blue satin, whilst a fresh pomander hung from the roof and scented it with the tender sweet scent of orange and clove. Already she had discovered where her Greville was, for George Romney—against his better judgment—had told her.

"But," he wrote, "I implore you do nothing foolish."

She smiled as she read it. Foolishness, rashness, what did these people know of life who refused to live it to its full?

She listened to the steps of the link boys, and the footmen with lanterns, and her own heart made a feverish drumming as though a wild music went on within her. This was perhaps the moment she had waited for, her meeting with her beloved again.

Yet when she arrived she was surprised that the house was so small; she would have thought that with Sir William's generosity to him, Charles could have afforded something larger. A man answered the door, and she swept past him and up the stairs to the room that, from without, she had noted to be lit. She rapped on the door imperiously, and heard his voice—oh, joy!—the adored voice of her master.

"Come in," he commanded.

Her heart was making a terrible noise as she opened the door, and, stepping inside, shut it, with the protesting man without. The room was lit solely by candles, and at the far end Greville, looking older and more haggard, was poring over a manuscript. He turned to look at her, then rose as though he could not believe his eyes. She saw him again in the fine fullness of his beauty, the long aquiline face that she had loved so much, the hair pressed back yet still with its waves and curls, the sensuously curved mouth that once she had thought to be shaped like a scimitar.

"Emma!" he exclaimed.

"Oh, dearest Greville, I had to come to you again," and she held out her arms, the clumsy folds of the enormous velvet cloak encircling both of them. But he thrust her away.

"You have done wrong. You should not have come here. Have you thought of your good name?"

Amazed at his coldness she challenged him. "Did you think of my good name when you sent me to Naples?"

"That is finished with."

"It is not finished with. You threw aside my love, and oh, Charles, I gave you all of it. I love you so much. I still do love you so much, that I would do anything in the world for you."

He made a little impatient gesture as though this irritated him. "Is your chair awaiting you? I cannot but think that this would displease my uncle greatly, and have no wish to fall into disfavour with him."

"You are short of money? You have but to say so and I will speak to William on your behalf. You shall not find me ungenerous. The love I bear for you is so great that I am ready to give you all that I have."

"I shall not ask you to plead for me."

She was unused to men who did not melt to her, and she had held so many in her arms, cherishing the happiness, that she could not grasp the reserve with which Charles faced her. She made a supreme gesture, laying aside the deep blue cloak, and hurling it to the ground, to disclose herself to him naked as she had been on the day when she was born. She stood in the dimness of the candle-lit room, the heap of blue at her feet, her lovely body poised, her hair tumbling in a riotous glory about her shoulders. Greville was stirred. He took a step towards her, almost as though he would have crushed her to him and avail himself of so much beauty; then he hesitated and held back.

"No, Emma, you mistake me, all that is over."

"Not for me."

"It is for me."

They stood staring at one another, she naked, and realizing that she had offered herself and had been denied. It had never happened before, and would never happen again. She picked up the cloak and wrapped it round her calmly. "Good-bye, Greville, for now I know. Now I understand, but because of the love I once did bear you"—she hesitated for a second—"you have only to call on me at any time and you will not find your Emma hard, nor cold as you have been."

She turned, walking swiftly to the door, and, opening it, she found that the lantern-faced manservant who had admitted her must have been trying to peer through the keyhole, for he had not yet become upright, and she tripped over him. He gazed at her lewdly with an evil grin, but, ignoring him, she went downstairs and out to her chair.

The great love was over. This was the end, for Greville had refused her. Had he shown one spark of human warmth she would have turned to him and never have married Sir William at all; but Charles had not warmed.

She confided her story to George Romney when she went to his studio only the next morning. In his arms she could tell the story and be sure of sympathetic understanding.

"I am painting you yet again, my poor, lovely, ill-used Emma. Emma shall have no fears, for life is only beginning for you, my sweet one, though in your pain for Greville you do not believe it."

"You have always been so good to me."

"And you to me, my inspiration and my goddess."

He started on his new portrait of her as "The Ambassadress," and she actually gave him a sitting for it on the very morning of her wedding day.

It was not a propitious day when she set out for Marylebone church to become a lady, for the sky was overcast and the little village of Marylebone looked very grey. She compared it ill with the gleaming beauty of the *palazzo* in Naples, where the sun seemed always to shine. Although the meadows were sweet with wild flowers, they lacked the profusion of Italy, and the size of blossoms so abundant with colour and scent. She had chosen a grey silk frock, and she wore at the throat a frilling of mellow lace, clasped by one of Mr. Pinchbeck's delightful brooches. Sir William had this morning sent her diamonds for her to wear in her ears, but Emma had put them aside, because she felt that to-day she would come demurely to the church like a young village girl, her eyes moist, and her hands holding a single white rose.

She walked up the aisle to where her groom awaited her, and she whispered her responses falteringly, almost afraid at this solemn ceremony; in the vestry she dissolved into tears, though whether it was because to the bitter end she thought with regret of the nephew who had meant so much to her, or because now she realized she would be famous and was awed, no one knew. She was the wife of one of the most illustrious ambassadors His Britannic Majesty had ever instructed to act for him.

When they came out of the church together it was a strange coincidence that the greyness had been dispelled, and now a fitful sunshine lit the trees and the hedgerows, so fragrant with elder flower in a cream of foam and the traveller's joy beside it. It was a propitious omen.

"May you never have cause to regret to-day," he said.

"May you never regret your second Lady Hamilton."

Her mother clasped her affectionately to her, and was the first person to call her "my lady," and now the day was indeed sweet. They dined in private together, and Sir William fitted the diamond ear-rings to her little ears "as becomes a lady in all senses of the word." They went into the country and spent that night in a pleasant old house which once he had owned. He had ordered first that the rooms should be made sweet with white flowers in profusion, for to him his Emma was the white flower of all time.

Later he came trembling to her room, feeling young again, almost voluptuous, a bridegroom at last. Maybe their union would be blessed with children? A son? He hardly dared to think so far ahead. Emma, for her part, prayed that she might bear him a son, because she knew that was what Greville feared most, yet with the same breath she prayed to be barren so that she should not harm her beloved by it.

"Oh, William, my own dear husband, I pray that I may never disappoint you nor harm you in any way. I ask only to be a true and affectionate wife."

He kissed her hair and face and pressed his lips to the warm whiteness of her body. "What have I done to deserve so much? You will never disappoint me, it is I who might disappoint you."

"Ah, no, my sweet."

"The past lies behind us. It is only the future that matters, and that is lit by propitious stars."

But she woke early to find him lying on his back, snoring raucously, looking very old by contrast with the first vivid light of the day. How wrinkled and sagging was his throat, for in the late fifties he had

241

aged immeasurably. She stared at the closed eyes that were sunken with age, and at the protruding bridge of his nose, and the flaccid jowl that had slipped down to the chin line. Sleep, intensifying the rigours or age, horrified her.

Yet he was so loving and fond, he had given her security and had made her a lady, which none other had done for her. She turned away so that she should not see the face that had suddenly become so distasteful to her, but nothing could silence the noise of that snoring. At last, unable to bear it, she slipped out of the room into the next one. Opening the windows wide she admitted the sweetness of the fresh young dawn. Flower scent and dew, the delicious perfume of moist grass and lush hedgerow, and the glory of the new day as for a bride.

There was no going back, no return, for she was his wife, and although she cared for him, it was never love. It had not been love for Willet-Payne, nor for Sir Harry; it had not been love for George Romney, though a firm and abiding friendship was there. It was never love for Pliny.

'But I shall not regret,' she told herself, and determined to tread the path before her, wherever it might lead.

XLVII

AFTER THE honeymoon, Emma and Sir William returned to London. She was now at the zenith of her power, believing that no one could refuse her, and her husband was basking in her affections. He took on a new vigour, and whereas when he had left Italy he had been a man in advanced middle years, now he felt to be young at heart again.

His first desire was to present his wife at court, for it was important that she should be accepted by the King and Queen, and should have the seal of royal approval before they started back for Naples.

"You have thought no more of Charles?" he besought her on the last night of their honeymoon.

"Surely you realize that the real cure for such a passion is the one only a kind husband can prescribe?"

"He was never worthy of you, my sweet."

She pressed his hand to her heart so that he should feel how rapidly it was beating. "Oh, William, all that is over. It is a book now closed for ever. How can I think of Charles, when I have William?"

If he had had any further doubts, they were ended. When she looked at him so contentedly with her magnificent blue eyes he could deny her nothing. And, because he felt to be confident, he invited Greville to dine with them on their return. Now, he told himself, he would show his nephew that he had picked the very flower that Charles had flung from him, and worn in the coat of an ambassador it was indeed a rare blossom. If Emma was startled to hear of the invitation, she gave no sign when Sir William mentioned it to her.

"I thought perhaps you would like to show him that now—as my wife—you have forgotten him?"

She nodded. "He left a simple village girl. Sometimes I almost feel that he trespassed on my innocence."

"Now you will show him Lady Hamilton."

"Thanks to you, dear William."

"I want you to be at your best for him, to look radiant, and you must spare no money."

"You may rest assured that I shall do everything you say."

She dressed for the occasion with the greatest care, for now she wanted her Greville to see her as a risen star. He had loved her as a modest violet, and she recalled the day when he had been so bitterly jealous

243

of her success at Ranelagh, and, returning to Edgware, she had deliberately donned her cotton frock again and had gone down to his study to abase herself before so beloved a master.

Now his modest violet had blossomed into the perfect rose, and the thorns of that rose could pierce his flesh, for it she chose to employ those means she could wound the man she loved. But in Emma's heart there was no anger. She cared enough for him to want him only to see her as the ambassadress she had become, and to know that she could so easily use any influence and power that she had in his cause.

She selected a silver gown with blue, and to go with it she wore a tiara of diamonds on her hair matched to a necklace about her throat. She shone as though the stars themselves had come to decorate her, and the knowledge of her complete security had given her a new dignity, so that she walked into the parlour like a queen.

Greville had been drinking with Sir William at the side, and he turned from the fireplace where the logs were crackling. It was cold for the time of year. He looked at her, wondering if she would have changed, but never had he thought that it could be this much. The last time that he had seen her, she had stood naked in his study, with the velvet cloak dropped to her feet and her lovely body rising urn-like from the folds. He saw her now coming slowly into the room, the diamonds ablaze in a hot snow of fire. She did not hurry. Was it his mistake that the bosom was a shade larger, the waist a little thicker, or did that feminine jealousy, against which he found it so hard to contend, warn him that time must in the end mar even this perfect beauty?

Sir William indicated her with a wave of his hand. "I believe that I am right in suggesting that you have met Lady Hamilton before?" He was a man well satisfied with the bargain that he had made, and could afford to laugh.

"I have indeed met her before."

She looked at him calmly. So she could play the lady! He wished that he had whipped her harder when he had her at his mercy in the study at Paddington Green. The memory stirred him for a moment, and his mouth quivered at the thought; she, seeing it, knew what he meant, and extended her hand for him to kiss, with the gesture of an empress.

"My dear Greville," she said.

"Your stay abroad has much improved you." He kissed the hand now so smooth and white; who would have thought it had fulfilled once so many and so menial offices?

"I have learnt much. My singing is better and my art master taught me painting. My dancing master gave me instruction in poise, though perhaps the greatest lesson that I have learnt is never to love too well. It is perchance a common mistake, but one that, fortunately, only the ill-bred slip into."

"Undoubtedly."

All the time Sir William was amusedly tapping with his golden spy-glass in his hand, and purring with approval like a cat. Emma was putting Greville in his place! What a good thing, what a very good thing! He laughed to see it.

They ate a leisurely meal, and at the head of the table she shone radiantly. She knew good foods and the right wines to accompany them, and could now talk on any subject. It was remarkable the progress that this lovely creature had made, and Greville must have regretted that, when he had had the opportunity, he had not availed himself of her. A servant came into the room just as the meal was ending.

"There is a messenger without from the Palace," he said.

Sir William ordered, "Send him in," for he had approached the authorities on the subject of Emma's presentation at the royal court and had anticipated a reply.

"The messenger is in your study, Sir William."

"Then I will go to him, if you will excuse me." He

rose, bowing stiffly. His wife, at the far end, smiled warmly under the tiara of diamonds, but Greville made no sound. In another moment they had the room entirely to themselves. He sat there for a while, then leaned forward upon the Sèvres plate scattered with the remains of a peach that he had just eaten.

"Well, my Emma. So you've changed. You have the laugh of me there."

She had been searching for cutting words that she could utter; now was her moment, in her hands was a veritable rod with which to flagellate him, but she had not the heart to use it. "You thought that I would never be Lady Hamilton?"

"I admit that. I never supposed that my uncle would marry you."

"Alas, dear Greville, you underestimated my power, even though I warned you. In Naples I am important, and you would be surprised at the way I am fêted and received. Next week I shall go to court."

"In England?"

"Most certainly in England. It is the right of the ambassador's wife," and there was that ring of autocracy in her voice.

"If I am not mistaken you may find Queen Caroline a trifle difficult. Her Majesty has not got as short a memory as some."

Emma should have been angry with him, but still she could not be, she knew that she cared too much. "It delights you, Greville, to remember," she said, "I know that."

"Once it delighted you also."

"That was all so long ago. There was so much heartbreak, so much pain. Oh, it was terrible when I realized that you had forsaken me."

"You believed that story?"

"But of course, what else could I believe?"

"Naturally my uncle made it sound good. I did not give you up willingly, my dear. My debts were like millstones that weighed me down."

"Please don't let's discuss your money. Where there is true love, money is entirely matterless."

"Yet it seems to have made an enormous difference to a village girl that I once knew."

He was looking at her with the ardour that she had never forgotten, and she knew that his warmth suffused her. Probably she would have answered sharply, save that the door opened, and Sir William came in. He looked anxious, for the message had not been a pleasant one, and, acting on his own conviction that it was the right thing to do, he was going immediately to the Palace. Emma was horrified.

"But, William, is it so urgent as to be immediate?"

"I'm afraid so, dear Emma. Take care of my guest until I return. You, Charles, will find that she is an admirable hostess and that there is nothing she does not think of."

"I have," he replied coldly, "always found her to be over-generous."

XLVIII

OUTSIDE THERE were the noises of the London streets, but inside there was the snapping of the log fire on the hearth, and the pulsating of their hearts. Greville was standing on the rug before the grandfather's clock on the wall, which struck the hours with a melodious bell.

"It is little to ask," he whispered. "Once you said you loved me and I behaved badly. I know that now. We all make mistakes, for human nature is frail. Oh, Emma, can you not bring yourself to forgive me and to cede me now that beauty which once I did not hold in high enough esteem?"

She could feel her throat working as she listened to him. Greville, of all men! He had never been a man in her life, but far more than that—a god, and even though she tried to tell herself that that was over and done with she found an emotion within her eager and glowing for him.

"But, Greville, I'm married now."

"My uncle will never know."

"Only that I shall know, and shall hold the secret in my heart and hate myself for it. He has been so good to me."

"Was not I good to you too?"

She turned away her face. If only he would not recall the sweet intimacy of that little home at Paddington Green; the garden with the grape hyacinths—she had been gathering them when she had met Sir William for the first time—the noise of the rooks cawing in the thickening trees, the confused scents of hawthorn hedges and elder flowers in the Edgware lanes.

"Those were other days, dear, dear Greville, and then we were happy."

"We could be happy again."

He came closer and drew her to him. His arms were commanding, and against him she knew that she was devoid of power because she loved him so well. She knew also at this very moment that, if he should urge his cause, she would be willing to leave her husband and follow Greville to the world's end.

"How is it that you have this power over me?" she asked.

He did not reply, but all the time his eyes stared down into hers, and he had that enigmatical smile about his lips, the smile that she had never really understood. He moved the silver frock from her shoulder and kissed the flesh until it bruised. She had dressed as a queen to impress him, she had crowned herself with diamonds, but none of this really counted. It was he who could command her, not she command him.

"I could make you come to me though the whole world lay between us," he said, and it was true.

Two hours must have passed by. Out in the street there were just the passing link boys with their torches, the sound of the men puffing and blowing as they carried home some city alderman distended with a banquet and nodding over his fat paunch. Inside the room it was very quiet, with only the crackling of the logs on the fire and Greville breathing heavily as he took what he asked.

"Oh, darling, we should not have done this," she said at last.

"We always were each other's."

"I know, but what would William say? Poor William, he is so much in love, and has married me in such good faith."

"He is rewarded. He has you at the head of his table, and, after all, he is an old man, he cannot expect everything."

"But, Greville . . . ?"

He drew her to him as there was the sound of a chaise being driven up the street, the horses' shoes chinking like music against the cobbles. "Listen, Emma, my own sweet, adorable Emma. If you had a child?"

"William is unlikely to have children."

"I said if *you* had a child, then you would know from which root it had sprung. It would inherit the fortune that I should have inherited. At least it would not be a usurper."

Their eyes met. In that moment she read his meaning and it astounded her. It had not been so much that he desired her body, but that he had been flouted that she should have come into his uncle's life and therefore stood between him and his inheritance. Now he had made sure. He had deliberately set his seal upon her with the idea that for him she would propagate a son. She turned, enraged, and beat him with her small clenched fists. She made no sound, for it seemed that in this she had been

249

stricken dumb, but she beat so hard upon his chest that both of them failed to hear the door opening, and that was when she turned in a wild fury, and hit him with the flat of her hand full in the face. He paled before the stinging impact, caught off his balance and reeling. His own hand went involuntarily to the smart, and then Emma wheeled round to meet her husband. The silver dress was creased and the tiara cock-eyed. She was no longer an imperious queen, as she had determined to be at the beginning of the evening, she was just a wanton who had quarrelled with her lover. She pulled herself together with an effort, and stood there, ashamed that quiet, gentle Sir William should come into the room with such an atmosphere.

"So you're still here?" he said to Greville.

"I waited to keep your wife company and then to wish you good-bye."

Sir William said little; he went over to the side to help himself to a drink. Hurriedly Emma straightened her frock and righted the tiara. "What happened at court?" she asked. "Did you have an audience with His Majesty?"

"Later I'll explain," and she thought that he looked pale and that his mouth trembled a little. At this particular moment he bore his years badly and looked very old.

"Then I will make my adieux," said Greville as he bent over his uncle's hand. He turned to kiss Emma's, his eyes met hers and she could have killed him for the look, hating to think that she loved him so much. "The Queen," he said softly, "has a long memory, my love. It has been rumoured before."

They watched him go; they heard the sound of his chaise dying away into the distance and then they came back into the room.

"William, dear William, what has happened?"

"I am sorry, my sweetest, but there are disturbing matters at court."

"At court?" She stared at him in surprise, for she

250

was so accustomed to being fêted that never for a moment could it occur to her that something might be amiss. "How do you mean that there are disturbing matters? Am I not to be presented next week?"

"His Majesty sent for me. He was extremely amiable, he could not have been kinder, but he spoke to me in confidence."

"He spoke of me?"

Sir William's eyes avoided her across the rim of the glass that he held. "I fear me, my dearest Emma, that it is Her Majesty."

"Her Majesty?"

"The Queen has intimated that she will not permit it. She is, of course, notoriously strait-laced, and always lends a ready ear to rumour. I can only think that she has been misinformed."

"But, William, you can talk to her?"

"I'm afraid, my dearest one, that is not possible. It is the royal prerogative."

"But if . . . if I am not received here at the court, what will happen when I return to Naples? Does this mean that now, even as your wife, I shall have no proper place?" She knew that she was going to cry. The evening had been bitterly disappointing, and the tears were welling up unbidden. He comforted her.

"My sweet child, do not take this too hardly. I think that it can be circumvented, though for the moment is would not be wise—indeed, it would be extremely unwise—to attempt to force the royal hand. Their Majesties have said no, and we must abide by it, but I promise you this is only for the time being."

Petulantly she explained, "The Prince of Wales appeared to be uncommonly taken with me when we met?"

"Perhaps rumour of that has been the cause of the trouble. But you must not concern yourself, my sweet; the King cannot live for ever, he has had a long reign already, and undoubtedly with the Prince on the throne, matters would be very different. After

251

all"—and he smiled indulgently at her—"there is Mrs. Fitzherbert."

"Oh, that woman! What difference is there between her and myself? The marriage is not valid, and she knows that it isn't valid, yet lives there as his wife. I did not even pretend about Greville. She is allowed her Prinny, why am I not allowed my Pliny?"

He took her into his arms and fondled her. He had been considerably ruffled by the affair, and although he had tried to hide it from her, he was dejected. He took away the diamond tiara, and unpinning her hair, let it fall on both of them. In the quietness of the room (where so recently she had lain with her Greville) he knew that whatever might happen outside, here he and his Emma could be completely happy.

XLIX

AT THE court of Naples, however, it was not at all the same thing, for here King Ferdinand himself was enamoured of the beauty of the new ambassadress, and his wife, Maria Carolina, accepted Emma happily enough. The Queen liked her, and Emma put herself out to flatter Her Majesty. She loved the royal children, too; there were a great many of them, in fact once Sir William wrote home jokingly in one of his diplomatic papers, "The Queen is in the best of health, and—surprisingly—not pregnant."

Emma's cup was a joyful one, because now she knew that she was the chosen friend and confidante of the Queen. Her beauty was universally discussed and approved, and she sat for portraits and was famous, so that people not only came to the court of

Naples to see Their Majesties, but also to see the lovely creature who had turned the heads of half Europe.

She heard no more of Greville; in fact it was during this period that she had little time, for her moments were occupied much with their guest, Lord Bristol, who for many years was Bishop of Derry.

"But he is so old," she told Sir William, after the first time that they had met.

"But amusing." Sir William had a lewd wit at times, an old man's wit, and he personally had enjoyed the banquet which had been lit by golden lanterns and served on golden plates. The Bishop had been in good form, refusing capon and maintaining loudly that he "hated all neutral animals."

Emma disliked vulgarity, and she had been annoyed to be set beside the Bishop of Derry. The Prince of Wales was on a visit here, and she had desired above all things to seize this opportunity to ingratiate herself in his good opinions and perhaps pave the way to her presentation when she visited England next year.

"Later," said Sir William, who having been flouted on this particular mission was anxious it should not be mishandled now. "Leave it to me for the moment, dearest Emma, and occupy yourself with the Bishop."

"But he is a little tedious."

The Bishop was a large old man, self-opinionated and with the most surprising disrespect for all religious matters. He was not even courtly to His Royal Highness, a resplendent figure in exquisite satin clothes and wearing the Order of the Garter in deep blue from his shoulder. This disrespect produced a scene.

A Mrs. Billington had been asked to sing (music being the order of the evening), and the assembly was arranged on slender gilt chairs in the great salon to listen to the singing. Emma sat beside the Bishop in deference to Sir William's request, and all the time her eyes were on His Royal Highness, thumping time on the arm of his chair, and smiling superciliously with self-approval; he was perhaps a little drunk. She was still nursing the quiet indignation that "the Fitzherbert woman" should attend court when she could not, and felt this point must be properly contested and the obstacle—whatever it was—overcome. But to-night there was very little opportunity.

The Bishop plagued her with his ponderous compliments, stroking her arms and openly admiring the firmness of the flesh. He was attracted by her so that he hardly listened to the singing.

"But, sir, surely you love good music?"

"I love women who are not good better."

She did not know how to answer that, and so let it pass, but it vexed her. Now the Prince, imagining himself to have a very fine voice, was spoiling the music by insisting on joining in. He was happy in his cups, and finding the evening delightful and the people pleasant. The city was hung with lights, and their reflection beyond the window reached far out to the Bay itself. He thrummed the arms of his chair and sang in a stupid, untrained voice. This annoyed the Bishop, who kept saying "Pish" to himself, but after a while he could hold back no longer, and turning abruptly to His Royal Highness, said, "Pray cease! You have the ears of an ass."

Emma was horrified and attempted to restrain him. "The Prince is our guest, and one must be polite to a guest," she urged.

Whether His Royal Highness had not heard, no one knew, for now he actually got up to sing, standing and rendering his absurd songs, whilst the company affected to be delighted. All save the Bishop! Despairingly Emma caught her husband's eye, because she did not know what to do and saw catastrophe ahead. When the music stopped and His Royal Highness, vociferously applauded, returned to his chair, the Bishop remarked in a voice that could be heard all over the room:

"This may be fine braying, but it is intolerable singing!"

It was Emma who escorted him into another room, and she was indignant. "Really, sir, how can you speak so before a royal personage?"

"Personages matter little to me, and I would rather be alone here with you than in company of all the royal donkeys in Europe."

"But, sir, it is our Prince of Wales!"

"I cannot see that the accident of birth makes a man wiser or more intelligent. In fact, I should have thought that to-night we have had proof positive to the contrary."

She did not know how to answer him and was amazed. He pawed her hand, his lascivious mouth twitching. "Please," she said coldly.

"I came to see a Prince reputed to be clever, and found him as I said—an ass! I came to see a lady reputed to be beautiful, and found her as Diana of Ephesus," and he kissed her hand. She was aware of yet another conquest, and startled by it, drew back, for Emma did not love old men. Her affections were for strong, sinewy limbs, and arms that could almost break her in their clasp.

"Sir, indeed you wrong me."

"I would that were possible," he said, and she saw the bawdy appreciation in his eyes.

It chafed her to be here in the ante-room, when she desired nothing so much as to be back with the Prince of Wales, but this old man had his arm round her, and now she knew that she had under-rated his strength and potency.

"Sir, you would not have me call the servants? Please to release me."

"I would make you my prisoner for ever."

She looked at him imperiously. "You may have heard rumours, sir, but rumour is for ever a lying jade. I am the wife of Sir William, and I intend to stay the wife of Sir William and no other." So, wrenching herself free from him, she swept in anger back to the salon.

Their Majesties were on the point of departure. Standing beside her husband, Emma curtseyed low. King Ferdinand looked at her with those lingeringly somnolent eyes that held lust in them. Maria Carolina was no beauty; he had married her when she was but fifteen, and the marriage had been arranged, as indeed was that of her sister, Marie Antoinette. The King had found it difficult to initiate so young and petulant a girl into the ways of marriage, and recently she had perturbed him by occupying herself with the intrigue and strategy that was seething throughout Europe.

"The Queen would do better to leave politics alone, and devote herself more to the artless companionship of the fair Emma," the King had said.

"Indeed, it has been a charming evening," purred the Queen, and gave her hand to Emma to kiss.

Alone at the side of her husband, Emma faced the Prince of Wales, his large moon face smiling seraphically at her.

"Good night, Your Royal Highness."

He swayed slightly, his bland eyes amused, his mouth moist. "It ith delightful to meet tho charming a lady, but tell me, Lady Hamilton, there ith thomething I would know. Thurely I have thet eyes on your beauty before? It could not path and leave no mark on my memory. Where did we meet?"

"I once lived in London, Your Royal Highness."

"You mutht undoubtedly live in London again," and he broke into titters of self-approbation.

"Alas, sir, I have not yet been admitted to the court life there."

He waved his gentlemen back with his handkerchief, and Sir William withdrew to the far end of the salon with his guests. Alone under the yellow light of the golden Venetian lanterns, these two faced one another. "Do I underthand you, thweet lady, that you have been denied admittance to our court?"

"Alas, Your Royal Highness, her gracious Majesty felt . . ." She dropped her eyes and stood there looking much as she had done when she most pleased her Greville.

The Prince tried to steady himself. There was something wrong here, and he knew that she wished him to right it. He clasped and unclasped his over-ringed hands, and Emma saw with distaste how podgy they were. Greville's had been long and slender, the hands of a true artist, but these were German hands.

"Other ladies attend court," said the Prince thoughtfully.

She mistook his meaning, and because she realized that the chance might be passing, she said, "Indeed, sire, I know she does," and instantly knew by the look in his eyes that he was displeased at her suggestion he might have spoken of Mrs. Fitzherbert.

"Good night, Lady Hamilton," he said.

She racked her brains to think of some way out, some means by which she might retrieve a mistaken step, but could think of none and could only curtsey low. She watched him linger for a moment to bandy words with Sir William, then she herself turned from the room and went alone to the balcony. Dawn was rising, and before her lay the Bay of Naples. Vesuvius—it had been a good deal more lively recently—was emitting red penants which rose against the translucent sky in little vivid tongues of fire. But for all the scarlet of the angry volcano, the dawn was still a fragile and exquisite creature of opal and pearl.

A Neapolitan lover from the *casa* of his beloved close by emerged and lifted his face to the rising sun. About him was youth and beauty and fervour, and so distressed by the older men with whom she had recently been surrounded, Emma glanced at him admiringly. His strength was that of fecundity. She felt a tap on her shoulder and saw that it was the Bishop of Derry who had followed her out here. For a moment he nauseated her, then she was possessed by the feeling that she had to confide in somebody, and turned to him.

"That odious prince! I tried to ask a favour of him, and this after he has bored us all the evening. And what did he do? He took offence."

The Bishop nodded, then a schoolboy grin came to his face.

"You used the wrong language to him, my sweet Emma. There is but one language that he understands, that is the Hanoverian tongue," and putting his fingers into his ears to emphasize their height, he laughed at her, saying, "Hee-haw!"

L

IN EUROPE life was becoming more hideous. Revolution had surged through France. The unoiled tumbrils joggled down cobbled streets, with the brave, pale faces of the aristocrats turned again to the sky that they were viewing for the last time. The shining knife of Madame Guillotine fell with a sickening scrunch and rose dripped red with the best blood in the country. Men and women died alike. Marie Antoinette, white-headed with her torture, but still a queen, drove courageously to her death with a shrieking crowd to laugh at her mangled body.

Death was cheap.

Now it seemed that slowly Europe was going mad, ravaged and raked with the illiterate, screeching mobs, who demanded blood, and more blood. Maria Carolina, who had far more foresight than her husband, was alarmed at what might happen in the court of the Two Sicilies, for the rabble was spreading across the Continent and coming towards Italy. There was a great deal of rumour about a young man, who was reported to be a virulent bandit, Napoleon Buonaparte, a Corsican, who was doing great things for the crowds. Nobody had ever underestimated the calibre of the Corsicans, fighting was bred in their bone.

"Alas, what would happen to us if the horror of France came here?" said Maria Carolina, closeted with Emma whom she trusted.

"We could be brave. There is always a way of escape."

"But this Buonaparte? He seems to be such a dreadful fellow."

"Before he conquers the world he has to fight the British Fleet," said Emma. She had the greatest faith in the sea and those who rode upon her. "I imagine he may find that more worthy a foe than he supposes."

"Ah, yes, yes, the British Fleet," said Maria Carolina, and she clutched desperately at some straw of consolation. For help, if help there were to be at all, would come from Britain. For that reason alone she must keep close to the affections of His Britannic Majesty's Ambassador, and what easier method of contact was there than through his amiable lady? Maria Carolina liked Emma; they were happy together, though, of course, there were moments when they did not see eye to eye. But on the other hand, Emma did not understand the King, feeling privately that he was something of a monster.

"But the English are always so calm; they never do understand people like the King," said Maria Carolina, when one day they were talking of his prowess at hunting.

Ferdinand had just returned to the *palazzo*, he had been out hunting and had killed eighty-one animals in a single day, amongst them a wolf and some stags. Now he was lying on the couch and enjoying a beautiful sleep there. Emma could hear him snoring. Returning to take wine with the ladies, he announced boastfully that in his dreams he had shot another eighty-one animals. To Emma, who was inordinately compassionate, this was a horror.

"One would have thought that he had shed enough blood for one day," she ventured.

This amused the Queen, who thought that slaughter was a sign of manliness, and had never been able to conform to the English dislike of it. The two women agreed amiably, only once did they fall out really disastrously.

Emma had become so friendly with Maria Carolina that she was given free access to the royal apartments. Emma accepted this and went in and out of the rooms as she wished, it never occurring to her that perhaps it might be foolish to take the Queen at her word. Her Majesty was in the habit of making rash concessions, and later repenting of them, but unfortunately never admitting this. She regretted having given Emma the key to her privacy, and had only done this because it had been at a moment when she was terrified about the fate of her sister, the conquering proclivities of young Buonaparte, and the hooliganism that was raging throughout Europe.

On this particular occasion when Emma called to see her with a huge bouquet of red roses gathered from the Ambassador's garden, the Queen happened to be in audience. A manservant, who was a steward of the royal household, stopped Emma in the doorway.

"Her Majesty is with an English lady and does not wish to be disturbed."

Emma looked at him amazed, and did not believe that she was not wanted. She was disappointed, for the flowers would fade if she delayed in delivering them to Maria Carolina. Acting upon impulse she thrust the man aside.

"Her Majesty will see *me*."

It was a great deal more galling to realize that the "English lady" was one to whom Emma took the greatest exception. Against her no breath of scandal had ever floated on the harsh air of public opinion, for she was a virtuous wife and a devoted mother. Although Emma had abandoned little Emily, now at school in the North, and paid for by Greville, there were moments when the thought of other women's maternity was as a barb to her soul.

"I will go in," she said, and forced her way into the royal presence with no further ceremony.

It was a foolish thing to do and an error that only the girl from Hawarden would have committed, and the Queen was outraged. Turning sheet white she ordered Emma to leave her presence at once, but confident of her own powers of persuasion, Emma went closer with her flowers.

"But I have brought Your Majesty these lovely roses," she said, and laid them affectionately in the royal lap. Now the "English lady" against whom no word of scandal stirred, should see what power Emma Hamilton had at court!

"I ordered that I was not to be disturbed."

"But that did not include Your Majesty's loyal friend, Emma," said she artlessly.

The Queen was so indignant that she lifted her hand and slapped Emma's face quite hard. Never had she been angrier! Emma stepped back, her hand going involuntarily to her cheek, then, before she could stop herself, her temper had risen and she had returned the blow! The attendants rushed forward to protect the Queen, and the English lady did the wisest thing that she could have done, she fainted!

That evening the chatterboxes were wagging their tongues, for news of the fracas had gone round the court, and even in the streets of Naples itself, where the merchants plied their *ciambelli* and their *gnoccis,* the tale spread. The Queen had been slapped in the face by the English *comtessa!*

What none of them realized was that the friendship had been so close that it had brought both down to the same level. The Queen had long ago lost her dignity and, where Emma Hamilton was concerned, there was no sense of royalty at all.

261

Ultimately an act of oblivion took place, and eventually reconciliation was the result. In his cups on the piazza, the King chuckled to himself. Women were all the same, and what did they know of fighting? If they were queens or bawds the same procedure took place, they scratched one another's eyes out one moment, and kissed one another the next.

That was life!

LI

IT WAS an anxious period of history, with the eighteenth century closing into the nineties, and with ruin everywhere. The fact that the strong-willed Napoleon Buonaparte had risen out of the bloodshed did not seem to be a happy omen. The French were now led by him, as they would—in their present mood—have been led by any strong *citoyen* who dared to ride over them roughshod. Their hands were drenched with blood, and they were drunk with murder. The horror of Madame Guillotine sickened Emma whenever she thought about it, and even when she bathed in the sunken marble bath at the *palazzo,* her thoughts would return to those diabolical tumbrils, creaking as they jogged the doomed to keep their bitter appointment with Madame.

There was nothing that one could do to help them, and she could never exclude from her mind the reminder of those faces drained of blood, and the appeal in the eyes that sought so desperately for one last look of the beloved *Bois,* and of the bright sky, so soon to be darkened to them for ever. For hope, and no hope coming to them. At that period despair ground them all down, and it seemed that nothing could stay the ravages of death.

Maria Carolina looked to England for aid, but England was an island held aloof by the moat which surrounded her. She had stood through the ages for traditional order and loyalty, and they felt that she was apart from Europe and was the only chance to save the chaos. Emma, under the orders of the Queen, sent messages of their plight to London.

"Je vous fais mon ministre plènipotencier," the Queen said.

But Naples was becoming more and more involved in the tide of anguish, and the mob, encouraged by small successes, took greater liberties. There was the morning when they were out driving, and Emma sat beside the Queen with two of the royal children in her arms. The carriage was bespattered with festering grapes and sour oranges, plucked from the dungheap and flung by the crowd at Maria Carolina herself. Emma sheltered the children against her bosom and tried to shield the Queen's dignity with her own small body, the coachmen galloped the horses forward, and so ignominiously they were joggled home in utter confusion.

"Where would I be without my dear Emma?" wept Maria Carolina, who, when she returned to the *palazzo,* collapsed completely.

Any French servants in the royal service were dismissed, for the disquiet had begun in France, and the King was loud in his reproaches of his sister-in-law. The horror had begun at the Bastille, and the Bastille was where it should have ended, but now it was too late. Too much had got loose.

In the September of 1793 things were growing a little quieter, and there seemed to be some kind of a lull in the rebellion that was surging through Europe. The Naples court, clutching at any straw wherewith to comfort itself, was smoothed into a feeling of security which did not really exist. Perhaps the worst was past? Although the greater brain of the royal pair, Maria Carolina had much of Marie Antoinette's argument, who, when she heard the mob screaming for bread, asked, "If they cannot get bread, why don't they eat cake?"

It was the little girl from Hawarden who comforted the great lady in the most tempestuous hour of her anguish.

"I will never leave Your Majesty."

"Oh, Emma, my faithful one. The dearest friend a woman ever had."

In the friendship with the Queen, Emma found some small consolation, for her marriage with Sir William was physically a failure. Although he could give her both position and power, and she accepted these two with open arms, he could never satisfy her body which hungered and thirsted. It was her glory that high personages who visited the court of Naples received her and counted on her to help them. Politically she swelled with power, and she would not have been human had not success turned her head, for she wrote glowingly to Greville, telling him of what was happening. Again and again she emphasized: "You do not know what power I have here," and it was true.

Now the Queen had developed a schoolgirlish infatuation for her, and relied on her. The King, always fascinated by the sweetness of her face, privately flirted and publicly acclaimed her, but her husband could only pet her like an indulged child, which might be flattering but was horrifying to one of Emma's desires.

She wearied of celibate nights when the exhausted old man snored so loudly. Sleepless, she would turn her eyes to the extreme beauty of the blue beyond her window, a beauty that only accentuated her urgent desire. The blueness of that tideless sea, the abundance of the stars, far lovelier and larger than she had ever seen them through the trees at Hawarden. The heady perfume of the flowers clustering about her balcony came into the room like the essence of wine, and was as intoxicating, and sometimes there would be the tender sweet music of a guitar, of dark fingers plucking the strings, or the *serenata*. It was an enchanting setting for love, and lying here alone, she wept for Greville. Youth does not last for ever, and desire dies with age. How bitterly she desired the assuagement of her hunger in the sterile beauty of those nights which she had perforce to spend so tragically alone.

Once, as she lay there staring out to the sea flecked with phosphorescence, she saw a man's dark hand touch the white roses that blossomed so freely about the balustrade. Starting up she stared out, wondering if she should call the guard or if she had dreamt it; maybe the desire for manhood had created of itself a ghost?

The hand gripped the balustrade and a face appeared; she saw a lithe body bestride the marble, and beheld a young man, his very youth an intoxicant to her. She knew that he must have evaded the guard and might even be a beggar, but he approached her, and kneeling beside her bed, took her quite savagely into his arms. They kissed recklessly without a word. When he had fused her with his own fire, she could not hold back, but surrendered herself to him and lay silent, with the stars winking through the uncurtained window, and the atmosphere pregnant with emotion.

Until morning they lay entwined together, and he, waking early, stretched himself. She saw by the light of dawn that he looked even more attractive. It was only the old who, with morning, grew haggard. Here were no yellowed dewlaps, no sagging jowl and flaccid skin in pappy hills and furrows. No bags bulged beneath his eyes, for he awoke with the sudden brightness of firm flesh and the proud determination to take adventure where and as he could find it.

He kissed her lasciviously, then he had gone, and she knew that it was good-bye. She longed to say one word but dared not, for already she could hear the changing of the guard in the courtyard of the *palazzo*. The orders were rapped out, and there was the ring of men's feet against the stone, so that it would not be safe for the bandit to delay his *addios* a moment longer. The phosphorescence of last night had left the sea and now it was an untouched blue. The violet shadows were fast lifting and the sun spearing the East with banderilleros of gold.

The man passed from her room with noiseless feet, and on to the balcony. For a moment she saw him poised astride the marble balustrade, with the white roses and the bougainvilleas in festoons about him. He waved a defiant hand and had gone. Only Vesuvius remained, ominously watchful.

He will return, she promised herself, and blamed her scruples that she had not flung pride aside and gone with him in search of further passion. Here there was nothing with which to drug her desire, for if Sir William even deigned to visit her, she found his clumsy and palsied attentions irksome. She was avid for youth.

As she finished dressing she looked up and saw across the Bay ships in full sail, moving majestically like white swans on the face of the water. Dropping anchor, they fired a salute, and she heard Vesuvius catch the echo and send it roaring like thunder back to them. For a moment she was afraid that the Frenchies had actually come, and now, in very truth, that abominable Napoleon Buonaparte would land and murder them all. Then, looking closer from the balcony of roses and bougainvilleas, she saw that these ships bore the English flag.

Sir William's messenger came for her at once.

"Sir William desires your ladyship's presence, my lady."

She went like a queen, her draperies stirred by the same little wind that had brought the Fleet into the Bay. Sir William was sitting there breakfasting on hot chocolate served in a golden samovar. He had a dish of sliced peaches and capon, and he glanced at her petulantly. After the *amour* of last night, he looked to her to be peculiarly old. Never had his face

266

seemed more drawn or yellow, never had his hands moved so stiffly.

"You sent for me, William?"

"Dearest Emma, we have news. Part of our Fleet is already here."

"I have seen it."

She saw that his wig had become awry, and it accentuated his appearance of senility; he looked like some sere old mandarin who has taken opium the night before and is not properly recovered.

"To-day, dear Emma, it is our duty to entertain a young gentleman. See, I cannot find his name . . . ?" He fumbled for his spy glass, set in marcasite and kept dangling from a watered silk ribbon slung round his neck. But his fingers were so stiffened that he failed to find it.

"Let me read it for you," said Emma, and at that moment she was impatient of age and thrilled only by youth. "Yes, here it is. The gentleman who will visit you is Captain Horatio Nelson. It is written here."

LII

SIR WILLIAM commanded his Emma to look her best, so she made an elaborate toilet. It was good fortune that the modiste had recently sent her three new frocks, and she selected the most becoming. Again she decided on the old rôle, the one that had never yet failed her, for she would be the simple girl with virginal charm who had come from the village at home.

So she chose the freshly made frock with its soft fichu and muslin frills. She picked out the pale blue sash that had almost become a uniform, for half Europe wore the same pale blue, calling it *"Bleu à la Emma,"* but none could match her in it, and sometimes she laughed at them. She went out into the marble palisaded garden to take a pink rose for her sash.

It so happened that the Bishop of Derry had arrived on a visit. He could never keep far from the *palazzo* where he was wont to express his heretical outlook, and he followed her ladyship into the rose garden, leering at her with those bawdy eyes of his which always asked more.

"We have company," said Emma, curtseying.

"If you count myself as being company it pains me. I had hoped that perhaps some day I might be something sweeter to your so fair ladyship."

He ogled her, but Emma was not in the mood for an old man's meanderings; she was fed with the fullness of a youthful passion, and for the moment did not think in terms of the senile.

"I was referring to the Fleet that has arrived and is now anchored. The Captain is lunching with us today."

"And who is the Captain?"

She thought for a moment, "See, what was his name? Oh, yes, Nelson. Horatio Nelson."

"Ah, of course."

"Is he well considered and esteemed?"

"Oh, yes, I suppose he is. He is married to a dull creature, a widow before they met, and he has little use for women. If that was what your ladyship was considering?" and again he glanced at her with doubt.

"You are wrong, kind sir, for her ladyship is happily married herself."

"Her ladyship is married," and he grinned, "if that is what you can call marriage when night after night her ladyship sleeps alone."

"It is still marriage and I am faithful to it," but her heart stirred strangely as she fastened the rose in her sash. He had guessed aright, though she much disliked his proximity to her.

He came closer. "Were you faithful last night?" he challenged her.

For one horrifying moment she was half afraid that he was the one who had sent the young man to her, and that he knew what had happened. Then wisdom overcame the foolish panic. Far more possible that it was a bow drawn at a venture and he did it to tantalize her, because he could not know.

"How could I be otherwise?" she asked.

"If I stayed at the *palazzo* your ladyship would be otherwise," he promised her.

She changed the subject quickly because he sickened her. "I understand that Captain Nelson has been sent to us to obtain six thousand men for fighting? It is a special mission from Lord Hood, but I imagine that he will have difficulty in recruiting so many from Naples."

"I hope he succeeds; they will be so many less to join the rebellious mob," for the Bishop had a poor opinion of the scum of Naples, "and I hear he is bringing his stepson, Mr. Josiah Nisbet, here. If he is as dull as his mother, then indeed he must be very dull indeed."

All the same Emma's eye brightened, for the thought of a midshipman was intriguing. "Doubtless," she said, "I shall find the young Josiah more after my own heart than his captain."

"If you like midshipmen."

"I like young men. Youth has always had a special appeal for me."

"The callow has never appealed to me, and in the lists of love I can promise you, my pretty lady, that it is experience which pays."

He pawed her shoulder with his big clumsy hands, pockmarked in brown flecks with his years. She felt that she could have screamed from the contact with him and coldly she returned to the *palazzo*. When she entered the house she saw that two naval hats were lying in the vestibule.

"They are here?" she asked the manservant.

"Captain Nelson and Mr. Nisbet arrived but ten minutes ago, *Excellenza*."

She felt a twinge of excitement because she could hear the men talking in the ante-room, and went herself into the salon to await them. As she entered she saw a young midshipman standing at the far end, smelling the white roses she had previously arranged in a crystal bowl. He must have heard her enter, for he turned, clicking his heels together, his dirk clanking at his side as he sprang to attention.

"Excellency," he said.

"You are Mr. Nisbet?"

"Josiah Nisbet, at Your Excellency's service."

He was better-looking than she had anticipated, though perhaps a little callow. His hair was straight and mouse-coloured, and, though brushed strenuously, it still refused to lie flat; his eyes were pale blue, his skin without much colour, but she knew that he had heard of her and admired her, by the very way that he stared, as though to drink his fill of her.

"Undoubtedly you found the conversation boring," she said in an attempt to put him at his ease, "and came in here."

"They are talking only of the men my stepfather wishes to take back with him."

"And you are very young, and find it tedious? There are other and so much more interesting matters of which one may talk. Do please be seated. Don't stand at attention like that, for I am an informal person. I hope that you and I are going to know one another very well," and she patted the couch so that he came across and sat down beside her, becoming interested in her.

"My stepfather thinks of nothing but engaging the French Fleet and destroying it. I, for my part, am not so eager."

"As I told you, there are other things."

She encouraged him to talk and he spoke of his home, and of his widowed mother, who had obviously spoilt him, but who, having married again, had handed him over to his new father "to make a man of him." Josiah had come to sea somewhat loath, but he had to admit that Captain Nelson was scrupulously fair and, although strict, was in a lot of ways surprisingly understanding.

"Except," said young Josiah, "he has little care for a pretty face, and I, Excellency, have every care," and he looked at her shrewdly.

"To admire beauty is a good fault," she said, and patted his hand encouragingly. He caught that hand and held it.

"I heard you were the most beautiful woman in the world, before we dropped anchor here. I told my stepfather so, but all he said was that he had no eyes for beauty. War, war, war, that is all he cares about."

"But he must have an Achilles heel."

"Then he keeps it prodigiously well guarded," said Josiah with some bitterness, for he resented the fact that his life should be bereft of feminine companionship and so occupied with the insidious duties of strategy and campaign.

"We will find it," said Emma.

She turned to smile at him. He was a youth budding into manhood, and all her affairs had been with men. His smile was the rather sheepish grin of a boy, but time would change that, and probably for her. She heard the men stirring in the other room, and the big cream and gold doors were swung open. She could see the long, diplomatic room with the far windows on to the sea, and there the *Agamemnon,* nearest ship of them all, her flags flying, her sails furled, silhouetted against the bluest of skies.

Sir William, walking into the room, had with him a smallish man with an intent face; the stranger rolled a little as sailors do, and he stared ahead of him at Emma without any interest, for his mind was

271

far away. She was piqued by the fact that it was noticeable that she did not entrance him.

"My dearest," said Sir William, "allow me to present Captain Horatio Nelson of the *Agamemnon*."

LIII

CAPTAIN HORATIO NELSON had come to Naples in seach of six thousand more men after he had taken Toulon. He concentrated on the work in hand, which was urgent, and had no eyes for the wife of the Ambassador, even though she were the most beautiful woman in Europe. Perhaps for the first time in her life, Emma had met a man who never so much as looked at her.

"He is a most remarkable fellow," Sir William told her.

"Does he never mention me?"

"I assure you he has been so occupied in showing me the plans of the ports, for he has a scheme ready by which he hopes to intercept the French ships . . ."

"He seems very dull. I imagine that Mr. Nisbet, although young, is far the more courteous."

In Josiah's company she could almost enjoy herself. She took him about as an honoured guest, showing him ruined Pompeii and Vesuvius. Together they visited the crater, ominous just now, and belching forth flame, so that the journey up the side was rendered deliciously unsafe. That stirred her spirit of adventure.

In her companionship Josiah changed. He had come to Naples in the *Agamemnon* as little more than a lout, and she transformed him into a lover. Under that callow exterior there lurked a deeply amorous side to his nature, and she knew it. They sat together in the little arbour built at the far end of the rose garden, with the most exquisite view beyond over to Capri. A blue madonna reigned over the arbour, her hands and face carved in crystal so that when they caught the light they gave the impression that they were made of water. There was alabaster in the room and the servants had orders always to sprinkle it with jasmine, so that about it lingered an enduring perfume.

It was here that Josiah pressed his suit.

"I love you," he said, kneeling beside her as she reclined on the couch. "You are the most noble and wonderful *Excellenza*. I have never felt like this before."

"I am much older than you are, dearest boy."

"What does age matter? What does anything matter?" For that was how he felt. Discretion was folly. With an engagement with the Frenchies not far ahead, he migh die; it would be tragedy to die leaving such loveliness untasted. She touched his brow with gentle hands. It was pleasantly satisfying to her vanity, but she was very much irritated to think that Captain Nelson should have no eyes for her. She knew that the feeble body of his contained a courageous and tremendous spirit, but that his mind was apparently always on duty. In some strange way she felt that, in availing herself of the stepson, she avenged herself on the stepfather, and it gave her a peculiar feeling of delight.

Josiah kissed her hair, and let it loose to flow about them both.

"Never have I looked upon anyone so beautiful. My mother told me of you—she had heard of your loveliness and was afraid lest my stepfather should fall victim to your charms. She warned him."

"She warned Captain Nelson?"

"Yes, as though he would heed! But don't let's talk of him, let's talk of ourselves."

He reminded Emma of the lover who had never said a word, but who had come hand over hand to

273

her balcony, in the blue-drenched moonlight of that over-lovely night. He had wooed and won her, to leave her without one single expression of his feelings for her, and to this moment she had no idea how his voice might have sounded, and was intrigued by the thought.

"You talk too much," she reproved Josiah.

The blood surged to his face as he wrapped his arms about her, kissing her until he hurt her. She felt a sense of exultation as they lay together, as though she walked the heights of conquest. His youth was hers. Yet later, when she watched the young man sleeping, she knew that those same heights had left a bitter taste in her mouth. What was the matter with her? Had she changed? She had not really wanted to take this boy, and yet had availed herself of what he had offered merely because his stepfather piqued her, and because her own husband left her so hungry.

At the end of twelve days the time came for the British Fleet to weigh anchor, Nelson having obtained his six thousand men, and he came to the *palazzo* to make his adieux. Emma watched him as he came forward to kiss her hand. In those penetratingly blue eyes there was no passion, only the look of a conqueror, for they were cold eyes, she told herself, and from Nelson himself a man—and a woman too—could expect no mercy.

"Your Excellency has been indeed kind to my stepson," he said, "and I thank you on behalf of my wife and myself for what you have done for him."

"You and I might have been friends, if duty had not called you so strongly?" she suggested.

Perhaps for the first time he noticed the desire about her body, and realized that certain forlornness in her eyes, as though she could not bear to part with him. "I shall return, Your Excellency."

"I shall await that moment with impatience, Captain Nelson."

"But first I must beat the French."

"You will." Her face was illuminated by the light

of prophecy. "I have the feeling under my heart that you will be the saviour of Italy."

He bent over her hand, clicked his heels and turned to go. If only he had looked back! she told herself, but he did nothing of the sort. Nelson was not the man who, turning a corner in life, looks regretfully behind him. She saw his shadow flicker across the marble floor, and heard the chink of his sword; and long after shadow and chinking had ceased there was the silence of the late-swooning afternoon, and she knew that something had changed completely in her heart. She must be crazy!

Horatio Nelson was a smallish man; he was not even attractive to look upon; he had none of Willet-Payne's virility, none of Greville's Grecian beauty. He had not cared for her, he had in fact left her to be seduced by his stepson whilst he discussed strategy with Sir William and the King. But at the same time he had left a lasting impression upon her, and one that she could not eradicate. 'I will make him love me,' she promised herself, flouted at the thought that he had not cared, 'I have it in my power and I will make him love me.'

What she had failed to realize was that calamity was close at hand, and the shadow of tragedy was about the court of Naples. The Queen was deeply anxious because of the Neapolitan Republicists and the disorder that was so rapidly spreading throughout Sicily. Unpleasant riots began and grew steadily worse. At all times there were alarming sounds to disturb the exquisite city, for a shot would ring out, or a yelling mob would surround someone who screamed in the very agony of death itself. Insurrection was on their doorsteps, and it was apparent to all who chose to think that Vesuvius was not the only volcano in the neighbourhood, and steps would soon have to be taken.

From the pulpits war against Jacobinism was preached, death to the French, and, although on ev-

275

ery hand efforts might be made, this was a tide not easily stemmed.

"It would be wiser if I dispatched my wife home," said Sir William, now looking to be a tired old man in the new crisis.

"I would not leave you."

"I appreciated that you might say that, my sweet and lovely girl, but it is my duty to protect an adorable wife."

Horrified as she was by the terror of the disturbance which she found surrounding her, Emma determined to see it through. "Where William lives, there Emma lives too," she vowed, and kissed him affectionately.

He fondled her in that fatherly manner of his. He loved her devotedly, believing her to be sweet and innocent, and he did not wish danger to touch her. She still refused to go, even though matters were growing more desperate in the city. In the *Mercato Vecchio* there was the hideous execution of Tommaso Amato, who died deprived of the solace of extreme unction, and soon sixty more Jacobins had died tragic and bloody deaths. The death chamber of the *Capella della Vicaria* had begun its gruesome work, and Emma shuddered every time that she thought of it; now it seemed that they were not so far from the groaning tumbrils which had creaked down the Paris streets to the guillotine in the square. Death was here in Naples, and although Captain Nelson might be achieving English triumphs in Corsica, here there were hideous wounds and blood gushed forth, so that the gutters were stained, and the cobbles were dark, and mouths tasted salty.

Maria Carolina grew more downcast from fear.

"Oh, Emma, where should I be without you?"

"I am grateful to be able to give Your Majesty any help that I can. We shall survive. I am convinced of that."

The Queen shook her head, and put her hands to her neck, clasping the throat that was already ageing a little. She could think of nothing but the way that her sister had died. "It is as though already I felt a sharp knife here."

"It will not come. I am sure that we shall escape the ultimate horror."

But the Queen was disconsolate, for she had gone to Mass on the Sunday after Ascension Day, when there had been a dreadful scene in the Forum in Rome. The Pope himself had heard for the first time the shouts of *"Viva la Republica, abassa il Papa,"* and instead of standing his ground, as might have been expected, had fled dismayed. This turn had distressed Maria Carolina more than all else.

"But time will help us," Emma insisted. "I vow that Captain Nelson will save us all, and you will see that I am right."

"Alas, I have the feeling that nothing can save us."

She turned her eyes to the window of the Palace, looking as it did to the side of Vesuvius, with the vineyards and the water in between in a long arm. The smoke was rising clumsily against the dark sky. It had been a distressingly overpowering day, heavy with heat, and now even Emma felt a strange weariness, as though every exertion was an effort. The sky lowered as for an electric storm, darkening ominously even though night was several hours away.

"Emma, what is happening?" asked the Queen, who had been so involved in the European débâcle that she had not noticed the conditions immediately surrounding her.

"I don't know."

For a moment they stood together and stared out of the window across the marble piazza to the sea. Then they saw the black sky lit as though by a titanic torch. It glowed crimson; out of the crater of the volcano there spurted a cascade of flame and fire. In the distortion of that redness the whole detail of the mountain was lit in a horrifying manner. The little houses were plain, even the vines came so close as though they were here in the gardens of the Palace and their fruit clear. Immediately following that hideous flame there came the deep resonant sound, growing in intensity as though a thousand cymbals clashed together in one echoing discord. With it the smell of burning. The first light dust was falling, a fiery dust, hot with the heat of burning cinders, and the red glow still illuminated the mountain so that they could see the wide black stream of lava rolling remorselessly down its side, engulfing everything it approached, and passing on lustfully for more.

"Vesuvius has erupted," gasped the Queen, and hid her face in Emma's shoulder. But Emma still stood there staring.

It had surely been sufficient that the hand of man had been against them; now it seemed that they were also faced with the hand of the Almighty.

LIV

THE ERUPTION was, fortunately, not a major one, though it was alarming enough in all senses, and brought desolation in its train. It did, however, for the moment transfer the minds of the Neapolitan Republicists to other matters.

"Maybe it was sent by Providence," said the Queen, "for indeed it has made people think again of God, and that is good."

The Queen could only think how loving Emma had been, how courageous, and showered proof of her favours on her. Delightedly Emma wrote to Greville, telling him of her popularity, of her efforts in the cause of distressed Europe, and how she hoped and prayed that the threatened danger was passing.

Admiral Nelson—as he had now become—was already in pursuit of Buonaparte's ships, and

I have, my dearest Greville, great faith and belief in him. He is indeed a great man.

It was on a hot June day that the British Fleet returned to Naples again, and Sir William first sighted their approach when he was having breakfast on the piazza, taking it early before the heat became too oppressive. He saw the van of the small squadron of fourteen, their sails gleaming like silver, nearing Ischia from the west.

"Look," he said to Emma, "here is our friend the little Admiral on his way to fight the French."

She rose slowly and stood beside the table, staring out to sea at the lovely apparition of the ships. "But, surely, if he has come here, there must be something that he seeks, and what could it be?"

"He will come ashore. It is our duty to do everything that we can to help him."

"Naturally." She still stood there staring, her eyes startlingly beautiful. It was long since Emma had indulged in love. Her husband was ageing very quickly these days, and asked nothing of her. He thought of bed as a place wherein to sleep, and where he could indulge tired limbs to restore them to vigour for the duties of the following day. Because of the conditions prevailing in Naples which made both of them exceedingly anxious, she had not dared to think of any men outside. Nowadays it was too dangerous to entertain the thought of young amorous youths who might climb her balcony to give her delight. Bishop Derry, it is true, had been attentive, but he was an old man and showing his years more with almost every day. Her yearning for youth was overpowering, and kept recurring like a besetting hunger in her heart. She thought with affection of Josiah Nisbet, who might be here with the Fleet. Last time he had been a mere boy, but the year that had passed would have strengthened him in manhood. Maybe to-night once more she would feel the sublime strength of a man suffuse her, and would lie locked in Josiah's arms, with his mouth whispering loving words in her ear. The thought caused her to tremble. Some women are born to be loved, and Emma Hamilton was in that category.

"He will come ashore?" she ventured.

"Of course he will come ashore, and undoubtedly to us," said Sir William a little touchily. "Where else should he go than to the Embassy?"

"Maybe he will stay some days?"

She had not realized how parched she was for some fountain of joy, and if Josiah came ashore, she could at least assuage the thirst that gripped her.

"Everything depends on the French. Nobody can say how long he will stay save the little Admiral himself."

The *Vanguard* dropped anchor.

Impatiently Emma waited for the first sight of the Admiral and his stepson coming ashore to pay their compliments, but when the boat put in, neither of them appeared. It was Captains Troubridge and Hardy who presented themselves at the *palazzo* of the Ambassador to His Britannic Majesty. To Emma, now fevered with impatience, it was irksome to be shut out from this conclave. She was avid to know what it could be about. Sir William was closeted with his visitors for some time, and when the interview was finished she was at last admitted with refreshments for them. As she entered the room she realized that something must have gone very wrong, by the dull look on their faces.

"And where is the Admiral?" she asked of the immensely tall Captain Hardy.

"The Admiral is occupied on board, Your Excellency," he said, as was indeed true, for the Fleet was in a ferment. These were eventful days, much was at stake, and if victory was to be theirs the Admiral was fast to his post.

"And you have put in for stores?" she ventured. Victualling was the only thing that she could think of, and shot a bow at a venture.

"Stores are not possible to obtain," said Captain Hardy, and his voice sounded both dull and lifeless.

"Not possible? But surely . . . ? What do you say, William?"

The old man moistened the corners of his purple lips with an anæmic tongue. He wished his wife would keep out of such things. He said with a little hesitation, "It is not easy, my dear Emma. There is our strategy to be considered, and we cannot afford not to think of the situation from every angle. We must do nothing that might involve us in war."

"But surely it involves us in a much more disastrous war if we allow the English Fleet to be worsted? That would not only be war, it would be defeat."

Her eyes were wide and she blazed with fire; at this moment she was immensely strong, and the two captains looked at her.

"She speaks very truly," said Captain Troubridge impressed that one whom he considered to be light should feel so deeply.

"I have my position to be considered, and it is a very delicate position," said Sir William, avoiding his wife's eyes.

"Then I will go personally to the Queen and ask this favour, for we are great friends. I believe that I can influence her, and in view of that friendship can persuade her to help the Admiral."

For a moment it seemed that the whole room was electrified, and Sir William sat there uncomfortably glancing at his wife from under lowered lids. The hyper-slight, delicate little creature with the face of a madonna had become indeed a minerva.

"How can one thank Your Excellency sufficiently?" murmured Captain Hardy. In fact he did not know what to say, for he had given up the cause as lost, for the Ambassador had been very difficult,

281

and he knew that if he failed then it spelt disaster to the Fleet.

"Send the Admiral to me," she said.

"But——" and then realizing the look in her eyes, "I will go back to the *Vanguard* and tell the Admiral what you say."

"And I will go to the Queen."

Her husband tapped on the desk before him. "Emma, I implore you to be reasonable. At this time of the day the streets are unsafe, and the rioters may be out and about. You might be stoned; you might easily be killed."

She did not flicker, only turned to laugh. "In fighting Buonaparte, Admiral Nelson might be killed. This is very little for me to do for his cause; if only I lose my life so that his fleet may be fed, then I shall do well. Do you suppose that I value my life so much?"

She walked out of the room triumphant. She knew that she could influence Her Majesty, and through the Queen, His Majesty himself, and had no doubts about the outcome of her mission.

Alone in the diplomatic salon, the three men lapsed into an awkward silence, Sir William staring at his papers, Captain Hardy towering over Captain Troubridge, and at last he was the one who spoke.

"Will England ever know what it owes to Her Excellency if she achieves her mission, for she will have saved the fate of Europe?"

Sir William looked at him ominously; he felt very tired, and there were moments when Emma made him feel entirely helpless.

"I very much fear that she will achieve her mission," he said, "for Emma is the most purposeful woman I have ever met. But remember that she asked a duty of you. She requested you to send the Admiral here. You must not fail her."

LV

ON HIS return to the ship, Captain Hardy confessed that, so far, his mission had failed, but that Her Excellency desired the Admiral to put ashore to speak with her. He was received without enthusiasm. Nelson, at the moment or, in fact, at any other moment, had very little use for women. He was at work in his dark cabin, which was so small, and he was still concentrating on his plans. It was his duty to foresee every eventuality to avoid being taken by surprise and towards this end he had been practically sleepless for nights.

Whatever else might happen it was of primary importance that he should now obtain food and water, for it was unthinkable that his Fleet could go forward into so bloody a battle as this one promised to be, and yet be harassed by matters of this kind.

The ship smelt sour. They had had a bad trip, with dirty weather, and had shipped a lot of water, with the result that the *Vanguard* was impregnated with the stench of saltily wet woodwork. In the hold, the last few animals lay awaiting slaughter, their soiled straw stinking of excretions which permeated the whole ship. But Nelson's courage never flagged; he felt that his duty lay to the course of battle, and that his captains should have been able to cope with the question of "vittles."

"Hell's bells, what can Her Excellency want with me?"

"Her Excellency has herself gone to the Queen of Naples to urge our cause. She was, sir, most determined, and seemed convinced that, Sir William having failed, she could herself get the vittles that we required."

Nelson looked at Hardy uncertainly, then his face brightened. "Was she, by God?"

"Sir William felt that it would be immensely difficult, if not impossible. He has aged considerably, and seemed to waver. He felt that there was some detail of international diplomacy which disturbed him, and he was singularly biassed against our plight. I think it rested on the fact that he has aged so much."

"Her Excellency? Has she aged also?"

Nelson did not know why he should ask it, and suddenly he recalled her on that last day when he had bade her farewell, and had visited the *palazzo,* for the honour of kissing her hand. He had thought her to be an essentially good woman in spite of rumours; she had been very kind to Josiah—the boy had never ceased to praise her—and now she seemed generously minded towards the Fleet! He knew that she had risen from a lowly position, and told himself that it was astonishing how admirably she graced the exalted one which she now occupied.

"Her Excellency was very beautiful," said Captain Hardy with cold prudence, for he had heard rumours of her ladyship's prowess in the bedchamber, and thought it extremely unwise to excite the Admiral's interest. Also he had once overheard young Josiah discussing her ladyship with another midshipman, and boasting that he had possessed her. How true this might be Captain Hardy was not sure, young midshipmen often strove to appear more captivating than in reality, but he had to admit that young Josiah's manner had been extremely convincing.

"You say that Her Excellency has already gone to the Queen?"

"Yes, sir."

"And you tell me that she demands that I—that I should go ashore to dance attendance on her?" He struck the desk forcefully with his clenched fist. A small man, he was now quite tremendous with his sense of power, his eyes were shining, his disarranged hair falling forward on his brow. "Why, in God's name, should I go to her? What does the woman want with me? I have other duties to fulfil, and this is no time to dally at the petticoats of Her Excellency. All the world is on the brink of war."

"Aye, aye, sir, but she seemed to be most insistent."

The *Vanguard* tipputed with the tide, slowly turning at her anchor. Nelson stood up irritated; he recalled again that lovely creature with the glossy ringlets, and those virginal eyes that had set all Europe agog. He hesitated. If indeed she had gone on his behalf to the Queen of Naples, then she had behaved very bravely, though he could not see why he should go ashore. The idea was preposterous. Then he recalled that the woman must have infinite courage, and such courage should be repaid with courtesy.

He said, "I'll go. Make a signal that I shall be ashore to-night."

The tide had turned!

It was not only for the *Vanguard,* riding at anchor in the Bay, but for Horatio Nelson riding out to meet his destiny.

He went ashore that evening.

LVI

EMMA HAD hurried to the Queen, who was only too ready to lend a willing ear. Emma convinced her that her throne, her crown, everything she possessed, depended on Admiral Nelsons meeting and conquering the French Fleet, and Maria Carolina was enraptured with the idea.

"He can do nothing unless he has food and water

for his men," urged Emma. Now her patriotism was fired, and she had the strength of a tigress. "Your Majesty must see how truly important this is. Men do not understand; they are so occupied with the affairs of state that they underestimate the matters which are really household ones, and we as women understand them. Starving men cannot fight to win and so save Naples, Your Majesty."

Maria Carolina looked at her. Her own eyes were swollen with weeping over her cause, and her face quite puffy with it. Latterly there had been further riots so that she dared not drive through the streets, for the sight of the Queen's carriage always seemed to cause a hostile stir. She turned to her favourite, realizing that she could trust Emma implicitly, and she put out her hand and clasped her friend's.

"I will speak to His Majesty."

"But now—now? You must speak to him now."

"His Majesty is not in a good mood, for they have assassinated Caballero. Only yesterday, oh, it was so dreadful, he was discovered with his throat slit, lying in the courtyard," and she began to cry again. Emma swallowed down her horror.

"We must not think of that now, for this is not the moment for moods. The French are waiting to do battle, and Admiral Nelson *must* conquer them. Your Majesty must snatch at the moment, because that is all we have, and the Fleet must be fed."

She held the Queen's hand fast; the arms were hooped with flexible diamond bracelets, through which brilliancy the skin looked old and freckled, and not unspotted like the marble-whiteness of Emma's.

"I will do what you tell me because you always advise me so well. Oh, Emma, how I rely on you!"

"My only desire is to protect Your Majesty."

She waited whilst the Queen went into the inner room to speak to the King. It seemed to be an eternity to Emma as she paced up and down the Queen's apartment, with the ornate furniture, the redundance of crowns on carpets and hangings, and the chairs on which golden leopards were crouched. She bit her lace handkerchief, for she knew that if she failed in her mission now, it might mean the subsequent failure of Admiral Nelson to conquer Buonaparte, and that in itself was unthinkable. She knew that Europe might totter under such a major catastrophe.

It was a long time before the Queen came out of the King's chamber, and now her eyes were moist and she looked quite bedraggled. She was alarmed, and Emma, who knew how short was the time, had little patience with a creature so sodden with tears and so fearful.

"I do not know what to say," faltered Maria Carolina. "He won't act, for he is alarmed that any move of that nature might involve him in a diplomatic crisis. He says that if Sir William cannot see his way to helping, then why should he?"

Emma stared at the Queen with a sinking heart, but it steadied again because of her own impulsive patriotism. "Oh, these men!" she said, and walking past the Queen went to the door and rapped on it sharply. She heard King Ferdinand's grunt, sanctioning admission, and went inside. Now she knew that she would have to employ every wile of which she was capable.

The King was lounging petulantly in a long chair by the window, and fanning himself with an ormolu fan. He was more paunchy than before, and as he lolled in the heat he exposed his rotundity grotesquely. His face was pendulous, and he looked at Emma with fish-like eyes (she thought privately, he has as little personal charm as a fish), and was without interest. As she approached and curtseyed, she wondered how he had ever contrived to have all those children, for she could never associate so indolent and lethargic a being with any lovely desire. Yet she had known him warm slightly to her, and told herself that this was the hour when he must warm

287

again. If the Fleet were to be fed and watered, King Ferdinand must be made to desire her.

"I crave Your Majesty's pardon."

"It is unusual to penetrate into the royal apartments so informally, Lady Hamilton." He spoke coldly, and instantly Emma knew that the Queen had been right when she had said that he was in a bad mood. He flung aside the fan, and picking up a golden tooth-pick, busied himself with exploring his back teeth.

"Sire, you did not call me Lady Hamilton last night."

"Then I was speaking with you as the personal friend of Her Majesty."

"Could I not be the personal friend of His Majesty also?"

She looked ravishingly beautiful, and even Ferdinand, cold as he might be, had to admit it. Her kerchief had become artlessly disengaged, and now floated with a delightful casualness to one shoulder, disclosing the swelling globes of her breasts; his eyes were fascinated by the boldness of the sight and centred thereon.

"What would you ask?"

"I come to throw myself upon Your Majesty's mercy," and she knelt before him beside the long chair. The King stared down at the breasts even more deliberately disclosed by her obeisance to him.

"Oh! All this trouble has started with regard to Admiral Nelson, I understand?"

"Admiral Nelson sets forth to save the world." Emma flung back her head challengingly, and now he saw her face close to his own. Her skin was clear as a May-day pool at dawn, whilst her eyes had grown luminous with their patriotism. At that moment Emma's face was lit by immortality, and before he could prevent himself Ferdinand had dropped his own lascivious mouth, pressing it on the ripe fullness of her moist one. She did not draw back.

"Your Majesty . . . ?" she faltered.

"I would do anything for you, sweet Emma," and his neck was going hot with desire. It was strange that suddenly she should disturb him so much.

"Then feed the British ships, Your Majesty."

Ferdinand began stuttering helplessly, but Emma laid her hand on his, and in her new mood she was compelling. Some of that fire of enthusiasm which lit her with such infinite courage now fused him as he sat there with her kneeling at his feet and his knees enclosing her. He could not gainsay her if he would have done, for he desired her so much as she pressed closer and insisted.

He rang the crystal handbell by his side.

"Give the order now, I implore you? There is no time for Your Majesty to lose."

If the Major-domo was amazed to see the wife of the Ambassador to His Britannic Majesty kneeling at the feet of the sovereign, and the sovereign so visibly stirred, he gave no sign of it, but received the order coldly.

"Your Majesty," he said.

"Oh, sire, how can I thank you?" With streaming eyes, Emma bent over the fat little hands of the weak King.

"You must not kneel to me."

"It is only right and proper, sire."

"Sweet, pretty one, that is not so."

He drew her up to him and closer still. Now all that she desired was to delay him, so that in thinking of her he forgot the order that he had given and could not cancel it until too late. For half an hour they stayed talking, and never had King Ferdinand enjoyed himself more. He kissed that palely sweet face again and again, and felt refreshed. He drenched himself in her beauty.

When she kissed his hand on leaving him, he felt suddenly old and deflated, as though the life had gone out of him. He had the feeling of frustration, and when his wife came to congratulate him on the effort he had made on behalf of the English ships,

her swollen face only annoyed him. He remembered
with resentment that he had been pushed into marrying a mere child of fifteen—he had had little say in
the matter—and their marriage night had been
marred because she had sat in the middle of the
bridal bed, and had wept bitterly, protesting that she
wanted her mother! He could not for a single moment imagine Emma Hamilton sitting crying in the
middle of a bridal bed, even at fifteen!

Emma returned to the *palazzo*; she changed her
creased muslin frock and brushed her auburn hair
until it shone. She went into her own room to receive
the Admiral when he was ashore. Sitting here and
looking out across the Bay to where the *Vanguard*
rode at anchor she had a feeling of complete
triumph. "My Emy has been a brave girl," her
mother had told her this very afternoon, and she had
been justified in saying it. Emma was immensely satisfied. She could see already the small naval pulling-
boats coming ashore to take in "vittles," and rowing
to and fro. No time had been lost, and this was entirely due to her.

They told her that the Admiral had arrived, whilst
on the piazza Sir William dozed. Emma had seen
him, a handkerchief laid across his face as one lays it
across the inscrutable features of the dead. The
handkerchief rose and fell with his raucous breathing, in little puffy hills at one moment, in cadaverous
valleys the next. She had looked at it with supreme
distaste, but it did not matter if the Ambassador
slept, so long as his wife did his work for him, she
told herself.

The doors opened. At the end of the long room a
flunkey announced, "Admiral Nelson, Your Excellency."

She stood up.

He looked very small as he strode up the room
with that rolling gait of his, and the gold lace on his
dark blue coat caught the sunshine as he came. She

saw him looking towards her not with the eyes of a man surveying the beauty of the woman whom he desires, but with the admiring eyes of one who honours a great diplomat.

"I have come to thank you, Your Excellency."

"Are the stores arriving, and fast?"

"Everything is in order. I understand from Captain Hardy that Sir William did not see his way clear to assisting us?"

"Sir William was nervous; he had some private diplomatic reasons, so I personally went to the Queen. I understood how great was your need, and that there was no time, and the Queen and I have been friends for years, so that she relies on me."

"You persuaded her, Your Excellency?"

"Alas, no. I failed. I had to interview His Majesty, and I persuaded him." She dropped her eyelids discreetly—not for the world would she have admitted to Admiral Nelson how she had succeeded, for it had taken every wile of which she was possessed.

"Every man of His Majesty's Fleet has reason to be grateful to your goodness of heart, Your Excellency."

He bent over the hand that she held outstretched to him. And as he kissed her he glanced up at her face again. Surely he had underestimated the quality of her beauty? Her cheek was more transparent than he had remembered it, her eyes more virginal. Her hair had about it a sheen which, so far, he had only associated with fine silks and satins. Now he found that with those beautiful eyes riveted on him, he was almost stammering. For a second he forgot the dark little cabin where he had worked so long preparing his strategy for the coming battle. He forgot the stench of wet, salty wood and the filthy straw under the few remaining beasts for slaughter.

"I am honoured, Admiral Nelson."

"I am proud to kiss Your Excellency's hand."

She motioned him to the couch beside her, and eagerly she asked of the approaching battle. She prayed that God would defend the right, for it would be a dreadful calamity should the Frenchies escape.

"They will not escape," said the Admiral. "My plan is to corner them. To draw off their fire, and then come round on the other side to surprise them."

"I understand that they are very clever."

He smiled at that. "They are clever enough, by God, and quick enough, and they have courage. But the English have that rare quality of doggedness which it will take all the Frenchmen in the world to conquer."

"How true!"

She knew that he inspired her. For the first time she appreciated how great was the soul in this little body, which burnt like a torch. He stayed for an hour then rose to go, and she knew now that she was utterly distracted that he should be leaving her to face an unknown danger.

"You will defend yourself? You will guard yourself, Admiral Nelson?"

"Indeed, have no fear on my account, Your Excellency."

"But I do fear for you," and she trembled with entirely womanly apprehension for him.

He kissed her hand, and looking down at it she longed ardently to delay him, if only for a moment. "You—you will come back . . . ?" she faltered, and the tone was that of a woman who was already half in love.

He drew himself to his little height and saluted her. "Your Excellency, I will return crowned with laurels or with cypresses. Have no fear on my behalf."

Turning, he went down the room without looking back. She recalled that he had never looked behind him that other time, and now when the door swung to, she knew that her cheeks were wet. Admiral Nelson had gone forth upon his lawful occasions to conquer the Nile.

LVII

NELSON HAD won the battle of the Nile.

He had become not only a national hero but world-famous. For the moment he had saved Europe, but he had suffered a severe wound, for being hit in the head he had been concussed, and fever following it, he had to face several weeks of ill-health not at all to his liking.

Emma was most enthusiastic in the letters that she wrote to him, and she told him in glowing terms of the tremendous jubilations in Naples at the thought that at last they were saved. Always over-impulsive, she was unstinting in her praise.

> My dress from head to foot is all Nelson; even my shawl is in blue with gold anchors all over. My earrings are Nelson's anchors; in short we are be-Nelsoned all over. Once more God bless you. My mother desires her love to you.

She had warmed considerably, and wrote to the hero who had told her that he would "return covered with laurels or cypresses." And when eventually he did arrive in the Bay, Naples was in *fiesta* on his behalf.

As the *Vanguard* dropped anchor, Horatio Nelson knew that he felt uncommonly ill. He had hoped to have conquered his malady by now, but he had lost a quantity of blood, and was still concussed, for there had been no time or place in which to nurse him. He was in no mood for national rejoicings, but unfortunately none were to know this as yet.

Flotillas of small boats decorated with flowers and

accompanied by a *serenata* set out to meet their conquering hero. Sir William and Lady Hamilton were with the King and Queen in the royal barge which was a bower of lilies and roses with the standard flying over it. Emma was radiant, for she knew that much of this honour of his was shared secretly with her. She had "vittled" the ships. The victory could not have been won without her.

When the hero of the hour appeared at the landing-stage, Naples surged forward in a frenzy of joy to meet him. They screamed their wild approval, hailing him as *"Nostro Liberatore."* Roses were showered upon him whilst rockets pierced the sky, dropping cascades of myriad coloured stars. But at the *palazzo* it was the British Ambassadress who, having become deeply concerned for him and realizing his need, helped him up the staircase to the apartments that she had ordered to be prepared for him.

She was shocked to see him so ill. "Here at least you must rest," she said.

She had indeed thought of everything on his behalf. The bed was drawn to the window so that he could watch the Fleet even where it rode at anchor, and therefore not concern himself on their account. From the moment when she had first seen him on board she had been distressed by his pallor and thinness. He seemed to have shrunk to nothing, and looked gravely ill.

"They have neglected you," she said.

"There was no time for anything but to do battle, Your Excellency. How could they think of me when more vital matters were so pressing?"

He was sick, and she promised that she would be his ministering angel. He had constant headaches and could not digest his food, so that she had, in fact, to obtain asses' milk for him. His whole body was racked, but she prescribed for him and tended him. She caressed his long hair, and worked a veritable miracle of healing, never sparing herself on his behalf. It was entirely due to her nursing that he was ready to appear at the state ball which was given at the Embassy in honour of his birthday.

"You needed a woman to attend you and make you well again," she told him.

Naples was *en fête,* and enjoying itself to the full. For a week it had been hung with coloured lights, and decorated with flowers and flags, and on this great occasion all personal grievances were overlooked. The huge ballroom was decorated with red roses as a special compliment to the country from which Nelson came. A special verse in his praise had been added to the National Anthem, and was sung vociferously. Everything was set for a great occasion.

But there was one person who could spoil the proceedings, and on whom none of them had reckoned, and that was Josiah Nisbet. Now a lieutenant, he had come through the battle in the belief that he had only to return to Naples to win again the attention of the woman who had meant everything to him. He had thought of Emma repeatedly, and of that happy hour in the arbour. Visiting his stepfather on the satin-hung bed, he had seen Emma beside him, coaxing him to eat and drink. He had turned pale, for he could not believe that he saw what was really happening, and felt maddeningly jealous.

"You have forgotten me?" he said to Emma.

At that moment she had been leaving Nelson's room, and she looked at the young man who once had attracted her. He was not wholly plain, but she knew now only too well that the fact that she had been starved of passion had been her greatest spur to that affair.

She said, "Do I remember you?"

"I am Josiah Nisbet, his stepson."

"Of course. I fear that the Admiral is not himself yet. He is very pale and thin."

"He should be well with so attentive a nurse as Your Excellency." Josiah said it with some venom.

She ignored it. Jealous young men said these things, but she could afford to forget. There were other women for him, for all Naples seemed willing to amuse the English sailors, and the best thing would be for him to find some light-of-love.

On the evening of the party Nelson was almost recovered, and Emma had a special frock for the occasion. When all the other women chose to appear crowned with diamonds and in their jewels, it was Emma who wore a simple wreath of field flowers, and so innocent a frock that it showed the others off to disadvantage.

She sat by Admiral Nelson on a dais, and from time to time her slender shoulders leant against his gold epaulettes, and the entire room realized that she had no eyes for anybody else. She was tenderly solicitous that he must eat nothing that could upset him, tasting everything first, even to his grog, and then handing him the cup.

"She has been goodness itself to me," he told the Queen.

"Lady Hamilton is indeed good. She is the most lovable of women. I shall never forget the day that she came to me seeking victuals for your ships."

"Without the good offices of Her Excellency, the battle of the Nile could not have been won," he said.

"I hope, Admiral, that England appreciates what their Ambassadress has done for them?"

"You may rest assured, Your Majesty, that I shall never fail to proclaim that the glory of the Nile lies at the feet of Lady Hamilton."

King Ferdinand, however, was fussy throughout the party. Although his Queen thought their troubles to be over, he was still very apprehensive as to the conditions prevailing in Europe. Also he was horrified that Nelson looked so frail. Obviously the man might very easily die and, if so, the Frenchies had only to gather together their scattered forces, and come back and avenge themselves. He hated the thought.

When the royal pair left, Emma persuaded the Admiral to rest a little in her room, lest he should be too tired. The ball was to continue until daybreak, and must be a considerable strain on one who had recently been so ill.

"You must rest for a short time. You are not yet strong enough to bear the continued efforts of a party that bids fair to last all night."

"You take too great care of me, Your Excellency."

"It is a national duty, and I accept it as a charge."

She took him out of the ballroom leading him most tenderly, and he with a patch over his eye, its darkness emphasizing the singular pallor of his emaciated cheek.

All the evening Josiah Nisbet had been watching them with jealous closeness and had missed no little gesture, no artless glance, no touch of the hand. He had availed himself of a liberal amount of grog, and the strong French brandy that was plentiful was fast drowning his discretion. He was his mother's own son, and never had approved of her second marriage to Nelson. He recalled with distaste the age difference—his mother was older than her new husband—and he was apprehensive on her account. Not only was he outraged because once he had himself possessed the exquisite body of Emma Hamilton, but because he believed his star to have been eclipsed by a far more famous lover, in the shape of his gallant stepfather.

Josiah had a suspicious nature, and now he was inflamed by jealousy. Also there was chatter and scandal running jauntily through the ballroom. The behaviour of the hero of the Nile and the charming wife of the Ambassador was commented on, and nobody was hesitating to talk.

"Apparently Her Excellency has no eyes for anybody else."

"I imagine that Her Excellency would give him anything; she probably has given him everything," with some laughter.

Flushed and angry Josiah stared after the couple who had gone out of the ballroom hand in hand.

"Where have they gone?" he demanded of Sir William.

Sir William was feeling very old; all this was too much for him, and he did not understand how such a junior officer could shoot questions at him. Coldly he explained that there was the urgency of rest for the Admiral who had been wounded in the battle, and that the thoughtful Emma had taken him to her room. He thought it incredible bad manners that young Josiah should drop the cup that he held and stalk purposefully out of the room, but then the new generation had no good manners.

Nobody needed to show Josiah the way to Emma's chamber. His face flushed and his hair ruffled, he did away with ceremony, and opened the door without any rap. He saw his stepfather half lying on the couch, with Emma kneeling beside him stroking his hair. Both turned and were dismayed to see their visitor.

"And what is the meaning of this intrusion, sir?" demanded the Admiral. But it was not to Nelson that Josiah looked.

Now he reeled across the room, for the French brandy had done its work, and he stood over Emma despising the beauty and very desirability that once had fired him. "This is your doing," he said. "You're just a common whore. Don't you realize that this man is married to my mother?"

Emma could not believe her ears! Blanching and completely startled, she sprang up, but she was not in time to prevent the hero of the Nile from closing with his stepson. He was in a most violent rage, and had underestimated his weakness from loss of blood. They grappled with one another, one drunk with anger, the other with passion, and they plunged down to the floor together. Emma was terrified for Nelson's safety, and horrified by the foul names that Josiah continued to call her; she screamed for help and thought that she would swoon with anguish. It was a dreadful position in which to find herself.

It was Captain Troubridge who heard the noise and came rushing into the room. Earlier in the evening he had recognized Josiah's condition, and had very nearly sent him back to his ship then and there, but something else had attracted his attention and he had postponed giving the order until too late. From something that Captain Hardy had let drop at the buffet, he had had a presentiment that there might be a scene, but was completely horrified to burst into the room to find Josiah rolling on the floor and fighting the Admiral as he would have fought a gunroom mate, whilst Emma cowered on the couch. Troubridge plunged into the very thick of the fight; already there was blood, and his own was to mingle with it a moment later, for Josiah split his head open for him with his first blow. Troubridge, now furiously angry, retaliated by knocking a couple of Josiah's teeth down his throat, and then picked him up.

"Get back to your ship," said he. "You're not fit to be ashore. You're drunk and a disgrace to the Royal Navy."

"So's he." Josiah was far too drunk to be discreet, and he said whatever came into his head. "Everybody knows that woman is nothing but a bawd, but she's turned his head with her whoring."

He would have continued, save that Captain Troubridge caught him on the point of the chin and he crashed like a Pompeiian colonnade before Vesuvius on the day of the eruption. He carried Josiah from the room.

"You can hold yourself in arrest," he said, but the young man never heard a word, nor did he come to until he found himself on board and in irons.

Left alone with Admiral Nelson, Emma saw him stagger to his feet, attempting to brush down his coat. She burst into tears because she felt so utterly helpless in this disgraceful situation. She did not think that she could bear another moment.

LVIII

THE ADMIRAL sat beside Emma on the couch; he felt very ill and shaken, but more than this extremely angry that it had ever happened.

"Please I do beg of you not to take this so badly. The boy is preposterous, and I'll have him flogged and court-martialled for it."

"Oh, sir, I pray you not to be cruel to him. He was very drunk and did not know what he said."

"He had no right to get drunk to the degree that he lifts a hand against his own Admiral, and calls you—the very best of women—the filthiest names."

"Alas, what must you think of me?"

"I can only think that I have never met a woman whom I could praise with more honesty."

She was still smarting under the hideous words that Josiah had used, and did not know how to control her weeping. "You must promise me that he shall not be court-martialled. It would only make public something that is far better kept private. No good can come of advertising such a regrettable quarrel, and to-night of all nights."

But the Admiral was a man and a sailor, and he was not so easily soothed by soft words. He did not expect his lieutenants to draw his blood, and was indignant. "He shall be beaten for this. By God, that confounded boy shall suffer for it."

"I do not wish it." Compassion swept aside any insult under which she had smarted. Once Josiah's body had united with her own, and in some way she felt that she must help him.

"Women are too soft."

"Oh, promise me that he shall not be beaten."

"But God knows that he deserves it. By all the laws he should be flogged within an inch of his life."

She put out a hand and touched him with the faltering and sweetly tender touch she always used. For the first time she spoke to him as a man. "Indeed, dear Horatio, do not speak so harshly. We have had some strong French brandy here and it went to the poor lad's head. He will suffer sufficiently in the morning for what he has drunk to-night, and surely he has had punishment enough?"

"I refuse to discuss it; all I want is to forget this most unhappy incident in our lives." But she had called him Horatio. He knew how it had touched him.

"I can forget only if you forgive the boy."

He came closer to her, for the conqueror was fast becoming the conquered. Emma was dreadfully distressed at the names that she had been called, and even more so in that she knew that most unfortunately they had been deserved. There had been too many men in her life, and because Nelson trusted her innocence, she wanted above all other things to keep up the pretence of it for him. He thought that she was an angelic creature, and she could promise herself that she would be an angel on his behalf.

In the small hours of the morning, with the dance so recently finished and only a few last guests left, he was afire with fury about Josiah, but before the actual dawn he would be afire with passion of another order.

"What Josiah says is the talk of evil sections of European society," she explained modestly. "I rose from nothing . . ."

"All honour to you for that."

"Oh, Horatio, I suffered such pangs. I was so poor, and often very hungry. Hunger is a terrible thing. I have slept on doorsteps for I had nowhere else, and when I got work I had to work very hard indeed."

301

He kissed the little palms of her hands held uppermost to him to see.

"But this may be said with truth, that since those days I have never passed a poor man by. Remembering what it is to hunger and thirst, to grow weary and despair, I have been generous to those in like unhappy condition. I have indeed."

"I am sure you have. You own all the virtues in one, dear, sweet Emma. A lamp in the darkness of this world, a star in a black heaven."

"The world is so jealous . . ."

"It has no need to be jealous of one who has everything, not only love and life and extreme beauty, but the blessed gift of virtue."

"That is what they would deny me . . ."

"It is because they do not know you. Only I know you, my beautiful, my dearest Emma."

He took her hands and drew nearer. Genuinely horrified by what had happened she began to weep again, and he kissed her. He had thought that the kiss would be a small thing, as his mouth closed on her cheek, but, warming, it crept down to her lips and suddenly fired by the passion of all time he could not stay himself. He did not think again if what the drunken Josiah had said was true; he thought of nothing save that Emma was lying in his arms, and was amazed now at the tremendous ravages of emotion she could stir within him.

"Oh, most beautiful, most exquisite one, how have I ever lived without you?"

"Horatio, you little know how long I have waited for you. I love my husband, but only as a father . . ."

"You would never love me as a father . . ."

"As a lord," she declared proudly.

Suddenly he remembered forcefully that he was the guest of the Ambassador, and as such could not become enamoured of his wife. Resolutely he set her from him. "I regret. This should not have been. Please forgive me."

She hesitated, dismayed. Was she then to be

cheated of the man she so desperately desired, and at the last moment too? She played a diplomatic card. "I am sorry too. Shall we go back to the ballroom? Not all have left as yet and they will desire you presence."

They returned. And now the flowers were drooping so that the scent of red roses and stephanotis had become almost sickly. Across the Bay the first warning of discerning dawn was at hand. People were drunk and the company thinning as these two, with the Ambassador, bade the last farewells. Now with the light of new morning, the finery that was so gay last night turned tawdry, the silver was tinsel.

When all had gone and the servants at work to get the rooms ready for the morrow, Emma went to her own chamber. She removed her clothes and put on a muslin wrapper, entirely diaphanous, and eager to disclose the long white curve of thigh and the angle of a slender waist. I shall go to him, she told herself.

To-night he would be too tired to sleep, for he always slept badly. Again she opened the door, and slipped down the passage to the apartments that had been given over to the Admiral's use. Nobody stirred. She rapped softly on the door, and heard his voice instantly, quickening her heart as in the old days.

"Come in," he ordered.

She went inside. The room was lit by the opal whiteness of a new day born beyond Pompeii. She saw him lying on the bed, and knew that he had been restlessly anxious. His features were sharpened by the light.

"I was afraid for you, dearest Horatio," she faltered gently. "The night has been oppressive and too long, the festivities have made too much demand on you, and I thought perhaps you might need a sedative."

It was only an excuse.

If he saw through it he gave no sign, but turned to her, his face radiant. He held wide his arms in a ges-

303

ture of acceptance as though he prayed her to come to them for shelter.

"Our dearest Emma," he said, and she went to him with never a sound.

LIX

NELSON AND EMMA were lovers.

In that daybreak after the *fiesta* in honour of the victor of the Nile and the liberator of Europe, before he could stay himself he had penetrated the chaste white temple of her charm. He stayed on at the British Embassy for three weeks, but he was never blinded to the fact that this was not peace. He was radiantly happy in Emma, but he saw war ahead. This was a breathing space, it was not complete victory.

"Sweet Emma, we have got to consider this only as an interlude between two great conflicts, for it is not peace. Believe me that, whilst Buonaparte is free, there is no safety for any single one of us. I must return to my work and nothing must stop me from it."

"But surely the immediate danger is over?"

"I regret that is not so. There might easily be a repetition of the French tragedy here, for Naples is the sort of place where that sort of thing happens. The King and Queen would lose their heads, and if an insurrection starts, I charge you with the duty of persuading them to flee."

"But Her Majesty would never agree."

"My sweet Emma, they must be forced. You have done so much for them that you must persuade them. Swear that you will do this?"

"At all times I will do what you command."

She adored him absolutely, and could never have

believed herself capable of this devotion. Although he still stood second to Greville in her life—he was the first man that she had really loved—her fervent patriotism now blossomed with the new physical desire, and she could not have thought that so small a man could exert so large an influence over her. He left her for sea again, and this time she said good-bye with real pain in her heart.

"I shall return if there is any symptom of a revolution brewing," he promised, "and you must not be afraid nor think that I shall be unmindful of you."

"How could I ever be afraid with Nelson?"

"You may even have to put out to sea with me."

"That would indeed be joy," she exclaimed, and kissed him rapturously.

As she watched the Fleet weigh anchor and set sail she was completely unafraid. The sails bellied in the little wind, and turned to silver in the sunshine. The only anxiety that ever concerned her was the fear that he might discover her past, for Horatio (as so many men in her life) still believed in her innocence. He will return, I know that he will return, she vowed to herself.

Once more the revolution broke out and this time with a surprising suddenness. Again there came the sharp sound of shooting in the streets, and the animal noises of a crowd out for blood. The gutters were filled with rotting bodies, their throats cut so that looking at them it seemed they had a second and revoltingly hideous mouth which laughed in mockery at the very name of death. The smell of blood mingled fantastically with that of red roses and the lemon magnolias. In her own room the Queen wept copiously, for this was what she had always feared, and made sure that she would be killed as her sister had been.

Sir William dispatched frantic but futile letters to London seeking aid, and even His Majesty was undecided as to the right course of action to be taken and the court dithered. During this period of indecision the mob became more and more vindictive, and threatened still more violent action. It was Emma who, as directed by Nelson, drew the Queen's attention to the disaster which might eventually overtake her children if she delayed.

"Remember the little Dauphin of France. Where is he now? And the Dauphiness? Where are those poor children? One may suffer with the greatest courage oneself, and act wisely in being unafraid, but what of innocent babes?"

"But to flee Naples would be to admit that we are beaten."

"To flee Naples alive is better than to die, and all to no purpose. Surely Your Majesty must realize that?"

"They would not touch a woman."

"Did they hesitate to touch the body of Her Majesty Queen Marie Antoinette?" asked Emma.

She had never ceased to distress herself with the thought of that most dreadful last scene, when the white-haired, but still proud young woman had gone to the scaffold with her hands tied like a felon's. She had held her head high as she looked with sad eyes on Paris for the last time, but the guillotine had the power to roll that same proud head in the dust with the others, to drench it with blood for the executioner to hold up to the cheering crowd; a head still hideously bleeding, a sight never to be forgotten.

Maria Carolina shuddered as she thought of it.

"Mobs do not keep their hands off women and children; they go mad, and then they do not know what they do." For Nelson had instructed Emma to persuade the Queen to flee, and at all costs she must be persuaded.

Once Her Majesty had been talked round, everything was planned, for Nelson himself would take them to safety in the *Vanguard*. Urgent messages passed between him and Emma, for the courteasan had now turned into the conspirator and was arranging everything. His Majesty still clung to the fantastic hope that even at this late moment, something would happed to stop the disturbance. The Queen was loath to leave the treasures she had amassed, she had much of her sister's love of finery, and for this would have held back, but the wave of revolution came on in a tremendous tide, and at last both of them realized that they could not stay.

Arrangements were completed.

Between the royal apartments and the little quay lay a secret passage which dived down into the very bowels of Naples. It had been built a couple of centuries before, then sealed up and unused, having remained that way; but Nelson knew of it, and when he was staying at the Embassy insisted that it must be reopened. The fetid place had been full of foul air, and the first men who had started working there had died from it, but life was cheap, and nobody enquired too closely. A gruesome, dank place, it stunk of moisture, of human excretions, and of bad air. But, having once been opened up, the months had made it safe, and now it afforded a definite means of escape.

The *Vanguard* lay off again.

Sir William left from the back door of the British Embassy, whilst his carriage, surrounded by the screaming mob demanding blood, waited at the front. Emma was in her element, for, being born completely fearless, she adored adventure. She changed into quiet travelling clothes and set out to meet a hero who delighted her. That fact that a storm was blowing up, and a high wind was lashing the sea on to the land, did not agitate her in the least. At the appointed hour there was a ground swell, and already in the royal apartments (where they were awaiting the signal to start from Count Thurn) they could hear the thundering noise that the defiant sea was making.

It was Emma herself who carried the youngest Prince Albert in her arms when they went down into the hideous underground passage where Nelson was to meet them. The Queen wept and stumbled, and was terrified, for she could hardly see for her tears. Servants carried lanterns and tried to make the progress easier, whilst His Majesty protested against the folly of the whole journey. He was a poor sailor at the best of times and had the most unhappy misgivings as to what was to come.

The passage smelt sourly of wet weed and moisture. Rats scuttled across the causeway, amazed to be disturbed, and this agonized the women. They could only claw their way in single file, lantern bearers doing their best to point out the crevices in the stones, and help where they could, but the slipperiness of the foothold made every step a danger.

"If we escape with no broken bones, we shall indeed be fortunate—more so than I anticipate," said His Majesty.

A claustrophobic terror now possessed the Queen, who became hysterical, and would have turned back, save that Emma, carrying little Prince Albert in her arms, pushed her ahead and actually refused to permit her to return.

Suddenly, as they rounded the corner of what seemed to be an interminable passage, she saw Nelson and his party coming to meet them. The light glittered on cutlasses and pistols as the men approached, and seeing whom they were meeting, the naval consignment halted as a man and sprang to the salute. It was Nelson who stepped forward to greet the weeping Queen, and solemnly kissed her hand.

"We should never have started," she wailed.

"Your Majesty will soon be safe, trust your royal person to me."

Exhilarated and uplifted to hear his voice again Emma went on with the young prince lying against her breast. The boy had been ill all day, and at one time they had even entertained the idea of postponing the adventure because of him. But, during the afternoon, the window of the *palazzo* had been smashed by a piece of masonry that a defiant mob had hurled through it, and it had terrified the Queen. Emma carried the little prince as carefully as she could, slipping on the wet weedy surface with the dark sewer plunging beside her, soothing him solicitously, but herself disliking every moment of this difficult progress. At the far end of the darkness, at last, she perceived a pin-point of light.

"We are nearly there, it is little farther," said someone.

The light grew larger, and nearing it there came with it the clean smell of the sea, and the angry sound of it as it lashed the quay itself. They could not welcome anything more. Now they could see that beside the mole a barge was awaiting them, and the British bluejackets were at hand. They came forward to help the party, and drew them into the boats, where Nelson spread his boat cloak for the Queen, and taking Emma's hand helped her aboard. Until this moment they had not touched, nor had he looked at her, and now it seemed ominous that hands and eyes should meet at the water's edge, with the spray on their lips.

"You have indeed been good," she gasped, but the wind carried her voice away.

The boat bobbed like a cork, so that it seemed as if the city of Naples jigged and danced to them. Above all the noise of the wind and water they could hear the mob shouting. A fire had started in an ugly glowering mass on the horizon, and grew apace, so that Maria Carolina hid her face in her hands. If for a moment she had any doubts left about the wisdom of her flight, they must now have been dispelled, for the *palazzo* was ablaze.

She sat beside His Majesty in a final but pathetic attempt at dignity, and as they sat there there came the sound of a great explosion very near at hand, so that the earth shook under them. The order was given to "shove off."

In another instant the boat had put out to sea, rising and falling; the oars were plunging rhythmically, the spray in the faces of the men, and the royal party was setting out for the *Vanguard*.

LX

NEARING THE vessel there was still the horror of a rope ladder to be negotiated in the storm. One by one the passengers were swung up it, the Queen protesting bitterly. Emma went up lightly and without difficulty, her eyes bright with the spirit of adventure, her skirt blown about her, her hat lost, so that her auburn hair almost blinded her.

Sir William was already inboard, having been brought off by another boat, and they were bustled across the deck in the teeth of a gale against which they could scarcely stand. Below it was airless, with the horrid stench of bodies, of wood that had been soaked in salt, and of the animals in their byre, but it was sanctuary.

Emma still clasped little Prince Albert to her, whilst the Queen carried her six-weeks-old baby; the four little princesses were put to bed in one bunk, but before very long it was obvious that everybody was going to be very ill, for the sea was not to be kind to them, and the *Vanguard* was moving considerably.

She put out to sea on the morning of December the twenty-third. It was the first chance she had to weigh anchor, and directly she came out from under the lee of the land, she began to plunge and roll more violently than she had done before, which they had thought quite shocking enough. Emma was not sick, but she was deeply anxious for the Queen and the royal children, who were now far too ill to see after themselves. Against Nelson's orders she came on deck on the Christmas Eve, in the middle of a severe storm. He saw that she was there and scowled at her, but she ignored it. Then he went to her.

"I told you to stay below," he screamed against the wind. "I will have my orders obeyed in my own ship."

She turned and laughed at him. "If Nelson is unafraid, why should Emma be?"

"I am unafraid because this is my job. It is not yours. I fear that you must be very tired, and understand that you have not rested since you came on board."

"There is no bed," she said, "but it is not so bad for me as for the others, for they are very sick. I have the greatest fears for little Prince Albert."

"Sea-sickness seldom kills."

Down in the bowels of the ship the bluejackets were singing Christmas carols, and she could hear the sweetly familiar tunes coming up to them as she and Nelson went down the ladder into the warmth below. The music made her lips quiver and he saw it.

"Oh, sweet Emma, women should never put out to sea; the weather has been cruel to us; maybe Christmas Day will be kinder," he whispered.

But Christmas Day was more unkind.

Although at night they were to reach Palermo, their sails torn to pieces and all the men standing by with axes to cut down the masts if need be, disaster of another kind had overtaken them. Everybody was intolerably sick, and there was little that could be done for them. The ship stunk with vomit. Little Prince Albert had spent most of the time in Emma's arms, and was persuaded to take a little food at midday, after which he went into violent convulsions. Nelson himself came rushing to Emma's aid.

She was sitting on the deck of the cabin with the boy in her arms, her eyes streaming, and he thought that he had never seen such a wonderful picture as she made. She bathed the child's brow, whispering encouragingly to him, and at the same time trying to soothe the unhappy Queen who lay in the bunk with her baby actually at her breast.

"I cannot save him," said Emma, lifting pathetic eyes to the man who loved her, standing awkwardly by.

"I am afraid in the face of death we are all helpless."

She clasped the child, his face turned purplish blue with the convulsion and a froth dribbling from a corner of his ashy mouth. She wiped the mouth tenderly and began to whisper a paternoster to him. The heart of Nelson was distraught at so tender a sight. He had never had a child, for his wife had always been coldly distant and their marriage had remained unconsummated. She had already borne Josiah, suffering agonies at the time, and she could not bear the thought of a repetition of it, and had said so on their wedding night. He would never forget the coldness of her eyes, looking as though they were made of ice.

The little prince stopped breathing, and reverently Emma closed the half-opened eyes with her fingers and kissed him, her face wet with tears.

"He cannot be dead!" screamed his distraught mother.

Still sitting there, with the ship rising and falling and the prone bodies of the other royal children prostrate about her, Emma looked up falteringly to Nelson.

"What do I do now, Horatio? They must not know."

He helped her to her feet, the dead child still in her arms, and she pretending that he slept so that the others might not be dismayed.

"Oh, Emma, what courage!" he whispered.

The need for sleep so possessed her that she was drunk with it and reeled. They came out of the cabin, and he summoned an officer who took the child from her, then he led her to a corner of the deck and, removing his coat, laid it down to make a bed for her.

"I dare not sleep," she faltered.

"Nonsense! Nelson himself will be your sentry."

"But, Horatio, that poor little boy?"

"His troubles at least are ended," he answered almost grimly, and laid her there, standing beside her. The last person she saw was Horatio himself, keeping watch over her, and when she woke, hours later, she was alone and the ship had reached Palermo safely.

The Queen was not so prostrate with grief that she refused to go ashore, and ultimately it was Nelson who accompanied her and the princesses privately to the land, taking them to the old palace of Colli.

"I shall be at the British Embassy," Nelson told Emma. She had not realized that he would leave them and that landing meant parting.

"Then you are not staying with us?"

"Indeed, for the time being, if you need me?"

"Oh, Horatio, how I need you! That journey distressed me quite dreadfully, and the loss of the little prince."

"There is always the future."

"I know, but—look at that——" and she indicated Sir William, who, having suffered a three days' bilious attack, was extremely querulous. He had sent all his art treasures on to Palermo in the *Colossus*, which had been lost in the storm, and he could not recover from the shock this had given him. He was old, and showing it more every day, and he found it a very poor consolation that he had done his duty, or that a loving wife was making the new Embassy attractive for himself and the honoured guest they had with them.

He had no idea that Nelson and his wife consorted nightly. Sir William had no thought of love, and did not trouble himself about it, but every night the Admiral came to Her Excellency's room. He would slip inside the door and creep across the floor to the canopied bed where so much beauty lay exposed for him. The loveliness of Palermo lay beneath the wide windows, but neither of them looked at that loveliness, for they had eyes but for one another.

Wrapped with her arms about him in the sweetness of the night, sometimes she wondered what would be the end of it all.

"There is your wife, dearest Horatio?"

"She is very cold. She would never sanction any warmth in our marriage."

"My love, my poor, poor love! Never shall you chide your Emma on that score."

"Never," he agreed, and kissed her again and again.

Below the magnolias which smelt so exquisite, a man was singing tender music, and its sweetness seemed to fit in with the spirit of the hour.

"To think that you kept all this beauty for Horatio! Through all those lonely years, till now."

"Sir William . . ." she whispered.

"I think Sir William was more your father than lover," and again and again he kissed her warm white throat and the curves of the breasts which rose beneath it.

"Yes, that is true, he was always like a father to me and I felt as for a father for him," and she sighed. She would never be able to confess her love of Greville, which had been such anguish, and how he had sold her to Sir William. So she had been passed from one to another, and—worse—the same thing had happened earlier in her life. Horatio Nelson was of a mentality which would fail to understand the mysticism of Dr. Graham and his Celestial Bed; he would never understand her fervent longing to save her cousin from the press gang, which had sent her to lie with Willet-Payne. That was long ago, so long ago that it is doubtful if she even remembered the face of the golden-haired groom in the straw, or of Andrew staring in at the kitchen window when her mistress had whipped her so ignominiously; but she did remember Greville, her dearest, devoted Greville, with the strange treasures that had delighted him, and his

314

curious methods of correction. For the moment none of this mattered to Horatio, for he did not suspect it, and would have refuted any accusation with his own honour.

"All I ask now is to possess and to be possessed," he said as he clasped her to him.

"Ah, if I could but make you truly happy!"

But in their hearts both of them were secretly disturbed as to what Lady Nelson's reactions might be. Both knew that Sir William was growing old in diplomatic service, and he would ere long undoubtedly be recalled. Then what would the outcome be?

"I shall never give you up," declared Nelson, and he spoke with a passion she believed.

"I shall count the world well lost for the joy of making happy so great a hero."

"But there will be difficulties," he said.

Political matters he did not question, but difficulties with the country recurred in his mind. He was determined that England must know what Her Excellency had done for the Fleet. Europe knew it, for he had never ceased to proclaim it. Wherever she went she would be fêted and treated as one of the greatest women—if not the greatest—of her time. But how would it be in England? For he foresaw trouble in Norfolk with his wife.

"She must love you very much," whispered Emma, raising her limpid eyes to his.

"In her own way, but her way was never my way. Don't let's discuss it."

For now he could not trust himself to speak. In loving Emma he was betraying the woman who had stayed at home, and in his heart he appreciated that Josiah Nisbet had every right to be angry. He had laid his finger on the true pulse of the situation when he had declared that Emma was usurping his mother's place.

"But it is not good to look at to-morrow, when to-night is so sweet," urged Nelson.

"If I had thought of morrows, I suppose I should

never have been able to bear to-day," she answered, and let her arms curl about him. He was hers, entirely hers, and she was not afraid of any indignant Lady Nelson who might make life irksome when they returned.

Emma was far more afraid of the road which lay behind her, and she suffered tortures memorizing the black marks that had been chalked up against her virtue. The men who had held her as closely and as passionately, and who had drunk so freely from that same fountain. Nelson still believed her to be good. What would happen if he ever discovered the truth? And when they returned to London there would be plenty of jealous tongues in that great city prepared to chatter of what once had happened to Emma Hart.

Emma Hart, now Her Excellency. That was all a long way off.

LXI

IN EIGHTEEN hundred Sir William Hamilton was recalled, because his time abroad was finished. Now he would be entitled to take a pension and would settle down to live the life of an ordinary gentleman of London.

Emma did not know if she were glad or sorry. Exquisite gifts were showered upon her, even upon her mother too, but before they actually returned to England, they decided they would go the round of the European courts, and on this—which was practically a royal trip—Lord Nelson would accompany them.

They visited Vienna, Florence, Trieste, Dresden and Hamburg, and everywhere they were received with a tumultuous welcome in honour of the hero.

None of them realized that at home in London the ugly jade rumour was at work, and that her good name was being bandied from lip to lip.

She kept saying, "It will be wonderful in London," though she did get faint sinkings of the heart when she recalled that perhaps there, Horatio would have to return to his own wife, and it might be very difficult when Fanny Nelson met the three of them together.

As they neared the coast of England in another terrific storm, Nelson held Emma to his heart. "There it is at last," he said, "the little lights of Yarmouth town, and Caister beyond."

"After so long," and then, with some fear, "Will Fanny be there?"

"I expect so."

"Oh, Horatio, at first it may be a little difficult."

"Difficult only because she is not an easy woman. She is aloof and strange, but we will have courage."

However, when they landed, Lady Nelson was not on the quayside. The mob surged round only over-anxious to give the hero the welcome they felt he so richly deserved. The carriage was dragged to the Wrestler's Inn, where troops were paraded and a banquet held for Nelson. Emma was in her element. She adored to see Horatio fêted and praised, for in some ways it actually reflected on herself, she having been the power behind him. Ipswich gave them a far greater welcome, and Colchester outshone Ipswich, but at neither of these cities was his wife present.

It was only when they got to London one rather dismal Sunday that Emma had her first suspicion of a current which ran under all this. Nelson was wearing full uniform and looking very tired, and all three of them drove almost as one family to Nerot's Hotel.

('I'm home again,' thought Emma. 'Home to this very hotel where once——' and then she held her peace, for the past still had the power to stab her.)

Greville was awaiting his uncle. She saw him the instant that she alighted from the carriage, and was in many ways horrified to find that he still had the power to stir her very considerably. He had aged a little, but she was amazed to see how beautiful he still looked as he stood on the step of the hotel, his hat in his hand and his wig exquisitely combed.

"My dearest Greville," she exclaimed, and clasped his hand, whilst her voice became broken with emotion. "Your uncle is well, surprisingly so after the trip we have had, because the weather has been really very bad. He is naturally a little tired. . . ."

"He looks dreadfully tired. And is this . . . ?"

But Nelson had given him one look which penetrated right through, and then pushing past them both without a word, went straight up the stairs. His wife was staying at the hotel with his father, and he went to their suite. He knew that the moment had come when this thing had to be thrashed out, and Emma knew it, but she turned enthusiastically again to Greville.

"Wherever we have been we have made a positively royal progress. It has been so stimulating, and he has been so wonderful."

Greville must have realized that she had changed. At her fingertips she had power, and although she had written constantly emphasizing this to him, he had always allowed for her tendency to exaggerate, her excess of impulsive *joie de vivre,* and had never thought that now she might be all-powerful.

"You are more beautiful than ever."

"I have been so happy. My dearest Greville, I have been so very happy."

They went to their rooms where Sir William could rest and have food. The old man nodded in his chair; he seemed to have shrunk in stature, and huddled there, smiling blandly, as though he only half realized what was going on around him.

"People say that Lord Nelson is in love with you," Greville told Emma in a low voice.

"I have the honour to believe that indeed he is."

"Once I was in love with you." Artlessly he

318

flicked her hand quite sharply with his own. She knew what he meant, and turned surprised, her mouth working a little. Even Her Excellency was not proof against that reminder.

"Oh, Greville, that all seems to be so long ago."

"I was a hard master."

"No, Greville, never. I always loved you." That was the truth.

"How different the past might have been, my sweet; but you married to spite me."

"I warned you, if you recollect?"

"And I did not heed that warning. Much of this has been my own fault, but I swear that you were always the sweetest of mistresses."

She said nothing. Perhaps until this moment she had been unaware that so much of his power still remained; it seemed to have been so long ago. They ate and drank, and later Greville returned to his home in Cleveland Row, and Emma was left alone. Nelson came downstairs again to her. She knew that something had gone amiss by his appearance. It was not merely bodily fatigue, his iron will could always conquer that, it was that a certain fire in his eyes had been quenched.

"Well?" she asked.

"I am afraid that Fanny is being extremely difficult."

"What has happened?"

He walked up and down as he was used to doing on his quarter-deck, turning automatically and strutting back, then turning yet again, his hands behind him. "God! That this should have happened! Apparently there have been rumours flying about. Josiah lent a hand with it. I could not have believed this possible."

"About us?"

"Yes, it's diabolical, and quite untrue." Then he checked himself, realizing that was not quite accurate. The rumours were untrue in some ways, but he was in love. He would never forget his wife's coldly calculating eyes and her pallor. Possibly her anàmic face presented a vigorous contrast to the colourful beauty that had gone to his head during the past few months.

"The woman's name is on every lip in Europe," she had said, and her tone had the sting of frost in it.

That had been a horrible interview. His proud but anxious father watching from the background, and his indigant, rather repellent wife (primed by her son who had left little to her imagination) staring at him with no interest.

"Oh, Horatio, you ought never to have known me," said Emma, distraught that so much should have happened on her account and not knowing what to do next.

"Not to have known you would have been not to have known life itself," he answered. "Oh, no, my dearest, that would indeed have been the outer darkness."

But the first faint anxiety was pricking Emma's bosom, and she thought that she had seen the red light of danger. When, on the morrow, the three of them were dragged in their carriage by the citizens of London to the Lord Mayor's banquet for the sword of honour to be presented, Lady Nelson was—very pointedly—absent. Even Sir William remarked upon it and thought that it was "a grave pity." But he was tired out, and gabbled foolishly, soon forgetting what had concerned him so much at the time.

"It can't be helped," said Nelson curtly. "She is the most unreasonable woman."

Far more worried than either of them was Emma, who knew that to her surprise she was inclined to weep about it. She realized that this extraordinary state of affairs could not continue, for every lively tongue in London would lay on to it, and in the end all would suffer for it. It was she who suggested that it might help considerably if they all appeared at the theatre together, and so give the direct lie to the stories that were flying the rounds.

320

"Very well. I will command Fanny to attend with us."

"Oh, Horatio, would that be wise?"

She could not imagine what ailed her, but she felt so depressed. She wondered if she had over-fatigued herself with the irksomeness of the long journey, and therefore was allowing the present state of affairs to prey on her mind more than was reasonable. But she felt very sick.

"Fanny has got to come to heel."

Emma dressed herself with particular care for the threatre, knowing that a great deal depended on this. She chose a frock of deep blue spangled with stars, and she hoped that her personal charm would win over this wife who seemed to be so reluctant to meet her. Self-confidence was always one of Emma's strongest suits, and she felt sure that she could and would conquer Lady Nelson's prejudices.

They met in the vestibule of the box, Emma's first thought being 'How could he have married her?' and Lady Nelson's a stab of jealousy at the extreme beauty of her rival. Emma held out both hands warmly, and rushed to clasp those of Lady Nelson.

"I have wanted to meet you so much, so very much."

From the Ambassadress such a greeting was one that would have delighted, but from Emma Hamilton—as she now was—it meant nothing, and Lady Nelson made no reply, merely staring at her with accusing eyes that never flickered.

From beyond came the ponderous music of the theatre and the sound of the audience who were all impatience for the show to begin. Nelson pulled back the plush curtains and went to the edge of the box, which was the signal for the house to rise, cheering itself hoarse. He saluted and smiled, drawing Lady Hamilton to the front with him on one side and his wife on the other. The crowd looked on the beauty of Emma, not to the pallor and frigid displeasure of the other woman, who saw it at once.

321

At that particular moment when she believed that their troubles were over, Emma felt so overjoyed that she nearly fainted. She had to sink down into the chair that had been put in readiness for her, and a few moments later, when the attack of dizziness had passed, she saw Lady Nelson looking at her, and then turning to Horatio.

"Horatio, I refuse to stay here," she said, and her voice was extremely bitter.

"You will do as I bid. The country expects it of you, and I expect it of you. I command you to stay."

She looked at him coldly, probably the only person in the whole of England who dared to disobey the little Admiral. She said, "England may not know, you even may not know, but your mistress is pregnant, and by you!" Then she turned and left the box.

That was when Emma dropped down in a swoon.

LXII

HORATIO NELSON had not known it, and Emma had been doing her best to hide what were her worst fears. Now it was more than ever urgent to conceal what was happening. An accouchement could only give truth to the chatter, and must be concealed at all costs. One merciful providence was that Sir William was quite suspicionless, only thankful to be home at last, and already negotiating to possess himself of Number Twenty-three Piccadilly, a small, comfortable house which faced on to the Green Park.

But there was another singularly awkward matter of which, as yet, he had not dared to speak and which occupied him considerably. He had reported to the Foreign Office, as was proper, and had gone to the Palace to kiss hands. He had acquainted His Majesty with the fact that both he and Lady Hamilton would be paying their proper respects, whereupon His Majesty had chilled visibly. He had remarked that he had the greatest esteem for the valuable work that Sir William had done when at the Court of Naples, and at Palermo, and was indeed most grateful. Unfortunately, seeing the way that gossipy tongues were wagging (and naturally with an eye on the past), Queen Caroline did not feel herself disposed to receive Lady Hamilton.

This had happened before, of course, but Sir William had for the moment forgotten it, and hoped that the King had also. He did not know what to do. He realized that Emma probably had no thought of a wave of public opinion against her; she had been so fêted and admired, she had been the darling of the crowd so often, the confidante of the Queen of Naples, and had undoubtedly saved the British Fleet for Nelson in his hour of need, that she would have no conception of what was happening. Sir William was at an impasse. He did not know how to behave in such circumstances. He bowed low. It is impossible to quibble at the royal displeasure. Not for a moment did he imagine that a single word of the scandal was true. Emma was not Horatio's mistress, and never had been, he could swear. It was just the lewd minds of people who did not know any better, and who had started this absurd story going the rounds.

It was a shock to find the First Gentleman of Europe, who himself was scarcely as white as the driven snow, looking down his nose at the famous Lady Hamilton. Wonders will never cease, said Sir William, racked with rheumatic pains, and now seriously disturbed for the safety of his pension. The First Gentleman became attentive. Already there was a strong public feeling that the King's health gave rise to regrets (he was certainly very odd at times), and of course the removal of His Majesty might make matters more simple.

"If the father hates me, the son may love me," as Emma had once said.

But it was Lord Nelson who was now anguished. He had always longed for a child. In the early days of his marriage to Fanny, he had prayed her to give him children, and had been dismayed to find how far that was from her intention. Now suddenly—at the theatre of all places—he had discovered that he was to have a son or daughter of his own, and by his mistress. He drove back with the Hamiltons. Long after Sir William, fearing the approach of one of his distressing bilious attacks, had gone to bed, Nelson sat on in the sitting-room with his beloved. She looked both pale and ill, and was visibly distressed. Now she was making no attempt to hide her condition from him, but lay on the sofa, her eyes ringed with violet shadows, and her head heavy. She had not meant the matter to be disclosed so soon, intending to bide her time. Emma had few maternal instincts. It is doubtful if she ever worried herself as to what might have happened to little Emily, whom Greville had had educated for her. To Emma at the moment the thought of a baby was preposterous.

"My lovely and exquisite wife," said Nelson who was exalted at the prospect. "You have done for me what my own wife refused to do. Indeed, before God you are my wife and the mother of our child."

"Dearest Horatio, if only it makes you happy. . . ."

"I can scarce believe such happiness." His was indeed the simple ambition of the country boy who, being born and bred in a quiet Rectory, had dreamt only of his own hearthside and of his children. "My angel, how shall we manage?"

"My mother will attend me. Oh, Horatio, you little know how fortunate I have been in having so sweet a mother."

"But the world . . . ?" for even then he was be-

324

ginning to dread the ugly taint of scandal coming closer, and recognized that it boded them ill.

"For the time being, I cannot keep the child here. I can make arrangements and will get it all planned," she said.

The woman who had helped to arrange the flight of the court from Naples was unlikely to make mistakes on a small matter like this one. He agreed to that.

"For ever we are bound together by this child, this little pledge of our love," he said ecstatically. "We are one, and you must know that."

"I only know that I love you."

Neither of them realized that the Prince of Wales was going to promote difficulties, for he had been particularly pressing at the party given by the Duke of Queensberry when Emma, in spite of everything, danced until the dawn. She was determined to deny the charge of pregnancy as long as she could, and by her conduct gave people the lie. It is true that the idea had crossed her fertile mind, that perhaps she could persuade Sir William to father the child, although he had not stepped across the threshold of her chamber for five years, but she might have persuaded him even now.

However, this ailed her, and it was Greville who discovered the truth. His one horror had been that Emma might bear a child to his uncle and so deprive him of his inheritance, and as before, he was too clever for her. He had always been too clever. He faced her the very day they went to live in their new house. Greville knew the truth, and because she loved him so well, she never denied the pregnancy to him.

"I presume that it is Lord Nelson's child?"

"It is, and before God I am his wife."

"If Lord Nelson had a child now known not to be his wife's, have you thought how much it would hamper his career? It must not be, for his sake alone. It must *not* be."

"I know, Greville, but is there any reason why Sir William should not have a son?"

Greville had been prepared for this, and coming across the room stood facing her. "I was your master once, Emma, and I could master you again. I swear by God that if you did that, then I would proclaim the truth to the world."

"The world would only think that you were jealous."

"That is not so, for I have taken precautions. Have you ever heard the name of Josiah Nisbet?"

"Horatio's stepson?"

"I had the honour to cultivate his acquaintance at my club, and he was most open. He told me much that would be very useful. Emma, I ask you not to force me; purely in my own interests I should have to pronounce my verdict on it."

She looked at him in dismay; he had always been able to manage her, and she could not deny it. He had held the whip hand and very often the actual whip to her body. Her eyes fell before his. "Oh, Greville, why is it that I have had to love you so much?" she asked quite pathetically.

His answer was nearer to the truth than she would have believed. "Maybe it is because women are always attracted to an unscrupulous man. It easily might be that," and he kissed her.

She would have sold her body again for that kiss, and could not escape her desire for this one man.

The new year was breaking. 1801 was coming over the horizon, and there was the battle of Copenhagen yet to be fought. Nelson took a tender leave of his beloved.

"How I hate deserting you to your pains, my sweet!"

"They can never be pains when they are borne for you."

"So brave! Such courage! You will write to me?"

"Every day, and never doubt me. Pay no heed to rumour, but have no fear for me."

"I fear only for your sweetly innocent heart, and hate the thought of the Prince of Wales and his friends hanging round this house."

"You must not be uneasy, for I have met their like before," and she laughed.

She sent him away with a smile on her lips. She had already booked an appointment to meet the Prince that very night, for she felt that their social future depended largely upon it. But she must be careful! As she dressed to keep the engagement she realized that she really did feel quite ill—she had never felt quite so bad with little Emily—did it mean that this was to be his son? The thought made her intensely proud.

LXIII

THE NIGHT that Horatio Nelson sailed off to beat the French in Denmark, Sir William Hamilton, raddled with one of his recurring attacks of bile, was retching intolerably in his room and feeling miserably ill, whilst his wife danced through the night in the arms of the First Gentleman of Europe.

The Prince of Wales was in a merry mood. He had at last, and after a very trying period of family misunderstanding, got his household cares comfortably settled. Mrs. Maria Fitzherbert was now living at Brighthelmstone, and the Princess of Wales was being tolerably quiescent at Windsor. But whatever else people might choose to say about him, he had at least begotten a daughter so that he could not see that public opinion could quibble. He had done his duty by the nation, and considered that everything was now amiably settled. He had a wife whom he saw as little as possible, and a mistress (who adored her "Prinny") whom he saw as much as he could.

In search of further amorous adventures, with the return of Lord Nelson from victories abroad, and Sir William Hamilton from diplomatic triumphs, he had found the beautiful Emma to be entirely after his own heart. Undoubtedly Emma had returned at the right moment to capture the inflammable heart of the Prince of Wales, for a new face did much to intrigue a gentleman who tired easily.

"Your attitudeth? I long to thee your attitudeth," he begged. "Thappho. Aphrodite. Venuth."

This was no moment for her attitudes, for within the next few weeks her child would be born, and Emma was appalled.

"I have to feel in the right mood, Your Royal Highness."

It took more than feeble excuse to put the Prince of Wales at a disadvantage, and he smiled at her benevolently.

"Very well. I will dine with you and Thir William. I thould much like to hear you thing a duet with La Banti. I would like to thee your attitudeth. Perhapth later, you and I, tweetetht of ladieth, could be alone?" He glanced at her, pleasure glinting in his protuberant blue eyes. He knew far more of Emma's past than did Lord Nelson, and he never thought of her as being innocent. Prinny was perfectly well aware that other fingers had already plucked the fruit and had tasted it. Being a man of the world and not merely an idealist, never for a moment did he imagine that she had put any reservation on her virtue. "It ith a royal command," he told her, and bowed with apalling stiffness. Tight-lacing made it difficult for him to unbend.

Ordinarily nothing could have been more to Emma's liking, even though her beloved hero was at sea, churning his way out to battle, even though the beloved Greville was at hand, and tough wisdom warned her of the folly of such a step; she had always looked upon George of Wales as being the prize any woman could desire. Also there was the small matter of Sir William's pension to be settled, and her own position at court. But for the moment she could do very little, because of the baby so shortly to be born and now—if she were not extremely careful—making its presence obvious.

It was impossible to risk discovery, and in terror she fled to Greville. She had always thought of him as being the most reliable of all her friends, for he never lost his head. He had all the diplomatic attributes, and with her husband's pension hanging in the balance, she could ill afford to ignore what the Prince insisted was "a royal command."

Greville looked at her as she stood before the Adams fireplace in his house in Cleveland Row.

"The old fault, my lovely Emma—you have been too charming."

"But, Greville, what do I do?"

"You will have to agree to the dinner and the entertainment, but it should be a comparatively easy matter to insist that the payment be deferred."

"The Prince is insistent. I doubt if we can put him off so easily. Oh, Greville, I am utterly terrified, and feel that I can go no further."

He took both her hands in his, and she knew that his voice was both tender and soothing. "My own, my very own Emma. I will arrange everything for you, and His Royal Highness shall actually be satisfied that the anticipation being made longer, it will be but the more enchanting when the hour comes. My uncle's pension will therefore be granted, His Royal Highness will be entertained, and the lady will not be molested."

She owed him a great debt of gratitude. Where would she have been without Greville? And with Horatio at sea she clung in desperation to him.

"Greville, I never wanted children, and cannot think why I, of all women, should be forced to have them. It is not that I mind the pain. I bear pain easily, it is that I do not want children to hamper me."

"I know, my sweet."

He stroked her hair and as she lay with her head on his breast she believed implicitly in him. Her loyalty to that one great lover of her life never failed.

Writing to Nelson she told him of the Prince who wished to visit her as if it were an amusing incident only to find that his jealousy was aroused so that he became almost distraught. He knew quite well the methods of the Prince of Wales, and although never for a moment did he doubt his Emma's honour, he believed that the persuasive manner of so reprobate a visitor might very easily make matters quite impossible for her. The letters that he wrote were those of an indignant adolescent, bursting to fight a hated rival even if it be his future king! Never had he been in a greater fury, as his officers and the bluejackets would testify. At this period he was completely unbearable, and all for nothing.

It was late January before satisfactory arrangements could be made for the royal visit and the banquet that it would entail. The famous cantatrice, La Banti, was to be there, the Prince pressing to hear a duet, and after all the arrangements were complete, Emma failed him.

It was one of those snowy days; she had become overtired when in the morning she had taken a chair to do some shopping. The tiredness did not wear off with her dinner, and Mrs. Duggan insisted that she should rest for the afternoon and so prepare herself for the evening. She lay in the half-tester bed which overlooked the Green Park, where the thorn trees were thick with snow. Dozing a trifle, and surprised at her bodily uneasiness, she awakened suddenly, for a sharp pain had shot through her as a sword. Instantly she knew that her hour was at hand, and it was the very hour when she had an assignation with His Royal Highness the Prince of Wales.

She was in labour.

She called her mother, and was dismayed. Whatever happened no inkling of what was afoot must go below stairs or reach Sir William's ears. Nobody was to know, and the doors must be locked. It was given out that her ladyship had a severe bilious attack and was constantly sick. She was not to be disturbed, and the presence of a doctor was not considered necessary, for her mother would attend her.

Behind those locked doors Emma, as courageous with pain as with the other events of her life, faced birth fearlessly, and never made a sound. Below in the ornate dining-room where the best napery and the finest silver were displayed, the Prince of Wales gave a masterful display of temper. He did not tolerate excuses, and never for a moment did he suppose that her ladyship was indisposed. He bit his nails and behaved like a peevish and indulged boy, until Greville had the wit to produce another fair charmer, obviously not as beautiful but equally frail-looking and seductive. And when the lady had paid compliments, at first received chillily, and when the wine had filled him, Prinny began to pay some small attention and finally hardly appeared to miss the lady of the house at all.

At about the same moment as Prinny finally decided that the second charmer had something to offer, Mrs. Duggan delivered Emma of her second daughter. She received the child and hushed its first cries against her breast, for no one must hear the sound of a babe in the house and so discover their secret.

"A girl?" asked Emma.

"A little girl, and so like him. So very like him."

The sweat of labour still pearly on her forehead, Emma raised herself on an elbow to view the small face half-hidden in the blanket. "You must not let her cry, Mam. Whatever happens no one must suspect what has happened."

"No one shall suspect." For the double doors were locked fast and here she and Emma and the baby

331

were at the three corners of one of the strangest triangles in history.

"They will tell Horatio?"

"I will let him know. And now, Emma, think for yourself, for you must sleep."

She turned over on her side, prepared to do all she could to aid herself for a speedy recovery, because she dared not be ill too long in case some suspected it. She was not to know that as she slipped into the exquisite sleep after her ordeal, the Prince of Wales was rolling on the couch with the fair charmer whom Greville had introduced hurriedly into the house; that he was very drunk and had apparently completely forgotten that he had come here to see our dearest Emma.

LXIV

FOR THE space of a week and not a moment longer did Emma lie in.

She had always been blessed with vigorously good health, and was now wholly determined to be up and about, and so give the lie to any scandalmongering tongue that might suggest that she had given birth to a child. She was aided and abetted in this by Greville, who, although she believed that he had been indeed "an angel of goodness," was contriving for his own ends. Whatever happened Sir William must have no heir.

Emma's second daughter had been born surprisingly in wedlock, and therefore in the eyes of the law she was the daughter of Sir William Hamilton and as such could depose Greville himself. This was a thought that he could not abide, and he was doing all he could to withstand it.

He played on the loyalties of the mother. It would, he said, affect Lord Nelson's entire career. Already she must have realized how cruelly people felt about both of them; what was more it would veritably affect the pension which Sir William had hoped to make considerably larger in view of his good offices at Naples. Far from it being larger, it had turned out at a considerably smaller figure, and the poor old man was utterly bewildered. He was at a loss to understand what had happened, and why people should behave so strangely about his wife.

"My dearest Emma, how few people have really understood your goodness and your innate sweetness," said the old man when sitting by her bed. He was completely unaware that in the very next room Mrs. Duggan was frantically hushing a young babe in her arms, and praying that it would not disclose its identity. Mercifully the old man was growing a trifle deaf.

The next thing to do was to rid herself of the baby for the time being, and in this Greville was entirely helpful. It was Greville who had satisfied both herself and Horatio by making arrangements with a certain Mrs. Gibson in Little Titchfield Street, who was to accept the babe even as her own, care for it, and tend it so that nobody would know from which roots the child had sprung. Money would be sent at certain dates, and visits could be paid whenever desired.

"I would not trust Charles Greville," said Mrs. Duggan, who had never recovered from her early distaste for the man.

"He has been so good."

"I do not believe in him. I would not trust him."

"But then you do not know him as I do," urged Emma, who could not believe a word against him.

It was a little difficult to get away from the house in the hackney carriage with the living babe in her arms, but one thing was certain: Emma and her mother had so far managed to keep their secret, and they did not intend to risk discovery on a small matter like passing through the hall with the baby on her way to her new home.

"I know," said Emma suddenly, "my muff! She is a tiny child and will lie in it quite easily. How fortunate it is that to-day muffs are worn so large!"

She walked past her own servants in the hall carrying her muff. She drove to Mrs. Gibson's with the child lying in her lap, and looking at her with *his* eyes. But Emma had never been maternally minded, and those bland kittenish eyes did not disturb her unduly. To her the act of love was more significant than the product of that love.

The house in Little Titchfield Street was tall and thin; the maid who opened the door saw only a lady who was frail-looking and who carried a large muff. In the sitting-room Mrs. Gibson herself was waiting. She took the baby into her arms and was kindly.

"She is not like you, your ladyship?"

"She is like her father."

"Yes, my lady."

But there was one point on which Emma had not reckoned, and that was Horatio Nelson's passion for his child. He was beside himself with joy when he heard of her birth. They had devised a code between them, Greville assisting, and by this means they could communicate with one another, and should those letters be intercepted their secret would remain concealed. Certain it is that Charles Greville was taking no risks. Nelson was purported to have a sailor called Thomson aboard, and Lady Hamilton was supposed to be seeing after Mrs. Thomson, who was pregnant, and who, on being delivered of a daughter, sent loving messages to the father.

The return letters were ecstatic; they were forceful with impatience to be home and to view the new baby. Thomson said that he rejoiced to think that the child was so like his Admiral, for many had remarked upon the resemblance between them. He desired that it should be called Emma, out of respect to dear Lady Hamilton who had been so very helpful, but apparently this did not meet with approval from "Mrs. Thomson," for Emma wrote back that Mrs. Thomson most particularly wanted her little girl to be called Horatia after the Admiral.

Meanwhile Sir William knew nothing of all this pretty byplay, being entirely and somewhat naturally occupied with his own accruing difficulties. As he had failed to obtain the increased pension, he had been trying to manœuvre himself back to Naples as an alternative, but Paget had already been sent out there, and this, his final project, collapsed on him.

"I should have loved to have returned there; I do not care for London now," sighed Emma.

"But I should never see you again if once you went," Greville suggested.

"But, Greville, too much has happened, far too much. I cannot think what happens next to us all."

"You stay here."

"Sometimes I do not believe it possible." She lifted her reproachful eyes to him. At this time Emma was changing a little. The lack of attention at the recent birth had not been helpful to her figure and for the first time she was looking older; she had thickened a little, and her breasts had dropped, but, although Greville noticed it, he said nothing.

"You must not leave London," he said, himself the serpent in her Eden.

Sitting beside him in the pleasant parlour, with the first snow of hawthorn blossom on the little thorn trees of the park beyond the window, she whispered that Horatio had made a suggestion to her. He was tired of everything. He longed to have her as his wife, and the child too, to himself. He chafed against the bonds that Lady Nelson drew so harshly about him, for she was completely relentless. He wanted to declare openly that this child was his, which was the last thing that Greville wanted, for—however much they declared to the contrary—the child must depose himself.

335

Horatio had written, begging that Emma would leave England, and at the same time he would quit the Navy. They could then go to the estate in Bronte that King Ferdinand had given him as a reward for his services. There he, Emma and the child could be blissfully happy for the rest of their lives.

"You would never do it?" said Greville.

"Why not? Like this, there is no real happiness for any of us, and surely you can see it?"

"But you could not, you dare not, ruin Lord Nelson's career? That would be a dreadful thing to do. You would be blamed for your selfish action through all the pages of history."

"But how can I see him? How can I ever be with him? He has no real home, and all London knows it if I visit him at Nerot's, just as they know if he visits me here."

Greville, never at a loss, said, "Listen, my sweet Emma. It should be possible to buy a small estate, somewhere close to London, somewhere where you and he could occasionally find peace."

"Yes, but where? Far, far better that I should go out to him at Bronte."

"And ruin his whole life?"

She turned in deep distress and clung to Greville. "Oh, my dear Charles, because you always were my dear, guide me! Show me the way. I don't know what to do and am so confused."

"Then trust to me, my dearest."

So it was Greville who discovered for them the property at Merton, which he may easily have had in mind when he first suggested the idea to Emma. It was a house that could easily be made into a veritable Paradise, an ideal home for a hero who, having added the fresh glory of Copenhagen to his laurels, did indeed need a country home. Merton Place was a smallish estate, with some pretence at farming, and Emma now delighted in furnishing it. Sir William promised to come down on frequent visits, for his presence would be necessary to conform to the proprieties, and even "Mrs. Thomson's baby" was installed there.

"It is the wisest—the only—thing to do," said Greville.

"Surely, dearest Charles, you are the most unselfish of men. You who once possessed me, to give me so gallantly to another."

"Perhaps, my sweet, I owe you a debt! I have not forgotten when you left me for Naples."

She looked at him.

Although she had reproved him and had even railed at him in her letters, the subject had never been opened in conversation between them. It was in his house in Cleveland Row that he spoke of it. She had come there to see him about some arrangements that he was making, for Merton Place was to be bought on easy payments. Outside a ragged woman was selling country bunches from a basket in the roadway, and the lovely scent of lavender was blown in through the open window.

"Oh, Greville, I blamed you so horribly. It was only because I loved you so truly."

"Enough to forget everyone save myself now?"

It was a moment of complete intoxication. His head bent over her, his arms not too impelling but just a little chiding, as they drew her closer. He must know that she could not refuse him, she told herself; she forgot all that lay between. For him she was in her first youth again, young and almost virginal, a girl in a muslin gown at Paddington Green, with the cawing of the rooks from the adjacent trees, and the scent of moss roses in the garden.

"My love, my own, own love," she whispered.

He bent his body closer to her. She had forgotten that he could be so ardent. She felt his breath coming in urgent gasps; it was long since she had felt the fire of his embraces, the crazily impelling beating of his heart above her own.

"Oh, my dear."

It did not matter if hours passed. Once again, and

after all these years, she gave herself—and readily—to the man she was to love for always above all others. The flower scent continued to drift sweetly through the room. They lay locked in one another's arms, not recognizing time or place, conscious only of one another, for naught else mattered to them.

Much later he unlocked his arms. She smiled at the beautiful face above her own, and she kissed him with her passion spent, so that it become the kiss of a sister.

"I always loved you most," she confessed.

"I wonder how much one can believe? There must be so many you have loved best of all."

"But it is true. It was always you, Charles, my own Charles," she cried a little wildly.

"The greatest truth is always a lie," he said, and he smiled at her with something sardonic in it. She knew that he did not believe a word that she said, and in her heart was immensely disappointed in him.

LXV

IT WAS strange that during these fateful hours everybody appeared to be occupied with their own concerns and none to them seemed to have any thought for Sir William. He was immeasurably lonely. When he had returned to London he had thought that he held something of an heroic position in the affections of its people; he had done enough for them in all conscience. The difficulties of life at the British Embassy in Naples were still fresh in his memory; the triumphant progress of his final tour, and the great acclamations that had been accorded to him, and to his wife, as well as to Lord Nelson; so that the sudden change in his fortunes was all the more bewildering.

He was quite stupefied to find that, now he was back again, not everyone in the great city was willing to receive his lady, and that amongst those particularly choosey people was Her Majesty herself. He had been more than disappointed about the insignificance of the pension that was offered to him, and after all he had done too. He was so chagrined that he became ill. Financial worries were piling up and affecting him, and the recurring attacks of bile were painful, and added to them there was rheumatism, with which the physicians seemed to be helpless.

He was more and more agitated, and at first, trying to use his influence with the right people, he had entertained a trifle wildly. He had thought the money spent this way was indeed money invested towards ensuring a more sufficing income. Now, finding the tide running so high against him, he began to despair, realizing that he would never be reimbursed for the duties he had fulfilled so satisfactorily.

When he had first applauded Greville for guiding Emma and Horatio towards buying Merton Place and equipping it as a home for the hero, he had not appreciated that many of his own pictures and personal treasures would be transferred into Surrey. In the strange triple alliance of himself, Horatio and Emma, he had been guilelessly content, seeing nothing amiss in it. Now some glimmer of greater understanding came to him, and he found that he was an outsider, for the intimate trio had already begun to split into a duet.

Sir William was an old man, and all he wanted was peace and quiet, and somewhere to rest his weary head. Emma desired none of these things, because already she had discovered that peace was rather boring.

"But, Emma, we are growing older," he said one evening when she had desired to be out and about and her husband had felt himself unable to stand the strain of further entertainment.

"You may be growing older, but I have many young years before me," she replied. He thought that he detected a sharpness in her tone, and did not realize that for her the thought of approaching age was disarming, if not something of a terror. She had put on weight a little, thickening at waist and hips, the result of amateur midwifery, and although she tried to pretend that this was not so, in her heart it frightened her.

"Oh, Emma, are you really wise?" her husband implored her. He knew the helplessness of his own position and feared the oncoming of senility to his mind.

"Once you trusted me completely, William."

"I trust you implicitly still; I always have done. I have the greatest faith in you, but life is not as it once was for us."

"Nonsense, it will change again."

"Surely you can see for yourself? Once we had so much and served the nation so well. Now somehow, in spite of all that we did, we are no longer popular."

He sighed deeply as he sat in the dark red chair which he had brought with him from Italy. Frankly he could not understand or fathom the ingratitude of a country for which he had always done his utmost.

"Matters are different," she agreed with reluctance, and wondered if in his heart he doubted her. Had he guessed that the great difference was that England looked upon her as Horatio's mistress, and nothing more? Other countries had not been so pernickety; they had glossed over a relationship which they believed came to every man, and had cultivated a wider outlook. But England was fundamentally prudish. 'It's the Queen,' she told herself, and was indignant.

Recently something infinitely more terrifying had happened to Emma Hamilton, and it was one of those things that she dared not admit, not even to her

340

dearest Greville. When she had been at her heyday in Palermo, she had met, during the course of her duties, a certain lawyer called Arnodeo Gibilmanna, who was a Sicilian. She had not noticed him much at the actual time, though he was a handsome young man, virile and energetic, with a flattering tongue. He had always had an amorous compliment for any woman, and was obviously an admirer of the fair sex. Also he had adored Emma, but always from afar. At that time she had been entirely occupied with the affairs of state, and with Lord Nelson, so that she never gave Arnodeo a second glance. Being a clever young man he did not press his suit for the time being.

Emma was by nature habitually careless. When she left Palermo she left behind her in her rooms a residue of letters, of half-used clothes and miscellaneous pieces of jewellery which were scattered about the place. She was impatient and could not be bothered with this sort of thing when she was so eager to return to Naples. Arnodeo, leaving nothing to chance, went through the things, returned the clothing and jewels to her, delivering them in person, and Emma was grateful. She accepted them benignly, allowing him to kiss her hand, and was a trifle—but only a trifle—encouraging. The letters he kept for a more suitable moment.

He brought these with him to London when he scraped together his somewhat depleted funds, staking all on one big bid for success. In 1802 he arrived in the city.

Arnodeo had thought that possibly Lady Hamilton might receive him as a lover; if she refused he had the means of putting force behind his plea. He knew that London had cold-shouldered her, and realized that the Prince of Wales, at one time said to have been making advances, was now reputed to have eschewed her. He had heard of her extravagances which had made life exceedingly difficult for Sir William, but more than all else he had heard of Horatio

341

Nelson, said to adore her, and who believed her to be innocent. Nelson supposed that he was the one love in her life, but Arnodeo possessed letters which proved him to be wrong.

Out in Naples the exquisite Emma had been particular about the men who loved her, but now she was growing a little older, and with age less beautiful; she had experienced the unfriendliness of London, and undoubtedly might look twice at Arnodeo.

He came to the Piccadilly home one warm September evening when Sir William had the bile once more, and when Greville's chair had just been carried from the door on its way back to Cleveland Row. Arnodeo did not leave unobserved the finery of the house, the handsomeness of curtains and hangings, and the good furniture that Sir William had collected whilst he was abroad. There was beyond doubt some money here, and if Arnodeo could not buy love he could most certainly lift some capital out of the place which would help his resources. Money would be acceptable, for he had all the Sicilian love of comfort.

Emma received him alone. She was a little warmer than she had been in Naples, and seemed to be pleased that he had remembered her, and spoke kindly. She was still beautiful, he thought, for Arnodeo liked his women to be plump. He started as he meant to continue.

"I loved you in Palermo," he said.

"I am flattered."

"There, so gracious lady, you would not look at me."

"Englishwomen do not look at other men."

"But other men do look at Englishwomen. And if I am correct you look at the gallant sailor. Now I also am of an amorous nature, and have come to you, sweetest, most desirable lady, with hope."

Although his dark eyes were certainly compelling, Emma felt distaste. She had Nelson and Greville; she

342

did not want more. "You are mistaken," she said frigidly.

"But no, I do not mistake," and he would have taken her hand, but she snatched it from him.

"You have in truth made a very grave mistake," and she rose to end the interview. She was so angry that she made no attempt to be discreet. "You must go away," she told him, her hand on the bell-rope.

"Stop!"

She was unused to commands, and turned with an imperious gesture that had all the hauteur of Her Excellency in it. "And why should I stop?"

"When you leave Palermo, you leave behind the letters, yes?" He tapped his bosom with significance and she paused. She knew that she was careless and might easily have done this.

"And . . . ?"

He produced the little packet and she saw at once that the top one had been written by Josiah Nisbet, that another was in Bishop Derry's writing. 'What a fool I've been!' she thought, and her heart missed a beat as she realized that she must not show fear.

"The great sailor would have interest, yes? He does not know perhaps how so obliging is his lady. The young sailor he say in this one that he come to your room; he laugh about the Admiral. The Bishop say what 'appen. The gallant sailor would have the very much interest."

Emma thought that she would faint. Her whole body seemed to be going limp, and whatever happened she knew that she must keep control of her senses. She tried to pull herself together. What an unscrupulous villain to know her so well! Of course Horatio would never understand it, because he had never thought that Josiah had once been in her life, she always indignantly repudiating the accusation and swearing that it was the vile invention of a jealous young man. Horatio had loathed Bishop Derry because he himself was a Godbearing man, and believed in the Deity, whom the Bishop swore he despised. Horatio had hated the heretical attitude, and would never forgive if he had in writing the bald fact that she had "obliged" the Bishop.

For a moment she could not refute the accusations because she was taken so completely unawares. She could not imagine how she would uphold the innocence she had never possessed in the face of such an accusation. She would far rather capitulate, pay the price of her carelessness, and send the rascal away.

"How much do you need?"

The sum that Arnodeo suggested was an intolerable one! Frankly it terrified her. "Silence is always expensive," he reminded her. "Have you not the proverb which say that silence is gold?"

"We have indeed, and you are proving to me the truth of it."

She tried to argue with him, but it was futile. He wanted money. He had for sale something which she, of necessity, must buy. He could afford to charge her what he pleased and she could not afford to quibble at the cost. In vain did she plead. She had not got so much, she said tearfully, and until Lord Nelson returned with his prize money she could not pay, for he had to reimburse her for furniture and fabrics she had bought in his name to furnish Merton Place. Already she had overspent madly, and had little money left.

"I knew that I was over-extravagant."

Until now Arnodeo had not heard of Merton Place, and was instantly desirous to hear more. Rather tearfully Emma explained that it was a country estate where Lord Nelson could stay when on leave, and she and Sir William were assisting him by helping to prepare it whilst he was abroad.

"I could be head steward there," said Arnodeo.

Common sense told her that it would be madness and, completely horrified at the suggestion, she stared at him aghast.

"You cannot say no," he told her, coming closer, his dark eyes latent with warning as he tapped the little bundle of letters. She hated the sound that they made, almost as if they laughed at her.

"You drive me to desperation."

"Dear lady, do not let me drive you over the precipice." He was now so close to her that she could smell the garlic that clung about him. "You will give me the money, yes? You will grant me the appointment?"

She could not refuse him.

LXVI

SIR WILLIAM was growing daily weaker.

Returning rom sea, Horatio saw a considerable difference in him for now he had turned a very bad colour, and walked only with difficulty, suffering from shortness of breath which came in distressing little gasps.

"Why did you not write and tell me?" he asked Emma.

"Indeed, being so constantly with him, I hardly did notice."

The poor old man endured yet another devastating attack of the bile which his physicians could not conquer. It was the spring of 1803, and in the house that overlooked the Green Park he lay in his Emma's arms. As always, she was both devoted and courageous in illness, holding him with infinite tenderness, and kneeling on one side of the bed whilst Horatio knelt on the other. The trio who had played so great a part in the diplomacy of Europe were together in this the final scene for the poor old man.

An April day was painting the park beyond the window in pastel colours, and Emma realized that this was no trio, for a fourth but unseen figure lingered beside the bed. In these, the last hours, she knew how tender William had always been to her, and repentantly mourned the fact that she had wronged him so deeply.

Forlornly she held him against her, then with a tragic gesture she laid him down knowing that the end had come.

Across the still body Lord Nelson looked at her. "Oh, Emma, what can I say?"

"What a man! What a husband!" She was completely stricken in her anguish.

"I trust that he has provided for you properly." He was voicing a fear that recently had possessed him, for he suspected Greville. Nelson might have a blind eye, but it had never been blind to the serpent-like influence of that man whom he detested.

"He will have done. William was always so abundantly generous and good to me."

"Never did a wife more richly deserve a reward." And he meant it.

Sir William was buried by the side of the wife who had died twenty-five years before, and when the will was read, everyone was astonished by the inadequate provision that he had made for his Emma, whom he undoubtedly loved. The truth of the matter was that Greville had helped his uncle to compose that will; he had sat on the other side of the table, and had instructed the tired old man with a word here, and a mere phrase there, but they had been sufficient to render invalid the good wishes, with the result that Emma was now left with very little.

It was not—as some busybodies said—that Sir William had hit back from the grave. It was that Greville, in solidifying his own position, had jeopardized hers. Already poor Emma was deeply in debt.

"How shall I ever face my creditors?" she asked aghast of the man whom she had always loved so devotedly. "You know that William promised that he would pay them for me, and so far only about two hundred and fifty pounds has been paid."

"But," said Greville, "the will particularly states that those debts are to be paid out of the arrears of pension that the Government owe him."

"They will pay it?"

"After everything that you did at the Court of the Two Sicilies, how could they refuse?"

"True. Yes, of course, that is very true. They couldn't." But she knew that her palms were wet with anxiety and her eyes lit as though by fever. She looked with the first tinge of apprehension at her beloved Greville. Could it be that her god was a devil? But the thought was so unworthy that she refused to encourage it. "Oh, my dear one, comfort me!" she besought him.

He put his arms round her, but his manner was not warm and, sensing this, she recoiled from it. It hurt her more than she could say, for he had gained so much. The house in Piccadilly was his, and to her amazement he demanded that she should leave before the end of April.

"But so soon! Charles, how can you do this? That gives me barely a few days."

"It isn't as though you had nowhere to go. There is Merton Place."

"Greville, what has happened to you? Why are you, of all people, like this to me?"

He made no reply, and it was as though something warmly vital had been plucked out of the innermost depths of her heart and replaced by a stone which weighed heavily.

She took a small house in Clarges Street, remembering that she was already in debt, but really Emma had little idea of how to economize. Her expenses were mounting up all the time, only in these days she was so accustomed to having money that she could not do without it. Luxuries were necessities, and deeper and deeper she sunk into trouble.

"Before I go to sea again," Nelson told her, "I want to see our little Horatia baptized. Now that Sir William has gone it should be easy."

"Of course."

They planned the baptism to take place three days before he sailed. They went to the church where she had been married, and there Horatia Nelson Thomson, as she was called, was baptized at two years old, with her parents and godmother acting as godparents. Horatio Nelson was very proud and he gave the child a most handsome silver cup as a memento of the occasion. It was now that the new trio had begun. Before it had been Horatio, William and Emma, now it was Horatio, Emma and Horatia together. They returned by post-chaise to Merton, driving through the country lanes that were sweet with flowers, and Arnodeo met them on arrival.

"I can't stand that fellow," said Nelson, and the words struck panic into Emma's heart.

"He is all right."

In the late evening they walked in the garden where the last lilacs smelt heady and the acacias drooped in cascades of white, sweetly perfumed blossoms.

"Dearest Horatio, I shall miss you so desperately whilst you are at sea."

"You have the child, my sweet."

"I know, and thank God." She had never thought that she would be grateful for the child of her own body, but it had turned out that way. She caught his arm closer, for her mother had advised her to tell him of a small matter before he departed. "And soon, quite soon, dearest Horatio, I hope to bear your son."

"You cannot mean . . . ?"

"Indeed, my sweetest, here in my body. Part of you lives again and breathes."

They stood beneath the flowering shrubberies, he believing that now he saw heaven in sight. A son to follow him! For a moment he could not speak, for a whole lifetime's ideals and fondnesses suddenly flooded him. Then he drew her to his arms.

"Oh, my dearest, my very dearest. I shall go forward to greater victories, murmuring your most precious name. A son! I scarce dare believe it."

"A companion will be good for Horatia."

"I tremble for you in your pains, my beautiful one."

She ignored that.

"I have my mother. Oh, how fortunate I have been in one so fond! And I am not afraid, so that Horatio must not be afraid for me," she told him.

LXVII

EMMA HAD always thought that whilst her husband lived the polite world could not ignore her completely, because of him. But, when his coffin had rolled away and the last clod of earth had been trampled down above him, there was no need even for the merest lip service any more. Lady Hamilton was—as she had always been—the mistress of the hero, nothing more, and there was frankly no need to mention her any more.

The doors of the big houses that had once been flung open so welcomingly to receive her, were barred. At the little house in Clarges Street few people called because none wished to know her. Perhaps, she told herself, it was a good thing that her pregnancy was delaying her at Merton Place, and that little Horatia, enduring an attack of the smallpox (it distracted her father), succeeded in keeping her mother out of town.

The baby was born in the early part of the new year. It was her mother who cared for Emma, but openly this time, for now there was no need for secrecy. Everybody knew that the child was coming and that it would be Lord Nelson's son. In the house and garden she was for ever seeing Arnodeo, with his evilly dark eyes on her, though he said little. She would have done anything to be rid of him, but did not know how to do this without incurring yet further trouble. Again the baby was born when the snow blew across the garden at Merton, falling thickly through the air, so that she could watch it as she lay.

"A girl," said her mother, when Emma heard the first shrill shrieking of the child.

"Not another girl?"

"Indeed it is." Mrs. Duggan had caught the child to her and was staring down into its fragile little face. "Another Emma," she said, "so like you as is absurd. You looked just the same way, my Emy, the first time that I saw you."

"He wanted a son," said Emma weakly, and now her heart was full at the thought that she had failed him.

Although Horatio was disappointed, the idea of a second child rejoiced him, and later on there might be a son. It might even be propitious, for Lady Nelson was in poor health and if she died then he could wed Emma and so the son would be born in lawful wedlock, which was what he wished above all things.

He was, however, never to see this second little one—baptized Emma, as he desired—for before the summer had waxed, the child, immeasurably delicate, had died.

Nelson took this loss deeply to heart, to have had a child and never to have seen her. Still Horatia was his only one, and he had a small grave to tend. No more. Emma could not have believed that he would behave so tragically about it.

Unfortunately she was amassing debts. The beauty that had been her great claim to wealth was beginning to decay, and she was for ever trying to conceal this. In many ways she was now showing the world the effects of her mode of life. Fond of food, she indulged herself, and her complexion went blotchy, whilst she kept on accruing weight, despite the potions that she drank. The birth of little Emma and her mother's faithful but inadequate attentions had not done much to coneal bulging hips and thickening waist-line.

Also Arnodeo was a constant drain on her resources, and try as she would she could not rid herself of him. She knew that Nelson loathed him, and because she was afraid of a scene between them, she brought him back to her house in Clarges Street. Here he immediately began to take liberties, and he was rude to her friends, in particular Jane Powell, who had come back into her life and was very loyal.

"I would dismiss him," Jane advised her.

Nothing would have been more to Emma's liking, but the trouble was that she could not dismiss him. The prospect of Nelson returning from sea and finding him now installed in Clarges Street was not a happy one, because he would agree with Jane that the man should go. In all probability he would interview Arnodeo for Emma, and what would be the result? It is true that she had bought the letters, but she could never be quite sure that she had obtained all of them, and Arnodeo kept on taunting her with this.

Once he had actually come to her room in the night, and she, starting up, had seen his lithe and sinuous body silhouetted by the moonlight against the wall.

"How dare you come here?" she had gasped.

He had dared. He had come to the end of the half-tester bed, standing there gripping the posts between his dark hands, and smiling at her. The whiteness of his teeth in the moonlight was fantastic and reminded her of some hiedously grinning corpse.

"You must go away."

"Others come to you."

That was an insult, and the horrible part was that she dared not refute it; even though she longed to strike him she had to control herself. So much—so

351

very much—depended on her management of this quite dreadful situation.

"I command that you go away."

He stooped and plucked at the flimsy gown which she wore, grinning as he saw the curves of her body beneath it, pearly in the bluish light of the moon. She squirmed away, grabbing at the satin quilt and wrapping it round herself, realizing for the first time that his attentions were ominous. It was unthinkable that she should be in her own room trying in vain to rid herself of a cheap Sicilian.

"You drive me too far, Arnodeo. Have a care or you will force me to give you up."

"You cannot," he replied, "for then you give yourself up too," and he laughed.

If only there had been Greville at hand to help her manage this impossible position, but Greville had withdrawn from her life, and for the moment she was seeing little of him. He had not even helped her to get the money owing from the pension, with which he had said she should pay her debts, and her imploring letters to him had brought no reply.

"Go," she directed Arnodeo, and reached for the bellrope. Now she did not care, and never had she struck a more effective attitude than at this moment, with her head flung back and the rope actually in her hand. He must have seen something autocratic about her then, for he made a strange sound, and turning left her with never a word. She had a bolt fixed to the door, but now she could not sleep at night because she was afraid, and finally fled for a time to Merton Place.

When she heard that Horatio was returning, it was in an agony of apprehension in case now something was disclosed. She determined that she would make some satisfactory move, for this situation could not continue as it was, but recently her brain seemed to have become less alert, or was it that she was more indolent? She did not know which. She took a chaise and returned to Clarges Street to arrange something.

The little house was much the same, with a score of bills littering her desk and awaiting her, and all manner of callers demanding her attention, callers that she dared not meet because of the financial difficulties with which they would involve her.

"Tell them that they will be paid. The Government is considering the matter of the pension," she told Arnodeo. It was the old story, and none of the creditors believed her, for the Government would never pay, and even Emma knew it. She had no means by which to force them. It hurt to think that once she should have been so generous in their cause and should now be treated in this manner, but there was no way out.

Arnodeo had been drinking. He had fallen in with rapscallion companions, and was fast becoming overconfident of his position here. He looked at her with audacious eyes.

"So you have come back?"

"I have returned to make a change all round," for he would have to know.

"But I stay here? I—I stay here?"

"I have not decided about that." Already he could hear by her intonation that she was afraid and shrunk from the job in hand.

"I have made the bad debts and I need the moneys."

"You of all people should know that I have little money. You see the creditors who come here. It is obvious that I have none to spare."

He gave a shrug of his indifferent shoulders. "Then you must discover more money, or else you must suffer."

Because she was so angry she made no answer but swept from the room. She could not pay him more, already he had bled her white. She spent that evening in the company of Jane Powell, for Jane could always give her courage. They were the same firm friends that they had always been and enjoyed one another's friendship and could still be happy together. Coming home later in her chair she was set down at her own door, and the manservant who admitted her had obviously been asleep, though it was not yet late. He looked scared, and when she challenged him said that there had been trouble in the street that night, with footpads and such.

"Nonsense!" she said, sweeping in, her costly satin gown brushing the woodwork and rustling as she went. "If I am not afraid of footpads, then you should not be."

She went into her own room where food was awaiting her. She sat down before the low fire and was thankful for the countrified quietness of the place. She was tired. It was an unhappy thing that nowadays she was realizing how much more quickly she tired than before, and that she was ageing. It was quite hurtful. The satin curtains before the window fluttered slightly. Some fool must have left the window on to the street open, so she got up and went across to it, pulling back the curtain. As she did so, a dead weight slumped forward, practically on top of her. It was the body of a dead man, his throat slit and gaping, with the blood still dripping down his cheap brocade jacket. He was limp as he flopped horribly on top of her.

She would have shrieked but stopped herself only just in time, for she saw that the face blanched above the yawning, crimson gash was the face of Arnodeo.

LXVIII

ARNODEO HAD been murdered in a street brawl by some of his rapscallion companions. His body had been pushed inside the first open window to get rid of it, the murderer not caring whose house it was, and only providence had propped it against the sill.

The blood spattered down the amber satin of Emma's frock, and with it there came the repellant scent of garlic and her own sick nausea at the thought of it all. Arnodeo collapsed on to the floor and she fetched cloths with which to stanch the wound, for, whatever happened, he must not be discovered here in her house. She had cause enough to murder him (if cause were required), and she was now unpopular enough with the public to find them set against her if they found out what had happened. She made a gigantic effort, gripping him under the armpits, and dragging him along the floor to the window again. The street was where he had come from, and to the street he must return. She was given superhuman strength in the emergency and strained every fibre.

She had never thought that the man could be so heavy, nor that a corpse could look so repulsive, and averted her eyes. When she had got him to the window, she had to prop him into a sitting position, with the wound closing as his head sagged forward, and the spurts of blood still issuing from it making a gulching sound whilst she peered out of the window to look into the street. It was empty. Thank God the watchman had come and gone away again. Eleven o'clock, and all's well! The chrysanthemums were blossoming in the little gardens, and she could smell the wood-ashy smell of them as she heaved the body up. She opened the window wide and dragged him forward, the final effort leaving her breathless. She was fortunate in the pathway verging downhill, for he, falling limply, rolled far from the window and into the gutter, where a dead dog already lay, its belly extended, pale blue and stinking.

She closed the window and locked it, panting with the effort. Now she saw that the blood had spurted all over her satin gown, dyeing the amber scarlet. She tore it from her, wiping down the marks with her hands, and then tore the skirt away. She burnt it deliberately at the grate, kneeling there in her petticoat, her bare shoulders exposed, not feeling heat or cold, as she fed the flames with the marks of her own complicity in the murder.

Nothing whatsoever must remain to tell the world of what had happened. She, who had always basked in public opinion and favour, was now terrified that the tide might turn the other way. The fire emitted a stench as it made small, gritty ash of the frock that recently had been so exquisite. Before she went to her room she glanced out of the window, but there the body still lay where it had rolled, and a meagre, half-starved cat had crawled from an adjacent house, and squatting beside it on lean shanks, lapped up the blood. The sight was quite revolting.

She did not care who had killed Arnodeo; in fact she was only thankful to know that he was dead. He had admitted to her earlier in the week that he had made some bad friends, and that he needed more money, and they had probably been the cause of it all. She slept late, and her servant bringing her in hot chocolate in the morning told her that the steward had been murdered, and two friends of his, with whom he had consorted last night, had been arrested. She thought of Tyburn with horror; she remembered the jaunty caps the authorities made those wear who were about to die, and she shuddered as she thought of them passing to their doom that way. But she had not murdered Arnodeo, and whoever had done it had been kind to her, and in her heart she was glad.

There was a letter from Horatio, which was a joy.

I have been appointed to the *Victory*. Is it an omen?

Further on he added that he would be returning to Portsmouth sooner than he had anticipated, and would be home with her and his darling daughter within the week.

Returning to Portsmouth!

Adventure, she thought, and her heart was lit with

356

sudden joy. She, also, would go down to Portsmouth and meet Horatio there. She felt that there would be enchantment in waiting for him by the side of the water (she had always loved the sea), and knowing that any moment he would come ashore and to her arms, never expecting to find her there.

She ordered the servants to pack her things and took the coach. She was glad to be away from Clarges Street and from the room which—to her—still smelt of blood, of the ash in the grate where her frock had had to be burned only last night.

"Is her ladyship wise?" asked the old servant. "There are such stories of highwaymen, and the Portsmouth coach is often held up in the lonely part round Hindhead."

"That would merely be more adventure," for now she did not care. She took her seat in it composedly. How fortunate she was to be travelling at all, for she did not think that she could have borne another night in that house in Clarges Street, with the memories that it held for her. Yet she would have been afraid to move down to Merton in case it incriminated her. Now she was being driven towards the port town, and soon the *Victory* would be coming up the Channel, and her dear one would have her in his arms.

On and on went the rhythmic sound of the horses. They changed and got fresh ones at Guildford, then started on again for Liphook. At the edge of the Devil's Punchbowl she saw a gibbet crucified against the skyline, and dangling from it a sunken body against the moonshine. She drew back startled, for it seemed that she and death met so often.

It was close to the very gibbet that the coach was held up, and it all happened on the instant. She heard a shot ring out, and the horses taking fright stampeded, to be jerked to a standstill by the coachman. Involuntarily her hand went to the diamond necklace that Maria Carolina had given to her, with the locks of each of the children's hair centred in separate sections. Assuredly now she would lose it!

She climbed down, disdaining two other women who wept dimayedly, and clung to one another, and the palsied old man who tettered and prayed the highwayman "to be merciful."

Emma Hamilton had never yet had to ask a man to be merciful to her, and she took her stand, her head flung back. The man who rode to her looked down from a black horse, and she wondered what manner of eyes flashed behind that mask, guessing that they were virile and full of life. His mouth was sensuous, but he was courtly with the manner of a gentleman.

"Your necklace, madam?"

"It was given to me by the Queen of Naples."

"I care not for that. Your necklace?"

"What if I refuse?" and she laughed up into his face. In the moonlight she was suddenly amazingly beautiful and he saw the face and recognized it.

"By God, are you not Lord Nelson's?"

"I am Emma Hamilton."

He thrust the pistol back into his belt, and the glint of a shooting star played on it like lightning.

He said, "I do not steal from the love of a hero. If it had not been you, I should have ripped it off you," and he bowed. They were two of a kind, and she recognized it; he plundered jewels, but she plundered human hearts. It was then that the wind caught the gibbet on the Punchbowl, and the dead, inert thing hanging there creaked and turned limply.

"Have a care," she said. "You must not let them catch you, or you will hang there, and you are too young and too much alive."

He came closer, taking her hand.

He swooped down from the saddle and touched her lips with his own; the diamonds of the necklace quivered in the moonshine like water rippling over the stones of a ford, but he left them. As she got back into the coach again, she knew that a young mouth had made her his. She knew that she was growing older and perhaps this adventure had the

salty taste of blood in it; she knew also that this
might easily be the last time that she set out to meet
her lover. The last time. . . . The words were ominous.

LXIX

IT WAS early morning with the dawn hardly broken
when the coach came over the Portsdown hills.
Emma had sat there remembering the mouth of the
man who had kissed her, a brave man and a valiant
one, for had he not refused the Queen's necklace
when his hand had been actually on it?

The Portsdown hills were sweet with the grass
smell, and they swept down to the sea where the rain
began. The grey roofs of Portsmouth shone wetly,
and there was the pleasant odour of the refreshed
grass and earth. The coach went jauntily up the cobbled streets and turned in at the George yard. A
maidservant who took Emma to her room knew all
there was to know, for the *Victory* was already lying
off Spithead, and his Lordship—God bless him, she
said piously—would be ashore to dinner at noon.

Emma put on her better frock, smoothed her hair
and composed herself. She felt invigorated. Adventure was the one thing that she had needed, because
it was life to her and she could not exist without it.
No matter if it were raining she would go down to
the sallyport, and see if she could get a boat and go
out to meet her lord.

She went into the street.

It was but a light rain that blew in her face, and
about it was the freshness of the sea and the acrid
sting of it was stimulating. She went through the sallyport to the steps with the jetty below. (Through

359

this sallyport naval heroes innumerable. . . .) An old sailor with tin ear-rings in his ears glanced up at her as she came, for it was unusual for a woman and especially a lady in a fine gown to penetrate here.

"Is that the *Victory*?" she asked.

"It is, God bless her, with the great little Admiral on board her."

"How much would you want to row me out to her?"

He looked at her incredulously, with the rain falling lightly on his tanned face and grey beard. Then he named a price and she promised him double. He helped her into the boat with her eyes sparkling and her heart thumping. She had forgotten the night before last with Arnodeo's revolting body, burning her dress in the grate, the coach-ride and the highwayman's kiss. She had forgotten everything save that now the cool wind blew in her face, and the oars creaked as they rowed, like the wings of giant swans, and she was pulling out to sea.

Out of the mist she could see the masts of the *Victory*, her figurehead leaning across the face of the waters, and her ropes swaying indolently in the wind. She was alongside now and had taken firm hold of the rope ladder and was going up it. It was like the old days, the exciting escape of Maria Carolina and the King, and the time when the little Prince Albert had died in her arms with the ship bucking like a half-broken pony and her ears drumming madly to the noise that the water made. She came up on the deck washed clean with water. Once again she smelt the queerly confused smell of below decks as they took her to his cabin. She begged the officer of the watch not to announce her.

"I have come to surprise him; I promise you that he will not be angry."

Against his better judgment he let her go unannounced, perhaps because of the tenderness in her eyes that were still beautiful. And even if her figure was spreading and her complexion blotchy, she still

360

retained that strange attraction which had always been her birthright. She went into the cabin. Horatio was sitting with his back to her at his desk, the chart sprawled before him and weighed down with an unlit lantern at one corner and a telescope at the other end. He was tracing something with a pencil and, hearing a noise, rasped out irritably:

"Who's there?"

"It is your Emma, sir."

The instant that he heard her voice he wheeled round, staring at her helplessly for a moment, as though he thought she was a ghost. "Emma!"

"You're not angry?"

"How could I be angry? Oh, my love, my own, own love!"

He strode masterfully across the cabin, and took her into his arms. Here it seemed none could touch them and no reproaches could come to them, for they were each other's. He caressed her hands, kissing her quite violently, for he had not thought to see her for so many hours yet, and here she was holding his hand, and laughing at his emotion.

"Sweet Emma, I have missed you so much!"

"And you were so occupied?"

"I think the greatest of all battles approaches, and I have an appointment that I must keep with the Frenchies. This time I have got to beat them, and to give them the thrashing of their lives."

She thought that he looked much leaner, older perhaps, for his face had become quite cadaverous and his lips lay in a more determined line.

"Don't think of that now, my darling, think of me, for I am here to be with you and bring you happiness. Think only of me, my dearest."

"I must find Villeneuve," he said.

She put her soft hands on his. "Not now, think only of me."

"You are never out of my thoughts."

They went ashore in his barge, sitting side by side, and at the sallyport a crowd had gathered to cheer him as he came, and seeing her, cheered her also. They went to the George and dined in their own room with roast capon and a trifle, the food that the little Admiral loved best. Once away from the *Victory,* he seemed to take heart and asked fondly after "Paradise Merton" and Horatia. And how was Clarges Street?

"Arnodeo is not there any more, for the night before last footpads murdered him in a street brawl."

"I cannot be sorry, for I never liked the fellow."

"Neither did I."

"Yet you befriended him? How like my foolish, fond Emma, to be sweet to a man that in her heart she despised," and he kissed her fingers again.

He would never know that she had had good reasons for befriending Arnodeo, that she had been only thankful to find him with his throat split and know that he would never speak another word to betray her. He had kept her perpetually poor, he had for ever been plucking at her apron strings, urging, cajoling and goading so that she had never had a moment's peace.

"So fair and so dear," he said.

That was a long night, with the moon coming up over the water and the little *Victory* silhouetted against the island. They lay together until the small hours, quietly talking to one another and he was blissfully happy. Any qualms that he might have had for his future (and recently for no known reason he had been beset with forebodings) seemed to have been pushed far into the background of things. In the foreground was the lovely face that had inspired him, the warm arms and tender bosom that had always received him, and the yielding, captivating body that he loved.

"My darling," she whispered, her lips on his throat, "where would England have been without you?"

"Without *you,* you mean. For if there had been more Emmas, there would have been more Nelsons."

She began to tremble. Long after, in the quiet of the Portsmouth night, she turned her face wet with happy tears to him and whispered, "That was the most wonderful thing that has ever been said to me, and I shall treasure it for ever."

LXX

THEY WENT to Paradise Merton and spent the time there. Both of them were uncannily aware that every moment left was now of vital importance, and they grudged sparing it to an outsider. Their two selves, the child, the gardens, the beloved rooms were all that they asked. And as the appointed hour for his sailing drew nearer, even Emma paled a little, for he had passed on some of his foreboding to her, and she was more afraid than she cared to admit.

She would not go aboard the *Victory* to say good-bye, for his relations would probably be there.

"No, my dearest, we will part here," she told him.

"I would rather it was that way, too."

"I wish it were not autumn," for the autumn had always held some message of extreme melancholy for her.

"And yet for every autumn there is a spring," and he reminded her of those other springs in Naples, when the wistaria flowered in mauve wonder over the piazzas, when the lemon trees were in blossom and the lilies growing wild perfumed the roadways.

"You have it in your power always to make me happy. Oh, Horatio, how much you mean to me!"

On the last evening of all they went to say good-bye to the little Horatia in her room, and afraid of waking the child went down to be alone together. Nobody was to disturb them. The soft green silk curtains were drawn on the night, and the leaves blew against the panes, making a whispering sound almost like the sea itself. Emma knelt on the floor at his feet, her arms about his waist and her head against his knee.

"We have parted many times before," he told her. "The more agonizing the parting, the greater the glory of the reunion."

"I know that. I know that you only go to return with fresh laurels. . . ."

"Or cypresses."

"No, my own dearest, my own . . ." She laid her face against his, praying that he might not feel how wet her cheeks were."

"My sweet."

But to-night he could not comfort her as she had hoped because his own heart was too heavy. They sat on, no need for words, only the clinging together as though defying the world to part them. Only tasting from one another and praying the hour to pass, for it was Gethsemane, or to be prolonged lest it might lead to Calvery.

At last there came the sound of the post-chaise horses on the drive and nearing the door.

"There!" she gasped.

She had been waiting all through the last hours in dread of that sound, and imagining it (as once she had imagined at Naples) as the tumbrils drawing through the streets of Paris. But this was not at all the same thing, she thought quickly, and had no association with tumbrils. She must not let her misery run away with her. He got up and was hurrying. She knew then that it must be complete agony for him, for usually he delayed a little.

"I must not be late."

"No, Horatio, of course not. I have never held you back, have I? I have always bid you go, and you have called me brave Emma." She hoped that he would not hear the sound of tears already in her voice.

He was girding on his sword.

"God bless you, my own, my dearest Emma."

He kissed her once again with a mouth that had gone stone cold with anguish, then turning before she had expected it, he strode out of the room. She rushed after him, but already he had crossed the hall, passing down the steps into the post-chaise. She wanted to scream as she clung to one of the pillars of the house, with the autumn wind blowing at her hair, and the leaves coming down in a whirl. She saw the post-boy whip up. She heard the sound of the horses' hoofs and of the wheels, and for one frantic moment saw the beloved outline of his profile against the window.

The coldness of the pillar to which she clung was the coldness of what life would be without him, and it appalled her. She had a ghastly premonition that with him the warmth had gone, and stone was all that was left to her. She tried to push her hand across her mouth, to stop the moan that was tearing itself from her, for Emma must be brave. The world looked to Emma, she told herself, and she must stay courageous in the world's eyes. The post-chaise had turned the corner of the drive and had gone out into the lane they loved so well, where in summer the honeysuckles and the eglantine twined about the hedgerows and Nelson had gathered them for her and had lain them on her breast.

Now every memory stung; it was no longer merciful.

She went into the house and her mother receiving her into her arms said never a word, but led Emma to her room, where in privacy they could weep together.

"He has gone before, my Emy. He will return."

"He has gone for ever. I knew it the moment when he began to say good-bye. This is the end," and she refused to be comforted.

It was days before she could even face the garden again. Days before she could remove the marks of

365

tears from her cheeks, and dismiss their swelling from her eyes. She did not go to Clarges Street for a time, because she could not face it, and it was much later that her mother persuaded her.

"He would rather you went there than stayed here where every memory reminds you of him and hurts. Horatio would not want you to be like this," she said.

It was mid-October when Emma came to London again, and warm with it. There was the usual pile of demands for payment, for her income was being held up, and Greville had not been helpful. The debts were still outstanding, and Merton had been a strain on her resources, helping with that lavish hand of hers. Also the prize money had not been wholly procurable. However, after this fresh great victory—never for a moment did she doubt that it would be a great victory—she knew that she would have the money to put everything right and would be thankful, for she could only hope to stave off the creditors but a little longer. So she wrote brave letters and charmed them by telling them that when Lord Nelson returned—and he would return—everything would be well.

About the same time that she was writing her pathetic little letters trying to keep the tradespeople in a good humour, Nelson laid a finished letter on his desk:

My dearest beloved Emma, the dear friend of my bosom, the signal has been made that the enemy's combined fleet is coming out of port. May the God of all Battles crown my endeavours with success; at all events I will take care that my name shall ever be most dear to you and Horatia, both of whom I love as much as my own life; and as my last writing before the battle will be to you, so I hope in God that I shall live to finish my letter after the battle. May Heaven bless you prays your Nelson and Bronte.

366

He had entrusted to his diary his last codicil, recounting her unrewarded services and commending her and Horatia to the generosity of King and country. And when he flashed the unforgettable signal ENGLAND EXPECTS—he did himself expect of England that his dear ones would not want.

His writings do down in history, his pen at that moment was lit by genius, hers was the pathetic one of a woman trying to stave off accruing debts which were encompassing her from all sides, and causing her immense anguish.

He died in the cockpit of the *Victory*.

Emma was not to know for some time, and London was not very cheerful. Clarges Street might be happier in that she was rid of Arnodeo, and could afford to make some plans for the return of her beloved, but the lack of money was terrible. Once she saw Greville, and reproached him for avoiding her.

"Dear lady, how can you think of such things? These days I am a very busy man."

"Once you were not too busy for me."

"Once we were both much younger."

She hated that barb, for age had never attracted her. She saw it as the end of everything that she valued most, romantic adventure, joy, the happiness that lovers could give her, warmth, vitality, even life itself.

"I am not as old as all that," she reproved him.

"We do not grow younger," and she saw that beautiful profile was slipping, and the throat—once so firm—now had pits in it, and under the chin the flesh was beginning to loop. She wondered if time showed on her face too, and put up a hand to touch it. She tried to reassure herself, but the exquisite flesh was loosening and growing flabby, and time was marking her; she could not deny it.

It was the chaplain, a certain Mr. Scott, who was to break the dreadful news to Emma, but writing first to Mrs. Duggan.

Hasten the moment you receive this to dear Lady Hamilton, and prepare her for the very greatest of misfortunes,

he wrote. It was victory indeed for England, but for our dearest Emma it was complete defeat.

Late that night her mother came to her room where Emma lay reading and practising some of her attitudes, which lately she had thought much about and had started to learn again, for they had always interested her.

"Emy!"

"Yes?" and then, with that quick intuition that had never failed her, "Something is wrong? You have had bad news and Horatio is hurt?"

She rose in a burning agitation, her face having gone dead white.

"Emy, lie down again. Listen to me. You have got to accept this bravely, my dear, you have always had so much courage. Just bear it a little longer."

"You mean that he is dead?" and now she had no voice left. The colour had drained from her face, and only her eyes, grown very dark with the pain, stared helplessly at her mother. "You mean that Horatio is dead? They have killed him?"

LXXI

THAT CHRISTMAS was the saddest that England had ever known, for the body of the great little Admiral was brought home, and it was Mr. Scott who wrote to Lady Hamilton. He had been rowed ashore in the barge with the body, bringing it to the Admiralty and eventually to St. Paul's.

"I must go to him," said Emma, heartbroken in her Clarges Street home. "I cannot see my Horatio pass and not go to him."

"But how can you go, Emy dear? His family will be there, remember his family." Mrs. Duggan did not want further grief to be added to the enormous burden that Emma bore.

She did not go.

On January the tenth Lord Nelson went to his rest on a catafalque, with the figurehead from the *Victory* fronting it, and the sailors who would have died for him marching behind him. The whole of England seemed to be there to do him homage, save the two women; the wife who had never loved him, and the woman who had loved him too well.

But later, when the final chords of the organ had died away, and when the crowds had departed and had gone home, Mr. Scott, in a fever of apprehension, awaited someone at the side door, for he had to fulfil a promise. The street was hushed with mourning, every flag drooping at half-mast, and again snow was threatening, for the sky was leaden with it.

There came the sound of a chaise driving up Ludgate Hill; he heard it with apprehension, saw it round the corner and stop. This perhaps was going to be the most difficult task of all, he thought, as he went forward. Emma descended in heavy black, her face drained of every vestige of blood from weeping, and she led Horatia by the hand.

"I do offer you my sympathy, my very deepest sympathy," he stammered, and put out a hand to take hers.

She clung to it desperately, but said never a word, for she was too grief-stricken to speak. Together they went inside the cathedral. It was grotesquely silent; where recently the funeral march had filled it with immense echoes, now all was still. They went down into the crypt where the grave was as yet only half closed, for Mr. Scott had begged the men to wait. They stood back in an embarrassed fashion, knowing that this was the woman he had loved, and for that reason respecting her.

She went to the side of the grave holding the child's hand. Mr. Scott thought that she would fall, for she seemed to have become suddenly old, and was supremely changed. She stood there saying nothing, just looking down into the earth whilst the child broke into violent sobbing and had to be helped away.

Then with still never a word, Emma stumbled, as though she saw nothing and heard nothing and was aware of no one. In an agony of sympathy Mr. Scott went to her side.

"What can I do or say to help you? I do pray, dear Lady Hamilton, that you will remember his last signal, which was for all of us, including you yourself. England expects, and it still expects courage of you; the courage to go on."

At the door she turned, and, in a voice grown husky and quite unlike her usual gay, lively tone, she said:

"Thank you; you have done your best."

Those were the only words that she had said the whole time.

For weeks she lay seriously ill, and when she recovered it was to find that the bills were massive. Now there was a pile in the hall, and her whole estate was in difficulties.

"It surely can't be as bad as this?" she gasped.

"The money'll be found; they'll never leave you this way," said her mother.

"What'll I do? God, what'll I do?"

It was the same plea that she had written years ago to Greville, only now she had no one to turn to.

Merton Place was sold in 1808. With it went the memories of their love; the hero who had walked in the garden there with her; those lovely intimate memories which were all she had left of him. The new Lord Nelson was ungenerous, for one year he paid her nothing, and Emma was never able to recover from the time lost on that single year's liability.

She, Horatia and her mother had become wanderers on the face of the earth. They flitted about from one creditor to the next, always escaping, always remorselessly pursued. She wrote imploring letters to those who in her hey-day had been glad enough to cadge favours from her. Maria Carolina in Naples (who owed her life to Emma's good offices, and had hung her with diamonds, swearing everlasting friendship) had turned a deaf ear. The country which owed her such an enormous debt turned discreetly quiet on the subject of Lord Nelson's codicil. The hero could not have entrusted his darlings to less worthy hands.

What shall I do, was now to be her constant cry.

If only she could educate her child as Nelson had wished, if only she could fulfil his desires, she would feel that at least she had done her duty. But she dare not allow herself to go into liquidation, and that was what lay ahead of her.

In 1810 her mother died.

Through all her successes and misfortunes, Mrs. Duggan had been beside her daughter. Emma truly loved her. She knelt by the bed unable to relieve her pain, unable to do anything, and when finally she was buried in that same Paddington churchyard which she had as a fair tea-maker, known in happier days at Edgware, Emma was almost paralysed with grief.

"This is the end of all comfort," she wept.

One by one everything that she possessed was sold. It had to go to keep pace with the inroads that her creditors made upon her, but through it all she prayed that she might be left without scandal touching her name, or—more important still—the name of Nelson's daughter.

To her horror the last die was thrown against her,

and in the autumn of 1814 Thomas Lovewell of Satines House, Barbican, announced the publication of "The Letters of Lord Nelson to Lady Hamilton."

"It cannot be true," she gasped.

Greville had told her. "We shall all figure in this horrible publication," he said.

"I cannot face it; you at least figure in it respectably. What will they say about me?"

"They will say that you were my mistress."

"Oh, God, Greville, don't you understand? It is never so bad for a man to keep a mistress, as for a woman to be one. You will be exonerated. It is I and little Horatia who will suffer."

But, as usual, Greville was only thinking of himself.

"What can I do?" she asked him again and again, and finally he snapped under her despair; he was angry at being dragged into something so publicly undesirable.

"What do I care what you do?" he asked, and marched out of the room.

That was his good-bye to her.

She stood for a long time staring at the door which was closed in the face that had withered. She stood in the shabby black that she wore for her mother, the one friend who had stayed staunch all her life. She saw no answer, for obviously she could not stay on in the country for the publication of this wretched book. She could not endure the goads, the innuendoes, the remarks about Horatia, his child.

"Where shall we go, Mother?" asked the little girl.

"I will find somewhere," and even as she said it a spark of the old Emma lit a torch of adventure in her. They would set forth together.

LXXII

THEY WENT to France.

Everything had to be arranged secretly and with the utmost haste in case the creditors, learning what was afoot, detained her. She was haunted by the thought of prison, and now had no sentimental faith left in the honour of a country which would so willingly leave her to starve.

She and the child left under cover of the dark and joined the boat near the Tower of London. It was one of those wild nights, but then she had embarked on other wild nights and did not fear a storm. There was the melancholy sound of the horses trotting them to the docks, and she could see the outline of the Tower, ominous and solid against the sky. And, as they came nearer, she suffered qualms beholding the miserable little boat in which she and her darling were to put out to sea.

She thought that she could lie down and stay like that until they got to Calais, but they spent three days on that dreadful journey, storm-tossed and racked, and she was seized with internal pains, so that when she arrived she was in a lamentable condition.

"It will be all right when we can get a doctor to you, Mother dear," whispered the child, who now had to manage everything.

They went to a hotel, but of course that could not last, for they had not the means, and the imploring letters that she dispatched to Lord Nelson and Greville remained unanswered. England had done with her. Now it was actual privation. Jaundice yellowed the once exquisite skin, and a dropsical complaint attacked her, so that with the Christmas of 1814, Emma Hamilton was dying.

It was pitiful that England could care so little, when he had instructed it to do its duty.

The child staggered out in the dark and pawned the christening cup her noble father had given her; she could scarce reach the counter to thrust it across to the little Jew who bought it. The miserable lodgings ill sufficed, for the landlady was for ever badgering them. Emma lay on the fetid bed, a dirty blanket over her, and beside her the small picture of Nelson and another of her mother, the only remnants she had retained from the wholesale wreckage of her life.

The child was distracted.

"Lord Nelson will attend to your needs, my poor darling, I *know* he will," said Emma frantically. She could not lose her faith in mankind entirely. "It is only myself that he hates, and God knows I have never thought ill of him, nor would I have done him an evil turn."

She lay there until the New Year's Day. Calais was *en fête*. There was a procession of torches through the streets and they flickered as they passed the window, recalling to Emma the *fiestas* in Naples, Palermo in carnival time. The fun it all had been, and she herself the belle of every entertainment. Again she dreamt of the ecstasy of lovers who had come to her and her own climb to the dizzy heights and conquering.

Suddenly she changed colour.

"Oh, Mother, dearest Mother," gasped the child.

A priest came, and so she drifted out upon the sea that she had loved so well, into eternity. She had asked to lie beside her mother, but that was refused her, for now there was only the money to bundle her into a cheap coffin, cover her with a tattered petticoat and commit her to the miserable Calais cemetery that before long was to become a timber yard.

The new year made that day a cheerless one.

Again a light snow fell, for throughout all the big events of Emma's eventful life the snow had always fallen. The undertaker hurriedly brought the coffin out of the house, with the unhappy little girl following it. It was then that there came a sound from the end of the road, it was a clicking of heels in response to a word of command rapped out, and the chafe of sword against stone.

"What's that?" asked the child.

Down the road they came, a contingent of naval officers from some of the English Fleet which happened to be in port. They had heard of the occasion, and knew that here went the lady who had fed and watered the Fleet at Naples, and they—the only ones in the world—did not forget the debt that they owed.

Down the road through the snow they marched, following the cheap, over-dressed hearse with the seedy undertaker's men who only wanted to get the ceremony through and done with. The little undertaker saw with surprise, as they swung down the roadway, the company of uniformed men marching as one, and following into the cemetery itself, there to stand beside the grave, the only mourners beside her daughter.

They had not forgotten the last signal.

The lovely body that had fascinated and intrigued half Europe was thrust in its deal box into a nameless grave. Some time later the Navy crept to the cemetery one night and put a stone above it. They alone still stood beside her.

Her life was over, her beauty had perished, deserting her as had most of the friends to whom her fault had always been that of over-generosity. The little ship bearing Horatia turned towards England, for a guardian had come to fetch her home, and as she stood watching the white wake of that boat and looking with red eyes towards Calais, she knew that for her a new epoch was starting.

Little more is known of her.

She left no mark upon the world, the creature of

such parents, born of so great and abiding a passion. The last picture was of a small boat plunging through the water, with the white plume of waves in its wake, and a child staring mutely out to a grave, already forgotten, in a foreign cemetery.

No more.